From the Chicken House

I can't help making this personal. What would be on my list if I had a week to live? Er … it's almost easy. But then I think of the people I'd never see again, the things I'd never do. (Anyway, no one can eat that many lobsters.)

Melvin Burgess brilliantly brings home the consequences of a momentous choice – to a world that feels like the day after tomorrow, where love, sex, crime and revolution all swing into play. It's intimate, thrilling and intense. Like life itself.

Barry Cunningham
Publisher

MELVIN
BURGESS

THE
HIT

Chicken
House

2 Palmer Street, Frome, Somerset BA11 1DS

Text © Melvin Burgess 2013
From an original idea by Brandon Robshaw and Joe Chislett

First published in Great Britain in 2013
The Chicken House
2 Palmer Street
Frome, Somerset BA11 1DS
United Kingdom
www.doublecluck.com

Cover design and interior design by Steve Wells
Typeset by Dorchester Typesetting Group Ltd
Printed and bound in Great Britain by CPI Group (UK) Ltd, Croydon, CR0 4YY

The paper used in this Chicken House book is made from wood grown in
sustainable forests.

1 3 5 7 9 10 8 6 4 2

British Library Cataloguing in Publication data available.

PB ISBN 978-1-908435-33-0
HB ISBN 978-1-908435-95-8

To Brandon Robshaw, Joe Chislett and Barry Cunningham
– my co-conspirators

PART ONE:
DEATH

CHAPTER 1

THE VERY PUBLIC DEATH OF JIMMY EARLE

With Jimmy, it was all about the fans. People often say a performer gave everything, but no one ever promised more for a show than he had tonight.

Adam didn't believe it, but he still felt part of something special. Jimmy Earle had been the big thing for years, his shows were legendary, but nothing before had ever been like this. People had flown from California and Beijing to be here. This was going to be the concert to end all concerts, the one experience no one could ever repeat.

'Like human sacrifice,' said Adam. 'They should tear his heart out, like the Aztecs. Now that would be cool.'

'You won't be making jokes if he really does it,' Lizzie said.

Adam shook his head. It would never happen. Jimmy had everything – wealth, youth, good looks, talent. You could understand the losers and lowlifes on the big estates taking the drug called Death. They had nothing and never would. Why not go for that one crazy week in the blazing light? But Jimmy Earle? No way.

'He wants to join the 27 Club,' said, Lizzie, excitedly. 'Brian Jones, Jimi Hendrix, Janis Joplin, Jim Morrison, Kurt Cobain, Amy Winehouse – and Jimmy Earle. All twenty-seven years old. That's what they're all so scared about it. Look at 'em!'

It was true, Adam thought, as they filed into the arena. There were security guards everywhere, big men standing in the aisles. They all looked on edge.

'He'll be remembered for ever if he dies tonight,' Lizzie said.

Adam grinned. 'Yeah. And we'll remember this concert for ever.'

'Gosh, buying tickets – something else you're good at!' she teased. Lizzie never let him get away with a thing, but he couldn't help boasting. The glory that was Jimmy Earle was Adam's glory, too, tonight.

'Where were you the night Jimmy Earle died?' he said, acting it out. 'I was there. I *saw* it.' He grabbed her hand. She smiled back and squeezed. Adam felt his head go. He fancied her that bad.

Lizzie was out of his league, really. They used to know one another years ago at primary school. They'd been good friends – hung out, gone to the same parties. Then his dad had to leave his job, Adam had to change schools, and they'd lost touch until they bumped into each other again in town just a couple of months ago. It was like magic – they'd got on in a flash, as if they'd never been apart all those years.

He'd been delighted and amazed when she let him kiss her a week later. In a world where there were so many people and so few jobs, it was serious stuff for someone rich to go out with someone poor. Families hoarded their wealth like dragons. So look at him now! He felt like the King of the World with her at his side. He'd bet not one of her rich friends could have got her a ticket for Jimmy Earle like he had tonight.

Actually, it was his brother Jess who had got the tickets for him. God knows how – Jess never went anywhere or did anything. No need for Lizzie to know that, though ...

They made their way towards their seats. The noise was already deafening. People were shouting at the stage, even though there was no one there to hear them.

'Jimmy, I love you!'

'Don't do it, Jimmy.'

'No, do it! Top yourself. Save me the price of your next crap album,' yelled a bloke near them. He sniggered at his mates, who laughed uncomfortably. A tearful girl yelled at him to shut up. A couple of rows down, a man offered to punch his lights out if he spoke up again.

The whole place was too hot, too edgy. Lizzie slipped her hand out of Adam's as they pushed through to their seats. She sat down and stared around her, trying to take it all in.

'Do you think anyone here's taken it?' she asked.

'Bound to,' said Adam.

Lizzie laughed nervously. *She's scared*, he thought, and realised that he was scared, too. Deathers were dangerous. They had nothing to lose. That was the whole point.

Death had started out as a euthanasia drug, to give the terminally ill one week of great quality life and a clean way out. No one ever imagined that the young would take it, too; but then, no one imagined what it would give the young – super youth. On Death you were better – mentally, physically, sexually, any way you cared to look at it. It was the biggest high there was.

So they said. And of course, at a price. Death cost thousands per tab.

And there was no going back. No one had found an antidote and most scientists didn't expect one to emerge. Jimmy Earle was a big star – the biggest – but in this respect he was the same as everyone else. If he'd taken Death, he was as good as dead. He'd been on about it for ages, in the press, on his website. The concert had been cancelled twice since he had announced that he'd finally gone and done it. The authorities were terrified. Death had already caused the biggest wave of suicides ever recorded among the under-twenty-fives. Only when he'd withdrawn his statement and sworn it was all just a publicity stunt had they allowed the concert to go ahead.

The question was, who was Jimmy fooling? The authorities, or the fans? Was he or wasn't he on Death? And if he was – *why*?

'The bucket list,' said Adam. 'Oh, yeah!'

'Not the point!' exclaimed Lizzie. 'It's not what you do,

it's how you experience it. Everything is for the last time. Every little thing matters. That's the point. When you enter the Death phase, life becomes so intense. Most people wait till they're old and tired. Jimmy decided to do it while he's still young …'

Adam snorted. 'That's such a girl thing to say. Did you *read* his list? I mean – come on!'

Jimmy Earle's bucket list was a thing of legend. It had cost over twenty million pounds. He had slept with a hundred girls in one week; at least twenty of them had come out of it pregnant. He had travelled round the world, eaten two kilos of caviar at a sitting, drunk thirty gallons of champagne, snorted a pound of cocaine, been into space, killed a man, hunted snow leopards, climbed Everest … the list went on.

Of course, it was a fantasy. No one person could have done all those things in a single week. Or could they? Death didn't just kill you – it loved you up better than ecstasy and boosted you at the same time. With strength, fitness and belief on your side, you could do anything.

Maybe, just maybe, it was all true.

Nah, though Adam. *Publicity, that's all it is.* But how great would it be if someone, somewhere, really had done all that stuff in just one week? And how much greater if that person was him …

Lizzie fixed him with a look. 'Would you do it, Adam? If you could have his bucket list? Really?'

Adam tensed up. He hated being put on the spot. If it was true, Jimmy Earle had done more in a single week than he would in his entire life. More girls. More fun.

More everything. That was an amazing thought. But what Lizzie really wanted to know was if he'd jump up and start shagging all the girls he could find. It was her he wanted … But if you only had one week to live – well. You would, wouldn't you?

'Dunno. What's your bucket list?' he asked her.

Lizzie smiled. 'I'd have sex with as many attractive people as I could find,' she said. And Adam, to his surprise, felt hurt.

She snorted with amusement. Winding him up. She got him every time.

It was all right for her. Her dad had a good job, she had it made. All Adam could see ahead was hard work, never earning enough to do what he wanted. It would have been different if he'd done better at the football trials he'd had a few weeks ago. He was a brilliant player, but now he was having to come to terms with the fact that there were too many others more brilliant than him.

But he wasn't beaten yet. Practise, practise, practise – that's what he had to do. He could still make it if he tried hard enough.

The arena filled. Everyone was so wound up. A few fights broke out, but they were quickly put down, often by other people in the crowd. Even now, with every seat sold, the concert could be called off at any second.

When Earle came on the stage, the noise welled up like a climax before a single note had been played. He held out his hands and waited for the uproar to subside.

'We're going to play you a few songs,' he said. 'And it's

going to be the performance of a lifetime.'

He turned round, lashed out with his arm, and the band burst into the first number. The crowd roared.

'He's great! He's so great!' screamed Lizzie.

'He's fantastic!' yelled Adam.

The people, the adrenalin, the noise. He'd never seen anything like it. He wondered if anyone ever had. Around them the crowd surged to its feet, and they jumped up with it, everyone laughing, weeping, yelling, dancing. And this was only the first song.

The concert was brilliant. Jimmy seemed to be singing his whole life up there in the space of a couple of hours. The noise got louder and louder as they neared the magic time – ten-thirty – when he was supposed to die. Death was accurate; you could work out when you were going to go pretty much to the minute. Was he mad enough – committed enough – to have really taken Death?

With Jimmy, you could never tell.

As the last few minutes ticked by, the band launched into their current single, 'Something to Live For'. Jimmy howled and strutted his way through the song. Ten-thirty came and he sang on. It was all publicity – of course!

But just when everyone was certain, the song died in his throat. He staggered. There was a gasp from the crowd. Jimmy almost fell, but then drew himself erect, and clamped the mike to his chest. The band petered out. Out of the speakers came a rapid beat.

Babangbangbangbangbabangbangbabababang bang.

Jimmy's heart. It sounded as if it was trying to hammer its way out of his chest.

BANGBABANGBANGBABANGBANGBANGBANGBANG.

The band started a countdown. 10 − 9 − 8 − 7... The crowd went crazy.

'Don't do it, Jimmy! Don't leave us!' someone yelled.

... 4 − 3 − 2 − 1.

Nothing.

Jimmy Earle looked up at the crowd and grinned. He spread his arms as if to say, *Fooled ya!* Then he tipped forward and fell flat on his face.

There was a moment of stunned silence. People stood at their seats, waiting for him to get up. Was it another trick? It had to be another trick. A beefy first-aider rushed on to the stage, flipped Earle over on to his back and started chest compressions. They could see it all up there on the big screens, a hundred times larger than life. The guy was pounding on Earle's chest like he meant to break his ribs.

The crowd started up again, a different noise this time – a deep, nervous buzz, punctured with shouts and screams, building quickly. Onstage, one of the guitarists crossed himself, unplugged his guitar and walked off. The drummer climbed down from his seat, came to the front and said something into the mike. They couldn't quite make it out, but it sounded like, 'Congratulations.' The crowd was getting louder by the second. Someone nearby yelled, 'I love you, Jimmy, I love you!' A girl just in front of them screamed, 'Take me with you, Jimmy! I want to go too!'

Some Red Cross people came running up the aisles but they didn't make it to the stage. Chaos broke out. The crowd surged forward and up towards the stage, trying to get to Jimmy. People were begging him to get up, begging him to live, demanding their money back. Security reacted furiously, lashing out, throwing people down.

In the middle of it all, flat on the floor, eyes wide open, beyond any excitement or fun or sadness or pleasure or pain, Jimmy Earle lay, his chest violently pounded by the big first-aider. The air was going in and out of his lungs, the blood pumping in all directions in and out of his shattered heart. Not one drop of it was ever going to do him any good again.

CHAPTER 2

MANCHESTER BURNING

The big screens blanked out so that no one could see what was going on, but it didn't stop the chaos. Things were being thrown. Shoes, cans, even bottles were flying through the air and down into the crowd. There were screams; people were getting hurt. Fights broke out, security was getting overwhelmed. It was turning into a full-blown riot. There were warnings over the PA that the whole place was under CCTV and vandals would be prosecuted but the violence didn't stop. It was doubtful anyone even heard.

Then there was another announcement – Jimmy was alive! It was just a stunt after all. *Everyone, just calm down, please.* It seemed to work for a minute or two. People milled around in confusion. After a short wait – there he was! Jimmy Earle, walking on to the stage, waving and smiling. But it was pathetic – it was obvious it was just a lookalike dressed up in his gear. If anyone had any doubts that Jimmy Earle really had died, those doubts were put to rest there and then.

Things got suddenly worse. Seats were being torn up and thrown about. People were trying to storm the stage to loot the equipment – it would be worth a fortune after this. But then the doors banged open and police came in, squads of them, storming up the aisles in full riot gear. They fought their way to the stage, turned to face the crowd – shields up, batons drawn – and began to edge their way forward. They were going to literally push the audience out on to the street.

There was another announcement; there would be a refund available online to anyone not prosecuted. The management apologised and asked everyone to leave quietly. At last, things began to calm down.

Herded by the police, the crowd began to shuffle towards the exits.

Adam and Lizzie had good seats, close to the front, so they were among the last to leave. They heard the sirens going off while they were still inside, and by the time they got outside, things were already kicking off. Thousands of over excited, upset fans, suddenly thrown out into Manchester on a Friday night, with nothing to do – there was bound to be trouble. The venue was safe, but now there was the whole of Manchester to run riot in.

Out on the streets, the atmosphere was electric. People

were running to and fro in groups, groups merging into gangs, gangs into crowds. As Adam and Lizzie walked towards Piccadilly Gardens, some kids chased past, barging them out of the way.

'Hey!' shouted Adam. But the gang had already gone. They walked on a few metres, and saw what it was – a shop window, smashed, and the police gathering to stop the looting. Someone stumbled past them with a huge cardboard box held in front of him, leaning right over backwards in an effort to keep his balance, like a man in a cartoon. Further ahead another gang appeared out of nowhere and started throwing bricks and stones at the police.

It was like a Jimmy Earle song turned real. His music had always been about love and sex, loss and hope, about rioting and looting and fighting back against poverty and failure – and here it all was, sizzling hot in the drizzle of a Manchester night. Tonight the streets belonged to his fans, and they were going to make the most of it.

Adam and Lizzie ran on. The city was in flames. The shops had given up the ghost, the windows smashed open, people running freely in and out. On the corner of Princess Street, someone was pounding the back doors of a van with a piece of broken paving stone. There were shouts and sirens, clouds of smoke, the stink of burning rubber and petrol. It was a war zone. But for what?

Adam felt dizzy with excitement.

'Looting! Hey, what about it?' he hissed in Lizzie's ear.

'Wow. Look at it. Look at it!' yelled Lizzie, staring about her with bright, big eyes.

'You scared?'

'No! I love it!'

Lizzie had lived all her life safe and sound, protected by her parents' money. Sometimes she felt as if life was going to grind to a halt. Now look! The city going up in smoke and here she was, right in the middle of it.

They made their way up Princess Street to Albert Square. It was heaving. There was some sort of struggle going on in front of the town hall, a mass of people fighting their way forward showing no mercy. The police were there, trying to hold them back from storming the building. They were acting more like soldiers than law-keepers, lashing out at people with their batons. But they were outnumbered, and the crowd against them was swelling rapidly. Suddenly they'd had enough and made a run for it, pushing their way out of the crowd, which parted to make way for them. A roar of victory went up, and the vanguard at the front began smashing the windows of the town hall and pounding at its heavy oak doors, trying to get inside.

The police re-formed a line and tried to push their way back to the town hall, but it was no good. The doors were giving way and people were already crawling in through smashed windows. The banks and the headquarters of the big companies around the square were under attack as well. Bottles and bricks were in the air. There were no peacemakers. Anyone who wanted out had already left; it was just the hard core now. In the shopping streets and malls around them, the looters were still busy at work, but here in the square, people weren't interested in widescreen TVs and crates of beer. They wanted more. They were trying to tear the whole city apart with their bare hands and start again.

And they were organised. From where they stood, Lizzie and Adam could see people wearing rat masks. Adam hissed in excitement. Zealots! Half madcap protest group, half armed rebels – right here in Manchester, fighting to take over the seat of the city government.

'It's not just looting,' yelled Lizzie. 'It's a revolution, Adam!'

Across the front of the town hall, there was a ripple of movement. They looked up as a huge banner, thirty metres wide, unravelled like a wave of water down the height of the building. It showed a gigantic rat clutching a can of red paint, staring angrily into the crowd, with the Zealot slogan painted red behind it: 'OUR DAY WILL COME!'

The crowd in the square roared their approval. Above the noise, an amplified voice boomed out:

'The town hall is ours. Free cheese for everyone!'

Around them, people screamed in delight. High up on the roof, they could see Zealots in rat masks looking down at the crowd. One of them shook a machine gun in the air. Was it real? Adam wondered. The Zealots were every-where – pushing back the police and hauling them off as if they were under arrest. One group had taken a jack-hammer to Barclays Bank on the corner; someone else was squirting glue into the locks of the NatWest. Loud music started blaring out a Jimmy Earle number, 'The Rats Are Taking Over'. The crowd around them jostled and surged. A man banged into them and thrust a handful of pills into their faces.

'What is it?' Adam asked, reaching out. Free drugs! Ecstasy, maybe?

'Sweeties,' said the man, grinning at them. 'Courtesy of Jimmy Earle. Last point on his bucket list.'

Adam handed one to Lizzie and they looked closely at them. On each pill, neatly printed in black, was a tiny skull.

'It's Death!'

'It can't be ...'

But it was. Everyone knew what the pills looked like. Adam could see the man moving on, passing out handful after handful of the deadly little pills. It must have cost a fortune.

And people were taking them. He could see them tipping back their heads and flinging the pill down their necks. 'Live fast, die young!' yelled the man. He laughed and threw a handful of the pills into the air. Around him, people scrabbled to pick them up.

'We could have taken it without realising,' exclaimed Lizzie.

Adam stared at the black-and-white pill on the palm of his hand. What would it be like to know – to *feel* like Jimmy Earle, for one brief, sweet week ...

He flung his hand to his mouth and grinned madly at Lizzie. He swallowed. She started back, shocked – but then he showed her the pill in his hand.

'You bastard,' she yelled, and laughed. She stared at the small packet of craziness in her palm. All those people, just swallowing it! 'Do you think it's the real thing?' she said.

'Could be, if Jimmy Earle paid for it. He has the money.'

They looked at each other, shocked by how tempting it was. They'd been there with Jimmy. They'd seen it, they were part of it! If they took Death tonight, they'd be living it, too.

'It's not worth it,' said Lizzie. She flung her pill into the crowd. Adam did the same. Death, on a night like this? He wanted to live.

Only, some people said, that was exactly what Death made you do ...

From some way off, they could hear sirens. Reinforcements were on the way. The city was a dangerous place tonight. There was the sudden rat-tat-tat-tat of machine-gun fire. Instinctively, Adam and Lizzie ducked. Up on the roof of the town hall, rat-masked Zealots waved weapons in the air. On another part of the roof, there was a small blaze of fire moving about. It stumbled a few yards, then fell; it looked like slow motion from that height and distance. The crowd gasped as the fire rolled down the steep edge of the roof, over the edge, and down to the ground.

It was a person. Self-immolation. There were the jokes about cheese and the rat masks, but the Zealots were prepared to die for their beliefs. Every few weeks some-one died, killing themselves with fire, or going up as a suicide bomb. It was crazy – but you couldn't help respecting them for their commitment to their cause: freedom and food for all!

Above their heads, the loudspeakers began to spit out

slogans: 'Equality! Freedom! Power to the People! Down with corporate profits and greed! The government is in the pockets of the corporations – fight for the right to govern yourselves.'

Fire arms spat out again from somewhere. People were running to get away. Adam and Lizzie dropped to the ground and followed the crowd out of the square and into Crown Street. Behind them, gunfire started up in earnest. There would be deaths tonight. This was no place for tourists.

Outside of Albert Square, there were hardly any police at all and the looting went on unopposed. The Arndale shopping centre was in pieces; you could walk in and just help yourself. People had brought in cars and vans to carry stuff away wholesale. Adam and Lizzie wandered about the blazing streets, diving in and out of the broken shops, following the crowds. They picked up some scarves from a looted department store, and the anonymity it gave them made them feel untouchable, as if they could spend the rest of their lives living off stolen food like beasts running feral in the transformed city.

Later on, the police came back to try to chase the crowds off and make arrests; maybe the war in Albert Square was over. Adam and Lizzie got caught in a camera shop and had to run for it with the uniforms on their tails. But the police got sidetracked by some kids smashing a car. There were so many crimes being committed tonight, they didn't know where to turn.

The night came to an end abruptly. They were tagging

along with a crowd running down one of the narrow streets, pursued by a couple of riot police, when another policeman dashed out on them from the side. Adam slipped sideways and got away, but the man grabbed Lizzie by the arm, and held on to her.

Adam stopped. He wanted to help, but he didn't dare go near.

'We were just watching,' he yelled.

The policeman pulled the scarf from Lizzie's face. To Adam, it looked like a film – the burly policeman, covered in body armour and riot gear; and slight Lizzie, hanging off his arm like a rabbit.

The policeman stared at her for a moment. 'For fuck's sake,' he snarled. 'You want to end up in the nick, you silly bitch?'

He flung her down into the road and stalked off back to the main road. Adam ran to help her up and dust her down.

'Time to go,' said Lizzie, shakily. Adam nodded. Beyond the fires, the sky was growing pale. It was getting light. They were both really shocked by their narrow escape. The last time there had been riots, people had been locked up for months just for being there. Lizzie suddenly dived into her pocket for her phone. It had been on silent ever since the gig. She looked up. 'Mum and Dad are going crazy,' she said. 'It's three a.m. They haven't got a clue what's been going on …'

Adam got out his phone, too. Same thing.

'We're in the shit now,' he said.

They both grinned sheepishly at each other.

'But that was great, wasn't it?' he asked.

'It was the best night of my life,' said Lizzie, fervently.

They kissed. Adam felt a thrill when their lips touched. Wouldn't it be great if they could go somewhere and make love now, while the fires still burned! But there was no chance …

'It's all changing,' Lizzie said. 'Not just here. The whole world. People have had enough.'

Only a few hours ago the future had seemed so fixed. All the money was owned by the banks and the big corporations, the economy was falling apart, there were no jobs, social services were a joke. For decades everyone had complained but nothing had changed. Now, suddenly, it was all up for grabs. The Zealots had shown the nation how to seize the future by setting fire to the present. Who knew what tomorrow would bring?

'When will I see you?' asked Adam. All he wanted was to stay with Lizzie. It was unbearable to think that everything was going to go back to normal as soon as they went home.

They wandered a hundred metres up the road, but they knew it was over – for tonight, anyway.

'I better ring Dad, get a lift back,' said Lizzie at last. She paused with her phone in her hand. 'Shall I ask him to give you a lift, too?'

'No way!' Her parents hated Adam. 'They'll kill me.'

She nodded and rang her dad, arranging to meet him on the Oxford Road, by the university, away from the trouble. Adam walked her there and waited with her. Her dad glared furiously at him when he turned up in his Jag.

Lizzie kissed Adam passionately on the mouth then ran to the car and drove off. Adam began the long walk home.

He felt jubilant. He was falling in love, and the future was his.

CHAPTER 3

THE MORNING AFTER

Adam could feel his phone buzzing away in his pocket as he walked. It was his dad.

'Where are you? What happened?'

'The police locked the town up. I've just got out now.'

'Have you seen Jess?'

'No.' Adam was taken aback. His brother was as straight as a stick of rock, working as a research chemist for Pak-Hilliard, one of the giant corporations that owned half the world. He was always there, always working, always earning. Their dad was an invalid, their mum worked nights at telesales. If it wasn't for Jess, they wouldn't be able to pay the bills.

'He's not come back from work. I can't get in touch,'

complained his dad.

'Must be doing overtime.'

'Not at this time of night.'

'Something to do with the riots, then.'

Adam was surprised, but not worried. Dull old Jess. What was he doing out so late, while the shops were burning, and rioters and policemen were dying on the street? Hiding in a basement, probably, working on some formula to make plastic gaskets last longer.

His dad was still up when he got home, standing by the kettle with a blanket over his shoulders, drinking tea. It was cold. He always turned the heating off when Jess was out. The Great God Jess. As soon as he walked out of the door, the shivering started.

There was still no news.

'You haven't rung Mum, have you?' Adam asked.

'Of course I have. She wants to know what's happened to her son.'

Adam groaned. His dad was always ringing her up at work with his stupid worries.

'You have to stop worrying about everything,' he said.

His dad shuffled from the work surface to the table, with a cup of tea in his good left hand, supporting himself with the other on the back of chair. 'You should be doing the worrying for me. I have nothing to do but worry,' he said, and smiled grimly.

It was a typically bitter little joke. Adam sighed. The old man was going to be up all night now, but there was nothing he could do about it. Jess was bound to be safe.

He'd run a mile at the slightest sign of trouble.

Adam went to bed thanking his lucky stars that he wasn't Jess. His life was going to be different. He'd glimpsed the future and the future belonged to him.

Adam was brought round the next morning by his phone alarm at ten a.m. Saturday morning: football. There was a text from Lizzie waiting for him.

'What a night! You and me, Ads! xxxx ps don't txt dad's taking my phone.'

Adam hugged himself and turned sideways in his bed to look at himself in the mirror on the side of his wardrobe. His blond hair was curling over his eyes. His skin glowed in the light coming in between the curtains. He smiled at himself. How could she resist? After he'd failed his trials for Man U and City, it had seemed that his life wasn't going to be the golden dream he'd always hoped for. But the tide had turned. The death of a rock star had made him shine.

But it wasn't just about Jimmy Earle. It was about Lizzie. It felt so right, being with her. But it was not just a romantic dream. The fact was, if they fell in love it could change his life. 'Money opens doors,' his dad always said. Adam closed his eyes and wished. He wanted so much to be in love with her and for her to love him, but he knew it was stupid. They were only seventeen. Anything could happen.

He sighed. Life went on anyway. He slipped out of bed, took a shower and went downstairs.

Jess was there of course. So was his mum, sitting with his dad at the table eating toast. Jess looked pale. His mum was exhausted, as usual, with dark eyes. Adam came across to kiss her good morning – except it was good-night for her. She always waited to see him in the mornings, even when she was desperate for sleep.

'What happened to you?' Adam asked Jess, helping himself to cereal and sitting down.

'I went into town for a drink and got stuck,' Jess said.

Adam laughed. 'You picked your night,' he said. Jess hardly ever went out – and then when he did, Manchester exploded!

'You need to be careful,' his father scolded. 'Anything could have happened to you.'

Adam was exasperated. 'What's he supposed to do, never go out in case there's a riot? Give us a break, Dad.'

'Adam's right,' his mum said. 'Jess needs to get out more.'

'Did you see it? The whole place was up in flames. Where were you?' Adam asked.

'We holed up in a bar,' said Jess.

'Didn't you even go out to have a look?'

'It was dangerous!' said Jess. It was typical. The world was changing – and he was holed up in a bar in a bar keeping safe.

'The Zealots were there. It was amazing! They occupied the town hall.'

'Looting and destroying property,' insisted his father. 'According to the TV, the Zealots were handing out Death. Irresponsible thugs.'

'It was paid for by Jimmy Earle. I didn't see any Zealots handing it out,' Adam said.

'I wouldn't put it past them,' said his mum.

'They aren't just looters,' said Jess. Despite the fact that he was scared of life, he was passionate about politics. It was just that he never did anything about it. 'Everything the Zealots do is about trying to make people think – trying to wake them up.'

'Yes – by looting and encouraging young people to kill themselves,' sneered his dad. 'Very political.'

Adam shook his head impatiently. 'They were on top of the town hall. The police came in after them. There was gunfire.' He shook his head at the memory. What a night!

'Nothing about that on the news,' said his dad.

Jess scoffed. Everyone knew the news was owned by the government. You had to look on the internet and on social media if you wanted to get to the truth.

'Well, I want both of you to stay well away from it,' his mother announced. 'Over twenty deaths in Manchester last night. And they think thousands of those pills were handed out.' She shook her head, appalled. 'I wonder how those young people are going to feel about that this morning?' She stood up. 'I'm going to bed,' she said. 'Keep the noise down, you two.'

That was to Jess and Dad, who would have argued furiously about politics for hours if they could. She went round the table, bestowing kisses.

Adam got up to go, too. 'Footie,' he explained. He cadged some money off his mum for bus fares, under his father's disapproving eyes.

'Waste of time,' said his father, as soon as she was out

of the room. 'Big fish in a small pond.' He looked up at the little TV rattling away on the shelf, and slurped his tea. Adam stood there, dumbfounded.

'I love you, too,' said Adam. He turned and left.

Jess ran out and caught him by the gate.

'What is it?' Adam asked.

'Nothing. Just – look after the old pair, won't you? Dad loves you really.'

'He's got a funny way of showing it.'

'Yeah.' Jess laughed self-consciously. He looked awkward. 'Take care, mate,' he said. He nodded.

Adam shook his head and shot off.

He seethed all the way to the playing fields. It had nearly broken his heart when he failed to get in to Man U or City. He was still hoping to get in elsewhere – Burnley, maybe. Blackburn even. But his dad treated him like a failure already.

The crooked old bus jolted and crashed its way across the potholes on the edge of the road. As Adam looked out, the posh bus went past, long and high in the fast lane, the one that carted the rich kids to rich school, with rich lunches in their bags and a rich education at the other end. Six years ago, Adam used to catch that bus. Then his dad had had an accident at work and everything had changed.

'We can't afford to pay for two of you to go to uni, and Jess is the better bet educationally,' his dad had said.

Adam hadn't minded at the time. He'd thought sport was going to be his way out. He wanted to fly, not toil. But now …

Big fish in a small pond.

At least there was Lizzie. But how long would ~~~

At the playing fields, everyone was talking ab~
Jimmy Earle and the riots. That was more like it. Man —
he'd been there! The boys clustered round him while he
gave the details of the concert and the events that
followed.

One thing was for sure — Earle had hit a nerve.

'Have you read his blog?' someone asked. 'He was high
the whole time. Off his face.'

'No! He didn't need drugs. Everything was hyper-real.
Like, he spent an hour just looking at stuff.'

'My idea of fun,' said Adam.

'You don't get it. You don't need big experiences if
you're like that inside. Everything is a high. He may have
only had one week, but none of us will ever experience
anything like he did, no matter what we do.'

'But the bucket list. *That's* what it's all about,' said Adam.

His mate Jack licked his lips. 'Do you really think all
those women slept with him? There were a lot of A-list
celebs there. I bet he doesn't even *know* half of them.'

'If you've only got a week to live? What sort of bitch
would say no to you then?' said someone else.

They laughed.

The talk turned to what they would do if it was them.
What would your bucket list be? Most of the lists started off
with sex. Names were mentioned. After that, drugs,
money, travel.

'I wanna stand on the moon.'

'Get someone pregnant.'

'Get rich.'

'What for? You're going to die.'

'So I can spend the money, you idiot!'

'Leave something so people will remember me.'

'Kill someone.'

'Who?'

'Someone bad. That way, at least you do something good.'

Shag a princess. Write a book. Fall in love. Blow up the government. Die with a smile on my face.

'Leave my family with enough money so none of them have to work ever again.'

Everyone nodded. Of course you'd want to do that.

'What about the riots?' said Adam. 'The Zealots were there.'

One of the boys shook his head. 'Bunch of losers, cashing in.'

'Ah, come on. They were attacking the banks. They took over the town hall,' said Adam. '"Free cheese for everyone!"'

The boys laughed uneasily. The Zealots were a laugh, but they were so deadly serious as well. No one knew what to make of them.

'They didn't hold on to the town hall,' someone said.

'No, but they had to send the army in. The police were fighting among themselves,' said someone else.

Jack nodded his head. 'This is big,' he said. 'When the police won't do as they're told, the government's in real trouble.'

An argument broke out between those who supported

the status quo, and those who believed the whole state needed to be overhauled and changed. Adam listened. All he wanted – all any of them wanted – was a life. The question was, where could people like them get one? Not in a world like this, where other people held all the cards, that was for sure.

Then the coach turned up, and he forgot about the Zealots and got going with the game.

💀

The amazing thing, Lizzie thought, was how quickly life went from total adrenalin rush to utterly boring. Last night with Adam she had felt the future in the palm of her hand. Every window smashed, every door kicked in had seemed to be tearing down the prejudices and conventions that hemmed her in on all sides. She'd left Adam feeling as high as a kite, climbed into her dad's car – and had to endure half an hour of misery straight away.

'Out with the low-life … destroying property … vandalising the town,' he'd ranted. 'What are going to do – give it all away and turn out like your precious boyfriend, with no future and no hope?'

'You don't know what you're talking about,' she told him. 'We were all out there trying to make something happen. It's about hope. Changing the future. Not hanging on to as much you can for yourself.'

'You have a future,' he told her. 'I just wish you'd grow up and realise it.'

At home she'd had her phone taken off her and was sent to bed like a child. She was too tired to argue. The next morning, the consequences were announced. There were never any punishments in her house, just consequences. She was not to see Adam again. She was grounded for two weeks. No pocket money. No internet connection. No phone for a day. No this, no that.

Grounded — at seventeen? What were they on? The sooner she left home the better.

Later in the afternoon, she'd sneaked out to a neighbour's house. They had a daughter called Sarina about her age. Lizzie wanted to use her computer to make a mobile call to Adam.

Sarina was not exactly sympathetic.

'Why do you care?' said Lizzie, settling herself at the screen.

'Of course I care. Your parents are friends of my parents. What if my mum and dad find out you've been using our equipment, when you're supposed to be forbidden to go on the internet?'

'Oh, leave it, Sarina! No one will know, will they?'

'I know.'

Lizzie flicked through, trying to find the site she wanted.

'Your parents have rights, too,' wittered Sarina. 'You can't blame them. Those riots caused millions of pounds worth of damage. You could go to jail …'

'I told you, I never nicked anything and I never smashed anything. It's not illegal just being there.'

There it was. Mobile4free.com. Lizzie clicked through and signed on.

'Anyone with any sense would have left at once. Mum

and I were going shopping in Manchester this week. Now it looks as though we'll have to go to Leeds instead.' Sarina peered over her shoulder. 'Lizzie, what's that website? That's illegal!'

'Sarina! This is important. It's my boyfriend. Are you seriously trying to get in the way of true love?' she asked, swinging round to face her.

'They can trace that sort of thing. Now we're going to get into trouble because of you!'

Lizzie put her hands over the keyboard to stop Sarina getting to it. The little phone icon did a dance in the middle of the screen. *Come on, Adam, pick up!* she thought. She had to talk to him. Suddenly she was terrified that somehow, for no reason, he'd gone off her in the night.

'Hello?'

'It's me.'

'Lizzie! You OK?'

'Yeah. You?'

'Yeah.'

There was a pause while they both grinned at their ends of the phone.

'Hey, guess what, Ads? I can't see you ever again. I'm banned.'

'Really?'

'You want to see me?'

'What do you think? I'm just missing you. It's like …'

Behind her, Sarina was fidgeting. Lizzie tried her utmost to pretend she wasn't there.

'It's like we had that night and now it's all wrong, being apart,' Adam said.

That was it. That was it exactly.

'What are you doing tomorrow?' she said. 'My cousin Julie's having a party. She's loaded – it'll be amazing! Mum wants me to go, she thinks I'll meet a better class of boyfriend there. I can even have my phone back.' She laughed. 'She'll tell Julie you can't come but Julie won't care. She's got this nicey-pie image but underneath it she's so, so bad …'

They agreed to meet up outside the cinema in Stockport. Lizzie would pick him up in her little Punto. And …

'And Ads?' she said. 'That'll be the night …' Then she put down the phone before he could say anything.

Sarina, who had been sitting there soaking it all up, stared at her.

'What did that mean, that'll be the night?' she asked.

'Mind your own business,' said Lizzie. But she couldn't help smiling.

Sarina smiled back. 'Are you in love with him?' she asked.

Lizzie ducked her head. She wanted it – but it was too soon.

'You won't be really, because you're too young,' said Sarina. 'You just think you are, I expect. But it's still very sweet. Have you got your contraception sorted out?'

'You know all about that, do you, Sarina?'

'I already had sex. Two months ago. It was with a boy I met at a party. We did it in one of the spare bedrooms.'

'Were you going out with him?'

'No. I was just curious.'

Lizzie laughed. She was an odd one, Sarina. But Lizzie was curious. 'Did you like it?' she wanted to know.

Sarina pulled a face. 'I expect it gets better as you get older.'

Lizzie made her way back home. Tomorrow night. Her parents had already agreed to let her go to the party. Julie was rich, and rich was good, as far as they concerned. They were hoping she'd meet up with some dull boy with loads of money. No chance. It was her and Adam, all the way. *All* the way.

The thought sent a little thrill of excitement down through her stomach. When they'd first met up again, he'd seemed a bit of a pain – thought far too much of himself. But now she knew there was so much more to him than that. And then last night. The gig, the death of Jimmy Earle, the riots afterwards, had blown her away. It had brought them together in a way she couldn't even describe – it was so thrilling.

Was it love?

She wanted it to be. Last night she had been sure it was, but what would it be like next time they met, in the cold light of day?

She climbed in through the bathroom window. *Let it be love*, she thought. She slipped past the sitting room, where her parents were watching rubbish on the TV. *Let it be love. Let it be something. Let it be anything rather than this.*

CHAPTER 4

COME THE FALL

Adam got back home happier than he could ever remember. '*That'll be the night*,' Lizzie had said. She could only have meant one thing. He felt like a kid on Christmas Eve.

It was Saturday night and he could have gone out with his mates, but he gave it a miss. He wanted to be fresh for tomorrow, and anyway he didn't have the money for two nights out in one week. His mum was still in bed when he got home, but his dad was up, fretting in front of the TV. Jess wasn't answering his calls again.

'So where is he now that's so secret?' he wanted to know.

'At work,' said Adam. 'He never picks up at work, you know that.'

It was infuriating. Adam was always allowed to do what he wanted, but Jess was guarded like the crown jewels. Adam never knew whether to be offended or delighted, but he was determined not to let his father's mood puncture his own.

'Hey, maybe he's got a girl. He doesn't have to report everything to you, you know.'

His dad grunted – the nearest he ever got to admitting he might be wrong. He flicked through the internet channels and found the news.

There were more riots going on.

'Again.' He shook his head. 'Manchester will be in ashes by the time they finish with it.'

But it wasn't just Manchester. The Zealots and some of the other rebel groups had put out a call for people not to loot, but to protest. And people had heard them. Crowds were gathering in Leeds, London, Birmingham, Bristol, Newcastle – all the major cites. There was a crowd of over twenty thousand already in Albert Square – far more than the night before. All sorts of people had come to show support – students, workers, the professions. It was the biggest protest for decades.

Jimmy Earle's death had started something. Discontent had been growing for years; now it had found a spark. Unrest was flaring up all over the country.

Once again, the Zealots had occupied the town hall and made it up to the roof; once again the police had turned up to try and get them out – but this time there were many more people getting in the way. There was no violence, no throwing bottles and bricks. The crowd just stood there, facing them down, standing between them and the Zealots. Someone had a huge banner up, spread halfway across the square: 'You Shall Not Pass.'

The police had made a commitment to the crowds, apparently: don't attack us and we won't attack you. So far, both sides seemed to be honouring it.

Adam was fascinated. Even his dad had to admit this was something new.

'Maybe now the government will act to do something for the ordinary man,' he said.

Adam got to bed late, after two. He went to sleep with a smile on his face. Tomorrow was the day. Big party. Rich people.

Him and Lizzie.

He had everything to live for.

He was planning on lying in late, but his dad came in at ten with a cup of tea and put it on the bedside cabinet by his head. He stood looking down at him until Adam couldn't bear it any more.

'What?' he moaned.

'Jess hasn't come back.'

'No, Dad!' Not this again. He curled back over. The whole house had to sit up every time Jess had a night out? It was crazy!

'Didn't you hear? Jess is missing. No call, no message, nothing. Get up, get up.'

'What for?'

'To help.' His dad turned and left the room. So

– 38 –

annoying! Jess had found a girl, at last, and turned off his phone so he didn't have to listen to their dad going on in his ear while he was on the job. So what? God's sake!

'You're bonkers!' he yelled.

'Come down. Your mother is up, too,' shouted his dad from the stairs. 'Does that make you start to worry now? Up, up! This is an emergency.'

Adam wanted to go to sleep again, but he was too cross. The old fool had woken his mum up as well. But it was a little odd, he had to admit. Jess always rang home – always always always. He dragged himself up and went downstairs to see what was going on. His mother was leaning against the kitchen counter, watching him as he came in scowling, still feeling grumpy from being disturbed.

'I think this time we have something to worry about,' she said.

His father, of course, had been up all night waiting and worrying. At about six in the morning he'd started to make calls. Eventually, about an hour ago, he had hunted down Jess's workplace, which was the one thing Jess had kept from him. It turned out that Jess had left four months before.

'He's been lying to us all this time,' said the old man.

'Not lying, necessarily,' said Adam's mum.

'What else do you call it? He said he was working there.'

'Maybe a white lie. Not wanting us to worry ...'

'He's probably just changed jobs,' said Adam. 'You know what you're like, Dad, always worrying. Maybe he got demoted or something. Less money, you know? He wouldn't want you to worry about it, would he?'

'He's not succeeded very well,' said his dad.

Adam looked hopefully at his mum. But this time, she was scared, too.

His dad tried to report Jess missing to the police, but they didn't want to know. He'd have to be away for over a week before they'd do anything. His mum cooked breakfast for everyone to fill in a bit of time, then went to bed, hardly able to keep her eyes open any more. It was a mystery, but Adam still found it hard to worry about it. Nothing ever happened to steady Jess, his boring older brother.

He was wrong. The answer fell through the letterbox at midday.

Adam found it on the mat – a plush white envelope with a black band around it. He knew what it was at once. He'd seen them on TV before. The Zealots sent them out to the relatives of fallen fighters.

Jess? A fighter? It was beyond belief.

The envelope was addressed to his mum and dad, but there was no stamp. It must have been delivered by hand. Adam opened the door and ran out into the street, but there was no one to be seen. Whoever had put it through the box was already gone.

He took it through to his dad in the sitting room.

'What is it?' his father asked, looking up at him, small and frail in his chair.

'The Zealots.'

His father looked terrified. He tore the envelope open

and scanned it. His face crumpled.

'This is impossible. Not Jess.'

He glanced up at Adam, then down at the implacable print that would never change its story. 'No, no, no,' he murmured. 'No, no, no, no.'

Adam read over his shoulder. At the top was the Zealots' logo – an angry rat with a pot of paint – but the slogan had changed. Before it had been 'Our time will come.' Now it read 'Our time is now.' Underneath, it announced that Jess Whitely had given his life in the fight for human rights and self-determination, at the Battle of Albert Square on Saturday night.

'One of their pranks,' murmured Adam. How could this be true? He knew his own brother, didn't he? But his heart was telling him he knew nothing at all.

His father struggled suddenly to his feet and ran up the stairs. 'Sharon, Sharon! They're saying our boy is dead. Sharon!'

Upstairs, Adam heard his mother exclaim sleepily. He sat down on his own at the kitchen table and waited to see what would happen next.

💀

The rest of the day was spent in a state of shock. His mother kept leaking tears, which, more than anything, began to convince Adam that something terrible had really happened. They went over and over everything they knew, but none of them could believe that Jess really was a Zealot. He'd got caught up in the riots, he'd been kidnapped, he'd been arrested by mistake. Any minute now he'd ring them up and explain everything. But the day went on and no call came. Adam's dad made more phone calls – the hospitals, the police, Jess's work again. The police came round as soon as they heard about the letter and emptied Jess's room, searching for evidence. They took all his stuff away, even the letter. They told them that they'd check dental records, DNA, anything else they could to try and match the remains they had collected in Manchester the day before.

'Remains?' said his father. 'My son will still have a face, won't he?' The policeman shrugged and said it was just procedure, but Adam knew what he meant. Officially, it was never admitted, but he had seen it for himself: a Zealot self-igniting on the roof of the town hall. There had been more last night apparently, setting fire to themselves on the roofs of the houses in two or three cities around the country. Could one of them have been Jess, staggering across the roof and pitching in flames down to the crowds below?

The day dragged on; the news sank in and became real to them. At about three in the afternoon his mother couldn't bear it any longer and went back to bed. Adam kept his dad company in the front room, trying to watch TV. They sat there staring at the screen, going through the motions, trying to distract themselves from the exhaustion of grief. His dad made cup of tea after cup of tea, and finally broke down sobbing, sitting in front of the latest news bulletin. Clumsily, Adam sat on the arm of his chair, put his arm around him and tried to comfort him.

'But where had he been going for so long?' his dad

said through his tears. 'He's been giving me money all the time. Where did he get it from? Tell me that.'

'Maybe the Zealots have been providing it for him,' suggested Adam.

His father shook his head. He could not believe it. For Adam, too, it was impossible to take in. All his life Jess had seemed so ordinary — colourless, even. Now it looked as though they knew nothing about him at all.

'What does it mean?' he asked his dad.

'For you?' asked his father. 'That's what you're thinking, isn't it?'

Every now and then his father came out with these mean little remarks. He should be used to it by now but they took his breath away every time.

'It means work. No more school for you. We have to find you a job. Unless you can find one for me, of course.' He held up his ruined hand and shook it in the air.

Quietly, Adam got up and went to his room to lie down. Some time later, he heard his father go in to see his mother and she began to weep again. He could hear his father's voice softly murmuring, trying to console her. He felt his own grief at the back of his throat like a hard lump, but there were no tears, not yet. He lay there for a long time, and tried to imagine what had happened, and what it meant, and found that he wasn't able to do it. After a time, he began to cry, too. Then he fell asleep.

☠

At about six o'clock, he woke up from an otherworldly dream and realised that he was late. Tonight was the night.

He had a party to go to.

As quietly as he could, Adam got up and began to dress in his best clothes. He knew he shouldn't go, but he also knew that he wasn't going to stop himself. Already, through the grief and shock of what had happened, he could feel the world closing in around him. No school, no education – no life. He was going to end up like his mum, working the phone at the call centre for fourteen hours a day. This party might be his last chance. As for Lizzie – anyone could see she was too good for him. He wasn't going to tell her what had happened, or what it meant. It was too humiliating.

Before he went out, Adam rooted around under his bed and pulled out the condoms he kept hidden in a little cardboard box. He put them in his pocket, all except one, which he took to an old electrical socket in the wall that had been disconnected ages ago. He unravelled the tiny copper threads sticking out of the wall and used one of them to pierce a hole in the condom. It was tiny; you'd never know. Sitting on his bed, he texted her.

'Getting ready to go,' he wrote. And then he typed in the magic words:' I love you.'

Such a little phrase, I love you. What did it mean? It meant, I want to spend my life with you. I want you to give me your life. Please love me back.

He got up and crept downstairs like a thief in the night. He caught the bus out to Stockport to meet her. On the way, a text came back.

'I love you too Adam.'

Adam put the phone in his pocket. The bus pushed

forward through the end of the day. He leaned his head against the window and felt tears leak out of his eyes. He wiped them away with the back of his hand. In his pocket the condoms were coming along for the ride – the good ones in the left one, the bad one in the right.

Of course he wasn't going to do it. Of course not. How could he do that to Lizzie? Even though, with Jess gone, she was his only way out.

CHAPTER 5

THE CONTAINER PARK

A young woman was being beaten up in a lorry container.

The container was one of several thousand in a vast open-air facility close to the railway line in east Manchester. The boxes were stored two, three or more high in long lines, row after row of them stretching off into the distance towards vanishing point, as if some gigantic autistic child had arranged them this way. It had. The child's name was industry. A few decades ago the place had been buzzing with activity, lorries driving to and fro up the aisles, forklift trucks lifting the boxes on and off the lorries, stacking them, storing them, emptying them. Now, with the recession in its twentieth year, all was still

– on the outside, at least. Hidden away inside many of the boxes it was a hive of activity.

The young woman doubled up from a violent blow to the stomach, but didn't fall down, as she was held up from behind. Someone delivered her a blow to the kidneys, another at the front punched her in the face. Then they let her fall. She hit the carpet with a thud.

'Ready?' said the stocky man with greying hair who was directing the beating.

The young woman shook her head, dribbling blood and spit on to the carpet. With a grimace, the older man stamped on her thigh and she curled up in pain.

From the inside, you wouldn't know they were in a container at all. It was carpeted, decorated with stripy wallpaper, furnished with a desk and executive chair, coffee machine and other office equipment. Around and about, other containers had been converted into dormitories, living spaces, more offices, a gym, cafeterias and several laboratories. This was a factory. They made Death.

Florence Ballantine sat back on his desk and gestured with his finger for the lads to carry on. Either the girl was tougher than she looked, or else she genuinely did know nothing about it, but Ballantine was certain of one thing: the Death that had been handed out in Albert Square on Friday night had come from his facility. There were going to be a whole lot of kids dying suddenly next week. That was fine by him – except that instead of buying it in the post-Jimmy euphoria, they'd got it for free, at his expense. That was another matter altogether.

The stuff had to be his. Apart from the fact that he was

the only man on the planet making cheap Death, he kept tabs on every single pill that left the production line, and he was several thousand short.

'Smack her in the kidneys or the tits. I don't want any damage to her beautiful mind,' said Ballantine to the heavy working on the girl. The last thing he wanted was for her to be unable to work. He needed her, at least for now. This girl and her friend, who had already been through this procedure, were Zealots, contracted in to oversee the manufacture of black market Death at Ballantine's facility. Why the rebel group would want to help him make Death was beyond him, but he certainly wasn't going to say no – at least until he'd worked out how to make it himself. But that was proving harder than he'd thought.

The heavy delivered a good one to the kidneys. The girl collapsed on to the ground, groaning, and was sick on the carpet. Fuck! Guys just didn't know how to deal out violence these days. The office would stink of disinfectant for the rest of the day.

Ballantine bent over her with his hands on his knees. 'Your boyfriend told us, anyway,' he said. 'We just need to corroborate his story. Might as well,' he said, temptingly. 'This is just violence. You wouldn't want me to tell these boys to step it up a notch, would you?'

'But I don't know!' insisted the girl, and she started to cry.

Ballantine nodded. One of the lads kicked her in the breast. She curled up around it, panting with pain and writhing around. But she still wasn't talking. It looked like she really didn't know.

In that case, it had to be one of his own guys who had stolen the pills. Ballantine could feel his blood pressure going up at the mere thought.

'My turn.' said a voice behind him. 'I got something I want to try …'

That was Christian, his son. Ballantine looked distastefully at him. He looked like a freak – forty-five years old and he dressed like a kid in baggy jeans, a baseball cap and a t-shirt with a picture of a girl in a bikini snowboarding. What sort of gangster dressed like that? Fuck's sake.

'You leave her alone,' he said. No way was he going to let Christian on her – he'd ruin her for good, knowing him. It was just his bad luck to have a psycho for a son. He peered into his eyes suspiciously.

'Are you taking your fucking meds?'

'Jesus, Dad, do we have to talk about this in public?' Christian whined.

'Is he taking his fucking meds?' demanded Ballantine, addressing a big man standing by Christian's side – Vince, his bodyguard.

Vince nodded. 'Absolutely, Mr Ballantine. Every day. I take them out of the packaging myself.'

Ballantine glanced again at his son, who was seething at being reminded in front of the boys that he was a psycho on meds. Then he looked down at the girl, who had got herself up on to her hands and knees, bleeding from her nose and mouth.

'I'm telling you, kid,' he said, 'if you're lying to me, it won't just be you. It'll be your family, it'll be your friends, it'll be the people you met on the bus coming to work this week. OK. Until we find out who's been stealing from me, you stay on the park. You don't go anywhere. You don't go for a shit without telling me about it. Now get her out of my sight.'

The girl was dragged out. Ballantine didn't like people outside in daylight, but it wouldn't do any harm for the rest of the staff to see someone limping about. Good for discipline.

One of the guys shook his head. 'Tough kids,' he said.

'Tough kids?' sneered Ballantine. 'They're chemists, right? That's both of them we've done good and not a word. They only got out of university a year or so ago, they don't have it in them. Which means, gentlemen, that one of you, or one of your staff – which amounts to the same thing – is stealing drugs off me. I am not a happy man.'

The guys shuffled their feet and looked anxious.

'We have a leak.' Ballantine thought about how angry it made him and he started yelling. 'Have you any idea what this operation cost me? This is a fucking big risk and I am being let down badly here. People are taking this stuff for free. You hear me. Fucking free. Jesus!'

'Mr Ballantine, those kids are lying. They have to be lying. Everyone else is watertight; they're the only ones we never worked with before.'

'Where did kids like them learn to take a beating like that? University? They teach getting beat up as a chemistry unit at university? No. So you better find out who it is before I do it myself, OK? Because when I do find out, I am going to sack whoever was involved, and I am going to sack whoever was in charge of them. It should never have got this far.'

The guys shuffled their feet awkwardly. Getting sacked from this firm meant losing a good deal more than your job.

'Back to work. Christian, Alan. Distribution. I want that drug on the street before it starts to occur to people that it's not a good idea to take it. And this time, I want them paying for it.'

Sulkily, the guys edged out and hurried off to work on their own staff. Someone was going to have to take the rap for this. All they were bothered about was that it wasn't going to be them.

CHAPTER 6

THE PARTY

When Lizzie received Adam's 'I love you' text, it took her by surprise. It didn't make her feel happy though — it made her anxious. How come? Wasn't it exactly what she'd wanted?

She did want it. But …

The thing was, it was so quick. She hadn't even thought about love until the night before last, when Jimmy Earle died onstage in front of them and they'd spent the night out on the streets, caught up in the riots. It had been the most amazing night. If he'd had said it then, she'd have believed it. But now, in the cold light of day, she was less sure. If this was love, she was still falling. Why did he need to rush in and make out it had already happened?

It made her feel cross, with herself as much as him. There were a hundred voices in her heart, and ninety-nine of them were overjoyed. But one was going, 'Yeah? You reckon?' And Lizzie being Lizzie, ninety-nine out of a hundred just wasn't good enough.

She picked him up at the cinema, and he looked dreadful.

'You OK?' she asked.

'Yeah, great, I feel great. Hey, I'm so looking forward to this,' he told her, and he shot her a smile so sickly, so unfamiliar, she was shocked.

By the time she got the car on the motorway she'd worked out exactly what was going on. He'd told her he loved her and now he was regretting it. Just like a boy. Just like Adam! One minute you were the centre of his world, the next he treated you like you'd pissed on his chips.

One thing was for sure – he'd still be wanting the shag she'd promised him. *See about that, then*, she thought. She pulled out into the fast lane and put her foot down, ninety miles an hour. Maybe the atmosphere would improve at the party. The sooner they got there, the better.

Julie's house was set back from the road, so they passed it twice. There were electric gates, painted black and gold, and a drive winding up through young rhododendrons. Then they turned the corner and saw the house.

'Da-da!' said Lizzie.

It was ridiculous. It was half mock Tudor, half Swiss chalet, but with turrets. Adam and Lizzie sat and goggled

– 53 –

at it. Was it fabulous or was it hideous? Adam had no idea.

'It must have been built by a footballer,' said Lizzie.

There was a bit of field set aside for the car park, full of expensive motors – a couple of Ferraris, an old Roller, any number of Porsches and Jags. Lizzie parked up and looked over at Adam. He gave her another ghastly smile.

'I love you, Lizzie,' he said.

'Ads …' she said.

'What?'

'Nothing.'

She got out of the car and led the way towards the house.

Lizzie's cousin spotted them as they came in and rushed over to meet them.

'Lizzie! You made it.'

'Julie! This is Adam …'

'Guys! Excuse me, I just want to borrow her for a moment – hey, Adam, get a drink, they're over there.' She waved a hand over to the left and moved off to the right, pulling Lizzie with her. 'We won't be long,' she said.

Lizzie just had time to turn a surprised smile on him before she was hauled away into the crowd and hurried up the stairs.

'You are not going to believe some of the people I've got at this party,' said Julie. 'They practically own the world!'

'Is this your parents' place? What happened to that nice house in Knutsford?'

'Daddy got seriously rich.'

'I thought he already was seriously rich.'

'He got seriously richer.'

'That was such a great house! This place looks like it was designed by a footballer.'

'It was!'

They creased up on the stairs.

'Do they know?' asked Lizzie. 'Your parents? Won't they go mad when they find out you've had a huge party here?'

'They're away in … on holiday somewhere. They'll never know. The cleaners will come in. Professionals.'

'But stuff gets broken. Stuff always gets broken. They'll know.'

Julie stopped and put her finger on the side of her nose.

'No one would DARE. I have people at this party who will absolutely deal with anyone who gets out of order. If anyone so much as sneezes on the trifle, they will literally get turned inside out.'

Lizzie laughed, a little uncertainly. 'What sort of people?'

'People you would not believe. I won't even introduce you to them. *That* sort of people.'

Julie was drunk, and her bright eyes indicated alcohol wasn't all she'd had. She pulled Lizzie into a little room, and fetched a mirror out of a drawer with several lines of white powder on it and a fifty-pound note rolled into a tight tube.

'Be careful. It's not cut.'

'What is it?'

'XL5.'

'What's that?'

'Rocket fuel. Try it.'

Lizzie paused, then bent down to sniff up the end of one of the little lines. 'Wow,' she said.

'Isn't it? Get this — I'm not paying for any of it. The booze — anything!'

'Who is?'

'Older men.'

'Julie!'

'Not *that* sort of older men. Not like they want favours. Like, I want a party and they want a party, and I have the house so they provide the drinks and the … nasal comestibles, you know?'

'Oh my God.'

'What?'

'My brain. My whole body!'

'Yeah, innit? Come on! I'll introduce you to some of them.'

'But not the older ones.'

'No! Not the older ones. Not the ones I won't introduce you to. The guys you're going to meet will all be top-notch, high-quality boyfriend material.'

'I have a boyfriend. You just pulled me away from him. Can I take some of this down for him?'

'That's not a boyfriend. In entertainment terms, he's a night in with a packet of crisps and a nice film.' Julie slipped her a wrap from the back of the drawer. 'I mean something with a bit more of a kick. I'm talking about nightclub boyfriends. I'm talking about boys who know parts of your body you didn't even know existed. That one is *so* off the shelf.'

'You're an idiot.'

'Come on! I'll introduce you.'

Adam had rarely felt so out of place. All around him, the beautiful people draped themselves on items of expensive but badly chosen furniture, or gathered in groups across the expanse of cream carpet. A girl in a pair of jeans that cost more than Adam's dad's monthly pension sucked on a joint and watched Adam's best leather jacket – it had cost over a hundred pounds second-hand – turn on his back into a laughable rag.

The beautiful people averted their beautiful eyes.

He made his way to the bar, a long table carpeted with bottles of every form of alcohol known to man. A barman in a white suit on the other side raised an eyebrow at him.

'Er. What do you recommend?' Adam asked.

A couple of minutes later he was standing with a pint mug in his hand, with a drink called a Zombie in it. A cube of sugar burned weakly on top of a mound of ice. He stuck a can of beer in one pocket and a small bottle of vodka in the other – he had a feeling he was going to need friends tonight – then headed off to find Lizzie. He found her soon enough, killing herself laughing with Julie in the middle of a crowd. Everyone was tall, slim, tanned and expensively dressed. By the look of it they were pretty amusing, too. Lizzie was having the time of her life.

He walked past a couple of times in the hope that he'd catch her attention, but she didn't notice him at all. In the end he just shouldered his way in among them, and went, 'Da-da!' as if he'd just pulled off a trick.

At least it got him some attention. The beautiful people stared at him, then burst out laughing. He had no idea if they were laughing with him or at him. Then they started jabbering away again, glancing sideways at Adam as if he was made out of mud. But Lizzie found time to squeeze his arm, before Julie dragged her off again.

'See you in a bit,' she hissed. She shoved a little paper packet into his hand, winked and vanished. Adam tried to make conversation.

'What do you do?' one of the girls asked.

'Still at school,' he said.

'What does your father do?' she said.

Adam thought about it, and decided he couldn't be arsed trying to impress. 'He used to be a stonemason, until he had an accident at work,' he told her, and watched the girl's face fall.

'You're joking.'

'Nope.'

'So you …'

'Don't have any money. Yet. Yet,' he said.

'So what are you doing here?' she wanted to know.

'I'm a tourist,' he told her.

She smiled. 'So we're …'

'Yeah. You're the zoo.'

The girl's face fell, for the second time. Adam waltzed off. It didn't feel great, but making a fool out of someone else was better than feeling like a fool himself.

He needed to pee, so he got himself to a toilet and

snorted up the entire packet of powder Lizzie had handed him.

Wow, he thought. Suddenly, he was in the mood to party. He ran straight out of the toilet and into the first group of people he could find. Everything was great! All his earlier anxieties about fitting in were gone. He was witty, attractive, full of ideas and jokes. In fact, he'd rarely felt so good in his entire life. His problems – Jess, his parents, his whole life – all disappeared into a sparkling fountain of happiness and well-being.

It lasted about fifteen minutes, going up all the time. Then – panic attack. It took him almost without warning. One minute he was chatting happily away to a girl in the hallway, then his heart began beating too fast, and before he knew it his head was about to explode and he could hardly breathe. He put out a hand to steady himself on the wall next to him. The girl he was talking to looked at him curiously.

'You OK?' she asked.

He looked back at her, his mouth opening and closing like a goldfish, with nothing coming out.

The girl laughed shrilly.

'Look at this guy,' she shrieked. 'It looks as if his brains are going to come out of his ears.'

Adam turned and fled, stumbling out into the garden, his heart going like a road drill, his brains boiling in hot fat. What was going on? That powder he'd hoovered up? And he'd been drinking cocktails. How many? At least three. He checked his phone for the time. They'd been at the party less than an hour and he was already so off his face he was hardly able to speak. How had it happened?

There was no way Lizzie could see him like this. He had to hide.

He headed off across the lawns into the night. There were lights around the edges of the flower beds, and a big, waxy yellow moon overhead, so at least he could see where he was going. Eventually he came to some water, with a dark, overgrown tree hanging over it. He crawled right under the dense canopy, where the thick leaves hid him completely. He lay on the ground in the dark shadows and waited for his heart to stop leaping around his chest like a rat in a trap.

Gradually, his breathing stilled, his heart began to beat rhythmically. But then, one by one, as if they were things he hadn't thought of up till now, the events of the day came crowding in on him. His parents weeping at home while he'd run away to have a good time. The pin-holed condom in his pocket – and Jess! Jess! Somehow he'd managed to forget about him altogether for the past couple of hours, but now the dreadful reality drove into his mind like an iron bolt. His lovely brother, gone, whom he'd thought he looked down on but in fact admired above anyone else. He'd thought Jess was someone he could rely on, even more than his mum and dad, but now he was dead and Adam had never even known him. Nothing was as it had seemed. All the hope and optimism of the past couple of days turned to despair. His life was ruined. He would never see his brother again.

Rolling over on to the dead leaves beneath him, Adam drew his knees up to his chest and held his breath. He hung on to the air as long as he could, but he had to breathe in the end, and when he did the tears came – great wracking sobs that tore at his chest, and which he was utterly unable to control. He lay in the dirt, bawling like a lost soul, astonished at both the intensity of his grief and the fact that he had somehow been so unaware of how bad he really felt.

☠

Julie was right when she said there were some interesting people at the party. In the space of an hour, Lizzie had been introduced to rock stars, drug dealers, lawyers, a high court judge, politicians and any number of hope-lessly cool people involved in various kinds of money management. It was fun, but she was getting worried about abandoning Adam. She and Julie were on the stairs babbling with an offshore accountant when she spotted him pushing his way across the room on his own. He looked lost.

Full up with XL5 and fizz, Lizzie's heart melted. He was a boy. He wouldn't know what a feeling was if it got down on its knees and bit his bottom. He was confused! Bless.

It was up to her to reassure him.

'Fun, huh?' said Julie. 'See anyone here you like … just miaow!'

'I told you, I already have a boyfriend.'

'Aw, you really like him, don't you? Are you …?' Julie rolled her eyes and rocked her hips.

Lizzie laughed. 'Not yet.'

'Are you going to?'

'I guess I am.'

'Of course,' Julie added, 'boys like that are just practice, you know? But it's a good idea to get a lot of practice in, if you see what I mean. So it's your first time with him? Has he been around much?'

'No. It's going to be his first time.'

'Oh my God!' Julie stopped dead and stared at her. 'And you …?'

'My first time, too,' Lizzie admitted.

'That's so sweet! Right. Come here.'

She dragged her off to a quiet spot on the landing, rummaged around in her bag, and dug out a key.

'I was keeping this for something special. It's the key to the summer house. It's in among the trees, there's a fridge, some champagne on ice. Nice little sound system. You know? It's very private, there's a huge duvet … the moon is out, it's by the lake. Hey! What d'you think?'

'Is there really a moon?' Lizzie peered out of the window – and yes, there it was, big and yellow, hanging among the trees.

'It's full, too, almost,' said Julie. 'Kinda cheesy, huh?'

'It's perfect!' Lizzie beamed and took the key.

Julie beamed back. 'Go for it, babe,' she said. 'Be gentle with him,' she called as Lizzie ran off. She sighed happily. Lizzie was so naive, she'd been worried about inviting her. There were some very dodgy sorts here tonight. But it was all right. She only wanted her sweet little virgin boy.

Lizzie spent the next twenty minutes running around the party with the key to the summer house in her pocket, trying to make Adam's dreams come true, and failing.

Irritating! Where was he?

She was aware she was being a little unfair – she'd been off on her own for ages, after all – but it did remind her that she was annoyed with him anyway. I love you. Really? Just like that?

Her mother had warned her that he was a gold-digger. 'I thought gold-diggers were girls,' she'd said.

'No, Lizzie. Gold-diggers are *poor*,' her mother replied.

Ridiculous. So how come she suddenly got the feeling he was trying it on? He was probably just desperate to get into her pants. Fine. So where was he?

She ended up on the mezzanine floor, where she hoped she'd spy Adam below, but instead she got pounced on by a pair of really odd guys – some of those older men that Julie had been boasting about, perhaps. One of them was a huge, powerful-looking man, built like a house. He was wearing a suit so sharp you could have tied his lapels to your shoes and skated on them. He looked hopelessly out of place at a party like this.

The other was somewhere in his forties, quite handsome at first glance, but you could tell as soon as you looked closely that he'd had loads of surgery to make it happen. The oddest thing about him was the way he was dressed, like an American teenager out of an eighties movie: baggy jeans hanging down his bum, t-shirt with a gory picture of Metallica on the front, trainers and, most ridiculous of all, a baseball cap with the peak halfway round his head. At first she thought it was fancy dress, but from the way he was preening himself, he obviously thought he looked cool. His eyes, which had trouble

– 63 –

meeting hers, kept dropping down to her breasts. All in all, he was one of the creepiest guys she'd seen in a long time.

It turned out that Vince, the sharp suit, was actually employed by the elderly teenager, whose name was Christian.

'As what?' Lizzie wanted to know.

Christian smiled. 'Whatever I want him to be,' he said. 'Right, Vince?'

'You bet, Mr Christian.'

'You mean he's some sort of servant?' she asked. 'Like Jeeves and Wooster? He's your butler?' She snorted.

'Kinda,' said Christian. 'And my bodyguard.'

'Wow,' said Lizzie. She looked at the sharp suit. 'What do you need a bodyguard for?' she asked.

Christian shrugged. 'I'm a rich man,' he said, gazing vaguely at her groin. 'Rich people get kidnapped, attacked, robbed. All sorts of bad things.' He shook his head. 'There are always people about who aren't happy about stuff.'

Lizzie thought about it. 'Would he take a bullet for you?' she demanded.

Christian seemed struck by this thought. 'Would you?' he asked, turning to Vince.

'That's what I'm paid for, sir,' said Vince.

Christian smiled. 'I pay him a fuck of a lot of money. He's carrying. Show her,' he ordered.

Obediently, Vince turned slightly away from the crowd, and opened his immaculate jacket, revealing a holster with a gun tucked inside. Lizzie was so shocked she almost choked on her wine.

'Me, too. But not a gun.' Christian lifted up his t-shirt to reveal a stout-looking knife with an odd, short blade.

'Why's the blade so short?' she wanted to know.

'Specialist item,' said Christian. But he didn't offer to tell her what for.

Lizzie was both scared and mesmerised. 'Wow. But what do you *do*?' she asked. 'How come all these people want to kill you?'

Vince coughed discreetly. 'A lot of people would think that was a silly sort of question to ask,' he said.

'Lizzie's not a lot of people,' said Christian. He smiled at her, revealing a set of teeth that looked at least twenty years younger than the rest of him.

Vince made a soft but exasperated noise, like an irritated parent.

Christian ignored him. 'All sorts of stuff. Drugs. Weapons.'

'You're a gangster?!'

He shook his head. 'Businessman!' he said.

'You don't look like a gangster,' Lizzie said to him. 'He does,' she added, nodding at Vince.

'I might be in disguise,' said Christian.

A joke! It wasn't all that funny, but Lizzie laughed anyway, out of kindness as much as anything. Christian was delighted; he beamed at her.

'I like you,' he told her, reaching out and touching her lightly on the arm.

It was a pass, definitely. 'That's very nice, thank you,' said Lizzie. Time to escape. She began to edge away but he plucked at her clothes.

'Do you want another drink?' he demanded. 'What do you want? Vince'll get it for you, won't you, Vince?'

'But he'd have to leave you on your own, wouldn't he?' Lizzie said. 'What if an assassin comes? Hey – what if I'm an assassin?'

'Are you?'

'No,' she admitted.

'I didn't think you were. So, what'll you have?'

Lizzie shook her head. 'Sorry,' she said. 'I've got to go and find my boyfriend. Another time, eh?'

'Hang on …' Christian fished a card out of his pocket and handed it to her. 'Give me a call sometime,' he said.

'Thanks. Great,' said Lizzie, brightly. She turned and made her way downstairs.

Behind her, Christian nudged his bodyguard. 'I like her,' he said. 'She'd make a good girlfriend. Follow her.'

Vince looked suspiciously at his employer. 'Sir, excuse me for asking, but did you drink your milk this morning?'

Christian was furious. 'Fuck you, Vince,' he said. 'This is a party. We do not talk about milk at a party. For your information, yes, I did drink my fucking milk, as you well know since you stood over me watching me swallow it. How much do I pay you, Vince?'

'A fuck of a lot of money, sir.'

'Right. So go and do as I tell you.'

'Yes, Mr Christian,' said Vince, and he edged his way into the crush after Lizzie.

CHAPTER 7

LOSING IT

She finally caught up with Adam in the entrance hall.

'Where've you been?' she demanded.

Adam gave her a wobbly smile. 'Couldn't find you. Went for a walk,' he said.

He looked really odd. He had leaves and mud on his clothes. 'What's been going on?' she asked.

He laughed awkwardly. Suddenly she was struck by a dreadful suspicion. Leaves on his clothes …?

'Looks more like you went for a roll,' she said primly.

'No! No, no. I had to lie down. I got in a mess. That stuff you gave me …'

'XL5,' she said. She looked at him more closely. His eyes were red. 'Have you been crying?' she asked.

'No!' insisted Adam. He hurt so much, he couldn't

admit it to anyone — least of all Lizzie. 'I just took too much of that stuff, that's all.'

'How much did you have?'

'All of it,' he admitted.

'All of it? Adam!'

'I had to go for a walk, it blew my head off.'

Lizzie hovered for a moment between anger and pity — anger because he'd hogged the lot, pity because …

'You're only supposed to have a tiny little line. It's uncut.'

'No one told me,' he said, and his voice sounded tearful. Pity won.

'Oh … Come here.' She linked arms with him, and planted a little kiss on his cheek. 'Poor soldier. Beaten up by drugs.' He grinned at her — another wobbly, uncertain grin. Sweet! 'Feeling better?'

'Bit better.'

He looked so upset, she laughed. 'Come with me.'

She led the way out of the house and down the steps. A bottle of champagne, some relaxing music, a snuggle up under the duvet. If that didn't make him feel better, nothing would.

The moon, the balmy air, the music drifting across from the house. Adam was pretty much out of his head, coming down now, in grief for his brother, his life, God knows what else and still feeling panicky; but even so, he knew that this had to be his time with Lizzie. He squeezed her arm. It was going right again. He felt really weird, but it was going right. With his other hand he touched the packet of doctored condoms in his back pocket. He was going to lose his virginity and try to make his fortune in one go. It was so pathetic he snorted in amusement at himself.

'What is it?' demanded Lizzie.

'I'm having such a good time,' he said; but it sounded like sarcasm. He hurried on. 'Hey, look. Why don't we sneak upstairs and find a room?'

But Lizzie shook her head. 'You just come with me,' she said.

'What for?'

'I want to go for a walk.' She guided him across the lawn towards the lake, but Adam held back. It was the wrong direction. He wanted the house, a room. He wanted sex.

'I've already been this way,' he said.

She shot him a curious look. 'Just for me,' she wheedled.

But he stopped walking. 'No, let's go in and find a room. You haven't changed your mind again ...' Despite himself, his voice was sounding sulky.

'Adam ... don't do this to me, not now ...' But he was already certain she was putting him off.

'You're always making promises,' he complained. 'And then you back off. It's always the same.'

'Adam, stop it!'

'Are we going to do it or not?' he demanded.

She let go of his hand and shook her head. 'You know what, Adam? No, we're not. Just ...' She turned abruptly without finishing and stomped off back across the lawn.

'You never had any intention of it, did you?' he

shouted after her.

She spun on her heel. 'This,' she said, taking it out and shaking it at him, 'is the key to the summer house. There was going to be champagne on ice, nice music and the moon over the lake. I wanted it to be like that, and all you wanted was a fuck. So find someone else to fuck. OK? Because it isn't going to be me!'

She stormed off.

'Liar,' yelled Adam. He stood still and watched her go, then put his head in his hands. Was it true? Of course it was true! He'd talked himself out of it. Everything was turning to shit. Everything he touched – everything he even thought about, he now realised – all turned to shit.

He had to make it all right. He had no idea how. Just beg her to forgive him. Tell her what a dick he was. Tell her how much he loved her, before she found out the truth and gave him the boot anyway.

Turning, he ran back to the house and through the crowds, searching, searching, searching for her. But she was nowhere to be seen.

It just went to show. You could have a perfect night in a perfect setting with the perfect moon by the perfect lake listening to the perfect music, but if you tried to do it with an idiot, it wasn't going to work.

Lizzie wasn't inside more than a few minutes when she bumped into Vince, who told her that the boss would like to have a drink with her.

'No, thanks,' she said. She went to sit in the loo for a bit to have a cry, and when she came out, Christian was waiting for her, with Vince by his side bearing a couple of very elegant-looking cocktails on a tray. She was so taken aback she accepted one and ended up tucked away in a bay window in one of the reception rooms, while Vince kind of floated in the background, which she supposed was what servants did. She was aware that were really rather hidden. What if Adam came looking for her? Well, let him look. He could find her if he tried.

Adam had not yet totally imploded into his own misery, but he wasn't far off it. He should have been at home, grieving with his parents. Instead he'd tried to trick his girlfriend into giving him a future for free. Grief, betrayal, self-disgust and an avalanching sense of failure was overwhelming him. He quickly gave up trying to find Lizzie, and was leaning against a wall, sinking fast, swigging beer from a can, when Julie passed by and spotted him.

'What are you doing here?' she demanded. 'I thought you were off with Liz. Where is she?'

'I don't know,' he said.

Julie cast an expert eye over the hopeless mess before her. 'You've had a row,' she said.

Adam hung his head.

'Shit. Where is she?' Julie grabbed him by the arm and trailed him off to hunt her down. They found her eventually, trapped in a bay window talking to a weird-looking guy dressed up in fancy skateboard gear. Adam cringed back, and glanced anxiously at Julie, who was staring open-mouthed at them. She began to hiss in his ear.

'Shit, shit shit. This is bad, this is bad. See that guy

talking to her? That's Christian Ballantine. He is completely predatory. I mean, the guy is a pervert, first class – and he's rich. No one can lay a finger on him. We have to get her away from him.'

Adam shook his head. Julie ignored him.

'You go in this way, I'll go round the other side. Pincer movement. You are such a dick,' she added in despair. 'See the big guy in the suit? He's a gorilla, trying to stop anyone getting near them. You have to sneak past him. You got me?'

Adam peered around the big man. 'Does she want me to?'

'Of course she wants you to. She's gone on you. She said. Go get her, tiger. Say sorry and get her away as fast as you can, before …'

'What?

'Before he gets off with her and … interferes with her. She's yours, isn't she?'

Adam licked his lips. The pitiful remains of hope stirred sluggishly within him. He was still in with a chance!

'And don't let the suit see you,' hissed Julie. She shoved Adam in the back and he went tottering off towards them, while Julie scuttled off to get round to Lizzie from the other side.

Jesus, she thought, *talk about the cavalry*. Christian was very rich, very weird and very powerful. He thought he could do exactly as he wanted. There was a good reason for that: he could.

💀

Lizzie was trying to work out how to escape again without being hopelessly obvious about it when Adam suddenly appeared at her side.

'Talk?' he said.

Christian twisted round and glared angrily at him. 'Where the fuck's Vince?' he demanded.

Adam tugged at her sleeve; Christian grabbed hold of her arm. 'You're not going anywhere,' he said.

Lizzie had had enough. The pair of them were manhandling her like she was some kind of sandwich filling. She yanked furiously away. Adam let go at once, but Christian tightened his hold. It hurt. That was it. Lizzie took a deep breath and did what she had been told years ago to do on these occasions – stared Christian straight in the eye and screamed as loudly as she could.

There was a shocked and sudden silence. All around them in the crowded room, people turned to look, saw who was involved, and turned quietly away again. In the silence, Lizzie let out a brittle laugh. Then things moved very quickly.

Adam stuck a drunken fist out at Christian and, by sheer bad luck, caught him on the ear. Christian let out a howl and Adam disappeared backwards. At the same time Julie materialised, beamed at Christian and pushed her roughly away into the crowds.

'What? What's going on?'

'No. No, no, no, no, no,' said Julie. 'You are so out of here.'

Adam, meanwhile, was on a short journey to the front steps, the back of his leather jacket clenched firmly in the huge fist of Vince. He carried Adam out of sight round the side of the house, dropped him on to the gravel and gave him a short but expert beating; one blow to the head to knock him down, a couple as he collapsed, and three or four kicks while he lay on the gravel. Finally, he stamped on his head. Then he went back into the house. Shortly after, Julie came running out, pulling Lizzie by the hand. Lizzie was in tears.

'Just give me back my keys,' she begged.

'No, you're not driving in that state,' said Julie. 'Here's Harold anyway, he's going to give you a lift home,' she added, as a car came up the drive.

'I wish I'd never come,' Lizzie groaned. The whole thing was so utterly humiliating. Messed about by Adam, mauled by Christian, pushed around the place by Julie … and now, to top it all, she was being sent home early.

'It's your own fault, Liz. That boy is a wanker, a real wanker. And then you end up getting chatted up by Christian Ballantine of all people …'

'He wasn't chatting me up …'

'Yes, he was! Your mum is right; you're like a baby. Those people are gangsters! They're dangerous. You don't have any sense at all, no radar. You're like a rabbit in the headlights. He spotted you limping into his territory a mile away.'

Lizzie blubbed helplessly. The car pulled up next to them, and Julie guided her into the back seat.

'I'll get the car back to you tomorrow, OK? Don't go anywhere. Straight home,' she ordered the driver.

'What about Adam?' Lizzie cried.

'I'll sort Adam out,' said Julie, grimly. 'And, Liz – don't see him again. He's a tosser. You're better than that.'

She shut the door, and the car pulled away. As it did, a figure staggered out of the shrubbery and ran forward.

'Lizzie!' screamed Adam, holding out his hands for them to stop. The car drove quietly round him and off down the drive. 'Lizzie!' he groaned.

Julie came marching up and shoved him in the chest.

'You wanker,' she yelled. 'You complete, total wanker. If I catch you anywhere near my cousin again I'll have you beaten up properly, you hear me?'

'I'm sorry,' wept Adam.

'You are so pathetic. Just … fuck off.' She stormed back to the house.

'I don't have any money to get back,' Adam called after her.

'God.' Julie rolled her eyes. She dug in her pocket and fished out forty pounds for him. 'Don't let me ever see you round here again,' she said, and disappeared inside.

Adam put the money in his pocket and went back to weep in the shrubbery for a while. Then he phoned for a cab home.

CHAPTER 8

GARRY

In the taxi, Adam continued to cry. The future had been smiling at him only yesterday. Now it was leering at him like a death's head, stinking, filthy and full of fear.

You thought I was yours? it leered. *Well, I'm not.*

What had he done to deserve this? It wasn't even his fault! If it was anyone's fault, it was Jess's. Jess, who had pretended to love his family. Jess, who had lived and died a whole other life without any of them knowing about it. Jess the liar, Jess the fraud. His parents had kept telling him just how important his brother was but he had never really taken it on board. Now he'd gone, and he'd taken Adam's entire life with him. Adam had trusted him, and he'd been let down. Suddenly he hated Jess with all his heart. He wanted to stamp him to a pulp, to kick him, hurt him, dig him up out of the ground and strangle him. Even more than that, though, he wanted to ask him – why? Why had he fooled them all for so long? Why had he lied? What had he been doing all that time?

Who on earth *was* he?

He would never know. Jess had pulled off the ultimate escape from all questions, all blame, all guilt, all pain. Perhaps the thing that made Adam more angry than anything was the fact that Jess had put himself so totally beyond reach, and there was nothing he could do about it.

His kidney ached. His ankle was swelling up and growing stiff, his face red raw from the gravel. He'd cracked a rib, too; it hurt every time he breathed. Lizzie was gone; he'd blown every chance he ever had. He found the little bottle of vodka that he had stolen off the table and swigged at it, ducking out of sight of the cabbie, who was already eyeing him suspiciously.

What next? Go home? What for? To begin his new life? What a laugh! He didn't need work, he needed answers. Someone out there must know what Jess had been doing all this time – known him the way his family never had. But who? In all those years there'd only ever had one girlfriend, a girl called Maryse who had disappeared to London when she was eighteen and never been seen again. There had been one or two school and university friends … Garry, for instance. He remembered Garry. Bearded bloke in a wheelchair. He'd even been round to the house a few times.

Now he thought about it, Adam was sure he'd heard

Jess and Garry going on about the Zealots a few times, years ago. Conversations and arguments with his dad, about how cool the Zealots were, how at least they were doing something. That sort of stuff.

He was a nice guy, Garry. Stuck in a wheelchair, but he never let it get him down. Played basketball.

And ... Adam knew where he lived. Sort of. On the way back from a trip into town with Jess, they'd called in to see him. A dingy little two-up, two-down in Fallowfield. Him and Jess had been good mates for a while. Garry was in on it as well – betcha! If anyone knew what Jess had been up to, it was him.

Adam wasn't sure exactly where Garry lived, only the street. Once he'd paid the cabbie and got out, he wasn't even so sure about that any more. The last time he'd been there was years ago.

But he was in luck. As he finished off the remains of the vodka and limped up the road a bit – there it was. He recognised the colour of the drainpipe, which was painted purple.

There was a light on upstairs.

He tapped on the door. No reply. He banged. Nothing. He stood swaying outside for a moment.

Fuck this, he thought, *I'm dying here.*

'Garry!' he bawled suddenly. 'Garry!' He began to weep again. No one appeared, but he thought he heard a noise at the window.

'Let me in!' he yelled. Above him, the curtains twitched. 'Where's my brother? What happened to Jess?

Garry! Answer me! You know. I know you know.'

He kicked at the door and to his surprise it bent easily. It wasn't much more than plyboard. He leant back and flung his shoulder at it. The lock broke through the thin wood and Adam stumbled in, gasping at the pain in his ribs. Upstairs, someone shouted in surprise. He was standing in a cluttered sitting room. There was a stairway with a stairlift through an open door opposite him.

'What the fuck's going on? Jesus …'

He ran and looked up the stairs. Garry was on his way down on the stairlift. 'Who the fuck are you?' he screamed. 'What are you doing here? Get out of my house!'

Adam ran up to meet him. 'I'm Jess's brother. What happened to him? He's supposed to have died with the Zealots. You know, don't you, you know …'

There was noise above him. Someone else was up there. He peered up. 'Who's that?'

Garry was furious.

'You idiot, the police could be round. I don't know anything, Adam – go away!'

Garry didn't seem able to stop the stairlift, and continued past Adam and down. He grabbed out at Adam's sleeve with one hand, fiddling with the controls of the stairlift with the other. Adam pulled away.

'You used to talk about the Zealots. Where is he? Who's up there? Is that him?'

'No, of course it's not him. Adam, come here, come down here and talk to me. Jesus, this fucking thing won't work!' Garry leant backwards and snatched at him as the chair carried past on its way down. 'Adam! How do I know what happened to him?'

'Who's up there? What's going on?' In Adam's addled brain, everything that happened was about him and his brother. He pulled himself free and went tearing up the stairs, while Garry, howling in rage and frustration, continued down at a snail's pace. Adam burst into the bedroom. Someone was on the bed, covered up by the duvet. Adam dragged it off. It was a half-dressed girl. She let out a wail, and ran out of the room and off down the stairs.

'Stella! Don't go. Come back. Stella!'

Downstairs, the door slammed.

'Adam!' roared Garry.

Adam stood next to the bed looking wildly around him. He was certain Garry knew something. He began ransacking the room, looking for some sort of a clue. On the bed, on the floor, on the chair, on the table … He pulled open a cupboard by the bed and something spilled out. A bag of pills. He snatched them up. There was another roar behind him. Garry, flushed with rage, was clinging on to the door, his hairy face distorted in a fearful grimace.

'You stupid little fuck,' he screamed. He staggered towards him, grasping for the bag. 'Give me that … give me it …'

Adam danced out of reach. Garry was dealing drugs, was he? 'Tell me what happened to him! What do you know?'

'I don't know anything. What's wrong with you?'

'You know what's wrong with me!' Adam, to his shame, began to weep again.

'You little prick, Adam. Give me that! What are you doing?'

'This can pay for it – this can pay ...' cried Adam. He pushed Garry out of the way, and the crippled man fell to the floor. Adam ran out of the room and down the stairs.

'Adam, no! You don't know what you're doing. Come back!'

But Adam was gone, out of the door, on his way. Garry's yells stopped abruptly. Adam ran on. He ran and ran and ran, until the adrenalin stopped and the pain in his ribs kicked back in. He bent over, gasping for breath. When he'd recovered enough to move on, he put the bag of pills in his pocket and crept home.

It was over a mile back, and every step was agony. Halfway, under a street lamp, he took the bag of pills out and had a better look.

They were unmistakable. Little white caps with a crude black image printed on each one. A skull and crossbones.

It was a bag full of Death.

But it couldn't be. Death cost a fortune, everyone knew that. What was a poor man like Garry doing with this? There must have been fifty pills in there. They were worth ... It was crazy! Thousands. Tens of thousands. Some sort of fraud? It had to be ...

Adam put the bag back in his pocket and carried on home. When he got there, the house was still. He crept upstairs as quietly as he could and lay on the bed. He stayed still, trying not to think. He tried texting Lizzie.

'I'm sorry. Please talk to me.'

Nothing.

'Please, Lizzie, please. I need you.'

He stared at the screen, texted again. The same thing.

That was it. It was over. He was never going to see her again.

Adam took out the bag of pills and held one in the palm of his hand. He turned the TV on. It was an old film. A man and a woman kissed. She rested her head against his neck and sighed deeply.

Some kind of scam, those pills. Not real. But the news had said it was the Zealots handing the stuff out at Albert Square. If Garry was connected with the Zealots …

Could be. Maybe, maybe not. Who knew?

Adam popped the pill into his mouth, but didn't swallow, just held it there. It was an answer, wasn't it? One glorious week. What else had he got to look forward to now?

'We need a place of our own,' said the man on the TV. The woman reached up and kissed him again. She sighed.

He could sell the rest of the pills and have the time of his life. Why not?

The pill was dissolving in his mouth. It tasted acrid. Adam reached over to the glass of water by his bed, took a mouthful and swallowed.

He lay there. What had he done? Not much, he thought. What had he got to lose? Not much.

A shit life.

He knew he should get up and stick his finger down

his throat, but he didn't. He lay there and lay there and waited to see if he would, but he didn't. It was a relief, really.

Then he closed his eyes and fell asleep.

PART TWO:
THE LIST

PART TWO
THE LAW

CHAPTER 1

DAY 1

When Adam woke up the next morning, it happened so suddenly he was astonished. His eyes snapped open. He felt so clear-headed. His blood was fizzing. He was happy.

What's going on? he thought – and there it was, the past few days laid out before his eyes with total recall, every second in high definition. The concert, the riots, Jess, the party, Lizzie, how bad he'd cocked it up, Garry, the girl, the stairlift … and then right at the end of it, like a car crash, smack into a brick wall … Death.

He'd taken Death.

Adam leaped out of bed and stared at himself in the wardrobe mirror. His eyes sparkled. His skin was flawless – even the little spots on his forehead had vanished without trace. He was going to die? Impossible! He'd never felt so alive.

But how come? There'd been a fight. He'd been pulped! He felt where his rib had been cracked. There was a small, sharp pain there. Last night it had been agony.

The battering hadn't been a dream. This was Death working its magic, filling him up to the brim with life before it took it all away. He was transformed. He was quick, smart and strong. He was capable of anything …

And then he was going to die.

Adam stared at his reflection. This was him. A week to live? He tried to imagine himself dead and gone, tried to feel the stab of fear that must be in there somewhere. But he was too full of life. This was what it must have been like for Jimmy Earle. Now he got it. He stared at his fingers, the whorls on the tips, the flesh and blood and bone of them. They were a miracle of engineering. He was a miracle. Life itself was a miracle. The pattern of the wall-paper, the colours on the carpet. Outside the window a bird sang. That was a miracle. The whole glorious pageant of life was beating, beating − waiting for him to start up and go. And he was a part of it.

One week, eh? Death was on his heels, was it? He'd out-run it, out-gun it, out-smart it, out-live it − and then welcome it like an old friend. He gasped as another rush sped through him, smooth, fast, flawless. And it was still getting better! One week was plenty of time to do all the things he needed to do. How much real living did the average person get through in eighty or ninety years? How long did they spend staring at the wall, ashamed, asleep, doped up, stupid, whatever? How many of them were truly alive, the way he was alive right now? How many of them understood the glory and beauty of it? Hardly any. Maybe none at all. One week was time to do everything in the world so long as you lived hard enough, fierce enough, young enough, true enough. The rest of it was just waiting to die.

The waiting was over. It was time to live – right now!

No regrets. Regrets were for the little people. Hope was for the angels. For one week, Adam was one of them.

He wanted to run out into the sun and start at once. Even sitting here, just breathing, just being alive was good – but the precious seconds were ticking past so fast.

The bucket list! His last deeds on earth. He grabbed a pencil and some paper and began to write.

Fall in love.

What was he talking about? He *was* in love! Start again.

Sex with Lizzie. Get her pregnant.

Yeah. He wanted to leave something behind. A son! He wanted a son. He'd always thought he'd have children one day. Not so soon – but now he didn't have time to waste. He had to *make* it happen.

Loads of sex with loads of girls. Several of them at once.

Too right! He had a lifetime of shagging to get done in one week. One girl wasn't going to be able to keep up with that.

What else? Money. Yeah. He needed some money to spend. The life he was going to pack in didn't come cheap. And … his parents! People were going to miss him. He had to make it all right for them after he was gone.

Get rich. Leave my parents and Lizzie with enough money so they'll never have to work again.

Unable to stay still any longer, Adam jumped up and skittered around the room. He was wasting time! He had to get moving.

He got back to his desk and finished the list with a flourish.

Drink champagne till I can't stand.

Do cocaine.

Drive a supercar round Manchester.

Kill someone who deserves to die.

Do something so that humanity will remember me for ever.

Die on the Himalayas, watching the sun go down.

Adam read it through. Yeah. It was a good list. It was a great list. It was a life's work, and it was doable. No problem. First off – Lizzie. Love. He wanted her at his side while he lived his last week on earth. He took out his phone and rang. No answer. OK. She was still cross. Yeah, well, so she'd had a bad time, so had he. Was he sulking about it? No, he was not. And shit, he was going to die!

He was going to die …

Don't think it, don't think it. Don't think anything. You don't dare. You have to live.

He texted: 'Lizzie, I love you! Got grt news! Rng me!'

What next? Money. Hey! He already had some. He rummaged about in the covers for the pills he'd stolen from Garry. Death. Magic! These were worth a fortune. He was going to be living like a god for the next seven days.

Adam leaned into the mirror and grinned at himself. Despite the life that was fizzing inside him, his face looked back at him like a grinning death's head. He stared in horror for a moment, then flung himself back into action. He put on his clothes and hurried downstairs. He had to keep moving, he had to keep going. But as he vaulted down the last three, he felt a hard, hot little fizz burrowing its way round and round his stomach. What was that …?

It was fear. Fear that he'd thrown away his one golden gateway into this stunning, unaccountable universe. Even now, when the drug was at its height inside him, filling his senses with love and joy, there was despair as well. It was part of the deal. Adam stood at the bottom of the stairs and panted with terror as he thought of how much he had thrown away.

There's no antidote, he thought. *Don't waste time even worrying about it. No regrets!* He swung round the banister and into the kitchen. *Don't think, just live.* That was what life was all about. That was what life had always been about, if only he'd had the courage. Well, now he had no choice.

Don't think. Don't care. Just do.

💀

His dad was sitting at the table studying something on the laptop. He was always taking courses, trying to find a way back into work. It was languages now. What a joke. His dad was rubbish at languages. He'd never liked study – his brain was in his hands, his mum always said. It was just fate that when he'd had an accident, it was his hands that caught it.

'Where's Mum?' asked Adam. She always waited to greet him, every morning.

'Gone to bed.' He looked up coldly at Adam. For a second Adam was confused – what had he done wrong? Then he remembered. Jess. The party. Shit.

'I'm sorry,' he began, but then he was angry, too. He had one week to live. What was he supposed to do, sit around holding hands with them because of bloody Jess?

'I don't understand you. Your brother is dead and you run away from us. This is a time we should be together,' said his father.

'He lied to us about everything, that's not my fault,' said Adam. He stood by the work surface, thinking *What am I doing here?* He was wasting time.

'Your mother is upset,' said his dad. As he spoke his eyes filled with tears and Adam's heart went out to him. He'd made his family his life's work. First his hands had been broken, then his oldest son had died. And now Adam, too, was going to leave him. What did the old man have left, out of the treasure chest of his life? A surge of love ran through Adam. He ran across and seized his father around the chest.

'It's going to be all right. I have a plan. Gonna hit the big time, Dad!' It was what his dad always used to say, back in the day.

His dad shook his head and pushed weakly against Adam's arms. He looked so broken. 'No, no, I understand how you feel, Adam. You having to leave school to support me. It's wrong. I've let you all down ...'

Adam laughed. His dad thought everything was lost. How wrong could you be? Brilliant! 'No. Really! I have a plan. We're going to make the big time.'

His dad's brow creased. 'Work ...' he began.

'No, not work. A proper plan. You'll see. I love you, Dad.' He leaned forward and planted a great big kiss on his dad, right on the smacker. His dad almost jumped back. They weren't a kissing family.

'Oh, my God!' he said. But then he smiled and hugged Adam back. 'I love you, too, Adam. I never say, but I do. Always remember that.'

For a moment Adam wanted to tell his dad everything, but he didn't dare. Instead, he turned and ran. 'There'll be enough money for everything,' he shouted over his shoulder.

Behind him his dad rose to his feet, alarmed. 'What are you doing? Come back! No trouble, Adam! No trouble ...' But Adam was out of the door and away, off to fulfil his destiny, off to make his dreams come true and turn the world into a better place for everyone who loved him. He had one week to do it.

You don't dare think and you feel so much and you feel so good and you're so scared, and you so much want to live but you're not going to. And the life is fizzling out of your fingertips and if someone came up to you right now and said, 'You can have your life back but you won't ever feel like this again — what would you say? Because this is Death. Death is the cost of life, of all this beauty and joy and love. No more joy for ever, not like this, not real joy ...'

No! No! No! Of course you'd say no. Yes to joy and love and beauty and

- 93 -

Death, and no to year after year of being half alive and never knowing what life is about. You have to look life in the face now. You have no choice. You made your choice when you swallowed that little pill. So no, you wouldn't swap this for all the world, you can't, not for your mum and dad whose hearts will be broken, not for Lizzie, not for yourself. Not for anything.

And you ride the bus so full of joy and tears and youth and life and death, you hardly know what to do with yourself, except that whatever it is, it has to start now, right now, because this is it, my friend, what you're doing now, right here, this moment, this one precious moment in time called now. It's all you have. Don't waste it. There's so little of it left.

The bus sped along. Adam tried not to think. *Regret it, forget it, regret it, forget it,* his brain sang, and sang and sang, all the way out to Wilmslow.

☠

Lizzie rose out of sleep like a turtle surfacing in a sewer. She felt disgusting – sick, headachy and anxious, too, as if the events of last night were still happening. Someone was banging on the window.

It had to be her dad. *Have some respect for the dying.* She pulled the duvet over her head and tried to ignore it. It would go away. The world would go away. Even this headache would go away, eventually.

No. Louder than ever! Unbelievable, what selfishness. It was right by her ear, right by her damn ear! In the darkness she ground her teeth. Monday mornings in the school holidays were not for consciousness. He knew that. He was being a bastard.

She lifted her sore head. 'Go away!' she roared. But

even as she bellowed she remembered that her room was way up high on the first floor. She peered over her shoulder. There was a gap in the curtains just big enough for her to see that the bastard was Adam. He was standing outside her window, grinning at her like a maniac.

Lizzie stared at him a moment, then laid her head back down. Clearly she was still asleep, dreaming.

The events of last night came avalanching back to her at the exact same moment as she realised that this was real. She clawed herself round and stared. Yep. Adam, balancing on her window ledge, twenty feet up – Jesus!

She started to leap out of bed to open the window and save his life, when she realised she had nothing on. Conscious of how pathetic it was to let someone die rather than let them see her naked in their last seconds, she wrapped the duvet round herself and shot over to the window. Adam looked completely comfortable. He grinned and let go of the window frame so that he fell slightly backwards, making her stomach vault inside her as she fumbled at the catch.

'You idiot,' she hissed.

She opened the flap at the top of the window, scared that if she opened the main one she'd knock him off. As she did so, the duvet fell half off her and she had to snatch at it. Adam smiled happily and let out a low whistle.

'What are you doing? How did you get up there?'

'I climbed.'

'No, you didn't.' Lizzie peered out. How had he done it? When she was little she used to look out of her window when she'd been locked in her room, imagining the climb down. There were a few old screws that had once been used for wires to hold up a climbing plant. Apart from that, nothing.

'How did you do it?' she demanded.

'Let me in,' pleaded Adam.

She had no choice. She opened the window. He stepped in and went to grab her, but she twisted away. 'You must be off your head. Get out of here!'

'Lizzie – please!'

'I mean it, Adam. You were a total shit last night.' She peered at him, aware that she looked a mess and, despite herself, feeling a bit of a tingle at his closeness to her, here in her bedroom, while she held on to the duvet to hide her nakedness.

'I know I was. But listen – Jess has died.'

'What? Jess …?'

'I was scared to tell you.'

'Adam …' Lizzie pulled a face and fell on to the bed. She was hardly awake. This was bending her brain.

'I've got to leave school. Dad has no money. Jess earned everything.'

Lizzie shook her head. 'I need some painkillers. Hang on …' She went to her table, still clutching at the duvet, and swallowed some paracetamol. She got back into bed, folded the duvet tightly around her and glared at him. Adam sat slowly down beside her and gave her a lopsided grin. Lizzie shook her head, but inside she felt a lot less cool than she made out. He had scaled the wall of her house to reach her window. It was like *Romeo and Juliet*. He was in her bedroom. No one knew he was there. He looked gorgeous. His blue eyes, a bit of a sweat on him. Actually, truth be told, he looked *really* gorgeous – more so than normal, and she had really fancied him right from the off.

And his brother was dead. Shit. It began to sink in. Something dreadful had happened. But how come he was looking so happy?

'Go on, then,' she said. 'This had better be good.'

As Adam's story unfolded, Lizzie felt a column of panic rising inside her. Jess dead. No wonder he was so weird at the party. Adam leaving school and getting a crap job. It all got worse and worse and worse, but normal worse. And then – Death. He'd taken Death.

When he said it, she laughed. It wasn't pleasure; it was fear. She couldn't take on what it meant. This sort of thing happened to other people. It was not possible that something like this could enter her own life.

'I don't believe you,' she said.

'I climbed your wall,' said Adam. 'Just the gaps between the bricks, with my fingers and my toes. I'm like – I'm alive for the first time. Really, really alive. Look.'

He had the evidence in his face, in his looks, in the speed and fire of him. But he had concrete evidence as well. He rummaged around in the little rucksack on his shoulder and pulled out the little bag of pills.

'Oh, my God.'

'See?'

It was true. 'Adam! What have you done?' It sent a chill of excitement and fear right through her. He was doomed

– and he looked so alive! 'Why did you do it?'

Adam looked appalled. 'Don't say that,' he said. 'I have my week, Lizzie. It's going to be the best week anyone ever had. And I want to spend it with you.'

'Oh, my God.' She put her hand to her mouth and shook her head. She wasn't saying no, but Adam nodded at her anyway – willing her, willing her, willing her to say yes! Yes to everything. He was breaking her heart – right now, breaking it in pieces. She could feel it cracking inside her. She hadn't even known she was in love.

'Say yes. Say yes,' Adam pushed on relentlessly. 'I want to be with you for the rest of my life. I love you,' he said. 'Just love me back. For one week. Say yes. Please, Lizzie.'

She heard the desperation in his voice and shook her head. 'What do you want from me, Adam? I can't save your life.'

'I don't want to be saved. I told you. I want to spend my last week with you. How can you say no?'

Lizzie clutched at her head. She was trying to think, but her mind shied away. 'It's too much,' she said. 'You're asking … I don't know what you're asking!'

'I'm asking for one week of your time.'

'It's not one week! It's your whole life! You're asking me to watch you die. It's like – getting married or something.'

'Pretty short marriage,' Adam said, and despite herself, she snorted with laughter.

'You're something else, Adam, you know that?'

'I am now,' he said, seriously.

She was about to tell him that he had always been something else, that he always had been worth it, but what was the point? It was too late for home truths. Lizzie couldn't help being flattered and deeply moved. He had one week to live and out of all the things in the world, all the people, all the places, he wanted her.

One week, she thought. So little time to live your life. Could she do this for him, and then just walk away and get on with her own life with only memories to keep her company? But what memories they would be!

An idea suddenly hit her. 'You've got a list, haven't you?'

Adam's eyes swivelled briefly as he tried to remember what was on it. How many girls …? 'I'm … still working on it.'

'Hand it over.'

'It's private, Lizzie.'

'Private? You want me to drop everything for you and what we're going to do is private?'

'I only did it this morning,' said Adam. 'It's not final.'

Lizzie put out her hand. 'Give.'

Adam dug in his pocket and pulled it out. He cast a glance over it. 'Sex figures pretty highly here,' he admitted.

Lizzie snatched it out of his hand and scanned through it.

'At least I'm number one,' she said. Then her eyes bulged. 'Pregnant? You want to get me pregnant? And then you're going to leave me to bring up a kid on my own? Well, fuck you!' She screwed the list into a ball, threw it on the floor. 'You're not even going to be there for the birth, you bastard,' she said; and again, despite herself, she started to laugh. It was just so ridiculous!

Adam grinned at her and picked up the list. 'It's just the first draft. Come on, Lizzie. I mean, wouldn't you want to leave something behind?'

'Yeah, but I'd like to be around to watch it grow up.' She shook her head. 'Pregnant,' she said. 'I can't believe you. Give me that list. Right.' Lizzie took the piece of paper and fumbled on her bedside table for a pen. She scribbled out pregnancy. 'OK?'

'Yeah, OK. Whatever you say, Lizzie.'

'*Sleep with as many girls as possible. Two or three at the same time,*' she read. She glared at him. 'Three girls at once. You think I'm going to do that for you, do you?'

Adam hesitated. 'Haven't you ever wondered?'

Lizzie's pencil hovered in the air above number two.

'Look,' said Adam. 'This week. It's got to be a total experience. Two hundred per cent going for it. It's not like normal, it's like, everything. All the stuff you would have done if you went to uni, or if you'd gone to war, or if you married and had kids or just went crazy. You know? You might say you don't want a threesome now, but what about for ever? Because that's what this is about – for ever.'

'For ever in a week,' said Lizzie. She shook her head. 'Suppose I say no?' she demanded. 'What then?'

'Then – I'll keep trying to convince you.' He grinned, weakly. 'I could become a pain.'

'Become? Huh. And if I say yes? All this – we have to do *all* this. That's the deal, is it? I have to do everything you want?'

Adam looked at the list. 'We can go through them one at a time,' he suggested.

'Thanks.' She scanned down it again. 'Kill *someone?*' she exclaimed. 'You want to leave me with a murder charge?'

'No!' Adam shook his head. 'OK, I hadn't thought it through. I mean, only if it was someone who really, really deserved it. Hitler or someone.'

'Hitler's dead, Adam. We're not going to meet Hitler.'

'A serial killer, then. We'd be doing everyone a favour.'

'Except me. It's not up to us to decide who lives and who dies.' She shook her head. 'I want to be able to say no.'

'Yeah. Yeah. No problem. We only do it if you agree.'

'We go through these things one at a time.'

'Yeah! I mean, you're in on it, too, right?'

'Right.'

Adam looked at her. 'You're saying yes.'

'No, I'm not,' she snapped. But she was, and she knew it. She turned to look at him sitting next to her, smiling and ... hopeful? No. Hopeful wasn't big enough. It was like his whole life, his whole world, his whole being depended on her answer. She held all that in her hand. That was it. He had put himself, all of himself, body and soul, into her keeping. It took her breath away.

'I love you, Lizzie,' he said.

Love — what was that? It wasn't like tripping over a brick and falling on your face in the road. Of course it had to be the right person — but you had to go for it, too, didn't you? You had to be prepared to jump in and drown. Someone, that special person, they didn't just come to mean everything to you by accident. Somewhere along the line, you had to give yourself to them, completely give yourself, be prepared to sacrifice *everything* for them. That was what Adam was offering, and that was what he was asking in return. That's what love was, wasn't it? Like Romeo and Juliet. Like Bonnie and Clyde. Your true love had to be worth more to you than life itself.

He'd climbed the wall to her window. He had one week to live and he'd come to her. He was going to take her places she'd never even dreamed of going. She was going to fall in love. It was going to break her heart. It might even kill her.

'Say yes, Lizzie. Please say yes.'

And he was gorgeous, wasn't he? Gorgeous and doomed and mad and so, so sexy. And yes, sometimes she felt she was going to go out of her head with boredom and … and …

'I can walk away whenever I want, right?'

'Anything.'

'I can say no.'

'Anything.'

'We do it one thing at a time.'

'One at a time. Anything!'

'And …' she paused. Adam was beaming at her, just beaming like a light had been turned on in his heart. She was that light.

'I love you, Lizzie,' he said again.

And she could have said, *Oh, come on;* or *Grow up;* or *Please!* Or just *I don't believe you.* But instead, she jumped up and wrapped her arms round him, and hugged him so hard, and he picked her up and spun her round in circles and crowed like Peter Pan.

'And I love you,' she said, fiercely. She pulled him to her and snogged him, stark naked there in her room with the duvet on the floor. And … *Yes!* she thought. She was going to help him have the time of his life.

CHAPTER 2

MR B

At about the same time that Adam was climbing the sheer wall to Lizzie's bedroom, Garry, from whom he had stolen Death the previous night, was on the receiving end of a very difficult phone call with a man he knew only as Mr B. It was the first time he'd dealt directly with Mr B – usually he only got to speak to his underlings, but today he had been handed on to the big man himself. For that reason, he knew he was in some very serious, and probably very painful, trouble down the line.

'I'm sorry,' he begged. 'I got robbed. It was random. This guy turned up and did the house over. What can I do? Call the police?' He laughed weakly at his own joke.

Mr B waited a moment before he answered. 'I'll pop round tomorrow and we'll discuss the situation.'

'You?' said Garry in surprise.

'I like to deal with any problems that arise personally.'

'No need for that, is there?' No answer. Garry let out a high-pitched giggle out of sheer nervousness. 'I'll have the money for you, Mr B, just give me a couple more days. I mean, even if I still had the stuff it takes a while to sell it. You're a businessman. You know that.'

'Tomorrow, eleven a.m.,' said Mr B.

'That's not fair!' cried Garry.

'Be there,' said Mr B, and hung up.

Garry sat still, staring at the phone in his hand. This was bad. He had been warned that Mr B was dangerous, but he had been a poor man all his life, and the prospect of using his old Zealot connections by getting his hands on some Death to sell had been too much to resist.

'I'm out of my league here,' he muttered, chewing the ends of his beard. He was in a wheelchair. What was he supposed to do? Run around trying to hunt for the little shit? It took him half an hour just to get on and off the bus.

He picked up the phone and made another call – a call he had been told to make only under very exceptional circumstances. He sat a long time listening to the phone ring, before it went dead. Then he rang again. And again, and again. He'd been sitting there for half an hour before he got an answer.

'This needs to be pretty important, Garry,' said a voice at the other end.

'Thank God you answered,' burst out Garry in relief. 'Something's gone wrong. You're not going to believe this.'

Garry ran through his problem, aware that he was getting an unsympathetic silence, right up until he mentioned …

'Adam?' asked the voice, incredulously.

'Yeah! The little shit. What am I going to do about that, then, eh?'

There was a pause. 'I can't help you.'

'Come on! I'm seeing that guy tomorrow. Mr B. You know what they say about him.'

'I can't jeopardise everything we've worked on for just for this.'

'Just for this? This is my life we're talking about. You're making the stuff, for God's sake. Just divert some my way.'

'I'm a Zealot, Garry. I follow the rules. I'm not going to steal from my own organisation.'

'It was getting handed out for free the other day in Albert Square.'

'That was an operation. Look, Garry, I'm abandoning my family for this. If I can do that to them, what makes you think I'm going to stick my neck out for you? I warned you what you were getting into when I put you in touch with Mr B and you accepted the risk.'

'I just wanted a life, you know …' said Garry.

'I've given mine up,' said Jess, grimly.

'You had a life. Me, it takes me ten minutes just to go to the toilet in this stupid house. The stairlift keeps breaking; it gets stuck going up, it gets stuck going down. You try it when you're dying for a shit. I just wanted a life. I just wanted things easy for a bit.' Pathetically, Garry began to weep. 'Just have a word with Adam. How will that hurt?'

'He thinks I'm dead. It'll stir up all sorts of nonsense if he knows I'm still alive. What was Adam doing round at yours, anyway?'

'He was looking for you, what do you think? He was in a pretty bad way – someone had really beat him up. He's desperate, Jess, your whole family is desperate. What did you expect? They think you're dead.'

'I am dead.'

'Please, Jess, please?'

Jess sighed. He hated this so much. A gentle person, he had to push himself to be hard. 'Maybe you just have to die, Garry. Quite a few of us are going to.'

'But not like this,' begged Garry. 'Anyway,' he said, a thought occurring to him, 'what do I say to Mr B? I know where Adam lives. Your whole family. I mean, you know, under torture? What about that?'

There was a pause. 'You're threatening me,' said Jess.

'No!' insisted Garry, but he was. 'Look, I'm not a bad man. I don't want to do this, but he might make me. You know?'

'Garry, you bastard, I did you a favour!'

'Look, just … don't make me do this, right? Now you know how it feels,' added Garry.

'I need to think.'

Jess put down the phone abruptly. Garry sat there a while longer. He wouldn't tell Mr B where Jess's family lived. He'd sunk low, but not that low. But if thinking he would got Jess out and trying to get those pills back, so be it.

He wheeled himself to the kitchen under the stairs to make himself a cup of tea.

💀

In a gym in the basement of a large house buried in a clump of woodland south of Manchester, Vince was lying face down on a mat with Christian on top of him, studying the back of his neck. Both men were dressed in judo gear. Christian rubbed his finger down the vertebrae and counted under his breath while Vince waited nervously for him to finish.

'Can I get up now, sir?' asked Vince.

Christian stood and let him up. They bowed to each other, then battle resumed. Christian threw Vince around a bit, kicked his arse a few times, got him upside down on the mat and punched him repeatedly in the back of the neck before he'd had enough.

'That's enough for today.'

Vince got to his feet, panting.

'You're out of breath, Vince. You need to do some more work on your stamina,' suggested Christian. 'You're getting too easy.'

'Sorry, sir. I'll do a run this afternoon,' snarled Vince.

'No.' Christian wiped his face on a towel. 'I have a job for you.'

'Is it the cripple the chemist put us on to?' asked Vince. 'We should never have done a deal with him. Do you want me to sort it out, sir?'

Christian shook his head. 'I'll deal with that. I have something else for you. I want you to get out there and find out where Lizzie's gone.' He shook his head. 'Running off like that. She could be in any kind of trouble.'

Vince paused, not sure who they were talking about. Then he remembered – the girl at the party the night before. 'Why are you worried for her, sir? She's not exactly your girlfriend, is she?' he pointed out.

'With that crazy ex-boyfriend of hers hanging around? I'm worried for her. Just do it. You can start with her friend who threw the party last night. Julie, wasn't it? Her. Sooner rather than later, if you don't mind, Vince,' he added, when Vince paused, looking at him curiously.

Vince shrugged. 'I'll get right on it, sir.'

Vince left his boss and went to his own room. Inside, he closed the door, stripped off and went to look at the mirror. Magnificent black bruises blossomed all the way up and down his body, but the most serious injuries didn't show up as much more than a puffy swelling on the back of his neck, where Christian had punched him at least once a day for the past nine months. Every time, the same thing. It was doing him damage.

Christian was a nut-job. He'd have been in Broadmoor years ago if it wasn't for the fact that he was the son of Florence Ballantine. In effect, Vince was less a butler/ bodyguard, as Lizzie had suggested, and more of a warder/butler. His job was to serve Christian hand and foot – including the procurement of 'girlfriends', when required – right up to the point where Christian went mad. Then – he should be so lucky – he had permission to restrain him.

Man! He wanted to restrain him so bad.

The big man finished his shower and went in to give Christian his afternoon milk before he left. There was the usual fuss. It went in phases. Just now, Christian was in a sulky phase. Vince would have loved it if he simply started refusing to drink it, because it was at that point that restraining measures might come into effect. So far, Christian had denied him that pleasure.

Even so, and despite the fact that he stood and watched Christian swallow the meds in milk twice every day without fail, his boss's behaviour lately was beginning to worry him. This girlfriend thing, for instance. It was a worrying sign.

Vince made his way out to his car, a classic model Porsche, and paused outside to make a quick phone call to his real boss.

'Mr Ballantine.'

'Vince. How's it hanging?'

Vince paused, unsure how to put it.

'It ain't easy,' sympathised Ballantine.

'He just beat me up on the mat again.'

'Wow. I've heard about beaten wives, but a beaten body-guard? Is there a members' group or something you could join, you know? Share experiences, that sort of thing?'

In the background, Vince could hear raucous laughter. He shook his head and winced. 'Always the neck. It's dangerous. He's going to do me an injury.'

'Aw, come on, Vince. You're a big boy. You can put up with a little pain.'

Vince paused, unwilling to admit just how much he

dreaded those daily sessions.

'Did you really drag me away to complain about your working conditions, Vince? Is he still taking his meds? That's the only thing that counts. Vince, please tell me he's taking his meds.'

'He is, Mr Ballantine. It's not that. It's … there's another girl.'

'So what's new? There's always another girl.'

'Yes, sir, but this one, he's calling her his girlfriend.'

There was a pause. 'And is she?'

'No, sir.'

'How do you know?'

'She keeps trying to get away, sir.'

Ballantine thought about it. 'Isn't that the sort of thing girlfriends just do, though, Vince?'

Vince sighed. Like father, like son. 'Not if they really like you, sir.'

There was silence. Vince could almost hear the shrug.

'You know what,' said Ballantine, 'there aren't many things normal about Christian, but the fact that he likes girls is one of them. It keeps him happy. And if he's happy, I'm happy. And – he's taking his meds! So long as he's taking the meds, it never gets that bad. Believe me – I've seen the results of no meds. You don't want to know.'

'It's not nice, sir. I had to help him with the last one.'

'Heheheh, it's a tough job, eh? Vince, how much do I pay you?'

'A fuck of a lot of money, sir.'

'And how much does Christian pay you?'

'A fuck of a lot of money, sir.'

'That's right. Now two fuck loads of money add up to … what? A fucking enormous amount of money, if I'm not mistaken. I'm using a technical term, here, Vince.'

'I know, sir.'

'How long have you been with him now?'

'Nine months, sir,' said Vince. 'Pretty much to the day.'

Ballantine nodded. Secretly, he was impressed. That was a record. 'Tell you what, Vince. I'll make you an appointment with my personal physician. Get the neck checked out. If it's really that bad, maybe we'll do something.'

'A holiday would be nice, sir.'

'Vince.'

'Yes, sir?'

'You're whining.'

'Sorry, sir.'

'I'm sorry, too, Vince, because I have a whole lot on at the moment without having to listen to my son's baby-sitter complaining to me about his very well-paid working conditions.'

'Sorry, sir,' said Vince, but the phone was already off.

Vince shrugged. You could only try. He cricked his neck and shook his hands. Pins and needles. Ah well. Meanwhile, he had a job to do.

He climbed into the car, and headed out to the M56.

Just a few miles away, Jess was leaning up against the side of a lorry container in the company of Anna, the girl who had been beaten up the day before. Both of them looked the worse for wear – swollen eyes, fat lips and bruises all over their bodies. Ballantine's men were professionals. Of course, nothing had been done that would stop them working.

Jess was seething. Anna listened sympathetically as he told her about Garry.

'So what are you going to do?' she asked.

Jess glared at her. 'What *can* I do?'

'Go and sort it out.'

'I can't, you know I can't.'

'Yes, you can.'

'Even if I wanted to, we have our orders. Stay here until we get a new mission. That's what I'm doing.'

He fumbled in his pocket for his cigarettes. His hands were shaking, he was that upset, but he wouldn't lift a finger to save his own brother. He was such a bloody soldier, Anna thought. Always followed orders, never crossed the line unless he was told to. The Zealots were his whole life.

'It's your brother,' she said. 'Don't you care? And keep your voice down,' she added. She nodded sideways at the guard leaning up against a nearby container, who was watching them with interest. They'd started off as employees, on loan from the Zealots. Now, they were more or less prisoners.

Jess took a breath and forced himself to speak matter-of-factly. 'I'm not putting everything at risk just because my brother is an idiot,' he said. 'I've made the break. That life is over. I'm dead as far as they're concerned. What would be the point of showing myself to any of them? I'm going to be dead for real in another week or so.'

'You'd get Christian off their backs. I'd say that was a

pretty good start.'

Jess ground his feet on the tarmac in his agitation. 'I've made the break,' he repeated. 'They're on their own. It's up to Adam to look after them now.'

'Doesn't sound as if he's doing a very good job of it,' said Anna.

'He's a selfish little—'

'He's young,' she said.

Jess puffed furiously on his cigarette in agitation. So passionate, so clever, so committed. But there had to be time for yourself and those who mattered to you as well, or what was the point?

She glanced at the guard, who had relaxed back against the container, smoking a cigarette of his own. 'We can get out of here if we want to,' she said. 'They think we're a pair of geeky kids. I've been keeping an eye out. No problem. You could go out and —'

'No! We have our orders.'

'Jess, who's going to know?'

'I'd know.' He sank down on his haunches against the container, to make himself stay still. 'They think I'm dead. That's how it's going to stay.'

Anna sank down next to him. For a while they smoked in silence.

'I had a message from Command,' she told him.

'Did we get a target?' he demanded, eagerly.

'No. Just to stay here and make sure the production goes smoothly. They want as much drug out on the streets as possible until next Friday.'

'See?' Jess nodded. Point proven. Orders.

'Big day, Friday,' said Anna.

'Yeah. It's still growing?'

'Oh, yeah. Big rallies in all the major cities. Not just thousands – they reckon hundreds of thousands of people are turning up. They've called for a general strike. It's incredible. And Manchester's at the heart of it.' Anna shook her head. 'Just a few klicks away. And we're stuck here missing it ...'

Jess looked at her excitedly. 'It's started,' he said. 'What do you think?'

'Maybe.'

'I think so. I really do,' he said.

Anna grinned. She licked her lips and said it: 'Revolution.'

The magic word. What they'd been working for all their lives. What they believed in, what they hoped for, what they lived for. What, as Zealots, they were going to die for.

The Zealots were always asking for volunteers. Both Anna and Jess had made the offer, and the offer had been accepted. Self-immolation, maybe, although that was less likely now that things were moving. It was a great way to attract attention, but once you had the ear of the people, it was time to act. Most likely, they would be asked to be bombs. Organisations like the Zealots always had a need for people prepared to die, to take out difficult targets.

This mission ended next Friday, on the anniversary of Jimmy Earle's death. The next mission: to die.

'Think of it,' she said. 'It's all happening just over there – and we're stuck here. Don't you think that's just crazy?'

Jess scowled. 'Orders,' he said.

'Oh, for fuck's sake, Jess. Tell you what – I'm not staying here.'

He looked at her, alarmed.

'Come on. A day or two. What difference is that going to make? We're a part of it, Jess. We helped make it happen. If I'm going to die for the revolution, I want to see it. Every night there's a protest, bigger than the night before. By Friday it could be millions. It's the future and it's happening right there.' She nodded across towards the railway line, where Manchester lay, the heart of the revolution. 'We deserve it. We have a right to be there.'

Jess pulled a face.

'Aren't you even curious, Jess?'

Jess shook his head slightly. Of course he was! But … orders.

'Get out there, Jess,' she urged. 'You've earned it. Jimmy Earle set it all off, but it wouldn't have spread like it has if you hadn't worked out how to make the cheap stuff. It's finally, finally dawning on people how bad things really are, that so many kids are prepared to kill themselves just so they can have one crazy week. That's down to you. Don't you think we deserve just one night out there with them? I'm telling you, I'm going. You should too – you must. See your brother. Get the drugs back so Christian is off your family's case. Spend a night out on Albert Square and get a taste of what you helped make happen. Then come back and no harm done. Why not? Just – do it.'

'No,' he said, as she tried to interrupt, 'I told my family I'm dead because I am, as far as they're concerned. This is how I do things.' He stubbed out his cigarette. 'Things can go wrong,' he said. 'Those orders are there for a reason. What if we got caught or shot? It would interrupt the supply line maybe. Anything could happen. If you're going, that's all the more reason for me to stay here to make sure the mission is carried out.'

'We could go together. Jess, it would be so good! Why not?'

He stood up. 'If you go, that's up to you. I'm staying here.'

He left, back to work. He made her want to scream sometimes. They were both going to be dead very soon. The world was full of things she wanted to do and never would. She was prepared to give them up – she would give them up. But meanwhile she was going to snatch her chances when she could.

Such a soldier, she thought. Such a monk, too. Pity. He was a good-looking guy. It was a pity all round.

'Time to go, miss.' The guard had stopped Jess from leaving, and was making him wait for her. She stubbed out her cigarette and followed them back towards the lab.

CHAPTER 3

HALF A VIRGIN

'The cost of champagne is shocking these days,' joked Adam.

There were walking back from the shops. Lizzie looked sideways at him. Shocking was right. The really good stuff, Cristal or Dom Perignon, cost over two hundred pounds a bottle. Two hundred pounds, for a bottle of wine! Even the usual posh stuff, Bollinger, cost over a hundred. But as Adam pointed out, what was the point if you weren't going to go for it? What was he supposed to do? Save up for it?

Except it wasn't actually his money. Adam didn't want to wait until they'd sold the Death – that could take days. Lizzie had suggested nicking it – great idea! It was exactly in the Death spirit. Storm in and take what you want. Go for it!

But everyone knew what happened to Deathers if the police got their hands on them. They locked them up, refused bail, and waited for them to die. His last week, rotting in a police cell? Come on! He wasn't going to risk his freedom every time they wanted to go shopping.

Save the robbery for the big time. There was another, safer solution. Lizzie just had to pop back to her house and pick up her savings book. Six bottles of Bolly – six hundred quid. She'd been saving that money for a holiday with her mates; now she was spending it on Adam. He was the one on Death – how come it was her acting like there was no tomorrow? It was typical Adam. She was doing her best to think what a privilege it was to be the One chosen by Him to spend His last week with. She just wished it wasn't proving so expensive.

They were on their way back to her place. Her mum and dad were both at work, they'd have the house to themselves all day. The perfect place to get so drunk on champagne they couldn't stand up. And, of course, to lose their virginity.

Nothing had been said, but Lizzie knew it was expected. In a way it was fair enough – they'd talked about it often enough. Even so, she was feeling resentful. Maybe she was being selfish. Adam had, let's face it, cornered all the rights to be the unreasonable one here. Even so, having agreed to go on the ride, she was now realising that somewhere down the line she had actually become the ride and it was making her feel sulky. At the same time she was feeling increasingly panicky at what she had agreed to.

This was all going straight over Adam's head, of course. He was having a great time. Once they got to her house, he started showing her all the things he could suddenly do on Death – bouncing a ball off the wall with his head while he spun in circles, walking round the room on his hands. He was hilarious and gorgeous, all at the same time, with his blonde hair hanging off his head and his face turning red as he waltzed around on his hands in her bedroom.

Lizzie giggled, feeling hysterical by now. She put five of the bottles in the freezer to chill quickly, fetched a couple of glasses from the kitchen and led the way up to her room, where she sat on the edge of the bed easing the cork out of the sixth bottle, while Adam cavorted around her.

Bang! Off went the cork. Adam cheered. Lizzie poured the wine and laughed at the bubbles frothing up out of the bottle, but inside she was horrified. What on earth was she doing, drinking champagne with a dead man? Because that's what it amounted to. His brother had just died and here they were celebrating – it was mad! He hadn't even mentioned Jess since he'd first told her what had happened. Where was the grief? When was it going to come out? What on earth was he going to do next?

Adam took his glass off her with a flourish. Celebration time! He knocked it back, then another, then another, all in about five minutes.

'Hold on. What about me? You're drinking it all.'

'No, we've five more to get through.' Adam tipped his glass up and licked at the drips. He was in a hurry. Lizzie grabbed the bottle and poured herself another before it all went.

She looked across to Adam, who was now doing a handstand in the middle of the floor and muttering, 'I love you, Lizzie Hollier, I love you, Lizzie Hollier, I love you, Lizzie Hollier.'

It didn't sound like love to her.

'How drunk are you?' she asked, suspiciously.

He flipped over on to his feet and beamed at her. He had a think. 'Not at all,' he admitted. He grabbed the bottle and looked at it. 'How strong is this stuff?' he asked.

'Wine strength, I expect,' said Lizzie, sarcastically, but Adam didn't hear. He was rushing off downstairs to fetch another bottle. Lizzie sat on the bed and sighed. Death seemed to be working in waves. One minute he was relatively calm, the next he was like a ping-pong ball on speed. It was exhausting.

I must stop being irritable, she thought. It wasn't fair on him. One week to live! It took her breath away. If only she'd known what was going on when they were at the party, she could have stopped him.

It was a thought that chilled her.

Adam came running back up the stairs with the bottle, popped the cork and drank straight from the bottle. The wine fizzed down his chin on to the floor.

'I don't feel anything yet,' he said. 'Can *you* feel it?'

'Yeah.'

He looked curiously at the bottle.

'Hey – maybe it's Death,' she said. 'You know. It makes

you super fit, right? Maybe it makes you immune to booze as well.'

'No!' Adam was genuinely shocked. Lizzie snorted in amusement.

'Your face,' she giggled.

It was hilarious. Death was supposed to help you have a good time. Instead, it made it harder. They both creased up laughing at the thought. Giggles. A sign of hysteria. That was even funnier and for several minutes they were both holding their sides, hurting with laughter. Gradually, it subsided. Lizzie realised she was feeling very drunk already.

'Do you think that's what it is?' asked Adam.

'Nah,' she said, although she did. 'It's because you're so excited, that's all. Sit down. You'll get sick before anything happens.'

'Before what happens?' He grinned at her.

'Before *anything* happens. Sit down here.'

Adam sat next to her on the bed. He put his arm around her and went in for a kiss.

'I love you, Lizzie,' he said. 'I love you, I love you, I love you.'

'Go on, let's do it,' she said. Suddenly she wanted to get it over with. Adam was busy with her boobs, then moving on already to fiddle with her jeans. She stood up, took them off, pulled her top off and got into bed with just her bra and pants on.

Adam got in with her and pulled his own clothes off under the covers. She did the same. Naked, he pressed himself right up against her, so she could feel him all along her body.

'That's nice,' she said.

'Gosh,' said Adam. He shook his head and made his eyes go big and round. She laughed and kissed him.

He fumbled around for a bit, then, too soon, he climbed on top of her and began to push. It hurt.

'Ouch,' she said.

Adam stopped. 'You OK?' he asked.

'It's all right, go on.'

He pressed a bit more gently and got inside her. He began to move and suddenly, without any warning at all, Lizzie remembered that he was as good as dead. It was horrible. It just froze her blood. She turned her face away and tried not to cry, but the feeling was overwhelming.

'Why don't you ... just stop it,' she said.

Adam froze in surprise, then rolled off. 'What?'

'I'm sorry,' she said. She didn't want him to see her cry. She turned her back to him. 'Feeling sick,' she said. 'Too much to drink.'

Adam paused, not sure what to do.

'Feeling really sick,' she said.

'Do you want a bowl?' he asked.

'Just let me lie here for a bit. Go downstairs. I'll be all right. Urgh,' she added.

'OK. OK.' He got off the bed and put his jeans on. 'It doesn't matter, Lizzie. It's all right, I don't mind.'

'I just drank too much. I'll be better in a bit.'

'Sure. It's OK.' Quietly, he left the room.

Lizzie glanced over her shoulder to make sure he was

gone. Then she let the tears come. One week. What on earth had she agreed to? It was going to be unbearable.

💀

Down in the kitchen, Adam was seething. Did it count? He'd been there – but for less than a minute. What did that mean? Was he still a virgin or not? He was some sort of half-virgin. It was so unfair.

'I don't have time for this,' he muttered. He went to the freezer, popped the cork on another bottle and took a hard swig. The wine fizzed up in his mouth and made him choke.

This wasn't fun. Nothing was working.

He raised the bottle again and, as carefully as he could, drank the wine down. It fizzed and writhed in his throat, but he kept at it until he'd finished off the whole bottle, all hundred pounds' worth. When he was done he stood there, feeling …

Still sober.

Lizzie was right. It was Death, making him stay sober. It was like some kind of trick. Would he have to spend four times the money to get drunk? Maybe six bottles weren't even enough? This wasn't right. He was supposed to be in the middle of having great sex and then passing out from alcohol poisoning, and instead, here he was, half virgin and still sober, without enough champagne to drink, while a naked girl lay upstairs in bed feeling too sick to have sex with him. How did this happen?

There was a laptop on the kitchen table. He opened it up and got on the net, surfing around for some info on Death.

He wasn't alone, that was one thing. Hundreds, maybe even thousands of people had taken the drug in Albert Square the other night. Next Friday, there were going to be an awful lot of people dropping dead at the same time. And it was still going on. Death normally cost thousands of pounds per tab, but it looked as if someone had worked out how to make it cheaply. Overnight, cheap Death was flooding on to the streets. It had begun in Manchester, but it was getting everywhere – London, Birmingham, Leeds, all over the country.

Everyone wanted to die.

This was all interesting, but it wasn't getting Adam a shag, was it? He found a Deather site he'd heard of before, regretit-forgetit.com. There was loads of stuff there – places to post your experiences, your thoughts, your requests, answers to your FAQs.

Requests. Yeah. He needed a backup plan.

'*Deather teenager wants girls to sleep with. I'll give you the time of your life, you give me the time of mine.*'

It was kind of crap, but it was also kind of true. Adam pressed 'post'. It was the right thing to do. You couldn't do half measures. You had to be sure. It was all about him. Me me me me me me. Lizzie would understand … but maybe not a good idea to tell her anyway …

He went on to the FAQs. There it was.

'*Can I get drunk or high on Death? How much will I need?*'

'*Yes, you can!*' the answer said. '*But Death means you'll have to drink more, faster. With drugs, quadruple your usual dose. With booze, same thing. Best thing – drink it down quick. Four bottles of wine will get you really drunk. Have fun!*'

Four bottles to get drunk, eh? Adam wanted more than just drunk. He wanted paralytic. Four bottles = drunk. Six bottles might just = not able to walk.

Lizzie was out for the count upstairs. No point waking her up. Day 1 was already disappearing fast. He needed to get a move on.

Opening the freezer, Adam removed the remaining three bottles of champagne and lined them up on the work surface.

Number one. He popped the cork, lifted it to his lips and drank carefully. The bubbles were a pain – they stopped you drinking the stuff! It was a pity he couldn't make it flat. Wait – maybe he could. Digging about under the stairs he found what he was looking for – a bucket. He opened all three bottles and poured them one after the other into it. Yeah! A bucket of Bolly! Now you're talking!

He stirred it to get rid of the bubbles, then, lifting the bucket to his lips, started to drink it down. Better. It was still fizzy, but much easier than straight out of the bottle. Now he just needed to get it down him as quick as he could to get the maximum benefit.

Fifteen minutes later, with much belching and glugging, the bucket was empty. Adam did an experimental stagger round the kitchen. Yeah! He was pissed. Pretty fucking pissed actually. But ... he could still walk – just about. Bloody Death! He'd have been dead by now otherwise. *Heheheheheh*, he thought. *Heheheheheh*.

Hang on. Seeing double. Feeling sick. Feeling very sick. Walk. Door. Get up.

He took two steps to the door and fell over. He tried to

get up and failed.

'Too drun to fucki stanup,' he announced, to no one. Then he was lavishly sick on the floor. Success!

And he passed out.

Adam awoke lying on the floor in a pool of cold sick. Lizzie was sitting at the kitchen table glaring at him.

'What happened?' he asked.

'You drank it all. You greedy bastard.'

'Sorry.' He picked himself up and tried to grin at her, but it was difficult when you had cold sick all down your front. 'You were asleep,' he mumbled. 'I didn't have time. At least that's one thing out the way.'

'Out the way?' she demanded. 'Six hundred pounds' worth of champagne out of the way? Thanks, Adam. Any more things you want to get out the way for me? My money, what's left of it?'

'You were ill,' he reminded her. 'And this is about me, isn't it? One week,' he reminded her. 'I'll pay you back, don't worry.' She was making a fuss – spoiling it for him. 'I'm going upstairs to shower. Hey – I'm going to need some more clothes, these stink,' he added, and ducked upstairs before she could answer.

In the bathroom, Adam sat on the bath for a moment. He felt sick and incredibly anxious. The hangover, it must be. He found some painkillers and whacked them down. Then he got undressed and climbed into the shower.

Don't think don't think don't think. Thinking about what he'd done with a hangover was dreadful; it made his stomach lurch. *Don't go there.* What next? Sex, sex was next. He should have done that by now. He had to get on — he had so much to do and so little time to do it …

The water flooded over him, taking the sweat and stink off him and washing it away down the plughole.

Don't think — but you can't help thinking because that's what your brain does, thinking all the time, it won't stop. Don't think of the future because the future is disappearing before your eyes. Don't think of the past because that's going, too —

All your memories, gone, all your hopes and regrets, gone. Wherever you look, death is everywhere; past, present and future, all gone, like water down the drain …

From the floor came a rattle of music. His phone in his jeans pocket. Leaning out of the shower, Adam picked it up and opened it up. A number he didn't know. He pressed answer and held it to his ear.

'Hi, Adam,' said a voice.

It came as such a shock, he reeled back and banged into the wall behind him.

'Who is it?' he whispered.

'Don't you know me?'

Adam didn't answer, not daring. It must be some kind of mistake.

'It's Jess,' said the voice. 'We need to meet up.'

💀

Lizzie was drinking coffee in the kitchen when Adam burst in with the news. Jess was alive!

She goggled at him. She couldn't keep up with this. First Jess was dead — now he was alive. Ten minutes ago

Adam had been lying unconscious in a pool of vomit. Now he was rushing round the room babbling like a lunatic.

'Adam, stop it!' He was practically bouncing off the walls. 'Slow down. Jess is alive? Is he OK?'

'Yes! I don't know. He sounded fine. He wants the drugs back.'

'What, the Death? How does he know about that?'

'Garry must have told him.' Adam paced up and down, trying to work it out. 'They said on the news that it was the Zealots handing out the free Death on Friday night.'

'Jess was a chemist, wasn't he?' Lizzie thought about it. 'This is deep, Adam. Jess must be wrapped up in it somehow.'

Adam shook his head. 'Why would the Zealots sell Death? Jess wouldn't do that.' Or would he? Adam was finding out how very little he knew his own brother.

'When are you meeting him?'

'In a couple of hours, in Platt Fields Park.'

'Ask him about the antidote,' said Lizzie suddenly.

Adam swung round to face her, shocked ... horrified ... hopeful. 'There is no antidote! You know that.'

'That's what we're told. But he'll know for sure ...'

'There is no antidote,' he hissed furiously. 'That's the point, isn't it? I'm going to die. Just get used to it. It's a good thing,' he added.

Yes, he wanted it! Yes, he welcomed it! But the words choked in his throat and to his shame, emotion hijacked him, and he burst into tears.

'Hey. Hey, hey – come on.' Lizzie jumped up, and he let

her fold him in her arms.

'I can't,' he told her weakly. 'I just can't …'

'Can't what?'

'I can't think like that. Hoping. What's the point when there isn't any hope?'

'But what if there is?'

'No!' He pushed her away. 'You don't you get it, do you? I'm going to die. I've got my week, that's all I've got. That has to be enough. It HAS to be enough. Don't you see?' He wept and raged at her.

'Look, Adam. No!' she cut in, when he was about to launch at her. 'Let's have this conversation now – just once. OK? Just once. Because, Adam, we do have to have it. I have to have it. I have to know. It's … it's part of the ride, OK?'

Part of the ride. Adam stared at her.

'If there was an antidote. What then? Would you take it?'

There was a pause. 'I can't think like that. I can't do that, Lizzie …' He screwed up his eyes and tried to squash the tears right down inside himself, where they didn't matter.

The tears were answer enough. 'So look. Ask Jess. OK? Just ask him. He's involved in this somehow or other. The Zealots, Death, everything that's going on. If he says no, fine. We get on with your week. But if there is, we – I – am going to try and get it. Not for your sake,' she insisted before he interrupted her. 'For me. Because I don't want just one week with you. I want more. OK, Adam? It's not just about you. It never was, it never will be. It's about me, too. And it's about Jess, and your mum and your dad. All of us. We've got to stand here and watch you go. I'll do it for you, if I have to. But if I don't, well then, we're going to try and save your life whether you want it or not. OK? Deal?'

Adam felt like she was breaking him in half. But – OK. For her. For Lizzie. Not for him.

He nodded.

'Good.' Lizzie smiled, and looked pleased. But what she was really thinking was if Jess was alive Adam had taken Death for no reason at all. And how was he going to react when he realised that?

CHAPTER 4

MEETING IN
THE PARK

Adam begged her to come with him to meet Jess, but Lizzie steeled herself to say no. This was between him and Jess, she told him. But it wasn't that, really.

The fact was, she didn't believe in an antidote, either. You never knew, you heard the odd story, you had to hope – but the evidence was all the other way. No. Adam was going to die. He was dying now, even while he walked next to her along the road, fizzing with life like no one she'd ever known. She'd promised to spend the last week with him and she intended to keep that promise, but it wasn't going to be easy. Nothing else she was ever going to go through – childbirth, love, sex, her own death – was going to come even close to this in sheer intensity. It was going to be heaven and hell rolled up into one big, angsty ball.

She wanted a few hours on her own just to get her head round it. They would probably be the last few hours she'd have to herself before he died.

Adam got on the bus, turned his tragic, white face to look her and grinned as if to say, *Yeah, this is what it's all about.* She stood and waved goodbye, then went back home to tidy up and pack a bag. There was no way she could stay at home. Her mum and dad could not be allowed to even guess what was going on.

Where they were going to hide out, she had no idea. This was going to require some careful planning. Once she got the place tidy, Lizzie sat down and turned on her laptop. The internet was awash with Death.

It was amazing. Kids all over Manchester were following Jimmy Earle into the night, and with them was coming the biggest crime wave in history. Robbery, rape, murder. Suddenly there were thousands of people roaming the streets with nothing to lose and nothing to win but one week of fun. The police were desperately trying to track down the source of the drug, but meanwhile, it was flooding the streets.

She found a comment about a Deather who had committed murder online. Wow. She found the video of it easily enough – it had three million hits already, and it had only been online for two hours.

It started off straight enough – a well-known female reporter talking to some kid on Death. She was asking him why he'd thrown his life away like that.

He grinned. 'How do you like it?' he asked the reporter.

'What do you mean?' the woman asked. In answer, the kid lunged forward and stabbed her in the stomach, hard. Lizzie jumped to her feet in shock. Murder – right there in her face. The reporter made a strange noise, half groan, half gasp of surprise. The kid shook the blade right in the camera – in her face, it felt like – splashing the lens with blood. The crew tried to grab him, but he was off, sprinting away, pushing them all back and escaping easily.

Why had he done it? But she knew the answer, sort of. This was a poor kid who'd had nothing all his life. Now at least he had as much as that reporter – more in fact, because she was dead and he had a few more days to live.

And because he could.

Her thoughts were interrupted by a call on her mobile. It was Julie.

'Dolly,' said Julie. 'How are you?'

'I'm fine,' said Lizzie absently, still shocked from the images on the screen.

'No, you're not fine. You're in the deepest shit you can think of.'

'What?'

For a moment she thought Julie had somehow found out about Adam. But it wasn't that. That guy at the party that Adam had punched? Christian? He was interested in her.

'So what?' asked Lizzie.

So what? Julie was furious. Did she have any idea who Christian was? Only the son of the biggest gangster in the north of England, which without doubt meant the whole country, since Manchester gangs were the worst of the lot anyway. Not only that, he was a dirty, sick pervert as well. These were the people flooding the country with cheap Death. Julie had already had a visit from his bodyguard, the big guy in the suit, wanting to know where Lizzie lived. This was very bad news indeed. Very bad. How had she been so stupid as to get talking to him at the party?

'How was I supposed to know? You invite me to a party with a gangster and then it's my fault?'

'I didn't invite him, he just came.'

'Why didn't you warn me?'

'Because any idiot can tell at a glance he's not all there!'

'Did you tell him where I was?' demanded Lizzie.

'No, of course not. Well, not everything. I gave him your email.'

'My email? You cow, Julie. Why did you do that?'

'Jesus. Lizzie! Why do you think? So I wouldn't get beaten up, for fuck's sake. God, Lizzie, you are being so selfish about this!'

Lizzie groaned. 'So now I'm going to get bombarded by pervy emails from that freak. Great. Did you give him my Facebook as well?'

'Lizzie, Christian is not interested in sending you pervy emails. He's not that sort of a pervert. He's more the hands-on kind. I doubt that you'll get any emails. What you will get is a personal visit as soon as he's worked out where you live.'

'Can he do that?'

'Oh, yes.'

'Shit. But what does he want me for? What does he want to do?'

'What do you think he wants to do? He wants to perve all over you, and don't ask me what that means because I don't even know.'

'Well … what do I do, then? Call the police?'

'You do not call the police on these people! These people practically ARE the police. No way. What you do is, you go into hiding. Give it a few weeks, he'll probably get over it and move on to someone else.'

'Go into hiding?'

'Yes. That's what I'm going to do and I'm not even the one he wants. Don't argue, Lizzie,' warned Julie. 'You don't have any choice. And your parents will have to hide as well. I'm ringing them next.'

'No!'

'Yes! You want them beat up and set on fire, too?'

Lizzie thought about it. There didn't seem to be much choice – and anyway, it might play into her hands. 'OK,' she said, 'but I'm not going into hiding with them. It'd drive me mad. I need a place of my own, for a while anyway.'

They argued about it for a bit, but in the end, Lizzie got her own way.

'But where?' she asked.

Julie had just the place.

💀

While Julie was explaining things to Lizzie, Adam was on the bus to the park, allowing himself to think about his mum and dad for the first time since he'd taken Death.

Speaking to Jess had sobered him right up.

Lizzie was right; it never was just all about him. In effect, Adam had committed suicide. He was in freefall to the rope's end. It was a long rope, but it was going to end all too soon and he wasn't going to be the only victim. As sure as a soldier firing a gun, he had executed the hopes and dreams of his mother and father as well. He'd ruined their lives by ending his own.

But! Maybe not. They still had Jess, back from the dead. As ever, Jess was the one who was going to go back and pick up the pieces. Once he knew what Adam had done, he'd have no choice. Everything would be back to normal. On Jess's shoulders would be heaped all his parents' dreams and hopes. Jess would provide them with grandchildren, help and support them in their old age, and give them the joy of watching their offspring growing old and wise.

Except it wasn't all back to normal, of course. There was one person for whom nothing could ever be changed again: Adam. By coming back from the dead, Jess had removed any meaning at all from his own death. Jess, the faker, had made even Adam's despair meaningless.

Unless ... could it be true, as Lizzie had suggested, that there might be an antidote? Everyone said it didn't exist, but there were some stories going round – that the manufacturers only said there was no way out because the antidote cost even more than Death itself, or that the government suppressed the truth because, face it, without the death at the end, this was just one really good drug.

Everyone would want it.

Hope. That's what Adam was feeling as he rode the bus across town. Hope. And hope, he was discovering, was the most terrifying thing of all.

They'd arranged to meet by a boarded-up shed that had been a ticket office for the boating lake years ago. When Adam saw his brother he went running towards him – he'd never felt so glad all in his life. But when he got close he felt angry again. He'd forgotten for a few seconds how Jess had betrayed him – betrayed the whole family. You could almost say that Jess had killed him.

They stood there looking at one another, not touching. Jess looked flushed, his eyes bright. His brown hair had been cut short and he was wearing unfamiliar clothes. A new Jess.

'You're alive,' said Adam. He didn't know whether to hug him or hit him.

Jess nodded. 'Have you got them?' he asked.

Adam was offended. This was his greeting, then. He took the pills from where he'd hidden them down his pants, and handed them over. Jess snatched the bag and looked into it.

'Are they all here?' he asked.

'One short.'

Jess shot him a sharp look. 'You didn't take it, did you?'

'Do I look stupid?' Adam said it before he could think. He knew at once that the lie wasn't going to be as easy to take back as it was to give.

'You sold it?'

'Yeah.'

For the first time, Jess looked Adam full in the face. He raised his eyebrows slightly. 'Someone's going to die, then.'

'What are you doing with this stuff?' said Adam. He wasn't going to take any stick from Jess. 'Did you help make them?'

Jess ignored the question. 'That was a stupid thing to do. You could have got Garry killed, do you know that?' he asked, stuffing the bag into his pants.

Adam stared resentfully at him. 'So it's all my fault, is it?' he asked. Jess didn't meet his eye. 'What's going on?' he demanded. 'Why did the Zealots say you were dead?' He paused a moment. 'Have you told Mum and Dad you're all right?'

Jess looked away, then back. 'I'm not going to tell them, Adam,' he said. 'And neither are you.'

'Are you joking?' Now he was getting angry. 'Of course they have to know. What are you playing at, Jess?'

Jess took a couple of steps back, out of sight of the path nearby. 'Keep your voice down. I'm carrying, remember?' He waited for Adam to step into the shadows before he went on. 'I wanted you all to think I was dead,' he said. 'It would have been easier that way.'

'Easier than what?' demanded Adam. How could anything be harder?

Jess grimaced and shook his head. He looked furious himself. 'It's not about you or me or Mum or Dad,' he said. 'It's about everyone. The human race.'

'We *are* the human race, in case you hadn't noticed.

Your bit of it,' said Adam, bitterly.

'Do you think I don't love them? Or you?' Adam looked away. Him and his brother had never talked about love before. Jess reached out and grabbed hold of his arm. 'You reckon it didn't break my heart to do what I did?'

'I know you broke their hearts, all right. Mum and Dad's.'

Jess looked appalled. 'I'm sorry, Adam,' he said. 'I really am, but you can't tell them. It'd only break their hearts again. I'm going to die. I said what I did to get it over with.'

Adam was horrified. 'What do you mean? You haven't taken Death, have you?' he demanded.

'No. Of course not. I volunteered.'

'What, to die?'

'I'm a Zealot. It happens. Self-immolation. Suicide bomb if I'm lucky.'

Adam was struck dumb for a moment. It was unbelievable.

'When?' he croaked.

Jess shrugged. 'Maybe tomorrow, maybe next week. Soon.'

'But it's stupid! It's pointless,' raged Adam. 'What good will it do? No one's going to change their minds because you set fire to yourself, or blow yourself up …'

But Jess was shaking his head. He'd heard these arguments a hundred times. Adam wasn't going to change anything by going over it again.

'The Zealots,' Adam spat. 'So you're helping them make Death, is that what it is? And it was you lot handing Death out in the square that night, was it? That's great, isn't it? All those innocent people dying. Did they volunteer as well?'

'It's a war, Adam!' insisted Jess. 'There's always collateral damage. And it's working. Have you seen the crowds in Manchester? People are heading out in their hundreds of thousands. This Friday, one week after Jimmy Earle died, it'll be the biggest protest yet. Maybe more than just a protest this time. The police are coming over to us, even some of the army. It could be revolution.'

'They've brainwashed you,' said Adam.

Jess made a dismissive gesture. 'That's what they want you to believe,' he said. 'But it's you who's been brainwashed. The government are running scared. They know their time is up. I'm prepared to die for what I believe in. That's not being brainwashed. Maybe one day you'll believe in something, too.'

'And what about Mum and Dad?' said Adam. Although, in his heart, what he wanted to say was – *What about me?*

Jess gave him a thin smile. 'You want to make it hard for me. You can't make it any harder. I'm doing what I *believe* in, Adam. The human race is going down the plughole. People have been abandoned so a handful of investors can make more billions while the rest of us sink into the mud. There's enough capacity in the world to feed, clothe and educate everyone, but it's all spent on banks and weapons. This is war. People get lost in war. Families get broken up. It happens.'

'It's not war,' insisted Adam. 'You're just saying that to make it sound OK. You didn't have to go. You wrecked my life, Jess, you bastard. I trusted you, and you wrecked my life …'

Tears of self-pity filled his eyes, but Jess was having none of it.

'Oh, don't start. How did I wreck your life? By making you get a job? You were always going to get a job. Stopping you getting a place in a football team? You were never going to get a place in a football team. Did you think I was going to spend my life working like a slave so you could dream about being a big star? Wake up, Adam. Sorry it was me who rang the bell. Smell the coffee. It stinks. What did you expect?'

Adam was aghast. Was that what his brother really thought?

'It's called real life,' said Jess, furiously. 'Welcome to it. They're not my rules; they don't have to be yours, either. Mum and Dad choose to follow them. I've chosen to fight back, and you know what, Adam? There's nothing to stop you fighting back, too. You have a choice, same as me. Same as everyone. We can all fight.'

'And desert Mum and Dad like you did?'

'Then do your bit and work for them! There's no space for dreams any more, not unless you're prepared to make them come true. Look around you!' Jess swung his arm up, no longer bothered if people heard him. 'People are dying. People are wasting their lives working for loveless bastards who own nearly everything already and still want more. Society is dying, three-quarters of the world is starving – and you want to play football.' He spat the words out in disgust.

Adam had no idea all this venom was in him. 'You never said ...'

'I said all the time. You didn't listen. None of you ever listened.'

Suddenly Jess grabbed hold of Adam and held him in his arms. 'I love you,' he said. His breath was hot on Adam's face. 'Don't ever forget that. And I know you're going to work this out and do what's right.'

Jess hugged him hard until Adam pushed him away and stood there looking savagely at him.

'OK,' he said. 'OK.' He was panting with emotion. He had one last card to play – the trump. He played it. 'That missing pill. What if I told you I *had* taken it?' he asked. 'What then? Then you'd have to come back.'

Jess frowned and peered into his face. 'And did you?' he said.

'I did. I took it. So what now?'

Jess stood there a while, thinking. Then he shook his head.

'Then you're a fool and I can't help you,' he said. He laughed, tiredly. He looked suddenly drained. 'Just ... at least make sure you get your full week in, if that's all you have left.' He pushed his way past to the path. He was going. Adam had played his final card, and Jess was still going.

'You don't care about me. You never cared about any of us,' he yelled after him.

Jess shook his head again. There was nothing more to say.

'Jess – wait!' Jess paused mid-step. Adam steeled

himself to ask the million-dollar question. 'Is there an antidote?' he asked.

'It's a one-way street, just like they say.' Jess looked at Adam one last time – a long, searching look. 'I love you anyway,' he said. He paused a moment longer. 'I wish I could help you, but I can't.'

He walked rapidly away. Adam stood and watched him go. *At any moment*, he thought, *he's going to turn round and come back and sort this out.* That's what Jess always did.

But not this time. He walked along the path and disappeared behind some shrubs. That was it. Goodbye for ever.

Adam stood there a while on his own. *That's it, then*, he thought. Then he left and made his way back to meet Lizzie.

💀

After leaving Adam, Jess made his way into Fallowfield to see Garry and give him the pills. It had broken his heart seeing Adam, but he wasn't going to let that change anything. He had given himself to the Zealots a long time ago, and what hurt him or pleased him was no longer his own concern. Anna had convinced him that he should have at least a few hours for himself and not the cause. He wasn't sure that she was right, but he had been unable to resist the temptation of seeing the drama unfolding in Albert Square – perhaps a foretaste of revolution itself, if things worked out. He had given his life for this. Wasn't it right that he should have just a brief taste of it while he had the chance?

It had been a mistake seeing Adam, though. It hurt too much.

After Garry he would go into town, meet up with Anna and have his one night of glory in the square, watching the end of despair and the beginning of hope. Then it was back to the container park, where Ballantine would doubtless have the shit beaten out of him and Anna – if she came back, that was. He suspected that maybe she had already decided not to.

As for his parents, he didn't dare even think about them. Adam had been hard enough. He wasn't strong enough to see them, too.

He jumped on to the bus on the Wilmslow Road and rode into town. He felt like crying. But what use were tears of sorrow when the most joyful day of all was just around the corner?

CHAPTER 5
COME THE REVOLUTION

Julie's solution to the Christian problem worked out just right. She was going to lend Lizzie a city flat belonging to a friend of hers who was abroad for a few months. It was perfect – not just for Lizzie, but for Adam as well.

The bus took ages and it was getting dark by the time she arrived in the city centre. The shopkeepers were pulling down the shutters, the police out and about, setting up roadblocks and forming lines outside important buildings. As she came down Portland Street, she saw a group of people wearing rat masks abseiling down the Bruntwood building. Outside, the police leaned on their cars and watched. You couldn't even be sure what side they were on any more.

Julie had her own flat on Deansgate, and Lizzie met her there to pick up the keys before going on to meet Adam at Piccadilly Gardens. She had spoken to him about his meeting with Jess earlier. He had sounded upset then, but by the time he arrived he was distraught – weeping, raging, ready to kill himself right then just to escape the knowledge of what he had done. Jess had raised his hopes – then snatched them away. Now he was staring right into the void. No more years, no more months, not even a whole week any more. No going back; no going forward, either. Adam was a teenage Peter Pan. He would never grow up. Just a few days of now, and then oblivion.

'It's the ride, Adam, it's the ride,' she kept telling him. He was living his whole life in one week – there were going to be lows as well as highs. Wasn't that what it was about? She hurried him along, keen to get him off the streets before anyone guessed what was going on. Manchester was heaving – commuters hurrying to get away before things got rough, and there were protesters everywhere – camping out in Albert Square and Piccadilly Gardens, marching up Deansgate, groups wandering round with banners or sitting outside the bars and pubs, waiting for the protest to start.

What would the night bring? Lizzie wondered. She'd heard on the news that people were calling for the government to resign. At this rate, there wouldn't be anything left to fall.

They pushed their way through the excited crowds towards the Northern Quarter, where the flat Julie had found for them was. The crowds were thinner here, but as they turned off a main road into a small street, they heard shouting behind them. A window smashed, yells, a scream. Lizzie turned to see a wild crowd rushing towards them.

It was young people, maybe a hundred of them, raging up the road, full of fury. Lizzie pulled Adam into a doorway. There was no mistaking the sense of power and violence hanging over them. An old man was knocked to the ground and trampled underfoot. A woman got caught in the rush; someone grabbed at her and pulled at her clothes, and she was dragged along after them. Their faces were twisted in rage – or was it despair?

What was wrong with them? Lizzie had never seen anything like it.

They drew level to the doorway Lizzie and Adam were hiding in, and stormed past. Lizzie buried her head and hid. *Not me,* she prayed, *not me.* They roared and screamed just a metre or two away – she was certain they'd rape her or even kill her if they caught her – but no one leaned in to grab her and in just a few seconds they were gone. She waited a moment before she peered out, only to see Adam trailing up the street after them. She darted out and grabbed his arm.

'Not there, Adam … this way.' She pulled him away, but he resisted and gazed after the crowd.

'Deathers,' he murmured.

Was that it? Lizzie stared at the pack as they tore their way up the road ahead of them. These must be the people who had taken Death in the square the night Jimmy Earle died. They'd gathered together somehow, and were roaming the city in a mob, tearing it to pieces.

She shook his arm. 'Is that what you want?' she demanded. 'To be like that?'

'They're like me. All together,' said Adam.

'I thought you wanted to be with me.'

Adam looked at her, shook his head, looked back. A siren called further up the street and a group of police cars sped past. Reluctantly, he turned away. Lizzie dragged him to the building where the flat was, and took him upstairs. *I'm a fool*, she thought. *I should have let him go.*

Inside, Adam was inconsolable. He buried his head in her arms and wept like a child. 'I just want to live,' he sobbed. She held his head and stroked his face. What could she say? There were no words of comfort for what was wrong with him.

'You'll feel better in the morning,' she said, and hoped it was true. He curled up next to her on the sofa, drank a bottle of wine that she found in the fridge, and gradually became still. End of Day 1 and they were both exhausted, distraught, miserable. Poor payment for a life, Lizzie thought. She woke him up long enough to get him to bed, then lay next to him, while he clutched at her and then, mercifully, fell asleep.

She waited until he was still, then got up and went to sit in the sitting room, feeling deeply shaken. She had never seen true despair before. Adam's eyes had been like black holes leading all the way to death. All the websites she'd checked out had mentioned this, so she was forewarned, but the intensity of it was shocking. There were going to be moments like this – more and more of them, she suspected.

The Deathers on the street had been the real thing, she thought, the ones with nothing to lose and nothing to gain, ready to die. The trouble was, Adam wasn't like that. On the contrary, he was just ready to begin his life. It was the selfishness of the suicide. *Look at me! I'm going to die. Pity me. Be with me. Do what I want.* Suicide – but with all the benefits of watching your friends mourn you.

'It's all about you, Adam,' she whispered.

She got up and went to the sitting-room window. It was all going on outside, but she couldn't see much – just police lights flashing blue somewhere and the glow of flames around a nearby corner.

She flung the window open and it came rushing in on her. Shouting, screaming, chanting, singing, cars revving, the wail of sirens. And somewhere, not far away, the pop and rattle of gunfire.

Lizzie felt a thrill. Was it really happening? The world had seemed frozen rigid, stuck in its old ways just a few days ago. Now, everything was melting and the future was being forged here, on the streets of Manchester, right before her eyes.

Only one thing was certain. The government might fall, food and money might became common property, the new order might be cruel or kind, tyrannous or democratic – but none of it was going to affect Adam. His time was already over.

It's going to be so exciting, she thought. She wouldn't leave Adam. She'd keep her promise. But it was hard, so, so hard, to be tied to someone already in the past, when the whole future was up for grabs. What a shame, she thought, that she was going to remember Adam as this selfish little beast, gobbling up everything he could, when just a short while ago he had been so sweet and kind. Which one, she wondered, was the real Adam?

But then, what difference did that make now?

CHAPTER 6

BEING NICE TO CHRISTIAN

Mr B rang the bell to Garry's door at nine o'clock sharp, which surprised Garry because he'd said he'd call at eleven. He knew who it was at because the caller leaned on the doorbell for a good minute. Who else could it be?

Garry was on the toilet at the time. He flung himself from the seat on to his crutches, levered himself to the top of the stairs, got in the stairlift and started the thing on its way down.

'Please please please please please,' he begged. *Please let him be nice to me. Please let this go as smoothly and as quickly as possible.* And of course, *Please make the stairlift work.* Mr B was the kind of person you didn't want to keep waiting.

'Coming!' he yelled, as cheerfully as he could manage. Halfway down, the stairlift predictably went into reverse and started on its way back upstairs.

'No!' Garry jabbed at the button with a stubby forefinger. Why him? Why his legs? Why his stairlift? At last, after a series of desperate pokes and bangs, the thing ground to a halt and sat there sulking for a full twenty seconds before carrying on its way down again.

Christian did not look amused.

'Sorry, sorry,' Garry babbled. 'The stairlift has a mind of its own. Up, down, all around. Heh heh heh,' he tittered, grinning like an over excited puppy as he backed away from the door.

Christian stepped inside. He tried not to look discomfited by the fact that the place was damp and dirty. That would be bad manners. Christian prided himself on being good-mannered and expected it in others. It was sad but predictable that Garry had left him standing at the door for so long before answering – an example of bad manners if there ever was.

'Come in, come in!' chirruped Garry, unnecessarily. 'Sit down. Tea? Biscuits? Piece of cake?'

'No, thank you,' said Christian, looking with distaste at the grubby kitchenette tucked away under the stairs. He himself only ever ate the very best quality takeaways or ready meals at home, and his house was littered with tin-foil trays full of half-eaten and fly-blown meals. Compared to that, Garry's place was almost clean. But there was a difference; Christian's house was covered with rich dirt, while Garry's stank of poverty. And poor dirt, as everyone knows, is so much dirtier and more contagious than the wealthy sort.

The poor, the poor, Christian thought. *They are always with us, but that doesn't mean you have to do business with them.* Vince was right. This man should never have been given access to expensive drugs.

Garry sat there smiling up at him, thinking *The rich, the rich! Always on the make. Well, just you wait, pal. In a few days our time will come and yours will end.*

'Cup of coffee?' he suggested.

'No. Just the money will do, thank you.'

'Ah, the money! I can do better than that. Here …' Garry dug about in his pyjamas, much to Christian's disgust, and pulled out the polythene bag with Death in it. He beamed. 'You know what? I'd prefer to give them back. I'm a bit out of my depth, to be honest. It's just not secure enough here. I'm going to get myself into trouble.'

'Yeah!' smiled Christian. And they both chortled briefly at the thought of how nearly Garry had got himself into trouble.

'Just one missing,' said Garry. 'And I have the money for that right here.' Digging into his pyjamas again, he came out with a handful of notes.

'Thanks for the offer,' said Christian. 'But we have a contract. I provide the goods. You pay for them.'

Garry flinched. 'Contract?' he said. 'You mean – legally binding?' He sniggered weakly at his own joke.

Christian nodded. 'Yeah,' he said. 'In a manner of speaking.'

There was a moment's silence. 'Please,' said Garry. 'I'm

not ripping you off. I know when I'm out of my depth. I'm giving you the stuff back. Please.'

Christian strolled round behind the chair and began to rub his fingers down the back of Garry's neck, feeling his way through the flesh to the bones beneath. With the other hand, out of sight, he took a short-bladed knife out of his coat pocket.

'What are you doing?' begged Garry. The massage felt almost nice. Nothing could have been more terrifying.

'Quad or para?' asked Christian, suddenly.

'Eh? Well, para, you know? Hands and elbows, but no knees and toes,' said Garry, twisting round to look at him and parroting a phrase his mother used to use when he first had his accident twenty-five years ago.

'Quad,' said Christian. He grabbed hold of Garry's head and forced it forward. While Garry squirmed helplessly under his grip, Christian raised the knife, took careful aim, and brought it down with a dull thud into the back of his neck. The blade sank in up to the hilt in the gap between two vertebrae beneath the skull. A thin stream of blood rolled down under Garry's collar, and he let out a muffled squawk. A shudder ran through his body. He twitched a few times and then ceased to move. Christian let go his head, which lolled at an odd angle on to his chest, and stood back to survey his handiwork.

This particular cut was something he'd been working at for a while. It was a tricky one to get right. He picked up one of Garry's arms and let it flop down like a piece of limp celery. So far, so good. But the guy was being too quiet. Christian bent down and looked into his face.

'How's it feel?' he asked.

Garry blinked at him but didn't say a word. Not good. Christian was going for a C4, severing the spinal column in between vertebrae 4 and 5. Quadriplegic, but the victim could still breathe – if you got it right.

He tipped Garry out of the chair and peered into his face. It was changing colour. Shit! He pushed him over on to his face and fumbled at the neck, trying to count the vertebrae below the head. The bastard had a fat neck. Christian hated fat necks. He had miscounted, done a C3 instead of a C4 and disabled his victim's breathing as well. Silently at his feet, Garry was suffocating.

Bugger! Disgustedly, Christian kicked at the limp body. This was the third time he'd got it wrong. It was infuriating.

He shook his head, popped the bag of pills into his pocket and headed off. He needed more practice. Next time for sure.

Behind him, unable even to struggle for breath, Garry watched as Christian wiped his expensive handmade shoes on the doormat, so as not to dirty the streets outside with the cheap crud from the grubby carpet. The door opened and closed; his murderer gone. Garry turned red, then blue, then white, and died with a murmurous gurgle some ten minutes after Christian had left the building.

CHAPTER 7

THE HEIST

Tuesday morning and Adam was sitting in the kitchen, happily tucking into bacon and eggs. The food was perfect and so was everything else. The day awaited his attention, the sky blowing grubby white and grey clouds across a pale blue sky solely for his enjoyment. Lizzie was in the shower – and he was in love.

Best of all, he was no longer a virgin. Adam grinned at the ceiling. Sex was great. He loved sex. It was, without doubt, the most wonderful thing that had ever happened to him, and he'd done it with the most wonderful person he'd ever met. If he'd been any happier he'd have just melted away with sheer joy.

Lizzie, Lizzie, Lizzie. 'I love you!' he shouted out over his shoulder, and he heard her shout back, 'I love you!'

from the shower. How lucky was he? Maybe they'd go and do it again in a moment. And again, and again … Wouldn't it be great just to put on some music and spent the day in the flat? Staying in bed, doing it, chatting, relaxing, doing it again … maybe go out for a drink later …?

But he couldn't. There wasn't time. He had to get on with the list.

Overnight, things had sorted themselves out in Adam's brain. That was Death for you – each day was fresh and new – the next twenty-four hours opened up like a whole new life spread before him.

He whipped out the list and scanned it.

Fall in love. Done!

Sex with Lizzie. Done!

Get her pregnant. Yeah, well. Worry about that later.

Loads of sex with loads of girls. Several of them at once. He felt guilty about it, but he knew he was going to check out that website, regretit-forgetit.com, to see how many bites he'd had. Lizzie would understand, one day.

Drink champagne till I can't stand. Done!

Do cocaine. Something to look forward to.

Drive a supercar round Manchester.

Kill someone who deserves to die.

Do something so that humanity will remember me for ever.

Die on the Himalayas, watching the sun go down.

He'd work on those later.

Get rich. Leave my dad and Lizzie with enough money so they'll never have to work again.

Too right. He needed money to make the rest of the list happen. That was today sorted out. He was going to get rich.

He'd done three out of ten already and it was only Day 2! Heroic. And more than that. Look at this flat – it was huge! He could have put 'live in a fabulous place' on the list and he'd have achieved that as well. Everything was modern, every luxury you could think of. Jacuzzi. A sauna. Yes, you heard – a sauna. And the view – you could see halfway across Manchester. This was living! The food he'd just eaten had tasted better than anything he'd ever had before. That was Death, his best friend Death, heightening his senses, making everything so much better, so much more real.

Lizzie came in in a gown and sat opposite him. Adam jumped up and kissed her. Dreams. He was going to make them all come true.

'You know these protests,' Lizzie said.

'Yeah.'

'How about going to have a look? Everyone's talking about it. It sounds like something might actually happen this time.'

Adam frowned at her. 'But it's not on the list, is it?'

'Leaving something behind you is. This is big, Adam. The government could be overthrown. The way you are, maybe you could do something to help it. Legacy, you know?'

Adam thought about it while he took a shower. Yeah, legacy was on the list. Some act of bravery or something, so he wouldn't have lived in vain. But how do you make a life count? Six days left. A thrill of fear shook through him and he found himself leaning on the tiled wall, gasping for breath. Fear; it took him by surprise every time.

And Lizzie, going into the bedroom to get dressed,

paused to listen in on the mind of a man with all his youth and love and energy to burn up in six short days, heard Adam murmuring, sing-song under his breath, '... don't think it don't think it don't think it ...' and she knew that the day wasn't going to be spent planning the overthrow of the state. Who would bother to vote, if they knew there were no more tomorrows?

She sat down on the bed and sighed. If it were up to her, they'd have spent the whole day just lying in bed, then gone to the protest in the evening. Romance, excitement and falling in love. It could have been wonderful. As it was ... well, the sex had been OK. It was like Sarina had said – it was something that would probably get better the more you did it. But it wasn't ever going to get like that with Adam. So she felt ... but then, what did it matter what she felt?

Adam banged in on her and grinned.

'Guess what?' he said. 'We're going to rob a bank!'

💀

There was a huge HSBC smack in the middle of town – no one would expect them to take that out. Adam would get a Death-powered stranglehold on one of the clerks, force them to let him in, open up the safe and make off with the cash. Easy.

It took Lizzie a good fifteen minutes to change his mind. There was a reason why no one would expect them to take on the big HSBC – it was like an armed fortress, for instance. Plus the fact that the Zealots were putting all the major banks and companies under attack. There were police everywhere, and armed guards all over the building. The centre of town was the last place to try to pull a heist.

Adam came up with another plan – Booze R Us on the Wilmslow Road, back in Fallowfield. While the revolution was going on round the corner, the smaller places out of town would be relatively unprotected.

Lizzie wasn't exactly happy about it. She knew that shop. The till and the booze were behind glass and you had to tell the shop assistants what you wanted. They got it for you and you passed your money through a letter-box-sized gap under the glass. You couldn't get anywhere near the cash.

'There's a back entrance,' said Adam. 'Whenever some-one on the staff wants a ciggie, they go out that way and leave the door open. All we have to do is take them out, stroll in and help ourselves.' He grinned. See? All you needed was the nerve and commitment to do it.

'So why do they go to all that trouble to keep people away from the booze and the till, and then leave the back door open?' Lizzie wanted to know.

Adam had the answer to that. He had the answer to everything. 'Because the system was designed by security consultants, but it's operated by monkeys. Simple. No problem. Loaded!'

They caught a bus on the Oxford Road and then walked round the back of the shops to stake the place out. They only had to wait a few minutes before the back door opened up and a tired-looking guy with limp black hair came out. He lit up his cigarette, leaning up against a wall by the door, which, as Adam had said, he left open.

'Let's go,' hissed Adam.

Lizzie glared at him. She felt sick with fear. 'You owe me,' she hissed.

Adam grinned back. 'I won't live long enough to be able to pay you back. Just go! You'll get a share of the proceeds, won't you? Let's go-go-GO!'

He stepped forward. Lizzie followed him, and they both ambled casually towards the shop assistant. Not casually enough. Maybe it was the way they were walking – maybe it was the way Lizzie had pulled her woolly hat down over her eyes so she couldn't be recognised that made her look exactly like a robber. Either way, the assistant seemed to know at once that they were up to no good. He was edging towards the door before they were halfway towards him. Adam sped up. The assistant jumped inside and slammed the door shut.

'Run!' yelled Lizzie, scooting backwards; but Adam hadn't given up yet. He threw himself at the door – and he was in luck. The assistant was still fumbling with the lock and it flew open under his weight. Lizzie came running in after him and found him in a store room, piled high with crates of booze, crouching over the terrified man, who was cringing on the floor.

'Don't hurt him!' she said.

'I'm not,' hissed Adam. 'Get in there – quick.'

She edged her way to the door at the front of the storeroom. On the other side was a short corridor leading through to the shop. She glanced back; Adam nodded and she made her way forward. Behind her, Adam forced the man flat on to his stomach. He felt so strong he could do anything.

'Stay still,' he hissed, 'and no one gets hurt.'

The assistant pressed his face to the floor and nodded. Inside, Adam could hear Lizzie banging about.

'I can't open the till!' she yelled. Then: 'Agh! Ads, there's someone else here.'

'Not my name, you idiot,' Adam yelled back. He hauled the assistant to his feet just as Lizzie came charging out. At the same moment, an alarm began ringing. Cursing, Adam pushed both Lizzie and the assistant into the shop. There, cringing by the counter, was an old guy, over sixty, grey hair, balding …

'Shit, Lizzie, it's someone's granddad, we're not going to be scared off by this,' snarled Adam, furiously. He shoved the first assistant into the older man and grabbed them both by the hair. He was so full of adrenalin, he could have wrestled a rhino to the ground.

'Open the till,' he yelled.

'No,' squeaked the old man.

Adam banged their heads together gently.

'OK! OK! OK!' the old guy yelled. He reached over and pinged the till open. There it was – the lovely money. Adam reached in, snatched a handful and kissed it. He scooped the rest of it out, then turned abruptly and dashed out, with Lizzie on his tail.

They ran and ran, the clanging alarm fell away behind them. No one gave chase – they were in the clear. After five minutes they slowed down and ducked into an alley to get their breath back and count the loot. They'd done it! How cool was that? Adam pulled out a big, fat roll from inside his jacket. He counted it up: one thousand pounds. Not bad. He shook the notes in Lizzie's face. 'We can blow this lot, then we'll do another one. We know how now,' he boasted.

Lizzie nodded, but really, she felt dreadful. Yesterday she was living at home being bored. Today, she had run away from home, had her first sex with her boyfriend who had taken Death, was being hunted down by a pervert gangster – she hadn't even bothered mentioning that to Adam – and here she was, committing a major crime with a prison sentence hanging over her if she got caught. She was out of breath, sick with fear and emotionally exhausted. It was all too much. She started to sniffle.

Adam put his arm round her. 'Aw. What's up?'

She looked at him. What's up? Didn't he even know? She started to cry properly – great gusts of tears, crouching there in the alley, while Adam waved the thousand pounds under her nose to try and cheer her up.

'Come on, Lizzie. We pulled it off! Hey – guess what?'

Lizzie shook her head.

'Did you see that guy's face when I banged their heads together?'

Lizzie looked up. Her lip wobbled. Adam nodded at her. *Come on, come on, come on! Please, Lizzie, just feel good. Do it for me!* To his relief, gradually she started to smile wryly and then wheeze with laughter.

'He looked like he was going to piss himself, didn't he?' said Adam. 'And how about that kid when I made him get on his knees? I reckon he thought I was going to make him pray!'

Yeah, hilarious! Lizzie began to giggle, although whether it was hysteria or proper comedy, she wasn't sure. They laughed and laughed, had to hold each other up but ended up rolling around on the floor anyhow. Finally, snorting and giggling, they made their way to a bus stop to catch a ride into town. The fun bit was, the bus took them past the shop they'd just robbed. It was even more hilarious. There were police cars, cops stopping people going in and out. It was great. They'd made fools of everyone.

The bus rolled on its way down the Wilmslow Road into town. Past the Curry Mile, past the Whitworth Art Gallery. Adam and Lizzie checked on their phones to see where to eat, what to do, what was on. They were halfway there when Adam realised they'd stopped for too long and peered out of the window. There was a cop car next to them. He stood and looked out. There was another police car pulled up in the road right in front of the bus.

He knew at once. 'They're on to us,' he hissed. He leaped out of his seat and ran for the stairs. Lizzie stood up – then sat down again. Adam was fast, he might be able to escape, but her best bet was to hide here among the other people in the bus. And – Adam had given himself away ...

💀

Adam almost fell down the stairs. At the bottom the door was shut. He ripped it open, and jumped out – right into the arms of the police.

'I'm guessing you must the guilty party,' one of them said. A couple of them grabbed hold of him, pushed him over and pressed him down into the road.

'Spotted on the bus laughing your silly heads off,' another said, and they all laughed.

It was hopeless. Adam was surrounded, face down on the pavement, his arms pinned behind his back. He peered sideways and up; handcuffs. Once they were on, he was stuffed.

He twisted suddenly and managed to get on his back. *You have to try, right?* He jack-knifed – shoulders on the ground, striking up with his feet – and caught one of the policeman square on the chest. The man went flying. Adam flipped down, got his feet under him – and he was hurtling off as fast as he could, vaulting over the bonnet of a car and away up the road. He ran – ran and ran and ran, the cops hot on his tail. One of them was a bit overweight – he didn't stand a chance – but the other was young, long-legged and fit. Even with Death in him, Adam was losing ground.

He was going to get caught – he had to do something! He dropped suddenly to the ground and curled up into a ball. The policeman banged his foot smack into his back and went flying. But that foot caught Adam bang in his kidney. He jumped up at once and tried to carry on, but he was crippled with pain. He staggered up the street, his legs buckling under him. The policeman was back up already. He'd skinned his hands and his face on landing and looked dreadful, covered in blood – but his wounds were just skin deep. He caught Adam easily, spun him round and shoved him down face first on the road again.

'You little shit,' he hissed, and punched him hard in the kidney. 'Unavoidable injury sustained during capture and detention.'

The other police came running up. They dragged Adam to his feet and marched him off to the police car.

They had Lizzie, too, standing there in her black woolly cap. Except, when he got close, it wasn't Lizzie. It was some other kid, a bit younger than Adam, with the same kind of clothes as her, looking anxiously at him as he was marched up.

'Tell 'em, mate,' the kid said. 'It wasn't me, was it? Your mate must have got away.'

'Sorry, Al,' Adam said. 'They got us.'

The kid stared at him as it sank in. 'You bastard,' he squeaked. 'Hey, he's lying, honest, he's lying, it wasn't me ...'

The police led them off to the waiting cars. 'It's a set-up!' the kid yelled, but the police just pushed him down into the car. Adam went in another one, and they drove off. Before he got in, Adam managed to glance up and saw the white face of Lizzie in the upstairs windows on the bus as it pulled away.

At least she'd got away with it. But as for Adam – that was it. He was going to get tested for Death, locked up, remanded with no bail. They only needed one week. He was going to spend the rest of his short life behind bars.

💀

The cell was a metal box – welded metal walls, metal door, metal floor, a metal bunk and a metal toilet in one corner. A small square of glass about half a metre thick let in a thin grey light, drowned out by a bright neon tube that was locked above him in a tough metal cage. It stank of piss and shit, and would have held a dinosaur, let alone one miserable boy. They left him there to stew on his own for half an hour – then, without warning, the door burst open and two big policemen stormed in, shouting and swearing, screaming threats in his face. For a few minutes the cell was full of loud abuse; then, just as suddenly, they went out and left him alone, leaving him shaken and more scared than ever.

That happened twice more; then the questions started. They took him to an interview room and told him how much better it would be for him to confess now. His mate Al, apparently, had already cracked and told them everything. His parents had been called and were waiting outside for him. His mother was crying; so was his dad. It didn't look as though they could afford bail, but he might get a deal if he talked now. Did he really want his parents to be sat there all night, worrying about him?

Then came more time on his own. More threats. A policeman came in and kicked him around the cell for a bit. Then more quiet, more screaming and shouting, followed by another beating. Adam kept his mouth shut, more by instinct than from any sort of plan. Eventually, hours later, a doctor came for the blood and urine tests. Afterwards, back in the cell, sitting on the floor breathing in the stink from the toilet, Adam's last hope died. This moment, this misery, was going to be the rest of his life.

Hours passed. Once again the police came and took him out to a small room where he was charged with robbery and resisting arrest. Then he was marched along a corridor, turned a corner, and emerged in the front of the station where his mum and dad were waiting for him.

He was confused. What about the blood tests? Didn't they know about the Death? The policeman was explaining to his parents what would happen next. The test results would be back in a week or so.

A week! He was free. Suddenly, he was filled with joy. He had never been so glad to see anyone, ever. He grinned at his parents, but they looked back at him dark-eyed, and almost at once, his spirits sank again because – what was he going to say to them? How could he ever explain what he had done to himself, and to them?

All three of them stood there like naughty children while the sergeant gave them a lecture about being good parents and a good son. His mum hugged him while his dad signed some papers, and he was handed over like a lost pet into their care.

The journey home was grim. The bail had been huge – more than they could possibly afford. But they'd found it for him somehow, out of love. His mum drove; his dad sat twisted round in the seat trying to talk to him, but Adam had nothing to say.

'Why?' his dad kept saying. 'Do you think this is going to solve all our problems? All you've done is make them worse. All that money for the bail.'

'It's not the money,' said his mum.

'Not just the money, no,' said his dad. 'But Adam – think! What are we going to do? How are we going to manage?'

Back home, his mum cooked him sausages while his dad sat at the table drinking tea. He went off to bed as soon as he could and texted Lizzie that he was out. There was no reply.

A row was going on downstairs – obviously about him. Some time later, his dad came up to say goodnight. He bent over the bed to kiss him, something he hadn't done for years. His scratchy grey beard on Adam's cheek reminded him of when he was little.

'You must remember that we love you, very, very much. No matter what, Adam. No matter what. We have each other first, last and for ever. But this has to stop. Robbing a shop! A poor man doing his job – you must have terrified him. You must accept the way life is and help us. You understand?'

Adam nodded.

'I want your word. Your word of honour, Adam, that this will stop.'

Adam didn't even pause. 'I promise. I give you my word. I'm sorry, I really am.'

'Good.' His dad nodded. For him, that was that. Adam had given his word. There would be no more questions or doubts. Only Adam knew that his word was worth nothing.

The old man paused at the door to drive his message home. 'I love you. I love you and this has to stop,' he repeated. He nodded once more, then left.

Adam tried to go to sleep – the sooner this day was over the better. All he wanted was that wonderful good-morning feeling that came when he woke up with Death fresh in his veins. But he knew his mum was going to come up to see him, too. Sure enough, ten minutes later, there was her step on the stairs. The door creaked open. She whispered his name to check that he was awake. He didn't answer, just lifted his head, and she came quietly in, sat on the bed next to him and stroked his head.

'I'm sorry,' he said.

'I know you are,' she said. 'I'm sorry, too.'

'What for?'

'This mess. It isn't what I wanted for my kids. Your dad handicapped. Me working myself into a shadow. And Jess, of course, especially Jess. But you know what, Adam? The funny thing is, I'm proud of him in a way.'

Adam was outraged. 'But he let us down!'

'He stood up for what he believed in. And maybe he's right – have you thought of that? Everyone's working harder and harder for less and less. So few people getting richer and richer, and the rest of us getting poorer every year. Kids killing themselves for a good time. Jess wanted to do something about that.'

'I can't believe you have any pity for him,' said Adam.

'I know he let us down. I'm angry about that, too, but at least he did it for a good cause. People are talking about revolution, you know. It can happen if we want it to. There are half a million people on the streets of Manchester right now, as we speak. Half a million! Something has to give.'

Adam said nothing.

'The thing is, Adam ...' She squeezed his hand and bent down a little closer, to try to push her words deep inside him. 'Life is still worth living. There are so many wonderful things. Having a job you don't like – most of us have to do things we don't like, but it's still an adventure. It's all waiting for you. Growing up, having children. Making love. Falling in love.' She smiled. 'It really is like they say in the songs. Love *is* the greatest thing. Don't throw it all away just because there are bad things as well. Life can be generous as well as mean. It can be joyful. Always remember that. Promise me, Adam, will you – always to remember that?'

More promises. Adam nodded. But he would keep this promise, he felt. He would remember her words until his dying day.

She bent to kiss him. 'Night-night,' she whispered.

'Night, Mum.'

Adam turned over as she left the room and lay there, keeping himself awake. He waited until the house had gone very, very still before he got up, let himself quietly out of the front door, and left.

CHAPTER 8

LIZZIE MAKES A DATE

On the bus, Lizzie escaped by simply staying put. No one seemed to realise that she was with Adam, or if they did, they didn't point her out when the police came up and took that lad downstairs. She sat quietly until the bus got into town, and went straight back to the flat.

That was it, then. Bang. Adam was as good as dead.

On her own at last, she burst into tears. What a couple of days! It was exhausting just sitting next to Adam, watching him foam over with life and knowing he was going to be dead in just one week. And now he was gone for ever.

She was relieved; she felt dreadful for feeling relieved. She was sad; she was angry. He'd let her down; she'd let him down … she didn't know what she felt.

She drifted about the flat, wondering what to do now. Her parents would be going crazy. She turned on her phone, which she'd kept off to avoid hearing from them earlier, and sure enough, there was a long list of calls and messages. *Where are you? What's going on? We just want to know you're safe.* It was the first time she'd been away from home without telling them. She had planned to be away a week, but it looked like it was time to go home already.

Life was going straight back to zero, she thought. Home. School. Mates. Mum and Dad. And all the time, Adam was in a cell waiting to die.

Not yet. She wasn't ready to go back yet. She turned on the telly and flipped through the internet to find out more about Death – and there it all was: the gangs rampaging round Manchester, the rumours about the Zealots manufacturing the new cheap Death. The stages people went through. It started off manic, apparently, in the first few days, then calmed down. That was when the despair hit home.

She wept again. It was impossible to think about Adam without crying. He had been a little shit these past two days, but that wasn't him – that was the drug. She dried her eyes and flicked through some more until she found what she was looking for. A page on a Deather site: The Antidote.

It was a no-hoper – but it was the only hope.

There were a lot of rumours, but no hard facts. A post by a journalist explained how an antidote was impossible, because of the way the drug bound itself to the brain. But then there was another by a guy who claimed to have actually taken the antidote after stealing it from a secret government lab. It was real, he promised. It was out there. You only had to look ...

And another post warning about this cruel hoax.

Who knew? If there *was* an antidote, she was in the right place. This was Manchester, where it was all happening. The police were pretty sure the illegal Death was being manufactured here. Not only that, but Lizzie had a good idea who might be involved.

It was dangerous, she knew that – Julie was scared by Christian for a reason. But it was Adam's life at stake. She had to at least try. If she didn't, she wouldn't be able to live with herself.

She had his phone number, too – he'd slipped it to her when she was talking to him at the party. She didn't want to lunge straight in, though, so she began by trying a cautious phone call to Julie first.

Her cousin was horrified when she heard that Adam had taken Death, but pleased that he had been caught.

'Thank God he's off the streets,' she said. 'Deathers are such wankers. It makes me angry. He deserves it. God knows what sort of trouble he'd have got you into. He was lucky to have you for just a few days. These people only get worse as it gets closer.'

She went on to tell the story about a couple who had been at her party who'd taken Death.

'It started off, they were so cool. Really Zen and that. Sitting about watching the sunset and being, like, in tune with the universe? You know. The next day, guess what? She catches him with a pair of prostitutes. He's like, "Hey it's cool, I'm just, you know, making the most of my last few days." Next thing, they're at each other's throats. From love to hate in two minutes. How Zen is that? She forgives him, just about, but now – guess what? Going with those whores has made him realise what he's lost! How insulting is that for a girl? Next day she finds him in the bathroom with his throat cut out, dead as yesterday's hamburger. So now she's got two days left and she's searching like, for the antidote, you know? Which doesn't even exist. How's that for fun? One more week on the planet? He didn't even make four days.'

'So that's right about the antidote?' Lizzie asked. 'You know that? There isn't one, right?'

And all she wanted was for Julie to say, *'No, there's no antidote. I know that for a fact.'* She pretty much held her breath, waiting for the feeling of relief when it came.

But instead, Julie got cross. 'Listen to me, Liz,' she said. 'The people peddling this stuff are very rich, very powerful, very greedy, and very dangerous. They will do anything they have to to get what they want. If there is an antidote, they're the only people who know about it, and they ain't saying.'

'So you're saying there might actually be one, then?'

'Don't you even dare think about it. You've just had one fuck of a lucky break. You had Christian Ballantine after you and a total loser for a boyfriend – and by sheer luck, both those things have been sorted out for you. So just leave it, OK? Bloody hell. What are you trying to do? You're seventeen. Stop acting like a silly little girl. Stay away from anyone – especially Christian – who has anything to do with this shit. Get it?'

'I hear what you're saying,' said Lizzie, non-committally.

Julie seethed and raged some more, but she had already made a number of fatal mistakes, including calling Lizzie a silly little girl, but mostly by confirming that Christian was involved in Death.

☠

Christian was delighted to hear from her.

'Where've you been? I've been trying to find you,' he cooed.

'Oh, round about,' Lizzie replied, vaguely.

'Shouldn't you be at school?' he asked.

'It's the holidays. Hey – I have a question for you,' she said.

Christian was lying in the bath. He settled down in the foamy water with a cup of tea at his side. He had been getting pretty peeved with Vince about his inability to find the new girl – and lo! Here she was, delivered right into his hands.

'It's about Death,' said Lizzie.

Christian paused, his cup of tea halfway to his lips. 'Why are you asking me about that?' he asked, peevishly.

'You said drugs. It sounded very glamorous,' said Lizzie. 'I just thought … you know …'

'OK,' said Christian. This girl was not only desirable. She was also dangerous.

'I was wondering if you knew if there's an antidote. I've been hearing there is one,' Lizzie said.

Silence, except for a little splashing.

'Because I have this friend,' Lizzie pressed on. 'This guy. He's been through a really bad time and he's gone and done it. Taken Death. I was wondering … you know …'

'I see,' said Christian. 'Well. We should meet up and talk about it.'

'Can you do anything?' she asked.

'If I could help you – and I'm not saying that I can – you'd have to meet me, wouldn't you? I mean, what do you want? For me to put it in the post?'

Despite herself, Lizzie felt a ray of hope.

'Are you saying there is?' she said, calmly. 'Just be straight with me.'

'Lizzie, this is a phone call. I can't talk about it here.'

'I have to know. I can't come to see you unless I know.'

'Put it like this,' he said. 'The things people can do today, huh? You know? The entire human genome. Particle physics. They made a man grow a new leg the other day, I read. Then they say they can't work out something like this. Strange, isn't it?'

'I knew it,' said Lizzie, calmly. 'I knew it. Everyone says there isn't but I knew there just had to be.'

'You think.'

'Don't you?'

Christian laughed. 'Yeah, matter of fact I do. You are going to have to come to meet me, though.'

'Can you get it for me?'

'We can't talk about it on the phone.'

'How much will it cost? I'll need to bring money with me.'

'More than you could possibly afford.'

'I can give you ten thousand. I have ten thousand,' she said. And she had. Various aunts and uncles had given her the money towards her university fund.

Christian snorted. 'Forget it. Nowhere near.'

'That's all I have.'

'Just come round. You won't need any money.'

Lizzie paused. 'Will you give it to me if I come?'

Christian laughed out loud. 'Oh, I'll give it to you, don't worry about that,' he said, and he giggled like a boy.

So it was that. She'd thought so. So – just how far would she go to save Adam's life?

'What exactly do you want, Christian?' she demanded. 'Just say it.'

'I want you, round here, right now. In my bed.'

'That's the deal?' she asked. 'Sex for the antidote, right?'

'That's the deal.'

'How long do I have to think about it?'

💀

Christian's house was right out in the country. Driving there, Lizzie was so nervous she actually stopped the car at one point and started back. But then she turned again and went forward. She was saving a life. What sort of a bitch would she be to let Adam die, just because of sex?

It was the old story. Boys went to the rescue with a gun in their hands, girls with their knickers in their pockets. So which was worse? This way, she thought, at least no one was going to get hurt.

When she arrived she sat in the car at the bottom of the

drive for another minute or two. *Last chance to back out.* Then she drove up and parked on the gravel in front of the house.

The house didn't help. It looked wrong. It was a great square thing, an old rectory or something. The curtains were all drawn, but some of them were half off the hooks. The paintwork was peeling, there was glass out in at least two of the upstairs windows, and a hank of ivy had been half pulled off one of the side walls and hung there like a piece of peeling skin. The lawns and shrubbery that bordered the house were wild and overgrown, but the gravel area in front had been carefully raked. Three highly polished and very expensive cars stood there – a Porsche, a Lamborghini and something else, she had no idea what. There were skid marks in the gravel as if someone had been doing wheelies. If it wasn't for the cars outside, she'd have thought she was at the wrong address.

She knocked on the door, which was opened almost at once by Vince, who didn't say a word, just stood aside to let her in. He was huge, she'd forgotten how huge. Standing next to him, she felt very little indeed.

Vince turned and led the way inside, still without a word. It seemed as if she didn't require the pleasantries any more. It made her feel like dirt. Maybe that was how prostitutes always felt.

They walked along an uncarpeted hallway, past a series of shiny but very dusty doors and expensive-looking wallpaper. The whole house was like that – beautifully decorated with lovely furniture, but filthy dirty. It stank, too, of stale food and old clothes.

Vince opened one of the doors and ushered her in to a huge sitting room – no carpet, one enormous couch and a table littered with old takeaways. Christian was waiting. He stood up as she came in.

'Hello,' she said.

'Hi, you look great,' he replied. He walked over and kissed her. She had thought there might be drinks or something, but no, he was straight in with his fat, wet, old-man's tongue. It was such a shock, she pushed him away and backed off.

Christian glared at her. 'Are you doing this or not?'

She nodded.

'Kiss me, then.' He stuck his face towards her and stood there like a sulky boy, his lips pouted, head forward. Lizzie dithered. Then he tutted irritably and came in again for another kiss, same as last time, full of wet tongue – a nasty porn kiss, she realised. But what had she expected? Romance? She had agreed to be porn for him.

Christian ran a series of little kisses down her neck that gave her the tickles. That was the icebreaker. Then he was easing the shoulder straps of her top down, pushing everything down below her breasts and grabbing hold of them. It was horrible enough for her to back away from him again without thinking.

'Are you going to be my girlfriend or what?' he demanded. 'You're not just playing me along, are you?'

'It felt funny,' she said.

'Oh. You girls,' he said, suddenly playful. 'C'm here, you.' He grabbed her again, kissing her and kneading her breasts roughly. But before he could get any further, they were interrupted by a knock on the door.

'Fuck's sake!' roared Christian. 'What?'

Vince peeped in. 'It's Mr Mindly at the door, sir,' he said.

'Mindly. Of all times.' Christian disentangled himself, wiped his mouth on the back of his sleeve and went to the window to look out, leaving Lizzie standing with her top and bra around her waist. Vince stood at the door, staring at her. As delicately as she could, she pulled her clothes up and bowed her head.

'Bastard!' exclaimed Christian. 'Coming to my house. How much does he owe us?'

Vince took out his phone and consulted it. He glanced at Lizzie.

'Never mind her. She's my girlfriend,' Christian said.

Vince shrugged. 'About fifty thousand,' he said.

Lizzie thought, *I shouldn't be hearing this, should I?* But it was too late now.

Christian glanced back at her. 'You get upstairs. Go and warm the bed up. It's the third on the left when you get to the top. Front of the house. Go on.'

Lizzie hurried up. Vince watched her up the stairs and into the bedroom before he went to the front door and opened it.

The room was big, freshly decorated and dirty. There were splashes all up the walls behind the bed, and the smell of rotting food coming from somewhere. She found it soon enough, on a tray by the bed – a half-eaten burger that had passed its throw-away date ages ago.

Lizzie threw it down the en suite loo, flushed, then stood looking at herself in the mirror above the grimy washbasin. The face staring back shocked her. She had never seen herself look so pale. Her eyes were like stones. Her top had been ripped at the neckline where Christian had tugged it down. She looked petrified.

It was time to run, wasn't it?

There hadn't been any talk about the antidote, either. She should have made him hand it over before he got her clothes off. And what if he was lying? Or what if he was telling the truth but then changed his mind once he got what he wanted?

She'd always trusted her instincts, but she had overridden them for Adam, and now she didn't know what was going on or how to cope with it. She was trying to be heroic, but what if she was just being stupid instead?

The smell of the rotten burger still hanging on the air made her gag. Suddenly, she'd had enough. She went quietly to the door, opened it a fraction and stood there, listening. Voices were being raised. An argument going on. She crept on to the landing and peered over the banister. No one there …

Then, just before she began to tiptoe downstairs, out of the blue, there was a single gunshot.

Lizzie jumped, screamed slightly, then froze, utterly unable to move a muscle. A door opened below her and Christian stepped out into the hallway. Behind him, he left a bloody footprint – just one. His left shoe was dripping gore. He glanced behind himself and got on one leg to ease the guilty shoe off.

'You idiot,' he said, speaking into the room he'd just left. 'That was too quick, much too quick for the amount he owed us. I could have C4'd him. And on the carpet. Don't tread on it,' he yelled suddenly. 'Take your shoes off. That's a good carpet. You should have shot him on the tiles, for God's sake. Look. What a mess.'

'He was going for his weapon, sir.'

'Was he?' Christian turned and went back in.

'His inside pocket, sir.'

There was a pause.

'That's his wallet, you fucking idiot. His wallet. Look, he has money in it. *He was going for his wallet so I shot him.* How would that look in court? Vince, you're an idiot. He was going for his wallet.'

The two men started to laugh and somehow, this sound brought Lizzie back to life. She had to get out – she was witness to a murder. She jerked back from the banister and ran lightly along the corridor to the back of the house. She was in luck – there was another stairway there. But before she could go down, another door opened below her and Christian came out, carrying his hands before him, covered in blood. She just had time to dash into one of the nearby rooms off the corridor as he came up the stairs. By sheer bad luck she found herself in a bathroom – exactly where Christian was heading. She just had time to climb into the bath, draw the shower curtain and lie down, before he came in after her.

Christian spent some time at the basin, washing the blood off his hands and trying to get some spots out of his t-shirt. Then he took a pee, shook himself and left.

Lizzie waited a few minutes before leaving the bath and going quietly to the door, which he had left ajar. Below, she could hear the two men arguing.

She had to get out. They'd kill her.

She made her way down the front stairs, but the door was locked, so she had to go to the back of the house, right past the room where they were arguing about the best way of getting blood out of the silk carpet. Her luck held, and she escaped through a kitchen window. All she had to do now was get round the front to her car and drive off.

It was getting dark. She was going to be all right! Keep to the bushes, avoid the windows; she was making it! She reached the front, and was just about to leave the shelter of the shrubs and venture on to the gravel drive for her car, when the front door opened and Christian came out with Vince behind him carrying something heavy wrapped up in black bin bags. Christian opened the boot of the Porsche. Vince dumped it in there.

Lizzie was tucked away behind some bushes. It was dusk, she was well hidden, no one could see her. Vince got in the car, started up, pulled away and as the headlights swung round they shone straight at her. She was picked out beautifully, white as a sheet, hidden badly behind what turned out to be a straggly tree.

'Lizzie!' Christian roared.

She turned and fled for her life, but got no more than a few metres before her feet were kicked out from under her. She crashed to the ground and was picked up before she had time to draw breath.

Christian carried her towards the house in his arms like a hero rescuing a wounded girl. He paused by the car where Vince was still sitting, waiting.

'You go on,' he said. 'I'll look after her.'

'She saw everything,' said Vince, and he drove off.

CHAPTER 9

JANET

Adam arrived back at the flat at half past three on Wednesday morning. Lizzie was nowhere to be seen. He texted and rang her; no answer. Where was she? He wandered from room to room like a lost child, looking for clues, but there was nothing. Then he got angry, and trashed some dishes and cupboards in the kitchen. He needed her! He rang again and raged and wept at her down the phone; then sent another text begging forgiveness, pleading with her to come back. He turned the TV on to try and distract himself, but it was no use; his spirit was in freefall. Seeing his parents had brought him face to face with the feelings he had been trying so desperately to avoid, feelings of failure, of isolation and worthlessness. Lizzie had deserted him, he had destroyed his parents' lives as well as his own; all he wanted now was for it to stop.

He contemplated throwing himself out of the window – he even went so far as to open it up and look down at the drop. He longed for the oblivion at the end of it, but lacked the courage to face the fall. He began a search around the house, looking for painkillers that might put an end to it all, but he only found a half-used packet of paracetamol in the bathroom – not enough to kill a baby, let alone a strong young man powered up by Death. He went to bed in the end, believing that the only reason he didn't end it all now was because he lacked the courage. He was woken up a couple of hours later by his mum and dad ringing him. He turned the phone off, leaned over the bed and was sick – literally, sick with fear. Then he turned over and went back to sleep.

💀

He woke up to a headache, and, he realised, a bit of nausea as well. What was that about? Death was supposed to make you feel great, wasn't it?

Don't make me laugh.

Then he thought – *Lizzie.*

He turned his phone on. There were a dozen calls and texts from his mum and dad, some from his friends. But from Lizzie, not a word.

She's dumped me, he thought.

He fell back on the bed. How could she do this to him? He was on Day 3 – it felt like Day 7 already – and she'd left him to it. The thought that he was on his own was so frightening that he lacked the courage to ring round and see if he could find her. He lay in bed for another hour, feeling too low to do anything, before he got up, showered, had some juice, put the TV on and sat watching an old comedy for a while. It was late morning by the time he finally tried to find her.

Her home. Nothing. It just went straight to answerphone. He tried Julie – she'd left them a number – but she wasn't picking up, either. Lizzie had told her what was going on. His number was coming up and they were all sitting there watching it, waiting for him to go away, thinking – *What a loser!*

He had a precious day in front of him and no idea what to do with it.

The comedy on the TV ended and the news came on. Suddenly the screen was full of scenes of people massing in the streets of Manchester. The crowds were immense.

Adam watched in amazement. Of course – the riots. Vaguely, he started to recall the scenes of unrest he had seen going in and out of town. Somehow, it had passed him by. It wasn't about rioting any more – in fact, riots were impossible with so many people about. The Zealots had been joined by other groups: trade unions, student groups, civil rights groups, you name it. The police had stated publicly that it would not engage in any actions against valid protesters. A general strike had been called for that Friday, the one-week anniversary of Jimmy Earle's death. Even the state-controlled TV channels were talking openly about it.

Revolution. Was it really going to happen? The crowds

massed in the streets and roared defiance. And sitting there so close to the heart of Manchester, Adam realised that the roaring wasn't just from the TV. It was coming from outside. He went to fling open the window to let the noise in – and there it was! The roar of a million throats. The TV was showing live action and he was there, right there, listening to it. Up and down the street below him, thousands of people were pushing their way forward, trying to get to the main protests in Piccadilly Gardens and Albert Square. Never before had so many people gathered in one place, all with the same aim.

'Freedom!' roared the crowd.

The future, thought Adam. But it had nothing to do with him.

He closed the window and went back inside. He didn't need to see this.

Of all the crap times in history to take Death! The world was changing. No one knew which way it was turning. None of it was any use to him.

He found the regretit-forgetit site and logged on. The first thing he went to see was his own posting, asking for people to sleep with. And – he had a hit! Yeah! Someone had answered.

'Hi *Adam,*' it said. '*I'm interested – definitely. I'm not posting a photo because I don't want my picture up for everyone to see, so you'll just have to take my word that I'm not hideous! I am a bit of an old lady, though – all of 25. I suppose that seems ancient to you, but if you fancy having a date with an older woman – let me know.*'

You bet he would. Adam picked up the TV keyboard and typed in a reply: '*Just let me know when you're free.*'

Things were looking up.

He flicked through the rest of the site. So many people were taking Death! He found a page where people were posting up their experiences. He settled down to read a few.

'Hey, to the guys at the BP Garage on Finland Road – thanks for the cash, hope no one gets in trouble. Sorry about the broken arm, big guy with the black hair!'

A robbery. Way to go, Adam thought. And, wow, how lucky he'd been to get away yesterday!

'I told my mum and dad today.'

A pang shot through him.

Don't think it don't think it don't think it … Quickly he flicked on to the next post.

'I finished saying goodbye to the world today. I'm leaving early.'

Wow. That one froze him to his seat. Leaving early? There was so little time anyway. He remembered how he had felt last night – but this was different. It didn't sound like despair. He flicked on to the comments underneath.

'You DICK! You threw your life away, man. DEATH is for living, not dying on!'

'What an empty, barren little life you must have had,' said another.

'But you guys don't get it,' said someone else. 'When you're ready to go, you're ready to go, it doesn't matter how old you are or how long you have left. I think saying goodbye is a beautiful way to go. What did you say goodbye to?'

And underneath it, the original poster had written, 'I said goodbye to everything that ever mattered to me, and I did it real slow.'

Adam leaned back and thought about it. It made sense to him. Not the killing yourself – not yet, anyway. That stuff about doing it real slow. He'd been rushing around like a lunatic. Maybe it was time to slow down. Lizzie had the right idea after all. *Everything is for the last time. Every little thing matters.* It gives things a different perspective. He'd been going at it all wrong – too fast, too rushed. Today, he thought, he was going to take it slow.

Say goodbye. Yeah. Take time. Take a look at his old school, at his home. He didn't want to see anyone – no friends, no parents. As soon as he did that the peace would be shattered, you could bet your life. Maybe he'd take a few pictures on his phone, post them up for people to see, so at least they'd know he'd been around. Hey, that was an idea. He could leave some messages for them. He could say goodbye like that.

Better than meeting them face to face.

The more he thought about it, the better it seemed. It was right.

Before he went, he checked out his message box again – and he had an answer already.

'*OK. See you in Piccolinos off Albert Square today at 5? I'll be the blonde with the blue coat. I'll know who you are. We can have a drink and if we don't like one another, we can say goodbye. If we do ... let's see, shall we?*'

'*We have a date,*' Adam answered.

Five o'clock. It was almost midday already. Today was going to be a good day. Take it all in, enjoy it. The smells, the sights, the sounds of some of the places he'd been familiar with during his time on earth. Saying goodbye.

He rang Lizzie again. Still no answer. That hurt him, deeply, badly, right down inside. But he didn't have time to let it worry him. He finished his cereal and went out to begin his day.

Adam intended to catch the bus straight to Fallowfield, but as he walked to the bus stop on the Oxford Road, he got caught up in the crowds. Hundreds of thousands were converging on Manchester for the protests. There were tents on Piccadilly Gardens, food stalls and soup kitchens were being set up. There were posters and banners demanding that the government must resign, that the banks must be broken, that the corporations that had become more powerful than states be controlled, that capital should be mutually owned. A couple of the big office towers had signs up saying 'FREE MANCHESTER'. It was a declaration, not a request.

People were coming to see the future re-cast. Something remarkable was going to happen, something that could change your whole life overnight. Adam felt as if he was in a dream, that none of this was really happening to him. It wasn't. He was immune from the future. This was for the living, not the dead.

He wandered among the crowds for a while, but he'd quickly seen enough and walked away along Portland Street. On the Oxford Road outside the Palace Hotel a running battle was taking place. The rebels were trying to take the place over, and the management had hired their own security team to see them off. People struggled in the lobby and on the pavement outside; and in the middle of it, a thin line of people waited for the bus – life still going on amid the chaos.

Adam joined them. He stepped on to the number 42 and rode away out of town. Things were much quieter out there, and by the time he got to the university you would never have guessed that less than a mile away the world was changing for ever.

As he entered his own patch, a sense of the amazement of life filled Adam up – how the world just kept on going on! With you or without you, it was always there. He got off the bus, wandered around, anxious in case he saw his friends or his mum or dad. His mum would be at work, of course, but the old man would be home alone now. He had to turn his phone on to take pictures, but kept the sound down, although it kept vibrating. He checked. It wasn't Lizzie and there was no one else he wanted to talk to.

He stood on the corner of Copson Street and the Wilmslow Road, watching the shoppers going to and fro. The old Romanian lady who sold the *Big Issue* was there, calling out to people. Yeah, life went on regardless. It was beautiful but sad, and he tried to take some comfort in the idea that it would still be here, doing its thing, whether he was happy or sad, or high or low, or living or dead. In the end, what difference did it make? After, he went to have a look at his school. Same building, same students, same teachers teaching the same lessons. His death was going to mean so little to the world. Even his parents were going to get over it. Life went on. What did it matter how and when you popped in and out?

Sooner than he expected he'd had enough. He didn't want to go back to his house but he did, anyway, just so he could have a picture of it and post it up, and his parents would know he'd been there, thinking about them.

On the way back, he stopped on the Curry Mile to eat – a favourite restaurant where he used to go with his dad, and once or twice with his friend Jack. He wondered if he ought to give a Jack a call, but it was already four o'clock. He had his date in an hour. He ate up, paid the bill, and caught the bus back to town.

As he got close, in among the big crowds, he started to worry that Piccolinos would be closed, but he needn't have worried. People still had to eat. With all these crowds waiting in the city centre, it was actually fat pickings for the restaurants.

He pushed the door open and walked in. It was half restaurant, half bar – not the sort of place he'd usually go to. People were drinking wine. It was too old for him, and he felt out of place at once.

His date – Janet, she'd called herself – had told him she would be the blonde wearing a blue coat; and right there, sitting at the long table that ran in front of the bar, was a pretty young blonde woman. She caught his eye, but she wasn't wearing blue. Adam looked around, but saw no one else. He looked back to the woman. She was patting the seat next to her. There was a blue coat lying on it.

Adam froze. She smiled and called across to him.

'Adam,' she said. 'Sit down? Want a drink? I'm having prosecco.'

'Yes, please. How did you know it was me?' he asked.

'How many seventeen-year-olds do you see in here? I wonder if they'll serve you?' She nodded to a waiter and asked for another glass. The man frowned at Adam.

'Madam, he looks very young …'

'Bring us a bottle of water and a spare glass, then,' she said, and winked openly at Adam. The waiter shrugged and went to fetch them.

Janet settled herself back on her stool and gave him a long look. 'You'll do,' she said, and she laughed. 'How about me? Will I do?'

'Of course!' Adam insisted. He would have found it impossible to say no under any circumstances, but he took the chance to look her up and down. She opened her arms to show herself off, and then laughed and blushed slightly. She was quite short with a neat figure, wearing a white blouse open at the neck, a black jumper and a shortish green skirt. He was already wondering if he was going to get to find out what was underneath it. The thought made him blush, and he looked up quickly to meet her eyes. Underneath her make-up, one of them looked bruised, he thought.

'Fine,' he muttered, and she laughed at him again, but it was a high, tinny laugh, because he'd sounded so gruff and uncomplimentary.

The prosecco arrived with the water. Adam studied her some more as the waiter served them. There was more bruising when you looked closely. Someone had beaten her up recently. There were some laughter lines around her eyes. But they didn't make her look old, he decided.

She waited till the waiter had gone, then poured Adam a glass of wine.

'The world's falling to bits outside, and he's worried about his licence. Cheers,' she said, holding out her glass.

Adam picked his up, and they tipped their glasses together and drank. There was a brief pause.

'I was worried it would be shut,' Adam said, gesturing around at the bar.

'The Zealots use it,' she said. 'And some of the other rebel groups as well. Oh, it's a hotbed of sedition in here all right. Full of spies as well, I expect.'

Adam glanced at the other people sitting around. Most of them were in their twenties and thirties. Well dressed. How could you tell what side they were on? He had no idea. But the thought alarmed him.

There was more awkward silence. Janet smiled tightly. 'I don't suppose you have much small talk, do you?' she said.

'Er – do you work in Manchester, then?' he tried, but she lifted up a hand.

'Sorry, my fault. I don't want you to know anything about me,' she said. 'Do you mind?'

'No. It makes small talk a bit tricky, though.'

Janet bowed her head in admission. 'You're not doing bad,' she told him. She laughed again, more relaxed. 'This is funny. It feels exactly like the dates I used to go on when I was a teenager. Oh my God, I used to get so uptight! It brings it all back!'

'Was it that awful?' he asked, because it looked as if it was. He felt vaguely insulted.

She thought about it. 'Looking back, I always thought it was awful. But now I think, maybe not so bad. What about you?' she went on. 'Do your parents know about … what you've done?'

Adam looked coolly at her. He'd thought he'd do

anything or say anything to avoid scaring her off, but now it came down to it, he had his pride.

'I don't want you to know anything about me, either,' he said.

'Touché!' she cried. 'And that is going to make it rather hard, isn't it? But I like a little chat, it's romantic, isn't it, sitting here with the city burning all around us and everything about to change. Like soldiers of fortune, aren't we? Or spies or something.' She smiled. 'And with nothing to say to each other.'

'I don't want to talk about my family, that's all,' he said. 'You can ask me about anything else.'

'Can I? But isn't your family the whole thing?' she said.

Adam shook his head. He didn't want to go there. They talked about the protests instead, and Adam told her how he had been at the Jimmy Earle concert that had started it all off. She was curious about that. 'I'd have given anything to be at that concert,' she said. She asked him a little more about himself, about school, about his friends, his girlfriend. Adam was waiting for her to ask the big one – about his decision to take Death. He'd prepared for it. 'I couldn't see any future I wanted to be a part of,' was his favourite. Something like that. But to his surprise, the question never came.

Finally, she quaffed her wine.

'OK,' she said. 'Let's go.'

Adam gulped and nodded. He emptied his glass and followed her outside. It was a chilly, breezy day, colder than it looked. She walked down towards Albert Square, but it was just too packed, so they headed the other way, through the narrow side streets towards the Oxford Road. Janet linked arms with him, dipped her head and smiled.

They checked into the Palace Hotel on Oxford Road, where there had been a battle on the streets earlier. It all seemed back to normal, the staff in their places, everything quiet. Maybe it had changed hands. If so, there was no way of knowing.

It was appallingly embarrassing going in – the staff had to know what was going on. To his surprise, Janet felt it, too.

'That was the walk of shame, wasn't it?' she said when they got safely into the lift. 'I was thinking all the time, they must be wondering which one of us was the prostitute.'

It was a huge room – four-poster bed, two sofas, a desk, a table and chairs. There was an en suite bathroom, with a bath that was long enough to lie flat in, and a separate shower. It was all oversized.

'Do you like it?' she said. She laughed and looked sideways at him.

Adam suddenly thought that he was supposed to make a move and took a step towards her, but she darted off to the cupboards and stared searching through them.

'Here!' she exclaimed. It was a mini bar in a little fridge in a cupboard under the desk. She took out a half-bottle of champagne, which she gave to Adam to pop while she found some glasses.

'I'm nervous!' she confessed. 'Isn't that idiotic?' She poured for them. They clinked glasses and gulped at the wine.

'Have you …' she began.

'What?'

'Done this before?'

Adam blushed. 'Yeah, of course. A few times,' he lied. 'You have, I suppose.'

'Not with a seventeen-year-old boy with one week to live. I'm a virgin myself in that respect.' She laughed again and took another glug of her champagne. 'Right. I'm going in the bathroom to undress. You get into bed and I'll come and join you. OK?'

Adam nodded. Janet scurried off into the bathroom. Adam dropped his clothes as fast as he could, hid in the bed ... and waited.

She wasn't long. She come out wrapped firmly in a white bathrobe, and made him look the other way while she slipped in next to him.

'This is silly!' she said. 'I'm supposed to be the sophisticated older woman, but I'm just so shy.'

'What are you shy about?' he asked.

'You!' She wriggled close and pressed herself against him. He felt her body all down his – breasts, legs, torso, her little rough bush against his leg.

She kissed him. 'You can touch if you like,' she said. She lifted his hand to her breast. He rubbed gently and felt her hard nipple in his palm. She put her hand down and touched him under the covers, and came in for a kiss. She tasted of wine. Then she sighed, relaxed, and pulled him on top of her.

Afterwards, they dozed briefly. Adam came round before her and lay there with her head on his arm, waiting for her.

So that was it. Second time, second partner. He hadn't had time to think about it much the first time with Lizzie, but now it reminded him a bit of those birthdays he used to have when he'd think – *So I'm ten now, or I'm thirteen,* or whatever, and he'd strain to feel a change, but it was never any different. Having had sex wasn't much different from being a virgin. Maybe you had to wait till you were in love. Maybe you had to wait for ever to feel anything other than what you were.

He remembered how his dad had told him something his granddad had said on his seventy-fifth birthday. 'I know I'm old,' he'd said. 'But I don't feel old. I feel the same as I did when I was eighteen.'

You just did stuff. You went on and did other stuff. But it was all the same. Maybe that's what Death was going to teach him. That it didn't make any difference after all.

But … it had been very, very nice. He felt guilty about Lizzie, but she'd left him, after all. He was hoping they'd do it again when she woke up, but Janet wasn't interested. She went to the loo, then came back to bed and kissed him on the lips.

'Thank you,' she said. 'I thought I was going to make you feel older, but instead, you made me feel like I was fifteen again – all shy and sweet and scared. But perhaps a little more confident this time. I loved that, you know.'

She propped herself up with the pillows and finished off the wine. Despite her claim that she wanted him to know nothing about her, she started chatting away about all sorts of irrelevant things – bars in London and Manchester, a boy she knew who might have been the love of her life but didn't seem to care, and how heart-broken it made her feel, and how she couldn't get over it.

'I don't think I ever will,' she said. 'Not till my dying day.' She threw back her head and laughed, then gazed sadly at Adam. He knew – he thought he knew – what she was thinking: that he wasn't going to get over anything. His was a story already coming to its end.

When he looked at her again, he saw that she was crying. He wanted to comfort her, but didn't know how. She leant over for a tissue, blew her nose and wiped her eyes. 'Getting sentimental in my old age,' she said. For some reason, perhaps because of the sex, or because of her tears, or because she had shared a secret with him, he wanted to share something with her as well.

'My brother's in the Zealots,' he said.

Janet turned to him. 'Tell me about him,' she said; and it was as if a plug had been pulled. His whole heart came flowing out of him – about Jess, about how much he'd loved and admired him and how angry he was with him now, and how let down he felt. About his parents, and how he'd ruined their lives and was too weak even to tell them he was sorry. And Lizzie, of course; how he'd said he loved her because it didn't matter whether he did or not, but now he thought he really did, but she was gone, and he couldn't really blame her, could he? How could he blame anyone for anything after what he had done?

And most of all, he talked about how he wished he'd never done it. He wished he could go back to a week ago. Life had seemed so terrible to him then, but in fact, it was so precious, so wonderful, so lovely – and he'd thrown it all away because it hadn't been what he expected, like a sulky brat throwing his teddy out of his pram. Now he wanted it back so badly but it was gone for ever, and no one could give it back …

Janet listened carefully, but didn't offer him any advice or ask him any questions. When he began to cry, she took his hand and stroked it and waited until the flood ended.

'Your brother sounds like a proper soldier,' she said. She sighed and looked across at the clock on the bedside table.

'What are you going to do?' he asked her. 'Can't you stay?' He didn't want to be on his own.

'The revolution,' she said. 'Listen!'

From outside came the sounds of chanting – half a million voices calling for change. 'I want to be a part of that, just for a few nights.'

A few nights? Did that mean … 'Have you taken it as well?' he asked.

'No. Nothing like that. Don't ask, I won't tell you.' She slipped out of bed and began to pull her clothes on. As she dressed he could see more bruises on her body, but he didn't dare ask what had happened. When she'd finished dressing she checked her hair in the mirror and came to sit on the bed next to him.

'Now, Adam,' she said. 'I want you to listen very carefully to me. I know the Zealots. No, don't interrupt me. I know some of them very well, and I can tell you something not many people can. There is an antidote.

You understand? And I can get it for you.'

She looked down at him, her face almost without expression, as if she was conducting an experiment on him.

'I don't believe you,' he said. But he was hoping so hard.

'It's going to take me a couple of days,' she said. 'But I promise, I absolutely promise I can do this for you. All you have to do is stay out of trouble for that long. Until Friday.' She stared down at him. 'Well?' she asked. 'What do you say? Do you want it? Or would you prefer to hang on to your week?'

Your week. She said it scornfully. Such a tiny measure against a whole lifetime.

'Why are you doing this?' he begged.

'Because I can,' she said. She was quite businesslike now, like a doctor, sitting there on the edge of the bed telling him what he had to do.

'But I only have four days left,' he said.

Janet smiled, sourly. 'And if it's not true, and I'm lying, you'll have wasted two whole precious days staying nice and safe. Except, Adam, they're not precious, are they? They're painful and horrible and nasty, because you're going to die when the world is about to change, goodness only knows how, and everyone is looking towards the future and you should have your whole life ahead of you. Well, I'm offering you it back. Do you want it? Tell me. No questions,' she said as he began to speak. 'I can't answer them. All you have to do is keep yourself safe and be here when the antidote arrives on Friday night. It's that simple. Yes or no.'

'But everyone says there's no antidote,' he whispered.

Janet bent down close over him. 'Everyone is wrong,' she said. She leaned right down and kissed him on the lips. 'Everyone except me.' She laughed. 'Do you agree?'

'Yes,' he said. Yes. And now he had admitted it fully. He had made the most terrible mistake possible. Above all things, he wanted to live.

'Good.' She stood up and smiled down at him. 'Thank you for a lovely evening,' she said. She picked up her bag and went to the door, where she paused and lifted a finger of warning. 'Stay safe,' she told him. 'It's dangerous out there. If I were you I'd stay here, right in this room. No risks, Adam – because I'm risking a lot for you. Understand?'

Adam nodded.

As soon as the door closed behind her he jumped out of bed and stood in the middle of the room, exalting, his heart beating in him like a drum. It was a miracle. He was going to live!

He grabbed his phone and rang Lizzie. He had to tell her! Wouldn't it be wonderful if she came round and spent these two days with him? She had to know. Everyone had to know.

'I'm going to live!' he shouted. His voice echoed around the room. He had never felt happier in his life.

CHAPTER 10

CAPTIVITY

At round about the same time that Adam was shouting hallelujah in his hotel room, Lizzie was sitting up in bed with a cup of coffee. Her left eye had swollen up until it was almost closed, and a trickle of blood was coming down her nose. She was very much aware that every time Christian lost his temper and hit her, she became a little more ugly. Becoming ugly was a bad move on her part, because, as he had pointed out to her after the last blow just a few minutes before, he was only going out with her because he liked her looks.

He didn't like her being afraid, either. It made her look stupid, and the way she flinched when he lifted his hand was just plain irritating. Which was a pity because the past day had been the most terrifying of her life. At the moment, she was concentrating as hard as she could on not spilling her coffee. Trembling apparently made her look like a spakker, and who wanted a spakker for a girlfriend?

Christian was standing a few metres away, getting himself dressed up in some new gear — baggy t-shirt, trainers, and a pair of designer jeans he'd just had delivered. There was a new skateboard as well. He was posing with it under his arm in front of a full-length mirror.

'What do you think?' he asked.

Lizzie licked her lips and tried to control her breathing, terrified that if she spoke she might burst into ugly tears.

'You don't like?' asked Christian. 'You don't *like*?'

'I, I, I, I ...' she began; and the tears came out — hot, ridiculous, humiliating, ugly.

'What is wrong with you, Lizzie?' demanded Christian. 'Look at this stuff — it's quality.'

'I need, I need, I need ...' she began, trying desperately to control her voice.

Christian rolled his eyes. 'What *do* you need, Lizzie darling?' he sneered.

'I need to go to the loo,' she admitted. She'd been dying to go for ages, but held back because going to the loo involved being humiliated. Being humiliated, in Christian's eyes, was almost as bad as being ugly.

Christian tutted. 'Vince!' he bawled. 'Girlfriend needs to go to the loo.'

There was a pause.

'Vince!' screamed Christian. 'Girlfriend! Toilet. Where the fuck are you?'

The door opened and Vince came in. He hoiked his immaculate trousers up at the knees and bent to pull the potty out from under the bed.

'You took your time,' complained Christian, turning back to the mirror.

'I was making a deal.'

Christian closed his eyes, tiredly. 'You're a servant, Vince. You don't wander around with a phone in your hand when you should be attending to me and my girl-friend and our needs. Duh.'

'Sorry, sir,' said Vince. He put the potty on the floor and stood up.

'Pee,' said Christian to Lizzie.

'Can I have some privacy?' she asked.

Christian shook his head. 'I'm your boyfriend. This is a servant. The rich don't worry about that sort of thing. I could get him to hold my dick when I pee, like that guy does for Prince Charles, and it would not be pervy in any way at all. It's how we behave at this level of society. Go on. Pee.'

She really was busting. She got out of bed. Her face was swelling up on one side. Ugly, ugly, ugly. Her hand was manacled to the bedpost but, by holding out that arm, she managed to reach the pot and squat on it. She bent her head and pretended she was on her own. At least she was wearing a nightie, even though there wasn't all that much of it.

Both men stood and watched her. When she was done, Christian threw her a box of tissues. While she wiped herself, he came over, flipped her hair to one side and bent her head down, revealing the back of her neck. On it was a series of lines drawn in black ink – C1, C2, C3, C4, C5. Lizzie knew exactly what it was he had drawn on her, as he had explained that if he did a cut at C3, she wouldn't be doing much saying no then, would she?

Vince bent over to have a look. Christian evidently felt he was disapproving in some way. 'It's my girlfriend,' he said, crossly. 'I can do what I want with my own girlfriend, can't I?'

Vince frowned. 'I thought we'd agreed that she wasn't your girlfriend, sir.'

'She's in my bed. That makes her my girlfriend.'

'Only if she wants to be there.'

'Fuck's sake. Lizzie! Do you or do you not want to be in my bed?' he demanded.

Both men turned to watch her.

'Yes?' she said, cautiously.

'See? Ah, this is boring. I'm going to play on my Xbox,' Christian announced. He stalked to the door, shaking his head with exasperation.

Vince stood watching him curiously for a moment, before picking up the potty and going to empty it in the en suite. Lizzie waited until he came back out before she spoke to him in a whisper.

'What do I do?' she begged. 'Please. Help me.'

Vince said nothing. He put the pot back under the bed and picked up her coffee cup. He headed for the door.

'Please, Vince. I don't know what to do,' she begged. She'd seen how Christian treated the big man; there was no way he could like it. He was her only chance.

Vince paused and looked back at her. 'Just act like his girlfriend,' he told her.

'Is that all? Will he let me go?' she wept.

Vince shook his head. 'It always ends the same way. But at least you might not get hit so much getting there. He's making you look a right fucking mess.'

He left the room. Behind him, Lizzie closed her eyes and tried to control her shaking. *Act like his girlfriend*, Vince had said. It was the only clue she'd had so far. Because – *Fuck this*, she thought. There had to be some way out of this. First off, though, she had to find some way of not being so hopelessly, pathetically, stupidly scared all the time.

After leaving Lizzie, Vince went down to the kitchen where he opened a cupboard stacked full of boxes of medicines. Christian was worrying him. Up to now it had been nice straightforward kidnap and violence. Now it was girlfriend. That was just plain weird. Something was going on, and he was willing to bet it involved the meds.

He took out a brand-new pack of pills, peeled the cellophane off and peered inside. All present and correct: right labels, right brand, right everything. He sighed. Maybe it was just the normal ups and downs of being a raving psychotic that was making Christian behave like this.

Vince popped a selection of pills out of their foil wrappers, crushed them in a pestle and mortar, and stirred them thoroughly into a glass of warm milk, checking to see that everything had dissolved properly. Then he went through to the sitting room to give them to Christian, who was glued to his game.

Christian let out a wail of exasperation when he saw him coming, but put out a hand to take the milk. Turning to Vince, he drank it, swilling it around his mouth and gargling noisily before swallowing it down.

'Mmmm, yum yum yum. Yeah. I feel so much calmer already.' He laughed, a high-pitched, insane giggle that could have been him being mad, pretending to be mad, or pretending to pretend to be mad in order to hide the fact that he *was* mad, or any combination of the three.

Vince stared impassively at him. He'd definitely have to see Mr Ballantine about a doctor's appointment, unless the nasty little fuck stopped being so weird pretty quick. They were due to go round to pick up more Death that Friday. He'd ask about it then.

And if you are pulling the wool over my eyes and I find out before then, Vince promised himself silently, *I will abso-fucking-lutely take the opportunity of bouncing you around this room until your balls go ring-ding-a-dong on your forehead. And that, sir, is a promise.*

'You're being a dick today,' Christian pointed out. 'Tell you what. I had a call from Dad. Apparently someone has reported my girlfriend as missing. Imagine that, Vince! I wonder what could have happened to her? I think you better go round and investigate the matter, don't you? Her parents probably. Pay them a visit. That bitch Julie, too. She gave the wrong address, didn't she?'

'She did.' Vince was always happier out of the house. He nodded. 'I'll get right on it.'

'You do that,' said Christian. 'See you later, big boy.

Lizzie and I will watch a bit of TV. Maybe have a bit of the old okey cokey, eh?'

'Enjoy yourself, sir,' said Vince. *Fat chance of that*, he thought. Christian had been impotent for years. He should have mentioned it to the girl, since it was bound to be her fault when he failed to get it up.

Whistling to himself, he went to get his car keys. A trip into town. Nice. Maybe after he'd paid a call to Julie's parents and found out where she lived, he'd have time to stop off with some mates and have a drink.

☠

Adam awoke the next day feeling cool, light-headed and very calm. He was in a large and beautiful room, with subdued but radiant light coming in through the windows. He didn't recognise any of it, but it was deeply comfortable. His head felt completely empty. He lay still for a while longer, enjoying the feeling but knowing somewhere inside that this pleasant state wasn't going to last very long at all.

Then he turned over and it all came flooding back. He sat up. He was saved. He was going to live! He just had to wait two days, but he had to have Lizzie here with him – he *had* to. He picked up his phone and rang her number. Again, she didn't answer. And now, finally, at last, he began to worry about her. If she'd really dumped him he couldn't blame her. But it wasn't like her to just vanish. She'd have said. Wouldn't she?

He left a message and started to ring around. Her parents picked up this time, but they had no idea where she was. That was odd. They sounded scared. Adam was getting scared, too. He tried Julie again. Still no answer.

It was almost lunchtime by the time anyone picked up. It was Julie. She didn't sound very pleased to hear from him.

'I'm looking for Lizzie …' he began.

'Oh, of course,' sneered Julie. 'You wanna know where your girlfriend is. Boy, that's good of you. You have SUCH a big heart. Well, let me see? Oh, yeah, she got kidnapped by a bunch of gangsters and then her parents complained to the police so their house got torched. Yeah – that was it.'

'What?'

'Hey! Lizzie is going to be soooo happy to hear about you trying to get in touch, in between getting beaten up and gang raped! That is just so nice of you. It's so much gonna make her day, you wanker.'

'What's going on? You're joking me. Stop it. Where is she?'

'And you want to know why, you pile of shit? Because she was trying to help you. She walked straight into their arms asking them if they made Death and if so, could she please have the antidote – which doesn't actually exist, by the way, I'm pleased to tell you – and they said, "Sure! – Yep. Just pop round and we'll chain you up and rape you for ever."'

'The police—' he said.

'The police know, you fuckwit, that's why her mum and dad got done over. It's also, incidentally, why my mum and dad got done over. They are in hiding. I am in hiding. It was probably the police who did it. You, Adam – just

- 213 -

you stay away from this whole thing, right? Unless you want the same sort of shit raining down on your family's heads.'

'Who's got her?'

'Oh, yeah, right, I was just going to tell you about that … Fuck off and die.'

She slammed down the phone.

Adam's brain started babbling away to him at once, giving him every reason under the sun to explain it all away. He rang back but there was no answer. He rang again – no answer. He tried Lizzie's mum and asked her about it and … yes, yes, Lizzie was missing and she was very worried about her, and did he know anything about it? For God's sake, they just needed to know that she was safe …

'OK, Jean, we agreed not to talk to anyone else about this …' said a voice. Her dad. The phone went dead.

Adam got up, put his coat on, went to the door, and stopped. Because …

Because if he went to rescue Lizzie, he'd probably die, too – and he had a life to live! Janet had promised him the antidote. A whole life, his life, was going to be delivered to his door tomorrow. He'd only just got it back. He wanted it more than anything else there was. Why should he risk throwing it all away?

It felt like he was going mad. He ran around the room, groaning to himself. How could this have happened? Lizzie wanted him to live, wasn't that why she'd tried to get the antidote in the first place? And now he was supposed to go and get killed all over again for her sake? It was wrong, it was all wrong. It felt as if his head was about to explode.

Suddenly, he stopped running and clapped his hand to his back pocket. The list. It was still there – it had been there all the time. He pulled it out and read through it.

Kill someone who deserves to die. Well, that was going to be the bastard who had kidnapped Lizzie.

Leave my parents and Lizzie with enough money so they'll never have to work again. These people were gangsters, they were bound to have huge amounts of money. He'd take it off them.

Do something so humanity will remember me for ever. No one would ever forget how he'd rescued Lizzie and thrown away his only chance for life in doing so. That was noble. Lizzie would never forget. That was what mattered.

There was still time. Three days. The list was back on!

There was so little time, so much to do. He was going to die, that much was certain. But this time, at least, there was something worth dying for. He ran out the door and off as fast as he could. The lift was busy, so he took the stairs three at a time.

PART THREE:
REVOLUTION

CHAPTER 1

TO THE RESCUE, HERE I AM

Julie was in her Manchester flat flinging the final few items into her suitcase when the doorbell rang. Who the hell was that? Her parents had managed to keep the address from Vince despite all his efforts, as her father's broken fingers showed. He and her mother had hastily organised a trip to LA and didn't want Julie to go with them. In fact, they didn't sound as though they wanted to see her again for a very long time indeed.

And Lizzie. Poor Lizzie! God only knew what that freak was doing to her right now. It broke her heart, but there was nothing she could about it. Lizzie was as good as dead. All Julie could do was try and save herself. It was goodbye Manchester and London, hello New York and LA.

And in a hurry. If Vince was looking for her, Vince would find her. It might take him a few days, but he'd get there in the end. The sooner she was gone the better.

Julie ran to the intercom by the door as quietly as she could and listened.

'Are you going to open it, or am I going to knock it down?' asked Vince.

Shit shit shit shit shit. What to do? Think! Escape. Where? The window? Too high. The corridor? Below, she could hear the front door burst open followed by the leisurely sound of someone ascending in the lift.

Panicking, she ran back into her flat, locked the door and ended up, ludicrously, hiding under the bed like a child. Vince knocked and waited about two seconds before breaking the lock and coming in. From where she lay on the floor, Julie could see his feet in the hallway as he took off his jacket and hung it up in a businesslike way by the door.

'Tell you what,' he said. 'How about, if you come out on your own, I don't hit you in the face?'

Julie knew it was as good as she going to get. She closed her eyes and crawled out.

'What's it for?' she begged.

'Reporting Lizzie missing.'

'It wasn't me.'

'Who knows?' said Vince, and got on with the beating.

Three minutes later, her ribs were broken all down one side, and her liver and kidneys might or might not have been ruptured. But Vince was as good as his word; her face was untouched. To look at her, no one would even know she'd been hit.

She coughed up a little blood and wiped it away.

'Is it over?'

Before he could answer, there was a tap at the flat door. Vince stepped into the bedroom, out of sight. The broken door opened and Adam put his face inside. Julie lurched to the door and pushed him back out before he got any further.

'Where is she? Just tell me and I'll go,' he begged.

'I have no idea what you're talking about,' gasped Julie. Even talking was agony. She went to close the door, but Adam put his shoe in the way.

'Look,' he said. 'I've got three days to go. I'm going to die. I've got nothing to lose. At least let me try, OK?'

'Piss off, Adam,' snarled Julie. But she didn't push him again. The fact was, he had a point. It wasn't a very good point, given what a tosser he was, but still … Julie was fond of her little cousin, and if she could throw her a lifeline, no matter how weak, she was tempted to do it. As she'd grabbed the door her wrist had bumped against Vince's jacket, hanging neatly on the hook behind it, and something in one of the pockets had rattled.

Keys.

'Piss off! she snarled again, and banged the door on his foot, giving him a big, fat wink at the same time. Adam, the idiot, took his foot away. She glared at him and rolled her eyes down. 'Put it back!' she mouthed. He did as he was told. Julie banged the door angrily on it, shifted to one side, and while her body hid the movement, lowered her hand quickly into the pocket of Vince's jacket and took out the keys. It was a long shot, but you never knew …

'Get your foot out of my door!' she screamed. She put her hand to his chest as if to shove him backwards, and dropped the keys neatly down his shirt front. Then she winked at him again, kicked his foot out the way and slammed the door behind him.

There was a brief silence, and then, to her relief, the sound of Adam's feet pattering away. Whether he'd work out what to do with the keys was another matter. She could only hope. But she'd done her best.

Vince stepped out.

'What did you give him?' he asked.

Julie shook her head. The guy was a monster. How had he seen that? She'd had her back to him the whole time.

'Nothing.'

Vince took hold of her by the shoulder and slapped her violently on the side of her face. He waited a moment before letting her fall to the floor, then picked her up by her hair and punched her in the nose. It broke. Blood spattered everywhere.

'What did you give him?' he asked again.

'My face, you promised,' she said.

'You won't be needing that any more,' he said. He slapped her again, even harder. She spun round like a top and collapsed. The side of her face began to bleed. Vince sat down on a chair in the hallway.

'You're in shock,' he told her. 'You need a minute to recover before you can speak.' He rolled his cuff up slightly to look at his watch. 'Minute's up,' he said. 'So what did you give him?'

Outside, a car started up. Vince stiffened.

'Your car keys,' said Julie, and she turned to watch the look of shock on his face.

☠

The whole conversation had been bewildering. Adam had some idea that Julie was trying to help him. But car keys? What good were they? Down on the street he pressed the 'open' button on the key ring and right next to him, a car bleeped and flashed its lights at him. And not just any car, either – a classic silver Porsche.

'Oh, man. Speed machine,' breathed Adam. That was another point on his list – drive around Manchester in a supercar. And here it was! The gods were with him today. He opened the door, got into the driver's seat, put the key in and started it up. It roared quietly, like a wave of double cream breaking on fine gravel. There was a pair of sunglasses on the dash. He picked them up and put them on. They were too big, but he still looked cool. That was the kind of sunglasses they were.

Experimentally, he ran through the gears with the clutch pushed down to the floor. He'd had a few driving lessons and a bit of practice sitting next to his mum in the family car. It was a long way from owning a licence, but Adam wasn't likely to let a detail like that get in the way of an chance like this.

He'd just got it into first when the doors to Julie's block of flats burst open and the huge figure of Vince came rushing towards him.

The guy who'd beaten him up at the party. This was *his car?*

With a scream, Adam slammed his foot on the accelerator. Crunching and snarling, the Porsche lurched off down the street, jumping forward in fits and starts like a crippled pig. The big man screamed at him and launched himself at the car, landing on the bonnet, his face gnashing at Adam through the windscreen.

The Porsche stalled.

'Nooooo!' Adam started it up again and bounced along the road, swaying from side to side. Vince, lying full-length on the bonnet, swung a fist at the side window on the passenger side. The glass crazed and turned opaque. At the next blow, his huge fist came straight through and started groping at Adam's throat.

Adam leaned away from him and revved the engine; the car shot forward – and stalled again. Vince fell off. Adam got it going once more, forced the gears accidently into third, and crept forward at a snail's pace over something in the road. Vince? The screaming indicated that, yes, it was. Finally, he got the gear/accelerator ratio right, and shot off like a bullet, the car roaring and swerving violently from side to side. He struck a glancing blow at a parking meter, a Jag and a bin lorry in quick succession – and then he was away, shooting forward in a cloud of black smoke and the stink of burnt rubber.

Behind him, Vince got to his feet. Adam had driven over his forearm. Even worse, he had crashed his car. Vince loved his car almost as much as his body. He let out a scream of rage. He was going to kill that guy, very, very slowly, and he was going to enjoy every minute of it.

Adam had no idea what to do next. He had Vince's car. Great! But what next? He pulled over and went through the glove compartment and rooted on the floor and in the back seat, looking for clues. He found several bars of chocolate, which he ate, but there was nothing in there to tell him what he was supposed to do next. He tried ringing Julie again.

No answer.

He sat there, chewing his nail. What was he supposed to do? She obviously thought this was going to help him. Did she think he already knew where Lizzie was being held? There had to be a clue in here somewhere?

He looked around the car again. CD player, sat nav, map in the back. He flipped though the map. Nothing. He turned on the sat nav. It was a posh one.

'Where do you want to go?' a voice asked him.

'Er … to Christian's,' said Adam.

'Going to … Christian's,' said the voice. It was a woman, with a Salford accent. In fact, it was Vince's mother's voice – a birthday treat for her boy.

'Turn the car round, son,' she said.

Adam did.

'OK. Next right. Off you go. And don't go too bloody fast this time!' the voice snapped.

Ignoring her advice, Adam pushed down on the accelerator.

💀

Lizzie's day had started off well enough with breakfast in bed – scrambled eggs and smoked salmon, coffee and croissants, made by Christian with his own fair hands. They had a pleasant chat, watching breakfast TV. The news was all about Death, the riots and the growing demos in the cities, calling for the government to resign. They toasted the big sales in Death with their coffee cups, scoffed at the Zealots for their revolutionary fervour, and shook their heads at the weakness of police in not getting tough on the streets and sorting it out.

Lizzie had been practising her girlfriend act, and felt that she getting the hang of it. Some of it was pretty traditional – stuff like sitting in bed filing your nails, talking about your next hairdo, or trying on new clothes in front of your boyfriend. In other ways, Christian was rather more modern. A good girlfriend, in his view, should be independent, smart, funny and sexy. The trouble was that Christian considered himself the very epitome of all those things and, as a result, he expected her to be in agreement with him about whatever he wanted to do.

It was a hard act to get right. The worst part was when he tested her girlfriending skills by closing his eyes and waiting expectantly for her to announce his own desires to him. It was terrifying. At best, she was only putting the next beating off a while. No matter how attentive she was, Christian was going to make a fool of himself sooner or later – and Lizzie was going to get the blame.

After TV came sex, which rapidly disintegrated into violence as she failed miserably to get him excited. Getting hit was another thing girlfriends did and she had learned to take her beatings in grim silence. The fact was, she was relieved. Getting beaten was horrible, but it was a good deal better than rape, in her view – especially rape that she had to pretend she wanted. At least this time she managed to protect her face reasonably well – she'd found out how important that was on day one, when she had been beaten once for making a stupid remark, and then again for being ugly.

After kicking her around the bed for a few minutes, Christian wandered over to the window to have a think, and decided, suddenly, that today was going to be a lazy day. Tomorrow he had to go to pick up some more drugs from his father's factory. Today they'd lie in bed, watch his huge collection of back episodes of *EastEnders* and just … hang out.

Great! enthused Lizzie. *EastEnders*. Amazing. Her favourite show.

Christian beamed at her. 'Mine, too! How amazing is that?'

Isn't it, thought Lizzie. Yes – she was definitely getting the hang of this. If only she could survive long enough to find a way to escape …

They were several hours into the afternoon when Vince rang. Christian was not happy about it.

'This better be good. He knows not to ring when I'm watching 'Enders,' he muttered. Lizzie tutted sympathetically. He put the mobile to his ear and listened.

'She gave him your car keys?' Christian was most amused. 'You're not very good with girls, are you, Vince? I'll have to give you a few tips. Me and Lizzie are here having a lovely day, aren't we, Lizzie?'

'Yeah – hush, not so loud, I'm trying to listen.'

'Hear that?' exclaimed Christian, triumphantly. 'Someone likes watching 'Enders with me. See?'

He paused the recording and listened some more, then turned red.

'Might be coming round here? How do you work that out? The fucking sat nav? You had my address on the sat nav? What else do you have on it? The factory? The map reference where you put the bodies? You idiot. Jesus.'

He sat there steaming for a bit, while Vince rattled on. Lizzie sat next to him, filing her nails and listening in as hard as she could. Someone might be coming round? She had to hold on to anything that might help get her out of here …

'Smack her about. Make her suffer. Then get your arse round here. In fact, get round here now. We can worry about Julie later on, when you've sorted this mess out. Jesus.'

He ended the call, stared at his phone, then chucked it savagely at the TV. 'Right in the middle of 'Enders,' he complained. 'Calls himself a bodyguard.' He got out of bed and got dressed. 'Guess what?' he told her. 'Your old boyfriend is coming to rescue you. How about that?'

'Adam?' A ray of hope shot through her. 'That's dreadful!' she exclaimed. 'He must be … not accepting that we split up.'

'I hate those sorts,' snarled Christian. 'Some kind of weirdo stalker. We'll have to kill him.'

But he was looking at her suspiciously. Had she done something wrong? A thought seemed to occur to him, and he turned to her with tragic eyes.

'Haven't you told him about us yet?' he said. 'When, Lizzie? When? You make it so hard, sometimes.'

'I have told him! He's just … won't accept. You know …'

Christian slapped her round the head, but just once. Then he stalked off to make his preparations for Adam's arrival.

Lizzie pretended to weep into the pillow, but actually she was jubilant. Adam! Bless him. In her heart she knew he stood no chance. In fact, he'd probably just make it worse. . But he was trying. He was trying and … you never knew. She had to hope.

Christian came back into the room with a few items. A golf club. A pair of tights. Some handcuffs, ropes, chains and a cigarette lighter.

'Sorry, sweetheart,' he said. 'It's for your own good.'

He got her out of bed, chained her tightly to a chair with her forearms and hands behind her back, and gagged her by stuffing the tights into her mouth.

'This is the plan. If he turns up, we stay very, very quiet. Let him get in the house and creep around a bit. Then, when I give the signal, you scream as loudly as you can. He'll come running up, I'll take his feet out with the golf club and then brain the little bastard. OK? Nod if you agree.'

'Mnng,' she replied. He looked at her. She nodded.

'But the thing is, Lizzie – don't deny it – I think you still have a little bit of feeling for that boy, don't you? Oh, I know you do,' he insisted when she shook her head. 'It's not that I don't trust you, but … well.' He flicked the lighter and waved the flame in her face. 'Just in case you need a little help.'

He sniggered, went to the window and leaned out, whistling a tune – 'Whistle While You Work'. You had to hand it to him. No matter how mad he got, he always kept his sense of humour.

Lizzie pulled at her bonds. It was hopeless. Whatever the next half-hour brought, she was going to be spending it sitting in the chair, watching. But one thing she could do to help; she was not, under any circumstances, going to scream. When Christian got the gag off for her to yell, when the lighter flame flicked, she was going to shout to warn Adam. On that she was determined.

💀

Adam was sensible enough not to drive up straight up to the house, but Christian recognised the engine as it approached along the main road. Some minutes later came the soft swish and thud as Adam slid up one of the big sash windows on the ground floor. Next, the creak on the boards as he tiptoed around. Finally the different creak on the stairs as he began on his way up.

Lizzie knew exactly what was going to happen and was prepared for it. Christian put the lighter under the soft flesh of her wrist in advance. As soon as he heard the creak of the stairs, he flicked the flame on with one hand, waited for the burn to get deep, then hoiked the tights out with the other.

'AaaaRRRRRGGHHHH!' she screamed. It was impossible. It hurt too much. Christian shoved the tights back in her mouth and went to hide behind the door with the golf club before she could get out another word.

'Mnng, mnng,' she groaned, shaking the chair from side to side. But it was too late. Footsteps thundered up the stairs, the door crashed open and Adam rushed heroically in. Christian, stooping low to take the swing from up behind his head, swung the club violently down on to his shins. Adam yelled in pain and fell like a rock. Christian stood over him and – whack! Right on top of the head with the club.

And that was that.

He came round to find himself tied hand and foot to a chair, his hands handcuffed behind his back. His shins were ablaze with pain, there was blood trickling down into his eyes, and he had a splitting headache. Vince and Christian were standing by the window having an argument about something and Lizzie was sitting opposite on another chair. Her face was covered in bruises.

'I uv ooo,' he said. He was gagged. She looked at him and shook her head. He tried again. 'Ang … urv … oo.'

'Shut the fuck up, will you?' said Vince. He came across and slapped him round the face with the back of his hand. 'You stole my car,' he said in tones of disbelief, and whacked him the other way, knocking him out once more.

When he came round again, the two men were still arguing, as far as he could tell, about what to do with Lizzie.

'Mr Christian, she is NOT your girlfriend,' Vince was

saying. 'A girlfriend does not have to be tied up and burned before she'll lure her ex-boyfriend upstairs so you can brain him. A girlfriend would do those things willingly. She'd be *happy* to do that for you. You wouldn't even need to ask – she'd offer. It would be her pleasure.'

Christian was finding this difficult to follow, and he was grinning, grimacing, twisting about, unable to make his mind up. Finally, though, Vince managed to convince him.

'OK! You're right. The bitch has been leading me on,' he said. 'Fucking cow, can you believe it? I could have been killed,' he said, and he bulged in rage at the thought. 'Fine. Kill her. Kill them both. Let's not waste any more time. Shoot them both, the little fucks, right now.'

But Vince held up a hand. 'Sir, that's just more bodies,' he pointed out. 'I'm always driving to and fro with bodies in the boot. If I can suggest something else – how about a pill, sir? The boy's already taken it. If we give the girl one now, we can drive them both out to the factory tomorrow, lock them up in a box … and that's that. No one's going to go digging about round there, Mr Ballantine sees to that. In a week they'll both be dead, and we can dump the bodies wherever we want. Everyone will think they're just one more pair of Deathers.'

Christian liked it. 'Yeah, yeah, good idea. Let 'em die in a box, see how much fun they have then. But not the same box. We don't want them to comfort each other, Vince. They can suffer on their own.'

'Certainly not, sir,' agreed Vince. 'I'll fetch the doings, shall I?'

'Yeah.' Christian grinned. 'Good. The boyfriend can

watch. Then I get to fuck her for the rest of the day – he can watch that, too. Cool, eh?' he said.

'Very cool, sir,' said Vince.

They did it with a funnel and water. Christian turned Adam round so he had to watch. He banged his chair and begged through his gag, but there were no offers he could make, no bargains to be struck. Vince tipped Lizzie's head back as far it would go up and pushed the funnel down into her throat until she retched. Christian dropped a pill in, then swilled it down with a glass of water. They stood there, holding it tight and stroking her throat while she gurgled, turned red and swallowed.

'All your fault,' Christian said.

Adam closed his eyes and wept. He'd failed. Lizzie was as dead as he was.

'Orry,' he said. 'Orree.' She didn't answer. Christian tied her gag back on and Lizzie bent her head and wouldn't look at him. What could she say? It was, as Christian said, all his fault.

While Christian was gloating over Adam and slapping him around a bit, Vince went to pick up his jacket from the bed, where he had put it out of the way as he worked on Lizzie. As he did so, he spotted the corner of a familiar box half sticking out from under the bed.

He bent to pick it up. It was Christian's meds. But what was it doing here? He kept the meds under lock and key.

Vince smelled a rat. He tore off the cellophane and opened it up.

The box was full of polystyrene. It was a mock-up. A very good mock-up. But what would Christian be doing with a mock-up of his meds …?

A light went on in Vince's head. Christian's increasingly bizarre behaviour … false boxes of meds …. The little git had been having fakes made up and swapping them …

'You sneaky little shit!'

Christian turned round from what he was doing, took one look and knew he was caught. Vince shook the box at him.

'How long have I been feeding you fakes? What was in those pills – sugar? It's straight to the funny farm for you, you little dick.'

'You're talking complete nonsense,' said Christian smoothly, and without another word, turned and dashed for the door. Vince let out a bellow and shot after him, catching him by the collar before he got out. To his delight, Christian swung one at him.

Vince had put some thought into how to do this. He couldn't mark the little toad too much, or Mr Ballantine would be on to him. He spun him round and delivered a series of knuckle punches to the back of the neck. Revenge, so sweet! One, two, three, four. Christian collapsed to the floor without a sound. Vince picked him up, punched him in the solar plexus – always a good number, because it hurt like hell, made you panic about your breath, and left very few marks. Then, he banged his head against the wall.

Christian flopped to the floor like a doll. Perfect.

Vince took out his phone and dialled Mr Ballantine. It was time for a much-needed holiday. Where to? New York, Paris, the Bahamas? He smiled happily – but he had made a serious mistake. He noticed that both Lizzie and Adam were staring at a point behind him, and was just realising what that meant when Christian, who had never lost consciousness, even for a moment, leaped on him.

Vince was a good half-metre taller than him, and Christian had to more or less run up him like a monkey, getting footholds on his calves, then his bum, until he was able to bury his hands firmly into his hair and pull himself right up on to the big man's shoulders. Wrapping his legs firmly around the big man's neck, he pulled Vince's head forward and down with one hand and with the other, groped at his belt for that deadly, short-bladed little knife.

Vince knew exactly what that meant. He let out a gargling bellow of rage and fear, and began dancing about the room and shaking himself like a bear, frantically snatching and groping at the deadly imp on his back. But Christian hung on tight and he couldn't shift him. Desperately, he ran backwards at the wall, crashing into it as hard as he could and knocking every ounce of breath out of his tormentor; but Christian had all the strength and passion of insanity and he clung on, snarling in his ear as they cavorted around the room: 'I'm gonna quad ya, I'm gonna quad ya. C4! C4! Yee-ha!'

Adam and Lizzie, tied firmly to their chairs, were only able to watch in amazement. Adam had no idea what was going on – all he knew was that neither Vince nor Christian was watching him. It was late, it was terribly late, but rescue was still possible. He had to get Lizzie out of the grip of this psychotic monster and back to the hotel in time for the antidote turning up. This was his chance – but what could he do, tied hand and foot to a chair?

Adam began to rock himself backwards and forwards. He had no idea what this was going to achieve, but he did it anyway, and eventually he rocked so hard that the chair tipped forward. He just managed to catch himself before he went right over and ended up balanced improbably on tiptoes, still sitting in the chair, bent over almost double. He had just a little play on his legs and, with great difficulty, was able to hobble across the floor like an insect towards the door. He got himself out of the room as far as the top of the stairs, before he paused to look behind him. Vince was busy trying to bash Christian to pieces against the top of the chest of drawers. Lizzie, sitting still in her chair, was gazing at him with big eyes over the top of her gag.

Adam shrugged. What had he got to lose? Twisting as he fell, he flung himself down the marble stairway and smashed, bounced and bumped all the way down.

Behind him, Lizzie stared in shock. What on earth was he doing, trying to kill himself all over again? And what did it matter, anyway? She was going to die. She listened as he crashed down like a stack of sticks; then there was nothing.

Vince ran past her, howling. Christian had finally got that nasty little knife out and was waving it in the air, screaming in triumph. Vince swung round, ready to back him again into the chest of drawers, which had a hard edge just at thigh level, when Christian suddenly brought the knife down with a loud thud.

The effect was instant.

The big man stopped in his tracks and stood swaying on his feet, expressions of surprise and horror equally lit on his face. Christian jumped down, like a boy dismounting a horse, just as he began to topple. He came down like a tree right at Lizzie's feet, his arms limp at his sides, striking the carpet chin first. He opened his mouth to let out a final bellow of rage and despair, but nothing came. His eyes flicked up to meet hers. Then he closed them and let out the tiniest, weakest, most helpless little sigh of defeat.

Christian bent down to examine the knife in the back of his neck, and then down to the big man's face. He put his hand close to Vince's mouth.

'Breathing,' he whispered in ecstasy. 'Still breathing.'

Then he went crazy.

'C4 – C fucking 4! I done it, you bastard. See you ring Daddy now. C4! C4! C4!' And screaming with triumph, he did a dance of victory around the prostrate body, while Lizzie, in her chair, wept and struggled and did her best not to scream. She was certain she was going to get it next.

It took Christian about five minutes to realise that Adam had gone. For some reason, it flung him into a complete panic.

'Where's he gone? Jesus. Where he is?' he wailed. He ran around the room, looking out of the window, under the bed, in the en suite. 'Where is he?' he begged Lizzie.

Lizzie shook her head, unable to speak through her gag. Christian stared at her for a moment, then ran out of the room and down the stairs. Below, the front door banged.

Lizzie couldn't stop crying. What next? She looked over at Vince, lying flat on his front, with the knife handle sticking out from the back of his neck. His eyes swivelled round to met hers and they stared briefly at one another, each as helpless as the other. Neither of them could move a muscle.

Then – a miracle. The door opened and Adam came hobbling in. Flinging himself down the stairs had bruised him badly, but it had smashed the chair up enough for him to tread his way out of it and make off. He was still gagged, his hands were cuffed behind his back and his feet hobbled by the short length of rope that had tied them to the chair – but he was free. He had managed to get back upstairs, hide and wait till Christian had gone out, and now here he was, hobbling to the rescue.

He ran up to Lizzie and stood in front of her, making weird noises through the gag. Lizzie did the same thing – the pair of them, gurning and grunting at each other. Adam gave up. He lay on his back, lifted his legs up and kicked her violently in the stomach. Lizzie doubled over with a groan. Had Adam gone crazy, too? He jumped up, turned round, flicked her gag up and started trying to shove his fingers down her throat.

'Adam,' she groaned, 'what are you doing?'

'Ergaggnng – dech,' he said. And despite everything, she knew what he meant. He was trying to make her throw up to get rid of the drug.

Yes! She nodded agreement and stuck her head out, while Adam groped down her throat with his fingers. She retched and gagged – but couldn't be sick.

She'd had enough. 'Adam,' she said. 'Adam.'

'Hmm. Ngg, ngg …' he groaned.

She shook her head. 'You came back for me.'

'Nggg. Ganng. A angoo.'

'Yeah, I know you love me. But, Adam, you have to go, right now.'

'Nnng? Gno … I …'

'Yes, you do,' she told him. 'Christian will come back, any time now. Get out while you can. I'm stuck.'

'Ngg,' said Adam. He shook his head. He was rescuing her! He wasn't going to give up. He looked desperately around for some way of getting her out of the handcuffs and rope. No key, no hands, no pliers, nothing. His gag was wrapped around his head, going tightly inside his mouth, so that although his tongue was forced down, his teeth were free. In his desperation, he bent down and started chewing at the rope around Lizzie's hands.

Lizzie sat there and watched the back of his head. Her face hurt, her body hurt. She'd been force-fed Death and she was going to die – and here was Adam trying to chew her free.

She started to laugh.

Adam looked sideways up at her. He wasn't finding this as funny as she was. He went back to his chewing. Lizzie shook her head. 'Adam,' she said again.

He looked up and honked piteously.

'You have to go.'

'Mnnh! Urrg, mmm,' he said, nodding again desperately around the room.

'Just – get real for once, will you? Christian will be

back in a minute. If he catches you here he'll kill us both. You're no use to me dead. Go! Rescue me later.'

Downstairs a door slammed.

'Go!' she hissed. Suddenly she was furious as well as scared. *Just once, Adam – behave.*

'Arie. I uf goo,' said Adam, and he turned and bounded across the room like a gigantic rabbit towards the window. He peered out. It was a long way down, and the window was locked.

Feet on the stairs. There was nothing for it.

He took a few steps back and made a run at the window at the very moment that the door burst open behind him. He crashed through the glass and went down in a sparkling display of shards, like a gagged angel glittering in the late-afternoon sunshine. Down, down, down ,…

He hit the ground feet first in a rose bush and tipped over in a tangle of thorns. He rolled away deeper into the shrubs as a volley of gunshots came from the window above. It should have been an easy shot – but Adam had an advantage. The sun was shining brightly on that side of the building, and Christian was blinded by the light. Adam crawled to his feet – hobbled, hands behind his back – and made a mad dash for the car.

☠

Up at the window, Christian cursed. He turned to look at Lizzie, gun in the air. Havering, he waved it in her face.

'What are you doing, you idiot?' she yelled. 'He's getting away!' It was her only chance. In his mind, she was either on his side or against him.

It worked. He cursed and ran to the door and down the stairs. 'The fuck! The fuck!' he screamed. The front door banged again and she heard him running across the gravel in pursuit of Adam. Lizzie held her breath to listen, her heart thudding like a machine in her chest. *Please God let Adam get away! Please God get me out of this. Please please please.* Tied hand and foot to the chair, she was unable to do a thing. She remembered what Adam had done, tipping the chair and walking away. She tried it herself – and fell sideways to the ground, her face just half a metre or so from Vince's. He lay there unmoving, eyes shut. She assumed he must be dead.

The sounds of gunfire receded. The room, which had been so full of shouting and conflict a moment before, became very quiet. There was only her own ragged, half-sobbing breath. Another shot, in the distance. A bird began to sing in the trees outside.

Miraculously, she was still alive, but on Death. That didn't sound all that optimistic, but you know what? It did mean one thing; she had nothing to lose.

If I'm going down, I'm going to take you with me, you bastard, she thought.

She started to sob again and forced herself to stop. She had to be strong. She had to act the girlfriend and stay alive long enough to get her chance to kill Christian.

Opposite her, quite suddenly, Vince opened his eyes. She screamed slightly – it was yet another shock – then caught her breath.

'Vince. You ... OK?' she asked.

His eyes rolled sarcastically. He tried to speak but his

voice was so weak, she could hardly hear it. With difficulty, she jerked her chair closer.

'What?'

'Kill me,' he was saying, in a tiny little voice. He had hardly any breath – just about enough, she guessed, to keep himself alive.

'Kill you? How?' she demanded. For a moment longer they stayed staring at each other.

'What do I do, Vince? What do I do?' she begged. 'Tell me what to do. Maybe I can get him back for you.'

Vince snorted derisively. Fat chance.

Lizzie bared her teeth. There had to be something!

'... phone ...' said Vince.

'What?'

'My phone.' He was looking sideways. His phone lay in the middle of the floor where he'd dropped it when Christian attacked him. It was an iPhone, same as hers. Yes! Jerking the chair with her body, Lizzie made it across the floor, turned herself round and took it in her hands.

Communication. Somehow, someone, somewhere. Adam – if he was still alive. Her parents. She jerked her way again across the floor to the bed, tucked the phone under it and got back into her place just the door banged below. Christian came slowly up the stairs and into the room, the gun hanging in his hand. He stood by her head and looked down.

He was a complete mess. His teeth were bloody and crooked in his mouth. His nose had moved sideways, his eyes almost disappeared in the bruises on his face. Vince had done a real job on him. Only his psychosis was keeping him on his feet. He looked so, so crazy.

'Your boyfriend is dead,' he said.

Lizzie had no idea if he was telling the truth or not. All things being equal, he probably was. But she had to say something quick, or she was going to be next.

'Good,' she said. 'That bastard has had it coming for ages.'

She was amazed at her own survival instincts. Christian didn't reply. He just turned to look at Vince and cocked his head to one side.

'It took you bloody long enough,' she said, driving on, trying to touch a chord in his madness. 'What kind of way is this to treat your girlfriend, leaving me here with this freak?'

Christian looked at her. He licked his lips.

'Girlfriend,' said Lizzie.

'Girlfriend,' he said.

'Yes, girlfriend. What else am I doing in your bedroom? I can't even do my make-up or file my nails like this. How about undoing me so I can make myself pretty for you?' She began to cry with fear. All she could do was hope that it looked like the sort of thing a girlfriend would do.

'Girlfriend,' said Christian again. Suddenly he jerked his arm in the air. 'Yeah!' he said. 'Right on!'

'Great,' said Lizzie. 'How about a cup of tea, then? And maybe a sandwich. I'm famished.'

On the floor, Vince smiled to himself. *Clever girl*, he thought. Christian nodded. He cocked the gun, checked the ammo, lifted it and shot Vince through the back of the head.

'We don't have time,' he said. 'We need to get moving. Things to do, you know.' And he bent down to untie her ropes.

CHAPTER 2

NEW ORDERS

Jess was lying in his box in the container park, hands behind his head, staring at the ceiling. Anna, after her taste of what was happening on the streets, had refused to go back and had tried to get him to stay with her, but he'd insisted on seeing the job with Death through to the end.

'Such a soldier,' she'd said. It was true but she had no idea how it broke him up inside to be like that.

Predictably, Ballantine had responded to him coming back by beating the shit out of him and then locking him up. At least before he'd been allowed to wander about with a guard. Now, he only got out each day for work. The rest of the time he was locked up in his box. Worse, they'd taken away his TV, his radio and his phone. Outside, the government could have fallen, Parliament could have closed, the world might be upside down wriggling its toes in the stars, and Jess wouldn't know a thing about it.

He had only one link to the outside world – his Zealot phone, the same make and model as his personal one. He held it tightly in his hand now, ready to stuff it quickly out of sight if anyone came in on him. He was dying to make a call, to Command, to Anna, maybe, and find out what on earth was going on outside, but he didn't dare. Ballantine's men had found and taken his only charger, and the battery was almost dead. He was expecting a call – had been for two days now. Surely, surely, Command was going to issue him with new orders? As things stood, he was still supposed to make his way out to the big rally tomorrow, and die for the cause; public immolation. Self-burning. But they weren't going to waste his life in protest now. Surely – and he prayed for the chance – they'd want him to fight.

Most days he could hear the sounds coming over from the city. Albert Square was less than a couple of miles away and with the wind in the right direction, you could hear the voices of tens of thousands of people in unison together, singing and chanting. It was the voice of the people – but how many? One hundred thousand, two hundred thousand? A million? He had no way of knowing.

Jess rolled over on to his front. It was driving him mad! Everything he'd worked for was coming real – and he was stuck in a box. Tomorrow was Friday, a week to the day after Jimmy Earle's death. There was to be a mass demo, a general strike. Maybe more. Who knew how things had changed since he'd been locked up in here? Most important of all, they would be making the big announcement he had been working towards all this time. He had to be there … but no way was Ballantine going to let him out. With Anna gone, he was the only one who knew how to make Death. They still needed him.

Jess lifted the phone in the air and weighed it in his hand, a little lump of hope. And at that moment – finally, after two days of waiting – it rang.

'Jess? You there?'

'Anna!'

'You OK?'

'Yeah. You? I can't talk long, the phone's nearly out and they've taken the charger. What's going on out there?'

'Oh, man, Jess, you should have stayed with me. It's fabulous! I don't think the world's ever going to be the same again.'

Jess groaned. He was missing it all!

'Can you get away?' she asked.

'No! They've locked me up. Taken my radio and TV. Tell me – what's happening? Tell me quick,' he begged, torn between wanting to know and wanting to save his phone for the orders he hoped were coming.

'Everything! The general strike is on. The police, the army, they're all coming over. People are marching on Westminster and no one is lifting a finger to stop them. Just a few army brigades holding out …'

It was true, then. 'It's happening?' he asked. 'It really is happening?'

'It really is. And tomorrow – the big announcement. It's planned for one o'clock. You have to get out, Jess!'

'I'm trying.' In his excitement and frustration, Jess got

to his feet and paced round the metal box that was his prison. He had to be there! But how?

'Look, I have to go. If they ring with new orders I need the phone …'

'I have your orders,' said Anna.

Jess stopped in his tracks. 'What are they?'

'Get your arse out of there!' she said, and she laughed. 'Just – get out here.'

'Really? They want me out?'

'Of course they want you out! What do you think?'

'But I volunteered for the death squad.'

'They've taken you off it.'

Jess felt his heart leap inside him. Life. Hope! It nearly knocked him down. He hadn't dreamed he wanted to live so much.

'Why?'

'Why do you think? Don't you know what you've done? Without you, none of this would have happened. They're not going to let you go if they can help it. They want you alive.'

Jess listened breathlessly. He'd thought he was going to die. He was ready to die. He'd believed he wanted to die – and now he'd been given life.

Suddenly he had a thought … 'What about Adam? Did you find him?'

'Oh, yeah. He's holed up in a hotel room.' Anna snorted in amusement. 'That should keep him out of trouble. He thinks I'm coming round tomorrow with the antidote.' She laughed out loud.

Jess felt his heart, which had been frozen for so long,

begin to move. Life. His family, waiting for him. He could go back to them. It was unbelievable.

'And you?' he asked. 'You're off the squad as well?'

'Not me,' she said.

Jess stalled. 'Why not?'

He could feel her shrug. 'I must be a bit more dispensable.'

'What do they want you to do?'

'I'm a bomb, Jess.' She laughed. 'A blonde bombshell, that's me.'

Suicide bomber. A lot better than burning. But ... a long, long way worse than life.

'When?'

'Tomorrow.'

'What's your target?'

'Classified.' She laughed again, wryly. 'Sorry, Jess.'

His phone began to beep. It was dying.

'I'm going,' he said. 'Will I see you again? Let me see you again.'

'I don't think so, Jess. Just get out of there. They can't send anyone to help you, OK? You're on your own. Get out of there any way you can. And Jess. Guess what. I just want to say ...'

And the phone went dead.

'Shit!' Jess looked at the stupid gadget in his hand – dead to the world. What had she been about to say?

Whatever. He was going to war. He was going to fight for the revolution. All he had to do now was get out. And that was easier said than done.

CHAPTER 3

DON'T CRY – KILL

After shooting Vince, Christian wanted to get away as fast as he could. He untied Lizzie from the bed and hurried her to the door, but she managed to stall him by pointing out she was still in her nightie.

'It doesn't matter,' he yelled.

'It does!' she yelled back. She nodded down at her body. 'For your eyes only.'

Grumbling but flattered, Christian allowed her to pick up her clothes and get dressed. In doing so, she was able to recover Vince's phone from under the bed.

Done! She was feeling good – strong, quick, clever. It was only while he was hurrying her downstairs to the car that she realised what was happening; she was feeling the first effects of Death. It was a feeling that was unlikely to last, but if it helped her get away from Christian, it was more than welcome.

Christian drove them into Manchester, where he kept a town flat on Deansgate for business purposes. The fight with Vince seemed to have unhinged him totally. Maybe he no longer had to pretend – maybe the beatings his head had taken against the wall had done some damage, but his mood was swinging dangerously between the sentimental and the violent. At the flat, they spent most of the rest of the evening watching TV, with Lizzie manacled to the sofa. Her coat with the phone in it was in the bedroom, hanging up on the door. She had no chance to get anywhere near it.

As the film progressed, Christian began muttering to himself, at first quietly, then louder and louder.

'Tomorrow we go to the factory,' he announced, to no one in particular.

'Where's that?' asked Lizzie, lightly.

Christian jumped and looked at her suspiciously. He'd obviously forgotten she was even there.

'Don't answer her,' he said. 'She's fishing. No, she's not! She just wants to know. You trust her?' he asked, incredulously. 'You trust her? Do I look stupid?' he shouted suddenly.

'I'm your girlfriend, Christian,' she told him in a cross voice, doing her best not show how terrified she was. 'Of course you trust me!'

'Do I?' Christian flailed around in a panic. 'You? But who else are you?' he demanded.

'Just me,' she said. 'Girlfriend. Girlfriend. Remember?

Lizzie. Girlfriend. When are we going to get some tea, Christian?' she asked, frowning. Getting him to do things for her seemed to help keep him away from dangerous thoughts.

Christian chewed at his knuckle, and came to a conclusion. 'She's all I have,' he explained to himself. He kissed her, and went to the kitchen to see what there was to eat. He came back with a single bowl of tomato soup, all he had in. He wouldn't go out to get any more because he was convinced that his life was in danger. Lizzie had no idea why. Probably it was pure paranoia, but maybe, just maybe, he was scared of Adam. She hadn't seen a body. It could be that he was still alive.

She could hope, anyway.

They shared the soup, but it was nowhere near enough and in an hour or so, Christian started to get angry about how hungry he was. Lizzie knew better than to offer to go out for him, and made a big fuss about how important it was that they stay put and hide from their enemies. That helped calm him down and convince him they were in it together. She helped him do a search of the cupboards, but all she could find was a single bag of sugar. She spent the evening making gallons of hot, sweet tea for them both, which they drank together, huddled up in bed, like children hiding from the ghosts. The hours and minutes passed slowly by. He beat her up twice; once at midnight, and again two hours later. Towards first light, he fell in love with her all over again and went to sleep in her arms, weeping sentimental tears.

Lizzie watched over him. He had chained her to the

bed and to himself. There were no weapons nearby. She wondered if she could strangle him, but thought probably not. It was tempting, but now was not the time. So she waited, watching over him, until at last she fell asleep as well.

☻

After he had crashed through the window in a hail of shattered glass, and pulled himself out of the rose bush, Adam dashed off with tiny steps into the woods, still hobbled and with his hands cuffed behind his back. He had hardly gone more than twenty metres or so when Christian burst out of the front door and began firing wildly through the trees in his direction.

He ran on as fast as he could, tripping and falling over every few steps, until it occurred to him that he didn't actually have to have his hands tied behind his back – he could step over them so they were in front then untie his legs. Why hadn't he thought of this before? As he paused to do it, he could hear Christian tearing his way through the tangle of woodland, bawling in rage, only twenty or thirty metres away. But he was heading the wrong way and obviously wasn't sure where Adam was. He bent, rapidly untied the rope around his legs, and fled. Now Christian spotted him and fired off more rounds, but his luck held. It was another two hundred metres to Vince's Porsche and Adam covered them at full tilt, with Christian, full of fury but out of his mind, tripping and cursing, screaming at him to stop, and letting shots off at every shadow he saw.

Adam got to the car and there was a dreadful moment when he thought he'd lost the keys. He fished desperately around all his pockets before he found them. He reversed out, burning rubber and grinding the clutch as Christian came out of the trees towards him. He stalled on the road; a lorry going past blared its horn and swerved to miss him. But then he got going again – and pulled away, nought to sixty in seconds. A couple of shots thumped into the boot – he could feel the impact of them right through the car – before he got out of range, driving fast to safety.

But it wasn't over. It couldn't ever be over with Lizzie still in captivity. Christian would be straight back there. Maybe he'd shoot her on the spot, but Adam was hoping that now she'd swallowed Death as well, he'd follow Vince's plan and let her live out her week. Either way he had to get back. The longer he left it, the worse things could get for her.

He stopped in a lay-by and waited a few minutes to give the impression he was gone, then turned round and went back. He parked the car well away from the drive and once again made his way up to the house, but he was already too late; the birds had flown. Only Vince remained, dead on the floor with a bullet wound in his head.

Adam had escaped. Lizzie was as good as dead.

That was it, then. He'd lost her and he had no idea how to find her. She'd been fed Death – and what on earth would her last few days be like, with Christian as her jailer? It didn't bear thinking about.

He wandered around the house, trying to find some kind of clue as to where they'd gone, but found nothing. Eventually he went back to the car and sat at the wheel, still trying to work it out.

Christian had been right about one thing. It was all his fault.

Where was he? Day 4; Day 5 tomorrow. Two days to go. He'd lost his life, ruined his parents' lives, and now he'd destroyed Lizzie's as well. Sitting at the wheel Adam began to cry, quietly at first, then more and more until he was sobbing out loud. It was getting dark, but he remained where he was, with nowhere better to go, nothing better to do, until, blessedly, he fell asleep at the wheel.

💀

The following morning, Friday, Lizzie's luck was still holding: Christian woke up feeling refreshed. He looked almost normal. They kissed, made small talk, watched TV. He even went out to buy stuff for breakfast.

As soon as he was out of the door, Lizzie was out of bed. The phone … just a few metres away, in her jacket hanging on the door. The bed was a huge oak thing that weighed a ton, and she had to drag it inch by inch behind her to get there. She typed out her text in a panic – the shop was only a few steps away and Christian could be back at any moment. She got as far as '*at the factory*' before the front door went. Back already! She had time to type out Adam's number and send, before desperately dragging herself and the bed back, wincing at the noise of the legs on the boards, certain she was going to get caught.

She chucked the phone under the bed and just about managed to get everything back as it was before he came in bearing croissants and jam. She smiled sweetly. Done! It wasn't much of a text, but it was a start. At least something had gone out.

They ate together, in bed with coffee. When it was done, Christian wiped his mouth and said thoughtfully, 'You know what, Lizzie? I think we need to get away. Just you and me. Big holiday. Thailand, maybe. All points east. Japan. We've always wanted to go to Japan. What do you say?'

'It sounds wonderful! When do we go?' she gushed. Christian beamed at her, and her heart quailed inside her. She had her one week – the most life could offer her now. How horrible it would be if she had to spend the whole time pretending to be in love with Christian. She wanted to see her parents, she wanted to see Adam – she had so much she wanted to do in those few, miserable days. For the first time, she began to wonder if it was worth it, this dreadful struggle to stay alive. She was going to die anyway, probably in a horrible way. Perhaps it would be better to get it over with at once. Anything would be better than this.

But not yet. She wasn't ready for that. In a few days maybe …

The holiday idea seemed to be a runner. Christian booked some flights to Tokyo. They could get a hotel when they arrived. It was all set – and then things began to deteriorate. He finished the calls, made them both some tea, which they drank in bed; but then he began to get agitated. The muttering started up. Lizzie tried to distract him by talking about Tokyo, but it was no use.

'You idiot!' he suddenly bellowed. 'You've forgotten the business.' He swung round suddenly and glared directly at her. Lizzie cringed down – it was a bad move but she couldn't help it.

'Don't call me a idiot!' he screamed. But he had turned away and was talking to someone in his head. 'Yeah, but you are, aren't you? You have business. What's Daddy going to say … what's he going to think … what's he going to do?'

Gibbering in fear, Christian turned his horrified eyes to Lizzie, as if begging her for an answer. At any moment it could turn to rage. She tried to smile.

'Er … we ought to get the business side of things sorted out before we leave, though, don't you think?'

Christian looked suspiciously at her. 'What do you know about my business?' he demanded.

'Nothing. But you always have some. Isn't there something you need to do? Weren't we supposed to be … going to the factory today?' she asked, digging into her memory as she spoke.

His eyes swivelled, anxiously. 'Factory … yeah. That's it. Right. The factory. Good girl. Good girl, Lizzie!'

He ran to kiss her, and then dashed off to sort things out. Lizzie had time to sob twice before he was back, ordering her to get dressed. They were going right now. This time, to her disgust, he stood over her, watching her like a hawk, and she had no time to pick up the phone.

Fifteen minutes later, after tying her to the passenger

seat of his car with several metres of rope, he was driving her east. The phone was still lying under the bed. She just had to hope that Adam was still alive and that, if he was, he would manage on his own. It wasn't a thought that filled her with confidence, but there was one thing, to her surprise, she felt confident about. If he was alive, he would try. She had no doubt about that. Adam was an idiot in many ways but this much was true; he was her idiot, and he would never give her up in a million years. She didn't think there was anyone else in the world she could say that about. And she wasn't sure she knew anyone else who had that, either.

What a thing, she thought. *And what a way to discover it.* It was just a shame that they had only days left to live. And with thought, suddenly, she was fighting back tears.

There wasn't much time to mourn, though. Christian, who was obviously very nervous about the trip, started to explain to her that he wanted her along for moral support.

'What sort of moral support?' she asked.

He rambled on, half to her, half to himself, but from what she could gather, he needed her to reassure his dad that he was, in fact, taking his meds; and that Vince was, in fact, not with them because he had another important job to do rather than having been murdered; and that he, Christian, was, in fact, as sane as the next man.

'No problem,' said Lizzie, brightly. She settled herself into the seat and looked out of the window. Adam was going to die, if he wasn't already dead, and she was going to die, too; she knew that. But with a little bit of luck, just a tiny wee bit of luck, she might manage to take some of the bastards who'd been making this horrible drug with her. Christian was there, at the top of the list, and his dad was right below him.

Why not? she thought. *This one is for you, Ads. Leave the world a better place, like it said on the list. Go for it!*

Christian looked sideways at her, his eyes rolling like marbles. Lizzie smiled back. *Don't cry,* she thought. *Don't cry – kill.* Even if she took just one of them with her, it would be worth it.

She was expecting a long ride, but very quickly they were driving through a strange wasteland of lorry containers. Lizzie was amazed. She had no idea that such a place existed so close to Manchester city centre. There were hundreds of containers, maybe thousands, some stacked on top of each other, all laid out in endless rows.

The car pulled up in the middle of nowhere and Christian got out. He stood there a moment, flexing his shoulders and looking around him. She thought, *Is this it? Has he taken me here to kill me?* But then he bent into the car and kissed her on the cheek.

'Won't be long, love,' he said.

'Aren't you taking me to meet your dad?' she asked.

'No.' Christian was most amused. 'No way.'

'But you said—'

'Don't be ridiculous, Lizzie,' he said. He shook his head irritably, and walked off. Lizzie watched him disappear behind a container. Suddenly she was on her own. She tugged at her bonds, but he'd tied her good and tight. Her hands were free, but there was no way she could reach round to the knots that had been tied behind the seat. She was stuck – and if she didn't take her chance now, she might never get another go.

There was only one thing she could do. She leaned across to the driving seat and pressed on the horn. Please God there really was someone there. The horn blared out into the silence of the container park. And it worked: All round her, doors opened in the containers. The whole place was full of people hiding in them. They ran towards her. One of them was Christian.

CHAPTER 4

THE DEATH FACTORY

Adam woke up in exactly the same position he'd fallen asleep in – sitting in the car with his head resting on the steering wheel. He felt dreadful – headache, nausea, aches, the lot. What had happened to that beautiful glad morning of Death? Why was he so shot? It made no sense.

He clicked the key in the ignition and checked the time. It was already eleven a.m. So late! He'd slept for hours.

And … Lizzie. He'd lost Lizzie.

He couldn't see any way out of it. It was Day 5 – Friday – the day Janet had said he should meet her and collect the antidote. Was that what he had to do – save his own skin? He might as well, if he couldn't do anything for Lizzie.

He felt so bad about it – but it would pass, wouldn't it?

He had it all back. His parents, his life, work – all waiting for him. He could go and wait for the antidote, and just get on with it. He'd have to live with what had happened to Lizzie, but he'd forget. He'd learn not to let it ruin his life. That's what happens. We live, we move on. We persevere.

Adam took out his phone and turned it on. As he expected, there were maybe fifty messages from his parents. Looked like they were going to be in luck after all. Loads from his friends too, who had obviously been brought in on the act by his mum and dad. '*Where are you, we miss you, we just need to know you're OK.*' He scanned through them.

Then, an unknown number. He opened it up. The message had two words: '*The factory.*'

Adam stared at it. Where had he heard that word before? Vince, was it?

He turned on the sat nav and said the word 'factory'. And up it came. Adam sat there, staring at it. It *had* to be from Lizzie. And now he had a choice. He could go back home to life – to all the things, good and bad, he'd thought he'd lost for ever. Or he could try to help Lizzie – and probably die in the process.

Adam sat there at the wheel, not thinking, not feeling, just waiting. As if somehow, if he sat there long enough, maybe he'd think of a way he could stay alive and bear to face it.

☠

Jess was in the lab running tests when the commotion started up outside. A car pulling up, a door slamming. It was shocking. No one, but no one, made any noise during the hours of daylight in the container park. Even Florence Ballantine avoided moving about by day, and he owned the place. Everyone in the lab, guards and techies alike, paused, got to their feet, listening, trying to work it out. Then, the horn, blaring like a siren – and off went the guards like dogs after a rabbit, the guns coming out, faces intent.

They left the door open. Casually, Jess strolled towards it.

'Hey, where are you going?' one of the techs yelled.

'Don't worry, just looking. Having a ciggie,' said Jess. He leaned against the door and took one out. The techies didn't like it, but it wasn't their business to stand guard over him. Besides, they were curious themselves. Some of them were already drifting over to the door after him to have a look themselves. Jess yawned, but inside he was burning with excitement. It was midday. He had one short hour to keep his date with Anna. Outside, in Manchester city centre, the crowds would be gathering right now. Even here, kilometres away, the noise was immense. Every day it had been growing louder – the roar of a million voices asking questions the government was unable to answer. It felt as if the whole country was there, just out of sight, waiting to claim the future. Jess had been given a chance to join them, to be with them – to die for them, if he had to.

All he had to do was get there.

He glanced behind him. Some of the techies were still watching him. Not yet … not yet. Steady. If he ran too early, they'd be on to him at once.

He leaned out of the doorway to take a look at what the fuss was. There was a car with a girl sitting in it who looked familiar. She was yelling, 'He's not taken his meds! He's not taken his meds!' at the top of her voice.

He knew her. Where had he seen her before?

Then he remembered. Lizzie, wasn't it? Adam's girlfriend. What on earth was she doing here? And if she was here, could Adam be far behind? But Anna had said he was in a hotel room. Jess groaned. *No! Not here, not here of all places. Adam! You idiot!*

There was a crowd gathering around the car. Christian Ballantine was there, bawling like an animal, batting at Lizzie with his hands through the window while the big guys tried to pull him off. He looked crazy, as if his brain was melting. The girl cringed back in the car, shielding her face with her hands. She'd already taken a few batterings by the looks of it. Florence Ballantine himself was out there, too, striding over with a face like a fist, wanting to know what all the noise was about.

The techies had stepped out past him to have a look – it wasn't the sort of thing you saw every day round here. No one was paying him any attention. Holding his breath, Jess silently slipped around behind the lab. As soon as he was out of sight, he began to run, weaving in and out of the other containers. After a few hundred yards he paused to listen. There was shouting. He'd been missed – but they had no idea which way he'd gone.

He began to run again. He was away. He was almost free. And … he was going to live! To Jess, it was a wonderful thing to give your life for something you believed in.

He had been living with the idea of his death for so long, it felt almost wrong, as if he'd been cheated, to have it taken away. But today was the day – the one-week anniversary of Jimmy Earle's death, the big announcement in Albert Square. Perhaps, too, it was the day the government would resign. It had to happen. If he could be there when it did, he would not have lived in vain.

But what about Adam? Jess loved him – but he loved the cause even more. It was a shame. He'd have helped if he could, but today was booked. Today was the revolution. This was what he had sacrificed everything for – his friends, his family, his own life if need be. He couldn't let anything get in the way – not even his own brother.

He ran fast towards the perimeter fence.

☠

For a few seconds, Lizzie thought they were really going to let Christian tear her to pieces. But the big guys pulled him off and then a shorter, older man, obviously in charge, turned up and started roaring at everyone. But it was Christian he was most angry with. He grabbed him by the lapels and bawled at him, 'Is that right, you little shit? You've not been taking your meds, is that right? Is that right?'

'Lizzie!' cried Christian, in a tormented voice. 'How could you? How could you?' And bursting into tears, he began to cry like a child.

Ballantine let him go. That kind of answered his question. For a moment, everyone stood around watching in embarrassment; but Ballantine had reckoned without his son's cunning. Christian suddenly lashed out, pushing the older man back, and ran off at full speed.

'Catch him, you dicks!' yelled Ballantine. Some of the men shot after him in pursuit. His eye fell on Lizzie, cringing in the car, waiting to see what was going to happen next.

'What's going on?' he demanded.

Lizzie bent her head on to the steering wheel. *Out of the frying pan*, she thought. But she wasn't dead yet. She looked up and smiled at him as calmly as she could.

'If one of your men will untie me,' she said, 'I'll explain.'

Ballantine gestured to one of them to cut her loose. He stood watching, arms crossed, scowling. 'So where's Vince?'

'Last time I saw him he had a knife in the back of his neck,' said Lizzie.

Ballantine paused and looked closely at her. 'Are you having a laugh? Don't try and be funny with me,' he told her. But he didn't look so angry any more. 'Bring her to my box,' he told his men.

'Yes, sir,' one of them said, still fumbling at her bonds. A couple of the other guys dithered a moment, getting up courage to tell their boss that the chemist had done a runner. Sorry, sir, but …

You could hear the shouts of anger all the way to the railway line, half a mile away.

Ballantine's container, to Lizzie's amazement, was fitted out inside like a posh office suite. There was a staircase leading up to the container above, and for all she knew, another one going up even higher. It was like a house.

The older man sat down behind the desk and told one of his minions to fetch tea and biscuits. It made her start to giggle, and once she started, she couldn't stop. They all stood around and watched her being hysterical for about five minutes, until she finally got control of herself again. Then the older man asked her again what the fuck was going on.

Ballantine listened very carefully to her, nodding, urging her to take more biscuits and more tea — very polite, very calm. When she paused in the middle and needed a pee, he got one of his men to show her upstairs to the toilet, and she took the chance to wash her face and sort her hair out. They were treating her nicely. She wanted to look good. Mr Ballantine looked like the sort of person who didn't respond well to weakness.

He shook his head when she was done. 'What can I say?' he said. 'I apologise for my son's behaviour. I'm sorry that he's treated you so badly, and I'm devastated that he made you take Death. I wish I could make all of these things go away, but ...' He spread his hands, in a gesture of helplessness. 'What can I say?' he repeated. He looked around at his men. 'Box her up,' he said.

'Box her up?' repeated one of the men. 'Are you sure, Mr Ballantine?'

'Of course I'm sure. She knows Christian. She saw him murder Vince. She knows about this place. What do you want me to do, put her on the next plane to the Costa Brava? I apologise,' he told her again. 'Like I say, I wish I could make all this go away, but I can't.'

One of the men took her arm. She stood up shakily.

'Box me up?' she asked.

Mr Ballantine smiled, reassuringly. 'It's not as bad as it sounds. Not like being buried alive or anything. Just putting you away in a container for a while. Just to keep you safe.'

Lizzie shook the hand of the man off her elbow. 'Safe?' she said. 'For how long?'

''Bout a week.' Ballantine shrugged. 'Like I say …'

'But – what about the antidote?' she begged. 'Can't you do anything?' She ran out of words. If they wanted to make sure she never told anyone what she knew, they were hardly going to help her live longer, were they?

'If it's any consolation, which I don't suppose it is,' said Ballantine, getting up as if to see her out, 'there's no such thing as an antidote. Death binds itself to the brain in the first few hours. After that, you're dead meat. Everyone agrees about that. I wish I could offer a better way of spending your last few days, but that won't be possible either. Unless you want a quick way out? A bullet?' he offered.

'Mr Ballantine,' complained one of the men. 'She's so young.'

'Only fifteen,' said Lizzie. She thought maybe taking a couple of years off her age would help.

Ballantine shook his head irritably. 'What is it with you guys? You're happy to shoot your own grandmothers, but as soon as you come across a girl a few months underage, you start making puppy eyes at me. Tell you what,' he told her. 'Spend a little time in the box, have a think. If anyone can work out a better way of dealing with the problem,

I'll be happy to look at it. Meanwhile – box her up,' he told the heavies. 'Don't forget – that bullet's still on offer,' he added, as she was led out. He was still trying to be nice.

It was just a short walk to the place that was going to be her final home and prison. Inside, it was pitch black. No lights, nothing. She turned round and looked at the man accusingly.

'Sorry,' he said. He shrugged, embarrassed, and pushed her gently inside. He paused a moment. 'You've had some pretty bad luck,' he suggested.

'You reckon.'

'You want me to drop by later?' the man asked. 'Mr Ballantine is a gentleman, he won't let anyone molest you, but he might look favourably on a date.'

'A date?' she said, amazed. 'You're asking me for a *date*?'

The guy shrugged. 'Your last week and all that.'

Lizzie shook her head. 'The answer's no. I've got better things to do … like sitting in the dark crying. You know?'

The guy stiffened. 'Have it your own way,' he said, and shut the door on her.

Left on her own, she did as she said – sat in the dark and wept. She had been holding it together for so long, it had to come out somehow. She had nothing and no one to help her. The phone had been left behind in Christian's flat, Adam was probably dead, and even if he wasn't, would those two words she'd texted really be enough to lead him to her? But – she wasn't giving up. She had Death inside her, souping her up. She finished her tears and started to feel her way around the box. There was some rubbish scattered around – some bits of old furniture that someone had dumped for the prisoners to sit on, perhaps. A mattress, a table, an old armchair, a dusty leather sofa.

She stood very still for a moment, getting control of herself, then went back to the door and felt her way round it. It was locked tight, so she began to feel her way around the walls of the container, looking for some kind of a crack or opening, no matter how small, that she could use to her benefit. She was full of Death. She was strong. She'd survived so far. There had to be something in here that could help her escape. Somehow or other, she was going to do it. And when she had, she was going to fulfil her bucket list. There was only one item on it – killing as many of these bastards as she could. And boy, she was really looking forward to that.

CHAPTER 5

HIDE-AND-SEEK

Adam was on the M56, hammering it towards Manchester. The Porsche was a mess – bullet holes in the back, a couple of windows smashed in. If the police got to see it, he was going to get done. His driving was improving, but it still wasn't all that great. Other drivers were making as much space as they could between him and them as he went swaying past them at 120 mph in the fast lane. The sat nav kept nagging him to slow down, but it didn't stop telling him where to go.

He drove more calmly once he hit Manchester – no point asking for trouble. But when he arrived at his destination, his heart sank. It was an industrial wasteland – miles of it! The sat nav directed him to a set of gates in front of acres of parked-up lorry containers and told him to drive straight on. But the gates were locked.

He got out and climbed the fence to have a look.

To one side was what looked like an abandoned waste disposal site. He could see heavy machinery — lorries, bulldozers, tractors — rusting where it had been left. Beyond them, a huge warehouse crumbled in the damp weather. In front of him was the container storage area. It just went on for miles.

Lizzie was somewhere in there ... maybe. He had no chance searching on foot; it would take him for ever. He needed the sat nav, which seemed to be working on a map reference. Only one thing for it ...

Adam reversed the car to get a decent run at the gate. He hit it at sixty miles an hour, ducking as he struck — just as well, as it took the roof off as he went through. He smashed the remains of the glass from the buckled window so he could see properly, and shot off in among the boxes. He heard engines behind him and peered back. Two motorbikes had pulled out and were on his tail already. Damn it! He went faster, wobbling furiously from side to side.

Adam's car was fast, but the bikes were more manoeuvrable and he was losing ground. He had to get rid of them. He twisted ninety degrees, skidding violently, clipped a container, put his foot down flat and powered up along the long avenues in between the boxes. 'Turn left. Slow down. Turn round. Turn right,' ordered the sat nav. Then — 'You have reached your destination. You have passed your destination.' Adam looked desperately around. What had he passed? There was nothing there —

just yet more containers sitting blandly under the clouds. He twisted the car round another ninety-degree corner and headed back up, but a bike appeared ahead of him. He cursed, swerved round yet another corner, then another, then another, braked to a halt and jumped out. At least he could hide on foot. He just had time to get out of sight before the bikers turned up. Peering from behind a container, he watched them dismount and come to examine the Porsche.

While the men conferred, Adam tried the door to the box nearest him; locked. So was the next one, and the next. Chances were they were all locked. Behind him, out of sight, the bikes started off again. But where were they going? Adam paused, not sure which way to run. It was a nightmare place for a chase, with a million corners but nowhere to hide. He could run, he could look, he could dodge – but he could never get out of the endless avenues in between the boxes.

He began to jog away, back to where the sat nav had told him his destination lay.

If Adam could have flown a kilometre into the sky and taken a view of the park from above, he would have seen that it was far from empty. There were a number of people moving about in between the boxes, each hidden from the other, like rats in a maze.

Jess was there, zigzagging his way across to the northern perimeter fence where the waste disposal site was. Like his brother, Jess paused to hide away when the bikes came close, and started on again as soon as they drove off. In the distance he could just make out the bells of the town hall chiming the quarter-hour; quarter past twelve. He had forty-five minutes before the announcement.

He hurried on his way. He, Adam and Christian at that point were all no more than twenty metres apart, but none of them had any idea where the others were. Jess heard someone scuff their feet on the tarmac, and paused. Who was that? Friend or foe? He paused again and hid, listening carefully, trying to make out which way the feet were headed and who they belonged to.

Ballantine's men were out as well – some walking, some on motorbikes and quads hunting Jess, Christian and Adam. Their orders for the kid who had broken down the gate in Vince's car were shoot on sight. Jess they wanted alive; he was useful. And Christian, of course, had to be taken alive as well.

Christian himself was still there. When Lizzie had busted him, he had run to the edge of the container park to hide and weep. He'd thought they were in love, and she had betrayed him like a dog. His heart was broken. It would never heal. She was the same as all the rest.

Now, muttering to himself in a low monotone, he was creeping his way back into the heart of the container park towards the secure unit where his dad had no doubt locked Lizzie up. In his hand he cradled his knife – the short, stubby-bladed thing that had seen Vince away.

'See how she says no then,' he muttered to himself. 'See how she does as she's told, with this sweet baby stuck in her neck. See you soon, Lizzie.'

A motorbike roared nearby. Christian froze, but it shot

past the gap in between a pair of containers ahead of him and vanished without the rider seeing him. Christian grinned. He had killed Vince, he had run away from his dad. Nothing could stop him now. 'Soon, soon,' he crooned, and crept forward.

Adam rapidly began to despair of finding anything among all those containers. It was hopeless. He was sure he'd gone past the place where the car had told him his destination was – but he had no way of telling, since everything looked so much the same.

He heard it before he saw anything: a low, muttering voice. But from where? He froze, unable to work out where the speaker was. But then a figure crept out in front of him from in between the boxes, its back to him. It was a man; but Adam recognised him from the strange clothes he wore.

Adam's first instinct was – run. Get some distance between him and Christian, who was the scariest person he had ever met. But where Christian was, Lizzie must be nearby. He peered out again. Christian had already gone. Adam had no idea which way.

He ran lightly forward. There. To his right. A scuffing noise. Bending low, he inched forward again. At any point he was visible along half a mile of box edges. Which way had Christian gone?

He paused to listen. Whoever it was, they were close – very close. Just behind that corner there …

He peered around the edge of the box – then jerked his head back. Christian was less than three metres away. He'd changed. It wasn't just that his eyes had gone dark, or that his mouth was slack. His whole face seemed to have altered shape, as his madness deformed him from within. He was squatting on the ground, head bent low, talking to himself. Listening closely, Adam could just about make it out.

'Let me down. Betrayed me. No, no, no. She was scared, you idiot, that's all. Too scared. Not scared enough. Betrayed!' he groaned in a hollow voice. 'Ask her. Kill her. *Ask* her! Why should I, what excuse is there? She was scared, she was scared. And so am I.'

Christian panted and sobbed briefly. From his hiding place just around the corner, Adam could hear his feet on the gritty Tarmac and was just about to risk a brief peep, when Christian actually appeared, crossing directly in front of him. Adam froze, but Christian, focused on his murderous intention, did not look to either side, and moved straight on. Adam held his breath, waited until he was a box or so ahead, and then, as quietly as he could, stole out after him.

After another five minutes, Christian stopped outside one of the containers. To Adam it looked no different to any of the others but Christian bent down and pressed his ear against the side of it. After a moment he bared his teeth, punched his fist against the metal wall beside him and stood up. Adam darted back out of sight. Then, there was the creak of metal and he peered out again.

Christian was rattling at a padlock attached to the container doors. He fished a gun out of his pocket, and, glancing anxiously about, struck at the padlock with the gun handle. It did nothing. After a couple of tries, he gave up, held the gun the other way, took aim, and shot the lock off. He opened the door, and squinted into the darkness.

'Lizzie!' he called softly. 'Lizzie! You there, sweetheart?' He leaned round the doorway, lifted the gun up and took aim.

Adam screamed, 'No!'

Christian jumped in surprise and swung the gun round towards him. Instinctively, Adam jerked backwards, but that was no good – he had to act. With a yell, he flung himself forward, zigzagging as fast as he could towards his enemy. Christian had the gun on him, following him with the barrel, taking aim, ready to fire. But before he could, the door burst wide open and Lizzie ran out, wielding a lump of wood. She flung herself straight at Christian, and with a wild swing caught him on the side of the head. Yes! Christian staggered a few steps, but he wasn't down. Lizzie paused, blinded in the sudden light, unable to see. Christian took his chance, and swung the gun into her face.

'Lizzie!' screamed Adam. The gun connected, Lizzie went down and Christian had her in his grip in a moment – her kneeling down, him behind her, her hair in his hand, head pushed forward. In the other hand, held high up in the air, was the short, stubby-bladed knife. He turned to grin at Adam.

'Don't,' he sneered. 'Daddy, don't. She's been a naughty girl.'

Adam rushed forward, but as he did a figure stepped out from behind the container. Christian must have seen

Adam's eyes move, and he began to turn — too late. The man clouted him on the side of the head and Christian hit the floor like a block of stone.

It all happened in a moment. Adam ran forward to Lizzie. She knelt as Christian had left her, still dazed, holding the side of her head where the gun had caught her. Adam put his arms around her, and looked up at the man standing watching them. It was Jess.

CHAPTER 6

RUN FOR YOUR LIFE

Adam stared at his brother in disbelief, struggling to make sense of his presence; but he had someone even more important to him there. Lizzie had had a bad blow to the head but the drug she'd taken was working strongly in her, and she was already getting to her feet. Adam helped her.

'Got your message,' he said, proudly. Lizzie groaned and shook her head, still dazed from the blow. Adam looked over to Jess. 'You turned up in the nick of time,' he said.

Jess scowled at him and glanced at his watch. Like Adam, he'd heard Christian making his way back into the park, muttering about killing the girl, and had dithered about whether to follow him or not. He'd had no idea that he was about to save his stupid brother. Now, he felt weak with relief that he had. But he'd severely damaged his chances of getting to Albert Square in time for the announcement.

Even as Adam spoke, there was the growl of motors somewhere near. They'd been heard. In the echoing alleyways of the container park, Christian's gunfire was proving hard to locate, but it wouldn't be long before they were discovered.

'We have to go.' Jess peered down one of the long avenues to see if he could work out where their pursuers were, but Lizzie had recovered enough to get her wits back and she was more interested in Christian, who lay flat out before her on the floor. This was the man who had held her captive and in a state of terror for two days. This was the man who had forced her to swallow Death.

'Bastard!' she yelled suddenly, and stamped on his leg. 'Bastard! Bastard!'

Adam grabbed her – 'Shhh!'

'What for? He's bloody murdered me,' she hissed.

Adam turned to Jess. 'He made her take Death, too. We need to get the antidote,' he said.

Jess shook his head.

'Don't you care?' demanded Adam. 'I know there's an antidote. You must know something about it. Jess, we're going to die. You have to help us.'

There was shouting – already so near.

'Look, you've got it so wrong,' Jess said. 'You're going to live. I promise. But we have to run – right now!'

'But—'

'Now!'

Jess ran. They ran after him.

Around them, the bikes revved and skidded on the damp asphalt. Adam and Lizzie had no idea where they were going, but Jess did. He stopped running and opened a door in one of the containers – '*In here*'. They ran in and he slammed it shut behind them. At once, they were enclosed in darkness. Outside, a bike sped by, but it didn't stop. They held their breaths and listened, as the sound of the other bikes grew fainter. They were safe – for now. Until they wanted to move on.

'We'll be OK here,' said Jess. 'Most of the boxes are locked, but the Zealots got this one opened up for us in case we needed somewhere to hide. Ballantine and his men don't know anything about it.'

He sighed and slid down the wall to sit on the floor. He was going to miss it – after all that! Beside him Adam reached out to touch Lizzie's arm.

'You OK?'

'What do you think?' she snapped.

'I'm sorry …' he began.

But she had other things on her mind than sorry. 'So what's been going on? What about the antidote?' she demanded.

'A girl I met. She said she knew the Zealots. She—'

Jess cut in. 'She doesn't just know the Zealots – she's one of us. And she wasn't telling you the truth: there is no antidote.' He pulled himself back up to talk to them. 'But you're not going to die. The drug you took is fake. I know. I worked out how to make it.'

Fake Death? Adam stared at his shape in the darkness. 'But that's crazy. Why?'

'For life,' said Jess.

But Lizzie wasn't having it. 'Oh, fuck off talking in riddles,' she hissed. 'Just tell us what's going on. So we're OK? Is that right? We're going to live?'

'Yeah. You're going to live. If we get out of this alive, that is.'

'But it doesn't make any sense!' said Adam. 'I felt so great. I was stronger, quicker. Just like they said. How come?'

'Fake isn't quite the right word,' Jess said. 'Adapted. This version does a lot of the things that the original does, but I found a way of stopping it binding to the brain. You get a come-down – a long come-down. You're both going to get pretty sick. But it won't kill you.' Jess smiled wryly. 'I could have been rich. It's going to be a pretty popular drug when people realise what's going on.'

Lizzie couldn't believe her ears. She had been through all this – for what? 'Are you telling me it was all some sort of stupid trick?'

'No! More than that. Have you any idea how many people have taken Ballantine's cheap Death since Jimmy Earle died? Tens of thousands. Over three thousand took it that first night. Imagine all those people out there right now, believing they're going to die. Believing they have no future. In the past week, nearly all of them will have found out the same thing – the thing you've found out,

Adam: that life is actually the only thing worth having. They don't want to die at all. They want to live and it's the one thing they can't have.' Jess laughed. 'And we're going to give it back to them. In spades.'

They could hear the excitement in Jess's voice. But Lizzie was outraged.

'So it was a lie,' she said. 'The whole thing, one big lie.'

'A good lie!' insisted Jess. 'You've seen what's happening out there on the streets. Things are changing – and this drug sparked it all off. It's shown people how much life means to them. It's shown them it's worth fighting for. People are taking a stand. Isn't that worth a lie, no matter how big? At one o'clock there'll be a Zealot announcement about it in Albert Square: "You're going to live." Can you imagine how people are going to feel? The hope? The world's been changing around them. Suddenly, they'll be a part of it again. Just like you two.' In the darkness, he tried to embrace them. 'It's life,' he said. 'You've got it back. The future is yours to take …'

Lizzie pushed him away. 'You took our lives away and now you're going to give them back? Great. Playing God. You are so arrogant. God help whatever revolution people like you are planning.'

'We didn't *plan* it. We never dreamed it would turn into this. We just lit the fuse. And it's not just us any more. There are all sorts of people getting into this now. Different rebel groups, the unions, political parties. Everyone's involved.' Jess moved to the door to peer out of the cracks. 'I want to be a part of it. You can join me, if you like …'

Adam was listening to Jess's confession in a trance. So the whole thing, his whole week, had been nothing but an illusion. The despair, the pain, the rage, the love, the fear – all for nothing. The raw emotions he'd been through – the emotions so many people had been through – had all been just to help the Zealots make a political point.

But what a point …

'What about the antidote?' he said. 'That girl …'

'Her real name is Anna,' said Jess. 'She worked here with me, but she got out. I asked her to see if she could find you.'

He looked at his watch. Half past twelve. He needed to be in Albert Square in half an hour. He was wasting time!

'But … why did she tell me to stay in the hotel?'

'People on Death take risks. A lot of people don't make it through the week. We were hoping that if you thought there was an antidote, you might keep yourself safe.'

'You didn't think of just telling him, then?' said Lizzie.

'No,' snapped Jess. 'We couldn't jeopardise the whole plan by letting that information out too soon. It could have ruined everything.'

'All that pain. All those people. You sick bunch of bastards,' Lizzie hissed. 'And what about the people who did die? Good job you won't have to explain yourself to them, isn't it?'

'There are always casualties in a war. I was prepared to die, too. I still am.'

'So you taught them a lesson. Bravo!'

She clapped, the noise echoing hollowly in the little chamber.

'We made a revolution,' said Jess.

'You don't believe that,' said Lizzie. 'If that's what it is, it was coming anyway.'

As Jess and Lizzie argued over his head, Adam sank down to the floor, overwhelmed by the whole thing. It was fake. It had been fake all along – but it meant he was going to live. Lizzie was going to live. A moment ago he had nothing. Now, he had it all.

Trees, he thought. *And ... Chocolate. And fresh air and cars. Apples and pears. Music. Jokes. Falling in love –* like his mum had said. *The whole damn adventure.*

'Being in love,' he said out loud.

'What?' said Lizzie.

'We're going to live. We get it all back. Everything! Cream cakes and summer days and new clothes, and ... Sunday dinners, and fish and chips. The lot!'

In the dark, Lizzie pulled a face. Adam carried on. 'Growing up and growing old and having kids and getting a mortgage, and getting your heart broken and scraping your knees, and bacon sarnies, and being bored and ...'

'Being a dick,' she said. 'And dragging people down with you and ... nearly getting them fucking killed!' she yelled.

'Yeah, my brother's a dick,' said Jess. 'And maybe I am, too. But you know what, Lizzie? He thought he had the antidote, but he came to find you anyway. He really does love you.'

In the darkness, Lizzie could just about make out Adam's shape. It was true; he really did love her. But after everything that had happened, she wasn't even sure how much she wanted it any more.

'Sometimes, Adam … you know what?' she said. 'What if love isn't enough?'

Adam just looked at her, dumbfounded, as if he'd never even considered it.

'There will be love,' said Jess. 'And looking after Mum and Dad. And working hard. And getting up on freezing cold mornings, and worrying.'

'Yeah. All that,' said Adam. He was sore, he felt sick – the comedown from Death was taking hold. But he was going to live. Nothing else mattered. He stood up and shouted out loud for sheer joy.

Jess smiled. Adam was going to be OK. He was pleased about that. But now he was in a hurry to get on.

'I have to go,' he said. 'You want to join me? Come on! Don't you want to be in Albert Square when they make that announcement? Or are you going to play it safe and wait until it gets dark?'

Adam looked at Lizzie. She shook her head angrily.

'Come on, Lizzie,' he said. 'You were talking about the demos. You wanted to take part.'

'Forget the past,' said Jess. 'It's over. This is the future, and it's happening right on our doorstep.'

Lizzie hesitated. She was furious with Jess, angry with Adam – but it was true. She wanted to be a part of the future as well.

'We haven't heard the bikes for ages. I reckon they've got Christian and packed it in,' Jess said.

Lizzie groaned. 'OK,' she said. 'But not for you, Adam.

It's because I'm not going to miss out just to make a point to you two twats. Understand?'

Adam leaped up to grab her, and she let him. Love, eh? Maybe. Maybe not.

'What are we waiting for?' she said. 'Let's go.'

CHAPTER 7

WASTE DISPOSAL

They headed off, pausing, peering round each container, running on. There was no trace or sound of the bikes or cars. Maybe, their luck was in. Within minutes they had arrived at a line of containers at right angles to the usual rows. They walked around them and there they were, face to face with the perimeter fence. On the other side was the waste disposal site, with old machinery rusting on collapsed tyres and the huge, open-fronted warehouse Adam had seen when he first arrived.

One look sideways and they stepped back. This was dangerous. A long line of boxes ran parallel to the fence right to the far ends of the park. The fence was high, about ten feet – climbable enough, but as soon as they stepped out they would be in full view for half a kilometre in either direction.

The question: who else was watching the fence?

The answer: Christian was.

After he had been brained by Jess, he'd woken up with a vile headache and an even viler temper. His beautiful looks had been ruined. Worse, so had his beautiful brain. He knew this by the fact that he was in a permanent rage, and because he was able to remember barely anything of what had been happening recently. Only one thing remained in his mind: betrayal.

Lizzie. That bitch! She'd told him that she loved him then given him up to his dad and now, to cap it all, she'd run off with another boy. They were all in it together. They all had to die.

He had no doubt he would get to kill his enemies. He had right and justice and a gun and loads of ammunition on his side. He guessed that they'd try to get out by the old waste disposal site – it was the quickest way out, and not bounded by either canals, or private sites like most of the other perimeters. He made his way there and settled himself down, tucked away among the line of boxes by the fence to wait. It wasn't long – there! Just a flash, a brief glimpse as they popped out to look at the fence. They dived back in fast enough, but it was them all right, only a couple of hundred metres away.

Now he was going to end it. They were going to run for the fence, and when they did, he'd be waiting for them with his gun and his knife.

Creeping down, low to the earth, Christian began to weave his way through the boxes closer to where they were hiding, to give himself a better shot.

'We'll get them, precious,' he said to himself; and giggling at his own joke, wriggled his way forward.

☠

'Over there,' whispered Jess.

'What?'

'A hole. See? The wire's torn.'

They peeped out. There was a hole in the fence about twenty metres further up from them – just big enough for a single person to squeeze through.

Still dangerous. But quicker than climbing.

'When I say go, we go together,' said Jess. 'On the other side, run for the warehouse – that's our best chance to hide if we need to.'

'OK,' Adam said. Lizzie nodded.

'Go!' yelled Jess.

They dashed out. Almost at once a gunshot rang out. Christian wasn't as close as he'd hoped – ten containers away. He should have kept quiet but the sight of Lizzie was too much for him. In a blind rage he rushed out towards them. 'Bitch! Betrayer!' he howled. He fired off more shots, but nothing hit – they were out of range. But not for long.

There was an awful moment while they struggled, one at a time, through the hole in the fence with Christian powering towards them. Then they were through and running in between the decrepit bulldozers, diggers and lorries, slipping on the wet ground underfoot.

'I'm coming!' screamed Christian. He had already reached the hole in the wire and was squeezing his way through, less than fifty metres behind them.

'The warehouse,' gasped Jess.

They rounded a heap of bleeding paint tins, in under the roof of the warehouse and straight into an enormous rusting heap of metal. The building had been used to store old white goods – fridges and freezers, mainly, sent here to be recycled long ago. The recession had come and rendered them valueless, so here they remained, a mountain of abandoned metal carcasses, towering above them up to the roof. Jess had hoped they could slip away through another exit, but the only other way out had been blocked by a landside of rusting appliances years ago. There was only one way in or out – and Christian was coming through it right now.

'The roof – we can get out up there,' gasped Jess. They had no choice but to climb. Christian, yelling behind them, paused to try a shot, but he was still too far off. He cursed and ran forward. He was in the shed with them before they had made it more than a few metres up the mountain of scrap.

Adam clawed his way up, but the cost of the adapted Death leaving his system was catching up with him. He felt nauseous and weak. The metal carcasses were often precariously balanced on top of each other and to make matters worse, not all of them been emptied before they had been thrown away. As they climbed, fridge and freezer doors swung open like stinking mouths, dribbling black slime, all that remained of food that had been rotting inside for years. The stink was overpowering. It got on their hands, on their feet, on their faces. But they couldn't stop. Another bullet whistled past. Christian was at the bottom of the mountain now. He stuck his gun into his waistband and began to climb after them.

'Bitch, I'm going to kill you, bitch! I'm gonna C4 you all …' His voice choked as he breathed in some vileness, but his madness had given him an inhuman strength and recklessness, and he didn't stop. Even now, clawing his way over the fridges and freezers, he was gaining on them.

It was a horrible effort. Their feet plunged suddenly into cavities, or slipped on a slimy surface. Underfoot, the rusting units tipped dangerously. It had to happen – an accident. As he pushed forward, Jess slipped; his foot jammed in a gap, caught tight in between two heavy units. He tugged – it refused to move. In a panic he tugged again and pulled it out – but badly wrenched. As soon as he tried to put some weight on it, it gave way under him.

Below him, Christian saw and grinned. 'C4,' he hissed excitedly, and then bawled up at them, an incomprehensible cawing of rage and madness that no one could make out. Jess lunged forward, desperate to escape, but he slipped and fell back down several metres. Christian screamed in triumph; Adam and Lizzie turned back to help.

'Go. Go!' Jess demanded. But Adam shook his head. He and Lizzie tried to pull Jess up after them, but as they did the area they were standing on rocked and shifted downwards. They were balanced on the side of a huge industrial chilling unit, some kind of ancient meat refrigerator, one of a cluster of several towering over them like small cliffs. The whole lot was highly unstable, tipping under their weight, shifting down.

'Get off this thing – maybe we can push it down,' said Adam. The three of them slid off the corner of the big unit, got down behind it, and pushed. The mass of metal moved a few inches – then ground to a halt.

'Together,' hissed Jess. They heaved again. Nothing moved. The unit had jammed.

'I'm gonna have you, you little fucks!' bawled Christian. He was no more than ten metres away, clawing, shoving and heaving his way towards them. They were hidden behind the unit, but he'd be on them in moments.

'Again!' said Adam. 'One … two … three … push!'

Together they heaved. The huge unit shifted, moved down, slid sideways slightly – and at last began to go. One more push and it was on its way, picking up speed, sliding down, twisting as it went, dislodging and crushing everything in its way, straight towards Christian. For a second it looked as if it was going to jam – but then the units under it crumpled and it shot forward. Christian leaped desperately to one side, but the unit was just too big to avoid and it passssed straight over him. For a second or two afterwards they could see him, looking curiously flattened and smeared into the metal beneath him. One of his arms twitched then the whole thing went – an avalanche of fridges. A great mass of them toppled down on top of him, with a grinding, crunching noise, like a metal river passing over a tin mountain. Distantly, caught up in the noise, they heard a scream, cut suddenly off.

The avalanche slowed, petered out, and stopped. Lizzie

stared down at the place where he had disappeared. It was over, wasn't it? Finally. Christian was dead.

She turned to look at Adam. 'Yeah?' she said.

'Yeah,' said Adam.

She grinned. 'He was on my bucket list, too,' she said. She whooped. 'Hey! High five!' They slapped hands.

'Sorry to break things up, guys – but it's not over till we're safely out of here,' said Jess. 'Ballantine and his men must have heard that racket. We just killed his only son.' He nodded to the top of the mountain. 'It's safer to go up, I reckon. There's ladders on the roof.' He glanced at his watch. Quarter to one. He still had time …

They began to climb the final leg.

☠

The heap of fridges and freezers was unstable now, and it was hard to see what they were doing in the deep shadows right up by the roof. But they made it OK. After that it was just a short walk across to the ladders at the back of the building. They were halfway there when a group of men appeared on the roof.

There was no chance of escape. They were fifty feet off the ground – it was certain death to jump. There were six or seven men waiting for them, all armed. One of them was Florence Ballantine himself.

Jess sank down, sat on the roof and hung his head. They had been so close – so close!

'Yeah, innit?' said Ballantine. 'Thought you'd got away with it. Fake Death.' He shook his head. 'Oh, yeah – I know. A couple of our, eh, *experiments* should have died a few hours ago. Wasn't difficult to work out after that.' He shook his head and wagged his finger at Jess. 'Clever boy. And look! I'm not even angry. Why would I be? This drug is going to be a whole lot more popular than the real stuff. You get a great week – and then you live! What's wrong with that? And it gets better! Despite your bad manners trying to run out on me, I still want to work with you. Son, you and me are going into business, only this time, you *are* going to show me how to make it myself, regardless of what your Zealot bosses say. Then – maybe I'll let you go. Maybe I'll let your brother go. Who knows?'

He smiled broadly.

'And as for you two,' he went on to Adam and Lizzie, 'only one question. Christian's around here somewhere – we know he came in after you. So. Please. Where's my son? Don't tell me you've done anything bad to him because if you have, that's going to make me very angry indeed.'

Lizzie licked her lips. 'He was chasing us,' she said.

'Yeah.'

'He was on the fridges last we saw of him,' began Adam. But Ballantine wasn't interested.

'What I'm thinking is,' he said, 'who to do over? I need the boy to put pressure on Jessie here. I guess that means – Lizzie, isn't it? Sorry, love. You're looking very expendable to me.' He spread his arms. 'So who's going to talk first? Before I start snipping the young lady's fingers off one by one. Or perhaps the boys here would like a go at her first. Hmm?'

No one spoke.

'I will find out,' said Ballantine. 'And you know that. So I'm going to ask you one more time: where's ... my ... son? Come on. No one got anything to say?'

'I have.'

Ballantine spun round. The voice, a female one, was coming from behind him. The slight figure of a young woman was standing at the edge of the roof by one of the ladders.

It was Anna.

'You! Stupid enough to run and then come back. So now I got the full set. You guys got her covered?'

'She's covered, boss.'

Anna smiled. 'Mr Ballantine,' she said. 'I know how to make this stuff, too. I'll show you – if you pay me.'

'And what makes you think I need to pay anyone?'

'It's easier this way. But I don't expect you to take my word. I have the formulae and the chemical route to it right here – minus a line or two, of course. That'll be put back in once I get my money. Here ...' Slowly, she lowered a hand towards her coat pocket and began to advance towards him.

'Stay where you are!' shouted one of the heavies.

Ballantine held up a hand. 'OK, let's have a look. Take it out,' he told her. 'But move very, very slowly. Understand?'

'I understand.'

Carefully, she put her hand in her pocket and took out a notebook. 'It's all here. All you'll have to do is follow the numbers.'

The gangster nodded. With her arms up, Anna advanced slowly towards him and handed him the book.

Ballantine flicked through it.

'I'm going to bleed a chemist to check this out,' he said.

'Then why don't we go and get one?'

He paused, then nodded. 'It's not going to do any harm checking it out. First things first, though. You two,' he said, turning again to Adam and Lizzie, 'this might – might – just let your brother off the hook. But – I still need to know where my son is.'

Over beyond the waste disposal site and the container park, there came a roar from the city. The speeches had begun in Albert Square. Even though the distance turned it into a dull murmur, you could tell it was a noise formed in a million throats.

Anna smiled. 'Listen!' she said. The gangster paused and cocked his head, and as he did she suddenly launched herself at him, seizing him around the neck.

'Run!' she yelled. Ballantine swatted out at her, catching her in the face, but she had a grip on his neck and was holding tight. Adam, Jess and Lizzie turned and fled. One of the men turned to give chase, but Ballantine was screaming at them to get the girl off him, and they all turned to help. She disappeared in a mass of bodies. It gave Adam and the others enough time to cross the short distance to the ladder, and begin to climb down one at a time.

'She's wired!' someone screamed. Adam, last down, paused to see what was going on. The heavies had fallen back, Anna had been pulled away from Ballantine and was on the floor. The gangster and his men were beginning to run, but it was too late. Anna got to her feet in an almost leisurely movement and opened her coat wide, to show off the odd-looking packets tied to her body. Adam saw her stand there for a moment longer, the little control box in her hand, her coat spread, head up, proud like the soldier she was. Then, she exploded.

There was a flash of blinding light ripping open the night and a dull boom. Adam ducked down below the wall and clung on to the ladder for dear life as the blast ripped across the roof towards him. Shards of blazing roofing plastic rushed over his head and high into the air, caught in a wind of burning dust and fire. But it wasn't a huge explosion; it didn't need to be. On the other side of the wall, the roof crumpled; Ballantine and his men fell down, down into the space beneath. Their bodies flamed and twisted as they descended, until the dust thickened over them and they disappeared for ever.

Anna had been given her target. The last thing the Zealots wanted was a gang like this working against them so close to the city. One of the first things they planned was to cut down on organised crime. The clean-up had begun.

The blast died down. Adam put up his head to see what was left. Most of the roof was gone. High above him, pieces of it were still falling, some still ablaze. A cloud of dust and ash was boiling in front of him but it was already settling, and through it he could see the city beyond.

'Adam! Are you OK? What happened?' Adam looked down to Lizzie's shocked face. Hidden below the wall, she hadn't seen a thing. He shook his head, unable to speak.

Jess hadn't seen, either, but he could guess.

'Anna?' he asked.

'She had explosives. She … just …'

Jess rested his head briefly on the rungs of the ladder, then looked back up. 'Move over,' he said.

Adam edged carefully on to the wall while Jess and Lizzie made their way up.

'Suicide bomb,' Adam said, in answer to Lizzie's horrified look.

'She blew herself up? My God, that's terrible!'

'She saved out lives,' Adam said. But why? he thought. She'd smiled as she did it. He could see her face now, gazing at him serenely in the moment before she detonated. He remembered her in the hotel room a few days ago. She had loved life, he had no doubt about it – and yet it seemed as if she wanted this. How was it possible that you could choose to die, while you still loved life?

'You don't understand,' said Jess. 'It's what she wanted.' He looked down in the smoking cauldron of dust below them, where the wreckage was still settling. The mountain of old appliances was moving again under the weight of the debris that had fallen on top of it and a new cloud of dust rose slowly below them. 'She was a soldier. She didn't do it just for us; she died as a Zealot, for something she believed in. Ballantine was her target. What she's done is noble. I'm not sure she even saw it as a sacrifice.'

'Noble?' demanded Lizzie. 'She can't know what she's done. She's lost everything …'

Jess was looking down with a tender expression into the open warehouse where his friend had died. He seemed almost pleased for her.

'Do you envy her?' Adam asked him.

Jess turned to look at him. The question obviously took him by surprise. What Anna had done was something he had believed for a long time was going to be his fate. There had been a time when he wanted it more than anything else in the world.

'No,' he said at last. 'I wish I did. But I don't.' He looked back down. 'God bless, Anna,' he said. 'You got 'em right on the nose.'

Across the other side of the container park, the town hall clock struck one.

Adam looked at Jess, stricken. 'You're not there,' he said.

'You know what?' said Jess. He pointed across the park. 'Grandstand view, isn't it?' Adam followed his gaze. The smoke from the explosion was blowing away in the wind and Manchester lay spread out before them. There was the Hilton tower, poking up above the city. There were the tower blocks, the shops, the cathedral, the town hall. It was a beautiful sight. Everything went very quiet.

'The announcement,' said Jess. 'They'll be making it right now.'

'I'm sorry you missed it,' said Adam. Now that they were all safe, he felt dreadful. They had survived – but beautiful, kind Anna was dead, and he had been through a week more intense than anything he could ever have imagined. What had it all been for?

'I haven't missed anything,' said Jess. 'I'm alive. I'm up here with my brother, and I can see the whole thing. Look at it! No one else is going to have a view like this.' He waved his hand again. 'It's the future. And you know what? For the first time, Adam, it's ours.'

But Adam was inconsolable. Lizzie took him in her arms. 'What is it, Ads?' she said.

'I made such a mess,' he wept. 'I ruined everything. I nearly killed you and Jess. I owe both of you my life.' He looked up at them. 'What shall I do?' he demanded. 'Tell me what to do with my life, and I'll do it.'

Jess shook his head. 'Just live it.'

'Yeah,' said Lizzie. 'Enjoy!' She paused. 'Listen! There it is.'

Across the container park, a great roar went up, louder than ever, as several thousand people realised they were going to live and that the future was theirs for the making. High up on the warehouse wall, Adam, Lizzie and Jess got to their feet and made their way down to join them.

ACKNOWLEDGEMENTS

The first I heard of this book was in a phone call from Barry Cunningham, boss of the Chicken House, with an unlikely story involving A-level philosophy students, their tutors, and an idea about a recreational drug that killed you in a week.

'And I thought – now, who do I know who doesn't mind working differently?' Barry said.

Intriguing ...

The Hit is an unusual book in that it has so many parents. It wasn't my idea in the first place. Some of the settings – in particular the container park – and most of the characters all started somewhere else. In some cases only the names are left and I hope I've made it my own, but it's a matter of fact that this book would never have been written if it hadn't been for other people besides myself. I feel like a sort of foster parent to it. Without a number of folk and their generosity in handing the baby over, I would never have had the pleasure of this story, these characters, or the fascinating experience of bringing someone else's baby into the world.

So more than the usual special thanks then, first of all to Brandon Robshaw and Joe Chislett, for coming up with the brilliant idea of using a thriller to touch on the big issues, as well as for so many of the settings and characters, and especially for the basic idea of a drug that kills you in a week and the wonderful response – how would you spend that week? Thanks are also due to their students for helping those ideas along.

Having a good idea is great, of course, but the other side of the coin is recognising it. Most of us in the course of our lives no doubt have countless ideas that would make good books, films and TV shows, but without the gift to work out which are good and which are bad ideas, you're no better off than if you never did. You need to be able to sort the seed from the fluff. So big thanks to Barry Cunningham for picking this idea out of many others, and then picking me out of many authors. Putting the right idea in the (hopefully) right hands is a rare skill, and I'm delighted to be on the receiving end.

Thanks as well to my editor Rachel Leyshon, for showing such great patience and making so many useful suggestions – a pleasure to work with.

And to Banksy for the Zealot logo inspiration, and everyone who worked on the book, cover, blurb, PR, the lot – thanks!

Melvin Burgess
January 2013

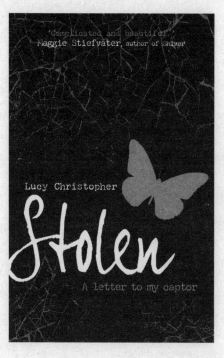

Human Kinetics

247 588

Library of Congress Cataloging-in-Publication Data

Kirkendall, Donald T.
  Soccer anatomy / Donald T. Kirkendall.
    p. cm.
  ISBN-13: 978-0-7360-9569-3 (soft cover)
  ISBN-10: 0-7360-9569-1 (soft cover)
  1. Soccer--Training. 2. Soccer--Physiological aspects. I. Title.
  GV943.9.T7K57 2011
  796.334--dc22
                            2011011402

ISBN-10: 0-7360-9569-1 (print)
ISBN-13: 978-0-7360-9569-3 (print)

This publication is written and published to provide accurate and authoritative information relevant to the subject matter presented. It is published and sold with the understanding that the author and publisher are not engaged in rendering legal, medical, or other professional services by reason of their authorship or publication of this work. If medical or other expert assistance is required, the services of a competent professional person should be sought.

The web addresses cited in this text were current as of May 2011 unless otherwise noted.

Acquisitions Editor: Tom Heine; **Developmental Editor:** Cynthia McEntire; **Assistant Editors:** Laura Podeschi, Claire Gilbert; **Copyeditor:** Patricia MacDonald; **Graphic Designer:** Fred Starbird; **Graphic Artist:** Tara Welsch; **Cover Designer:** Keith Blomberg; **Photographer (for soccer illustration references):** Tony Quinn; **Photographer (for exercise illustration references):** Peter Mueller; **Visual Production Assistant:** Joyce Brumfield; **Art Manager:** Kelly Hendren; **Illustration (cover):** Jen Gibas; **Illustrations (interior):** Precision Graphics; **Printer:** Premier Print Group

Human Kinetics books are available at special discounts for bulk purchase. Special editions or book excerpts can also be created to specification. For details, contact the Special Sales Manager at Human Kinetics.

Printed in the United States of America   10 9 8 7 6 5 4 3 2 1

Human Kinetics
website: www.HumanKinetics.com

United States: Human Kinetics
P.O. Box 5076
Champaign, IL 61825-5076
800-747-4457
e-mail: humank@hkusa.com

Canada: Human Kinetics
475 Devonshire Road Unit 100
Windsor, ON N8Y 2L5
800-465-7301 (in Canada only)
e-mail: info@hkcanada.com

Europe: Human Kinetics
107 Bradford Road
Stanningley
Leeds LS28 6AT, United Kingdom
+44 (0) 113 255 5665
e-mail: hk@hkeurope.com

Australia: Human Kinetics
57A Price Avenue
Lower Mitcham, South Australia 5062
08 8372 0999
e-mail: info@hkaustralia.com

New Zealand: Human Kinetics
P.O. Box 80
Torrens Park, South Australia 5062
0800 222 062
e-mail: info@hknewzealand.com

E5190

CONTENTS

PREFACE

Pele called it "the beautiful game." The simplicity of his comment about soccer has resonated among fans of the game for decades. The beauty of soccer begins with skill. Beautiful soccer means controlling an impossible ball, such as Dennis Bergkamp's 89th-minute goal in the 1998 FIFA World Cup or Maxi Rodriguez's chest-to-volley strike from the upper corner of the penalty area at the 2006 FIFA World Cup. Soccer's beauty is in the perfectly paced seeing-eye pass threaded through the smallest opening in the defense, which you will see anytime Kaka (Brazil) or Xavi (Spain) is playing. Or a solo dribbling run through the defense such as Diego Maradona's 1v7 run against England in the 1986 FIFA World Cup. Or the long-range cannon shot by Paul Breitner at the 1974 FIFA World Cup.

Then there is tactical brilliance. How about the 25-pass sequence to a goal by Argentina against Serbia in the 2006 FIFA World Cup, or the lightning-fast length-of-the-field counterattack for a goal by the United States against Brazil in the 2009 FIFA Confederations Cup final? Brazil's fourth goal against Italy in the 1970 World Cup is still considered a masterful display of teamwork, skill, and guile.

The objective of soccer is the same as in any other team sport: Score more than the opponent. This simple philosophy is enormously complicated. To be successful, a team must be able to present a physical, technical, tactical, and psychological display that is superior to the opponent's. When these elements work in concert, soccer is indeed a beautiful game. But when one aspect is not in sync with the rest, a team can be masterful and still lose. The British say, "They played well and died in beauty."

Soccer, like baseball, has suffered under some historical inertia: "We've never done that before and won. Why change?" or "I never did that stuff when I played." That attitude is doomed to limit the development of teams and players as the physical and tactical demands of the game advance.

And oh how the game has advanced. For example, the first reports on running distance during a match noted English professionals of the mid 1970s (Everton FC) averaged about 8,500 meters (5.5 miles). Today, most distances average between 10,000 and 14,000 meters (6 and 8.5 miles). There are reports that females, with their smaller hearts, lower hemoglobin levels, and smaller muscle mass, can cover the 6 miles attributed to men. The distance and number of runs at high speed have also increased as the pace of the game has become more ballistic and powerful. To those of us who have followed the game over the years, the pros sure do seem to strike the ball a lot harder now.

But the benefits of soccer extend beyond the competitive game. Emerging evidence shows that regular participation in soccer by adults is as effective as traditional aerobic exercise such as jogging for general health and for treating certain chronic conditions. For example, people with hypertension can see reductions in blood pressure similar to that seen in joggers. Blood fats can be reduced. Increased insulin sensitivity means those with type 2 diabetes and metabolic syndrome should see benefits. Regular soccer helps people, youths or adults, who are attempting to lose weight. A host of benefits are possible, all from playing an enjoyable game. An interesting sidenote is that when those studies were concluded, a lot of joggers just quit, but soccer players looked at each other and said, "Great. Can we go play now?"

The game is not as embedded in American culture as it is in other countries. Around the world, families, neighbors, and friends play the game whenever they can. In the United States, this neverending exposure to soccer is not as evident, so upon joining a team, an American child does not possess the beginnings of a skill set obtained from free play with family and friends. The coach may well be the child's only exposure to the game, requiring almost all coaching to be focused on the ball, which may neglect some basic motor skills and supplementary aspects of fitness.

In particular, the soccer community—and not just in the United States—has viewed supplemental strength training with skepticism. In addition, soccer players tend to view any running that is longer than the length of a field as unnecessary, and they avoid training that does not involve the ball. But give them a ball and they will run all day. The problem is many coaches apply the principle of specificity of training too literally ("if you want to be a better soccer player, play soccer") and end up denying players training benefits that are proven to improve physical performance and prevent injury.

This book is about supplemental strength training for soccer. When developed properly, increased strength will allow players to run faster, resist challenges, be stronger in the tackle, jump higher, avoid fatigue, and prevent injury. Most soccer players have a negative attitude toward strength training because it is done in a weight room and does not involve the ball. These attitudes were taken into consideration when the exercises in this book were selected. Many can be done on the field during routine training, and some involve the ball.

When a player or coach does favor some strength training, the primary focus is usually the legs. But as any strength and conditioning specialist will tell you, a balance must be struck up and down the body because the body is a link of segments, chains if you will, and the most prepared player will have addressed each link of the chain, not just an isolated link or two. Furthermore, those same specialists will say that while one group of muscles may be important within a sport, to address that group alone and neglect the opposite group of muscles will result in an imbalance around that movement or joint. Imbalances are known to raise the risk of injury. It has been known for years that strong quadriceps and weak hamstrings increase the risk of knee injury, but it is also known that athletes with a history of hamstring injury not only have weak hamstrings but also have poor function in the gluteal muscles. Weak hamstrings are also implicated in low back issues.

Many readers will review these exercises and select those that address specific weaknesses. The exercises in *Soccer Anatomy* are good choices to supplement traditional soccer training, but the concepts continue to evolve. These exercises are a good place to begin. With a regular program that uses systematic progression, players will improve aspects of fitness important for competitive play—aspects not addressed in traditional ball-oriented training. Players who want to keep playing and stay healthy with as few injuries as possible need to include some strength training. Players who neglect the strength element of training but want to move up to the next level will be in for a shock when they discover how far behind they are and realize just how much catching up is necessary. Should these exercises be considered the definitive list? Of course they shouldn't. Will conditioning professionals offer alternatives? Of course they will. But this is a good starting point with options for the coach and player.

The unique aspect of *Soccer Anatomy* isn't the supplemental exercises, as many other resources can provide suggestions. *Soccer Anatomy* takes you inside each exercise to show you which muscles are involved and how they contribute to proper execution of the exercise and to success on the field. The anatomical illustrations that accompany the exercises are color coded to indicate the primary and secondary muscles featured in each exercise and movement.

 Primary muscles   Secondary muscles

Use this information to improve your skill, build your strength and endurance, and stay on the pitch. Choose exercises that are appropriate for your age, gender, experience, and training goals. Even young athletes can benefit from resistance training. In preadolescent athletes, strength improvements come mostly from increasing training volume by adding repetitions and sets while using modest resistance (e.g., two or three sets of 12 to 15 repetitions on two or three nonconsecutive days per week). Excellent exercise choices for preadolescents are those that use body weight for resistance.

Resistance training, like any physical training, has inherent risks. As athletes mature, they are better able to process, follow, and adhere to directions that minimize injury risk. In general, when an external resistance such as a barbell or dumbbell is lifted, the set is performed to muscle failure. Exercises that use body weight as resistance usually have a set number of repetitions as a goal, although sometimes muscle failure occurs before the goal is reached. Depending on the training goal, the load must be individualized and age appropriate. Once you can perform the desired repetitions in a set without reaching muscle failure, increase the resistance by 5 to 10 percent.

Training goals will influence the workout program. Improving local muscle endurance requires high volume (sets of 20 to 25 repetitions) and low intensity. Hypertrophy training acts as the entry point to higher-quality training and requires 10 to 20 repetitions per set and low to moderate intensity. In basic strength training, the intensity is high (80 to 90 percent of capacity), but the volume is low (2 to 5 repetitions per set). Power training, which usually includes explosive movements, requires a higher intensity (90 to 95 percent of capacity) and a low volume (2 to 5 repetitions per set). In general, soccer players should focus on higher-volume exercises of low to moderate intensity, performed twice a week during the season with a focus on maintenance. Save strength and power gains for the off-season.

Safety is key when working out in a weight room. Always work with a spotter. Use safety collars on weights. Lift with your legs, not your back, when picking up weight plates. Drink fluids regularly, and use correct posture and form. Dress properly, and be careful not to drop weights. Consider keeping a workout journal to track your progress. Listen to your body, and don't work through joint pain or unusual muscle pain. See a physician who specializes in sports medicine. If you want to recruit help in the weight room, consult a certified strength and conditioning specialist (CSCS certification) or certified personal trainer (CPT certification).

CHAPTER 1

THE SOCCER PLAYER IN MOTION

Unlike individual sports such as golf, dance, swimming, cycling, and running in which the individual athlete largely dictates her own performance, soccer is a team sport. A team sport adds the dimensions of direct opponents, teammates, a ball, and rules regarding fouls and conduct that are applied during a constantly changing environment of individual, small group, and large group offensive and defensive tactics. A team sport such as soccer requires a range of complexity and intensity and physical and mental preparation beyond what is seen in many individual sports.

Preparation for competition in a team sport involves skill acquisition, tactical development, mental preparation, and physical training. Soccer demands its players to prepare nearly all aspects of physical fitness. As a result, a well-trained soccer player typically is pretty good in all aspects of fitness if not especially outstanding in any one aspect (in many cases, agility). A sprinter must have speed. A marathoner must have endurance. A weightlifter must have strength. Unlike these sports, soccer does not require a player to excel in any one area of fitness to be successful. This explains part of soccer's appeal—anyone can play.

This chapter focuses on the physical demands of soccer, but inherent in any discussion of the physical work required is the inclusion of some basic tactics. Tactics and fitness are intimately related. To know the players, one must know the game. Is a team's tactical performance the result of the players' fitness levels? Or does a higher fitness level allow the team to execute a broader vision of the game? That's soccer's version of the chicken or the egg question.

The Sport of Soccer

At its most basic level, soccer appears to be a game of nonstop motion. The adult game consists of two 45-minute periods that are played with a running clock. (In leagues with younger players, the duration of each half is shorter.) There is no allowance in the rules for the clock to stop. Although the clock runs continuously, the ball is not in play for the full 90 minutes. In general, the ball is in play for only 65 to 70 minutes. All those seconds when the ball is out of play—after a goal, before a corner, during an injury, when a player is singled out by the referee, and so on—add up. If the referee believes these circumstances are shortening the game, additional time, called stoppage time, may be added to the end of each half. One of the charms of the game is that the only person who knows the actual game time is the referee. Note: Some leagues, such as the National Collegiate Athletic Association (NCAA) and many high school leagues, control match time from the sideline and do allow the referee to stop the clock.

Since the game is not continuous, neither is the running of each player. People who study the movement of soccer describe several distinct actions: standing, walking, jogging, cruising, and sprinting. Cruising is defined as running with manifest purpose and effort, which is faster than a jog but slower than a sprint. The speeds above jogging are sometimes further defined as high-intensity running and very high-intensity running, which are further combined with jumping, sideways running, diagonal running, and backward running. A soccer player will execute nearly 1,000 distinct actions during a match. For the player, action changes every four to six seconds. When the running pattern is viewed like this, the game is no longer considered to be continuous activity simply because of a running clock. Instead, soccer is a hybrid of many actions, speeds, and changes of direction. Because the action changes frequently, it is not surprising that soccer players consistently score extremely high on agility.

Successful soccer is about how each team uses space. Soccer tactics can be summarized in a simple concept: When on offense, make the field as big as possible; when on defense, make the field as small as possible.

Ball Movement

The objective of soccer is the same as in any other team sport: Score more than the opponent. On average, 1.5 to 2 goals are scored per match. When counted over many matches, shooting success is pretty low. The overall shots-to-goals ratio is typically 10-to-1. At the 2008 Euro Championship, the average number of passes by a team was 324 per match. Because of the nature of the sport, ball possession changes constantly. Over 90 minutes, a team will have about 240 separate ball possessions. That averages to about 11 seconds per possession. (Remember, your team does not have possession for the full 90 minutes; the other team has possession, too.)

A ball possession can be brief with no completed passes or a long string of completed passes before possession is lost because of poor skill, an intercepted pass, a tackle, a ball lost out of play, or a goal. When plotted over thousands of matches, about 40 percent of all possessions have no completed passes, and 80 to 90 percent of possessions involve four players and three passes or less (figure 1.1). This explains why so many small-sided training activities are 4v4; it is the essence of the game.

If your team gains possession close to your opponent's goal, the number of players and passes will be less. This is an important concept. Forcing your opponent to make a mistake near its own goal puts your team at a distinct advantage. In soccer, goals often are the result of an opponent's mistake instead of a long string of passes by the attacking team. Strange as it sounds, high-pressure defense in the opponent's defensive end is an important offensive tactic. Because soccer is a hybrid of running speeds and directions, it also is a hybrid of possession and quick strike strategies.

In the English Premier League, about 80 percent of any individual player's possessions are only one touch (a redirect) or two touches (control and pass), with no dribbling. Also in the English Premier League, about 70 percent of goals come from one-touch shots, and

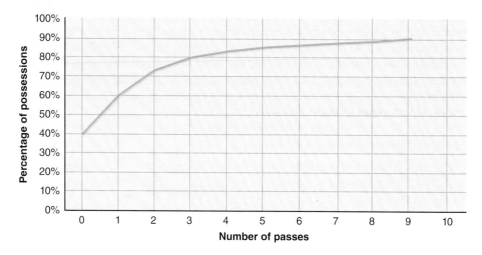

Figure 1.1 Number of passes per possession.

about two-thirds come from open play. The remaining come from restarts—fouls, corners, and penalty kicks (PKs). Combine these stats with the number of passes, and it becomes obvious that soccer is a passing game, not a dribbling game. The less dribbling and the faster passes are played, the faster the game overall.

Physical Demands on the Soccer Player

Many years ago, I asked someone how far a player runs in a soccer match and was told 10 miles. I did the math—10 miles in 90 minutes was 9 minutes per mile; this is doable. But a typical field is 110 yards (100 m) long, and 10 miles is 16,000 meters. That would mean I would have to run the length of the field 145 times at a constant 9-minute-per-mile pace to accumulate 10 miles; this is not likely.

Tracking a player's running distance isn't easy. People have used a paper and pencil coding system (at matches or while watching video replays), step counters, a GPS, and more. No matter what the method, getting the data is labor intensive and time consuming. Those who study the physical demands of soccer generally agree that the average running distance in adult male professional soccer is between 6 and 8.5 miles (9,700 to 13,700 m). Adult female professional soccer players run about 5 miles (8,000 m), but there are reports of female midfielders covering the 6 miles (9,700 m) males run. The total distance decreases in younger players, who play a slower and shorter game.

Since soccer is played at many different paces, the distance is divided according to speed. The general observation is that one-half to two-thirds of the game is played at the slower, more aerobic paces of walking and jogging. The rest is at higher, more anaerobic paces plus sideways and backward running. In addition, distances vary by position. Central attacking and holding midfielders cover the most distance followed by wing midfielders and defenders, strikers, and finally central defenders. Some call the slower paces *positional intensities* (get to the right place on the field) and the faster paces *strategic intensities* (make something happen).

Matches may be won or lost by a strategically timed sprint, so many select teams look carefully for fast, skilled, and tactically savvy players, understanding that endurance can be improved by training. In general, sprints in soccer are 10 to 30 yards (9 to 27 m) long and happen every 45 to 90 seconds. The overall distance an adult male professional player covers at a sprint is 800 to 1,000 yards (730 to 910 m), although in 10- to 30-yard (9 to 27 m) chunks. Hard runs (cruising) happen every 30 to 60 seconds. The time between these hard runs is spent walking, jogging, or standing.

The physiological load on a player when running at any speed is increased by about 15 percent when the player is dribbling a ball. Therefore, one simple way to increase the intensity of any activity is for players to dribble. Small-sided games (4v4 or smaller) that increase the number of ball-contact opportunities usually are more intense than games played in larger groups (8v8 or more) during which ball contact is less frequent and players have more opportunities to stand and walk.

Physiological Demands on the Soccer Player

Many attempts have been made to describe the physiological demands on the soccer player. A basic factor to observe is heart rate during a match. When a person goes for a jog, his heart rate increases rapidly and then settles to a plateau that stays fairly constant throughout the run. When this happens, oxygen demand is being met by oxygen supply. When the jogger stops, the heart rate slows rapidly to a new low recovery plateau that is still above resting heart rate until it finally returns to the resting level. The corresponding oxygen consumption is shown in figure 1.2 (page 4).

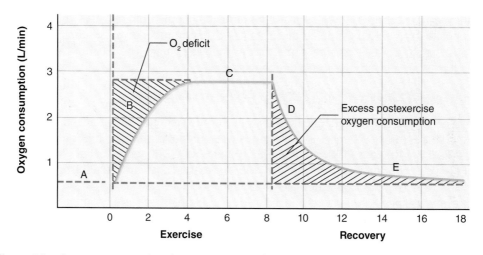

Figure 1.2　Oxygen consumption during exercise and recovery.

In a soccer player, a remarkably similar pattern emerges, and average heart rates are reported (figure 1.3). When the time scale is expanded, however, the pattern is quite different and reflects the intermittent nature of the game. The heart rate is rarely very steady during a match. Brief, rapid increases in response to faster runs are followed by rapid drops in heart rate during recovery periods (figure 1.4). Most reports show the typical heart rate range of a competitive adult soccer player is 150 to 170 beats per minute, with periods at or above 180 beats per minute. Most players work at 75 to 80 percent of capacity. Based on common interpretations of exercise heart rate, soccer is considered an aerobic exercise.

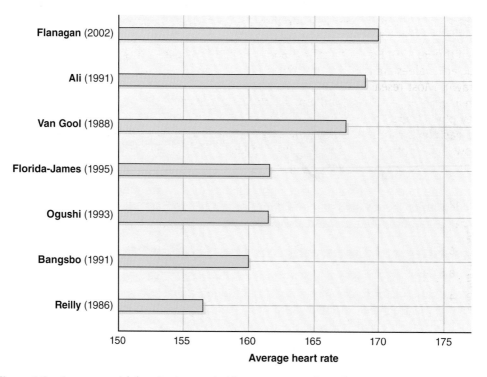

Figure 1.3　Average match heart rate reported by seven research studies.

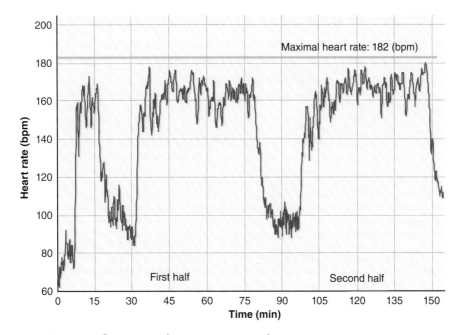

Figure 1.4 Heart rate fluctuations during a soccer match.
Courtesy of Dr. Peter Krustrup.

When the body works intensely, lactic acid is produced. Lactic acid is a product of anaerobic metabolism. Its buildup is perceived as pain (burn) in the exercising muscles, but lactic acid is rapidly removed during recovery. The resting level of lactic acid is around 1 unit. High levels for most people are 6 to 10 units. Anaerobic athletes such as wrestlers and rowers can produce lactic acid levels well into their teens or even 20s. Soccer does not require that kind of anaerobic challenge. Most reports show an elevated level of lactic acid during a match (figure 1.5), but it is hardly overwhelming considering the spectrum seen in sports. Lactic acid values are based on the time between the last intense run and when the blood is drawn. Most researchers sample blood at a fixed time (as seen in figure 1.5). If it has been a while since the last hard run, the blood sample could show a low level of lactic acid. A key physiological feature of a well-trained soccer player is the ability to recover quickly after each hard run, so it is not surprising that lactic acid values in soccer players seem to be low. Soccer players are able to get rid of lactic acid quickly because soccer training has taught their bodies to recover very quickly.

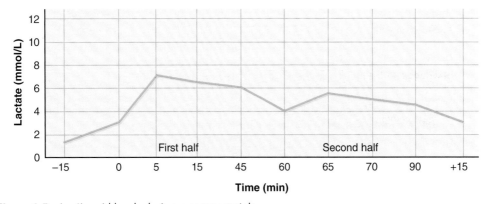

Figure 1.5 Lactic acid levels during a soccer match.
Courtesy of Dr. Peter Krustrup.

Understanding Body Chemistry and Soccer

To understand the demands of soccer, you need to understand the basics of energy. To perform mechanical work, the body needs fuel, which goes through a chemical process to provide energy. A car has one tank that holds one type of fuel, but the body has a number of fuel options found in multiple tanks. Fuel preference depends on fuel availability and the intensity of exercise.

Our bodies need energy, which we obtain from the sun through the ingestion of food. Technically we do not make energy; we transfer energy from the sun through food to the cells so the cells can perform their specific jobs. The currency of cellular work, exercise included, is adenosine triphosphate, or ATP. The adenosine backbone has three phosphates attached. Energy is stored in the chemical "glue" that holds the phosphates to the adenosine molecule. To get the energy, we must strip off a phosphate and release the energy, leaving a two-phosphate molecule called adenosine diphosphate, or ADP. Enzymes accelerate this process. Once the phosphate has been split and the energy released, we need to replenish our ATP warehouse by gathering enough energy to reattach a phosphate to that ADP. The body is constantly using and replenishing ATP. The estimate is that the total amount of ATP in the human body would probably fill something between a shot glass and a juice glass. This is why we have to keep refilling our stores. We are never completely at rest because the body always uses and replenishes ATP.

Released energy is used for many tasks. During exercise, energy is used primarily for muscle contraction, an enormously complex mechanism. The mechanical work of a muscle functions much like a ratchet. Each turn of the ratchet requires energy from a chemical source. Each turn uses energy, so the ratchet needs more energy to keep going.

Only about 40 percent of the energy available is actually used for cellular work, such as muscle contraction. The remainder is released as heat. The rapid breakdown of ATP during exercise to power all those ratchets heats the body. This heat needs to be dissipated so we do not overheat.

Anaerobic Metabolism

The word *anaerobic* means "in the absence of oxygen." We have two ways to produce energy anaerobically. One is simply to break down ATP and release the energy. If more ATP is needed, the body can take two ADPs and slide a phosphate and its energy from one ADP to the other to make a new ATP, turning the donor ADP into adenosine monophosphate, or AMP. Both processes are incredibly fast, but they drain the supply of available ATP almost as quickly. If there were any activity that ran this way exclusively, we would run out of fuel quickly, causing contraction to cease.

Once an ATP has been used, it must be replenished. The body does this by transferring a phosphate and its accompanying energy from another high-energy molecule called phosphocreatine (abbreviated as either PC or CP) to the ADP. This gives us a new ATP and a free creatine that must be resupplied with high energy for bonding a phosphate to be ready for the next transfer. If you were to sprint using only this as a fuel source (which never happens), the sprint might last 10 seconds at best. The simple ATP–PC cycle goes nonstop with each ratcheting of muscle contraction. There must be a continuous feeding of energy and phosphate to keep the cycle running, which is accomplished by the metabolic breakdown of carbohydrates (glucose) and fats (triglycerides) during exercise.

Another anaerobic way to produce ATP for the ATP–PC cycle and provide energy is the chemical breakdown of glycogen, the body's storage form of glucose. Glycogen is a long chain of glucose molecules stored in many places in the body. For our purposes, we will focus on muscle glycogen as the source. Glucose is a six-carbon molecule that is broken down into two three-carbon units. In the process, enough energy is generated to reattach a phosphate to an ADP molecule and make ATP. Actually, four ATP are produced, but the process needs two ATP to run, so the breakdown of a glucose molecule nets two ATP—not much. Because the process has a far greater source of fuel (muscle glycogen) than our juice glass of ATP, it can continue for a longer time, just not as fast and at the cost of lactic acid accumulation. When lactic acid, a product that causes a burning pain in the muscles, is produced faster than the body can get rid of it, the local tissue chemistry is altered. To prevent injury to the muscle cell, the metabolic process is slowed. This is one aspect of fatigue. If you were to sprint using only the anaerobic breakdown of glucose as fuel (again, this never happens), the estimate is that the sprint might last about 45 seconds before the chemical effects of lactic acid would cause the cells to shut down in an attempt to prevent cell damage.

Aerobic Metabolism

The aerobic breakdown of glucose proceeds through the process just described with one twist. In the presence of oxygen, lactic acid is not produced. Instead, the predecessor of lactic acid moves into a circular cycle that spins off carbon dioxide (those six carbons from the original glucose molecule need to go somewhere) and a number of compounds that carry hydrogen (those six carbons of the glucose molecule have hydrogen attached, and they too need to be dealt with). These hydrogen-containing compounds go through a process that transfers the hydrogen down a series of steps to the final acceptor, oxygen. Each oxygen molecule accepts two hydrogen molecules, producing water. During this transfer of hydrogen, enough energy is captured to transfer to an ADP, secure a phosphate, and replenish spent ATP. Depending on the details, the complete metabolism of a single glucose molecule produces 35 to 40 ATP.

But glucose, a carbohydrate, is not the only substance metabolized aerobically. Fat is a rich fuel source for energy. While glucose is a six-carbon molecule, a triglyceride has a glycerol head (with its three carbons and associated hydrogen) and three fatty acid chains, any of which can be less than 10 to 20 or more carbons in length. In fat metabolism, each fatty acid chain is cut up into two-carbon segments that each follow an aerobic path similar to the one taken by glucose to produce energy. Remember that a glucose molecule is split in half, and each half goes through the energy production process. A triglyceride, on the other hand, is far larger because of its three long fatty acid chains. If each of the three chains has 18 carbons and the process proceeds in two-carbon units (and do not forget the glycerol head), well, you can see the aerobic breakdown of a triglyceride produces far more ATP than does glucose, perhaps by a factor of 10 or more, with the same easily eliminated products of carbon dioxide and water. The problem is that fat metabolism is the slowest process.

We also can produce energy from the aerobic metabolism of proteins, but the amount of energy we get from proteins during exercise is pretty small. Most people tend to ignore the energy contributions of proteins to exercise.

The end products of the aerobic metabolism of carbohydrate and fat are water and carbon dioxide, both easily eliminated, especially when compared to lactic acid. In terms of the time needed to produce ATP, the aerobic breakdown of glucose and fat takes longer than the anaerobic metabolism of glucose and far longer than the ATP–PC cycle. Although speed of production is not its strong point, aerobic metabolism has the capability to produce energy for exercise for an indefinite period of time because everyone has an ample supply of fat.

Energy During Exercise

The interaction of all these metabolic processes can be complicated. At no time is any one of the metabolic processes or sources of fuel supplying 100 percent of the energy needed for exercise. The intensity and duration of the exercise dictates the predominant energy process and fuel. Intensity and duration of exercise are inversely related: The longer the exercise, the lower the intensity; shorter work is more intense. You could not run a marathon at your 100-meter pace, and you would not want to run a 100-meter race at your marathon pace.

Figure 1.6 helps explain this interaction. The X-axis is exercise time, and the Y-axis is the percentage of energy supplied by the various fuel sources. For exercise of very short duration, such as a 40-meter sprint, the primary fuel source is stored ATP and phosphocreatine, but a small portion of energy comes from anaerobic and aerobic metabolism of glucose. As the duration of exercise increases, up to around four minutes, the primary source of energy comes from anaerobic metabolism of glucose, but some energy comes from other pathways. Exercise that lasts four minutes or more is fueled primarily by aerobic metabolism of glucose and fat, with a progressively smaller fraction of energy coming from the other processes.

The amount of energy available from stored ATP and phosphocreatine is very small. The amount of energy from stored carbohydrate is greater but still limited. The amount of available fuel from fat is essentially unlimited. The fat that is stored within the muscle, that surrounds the organs, and that lies under the skin is far more than anyone would need for exercise. But remember, it takes time to obtain fuel from fat. It is estimated that if fat were the sole source of fuel for running, you could run at only about 50 percent of capacity—a walk or slow jog at best. Muscle glycogen also is a limited fuel source. Someone who runs out of glycogen will slow down because the main source of fuel is now from fat. Most people run out of muscle glycogen in the fibers recruited for exercise in about 90 minutes. Soccer players can therefore run out of glycogen during a match. To compensate, soccer players should follow the dietary recommendations to increase muscle glycogen that individual-sport athletes have wisely adopted. A combination of training and high carbohydrate intake allows the muscle to pack in more glycogen, allowing the player to go further into the match before running out.

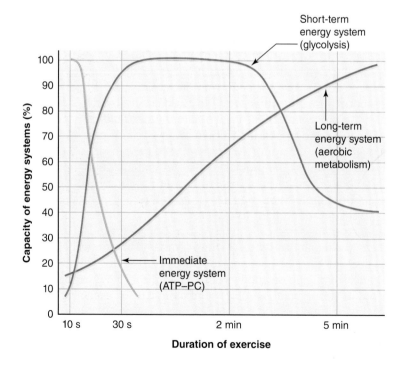

Figure 1.6 Relationship of exercise duration and energy systems.

Application to Soccer

Let's get back to the game. Remember, soccer is a game of numerous short sprints and episodes of high-intensity anaerobic work separated by periods of low-intensity aerobic recovery in preparation for the next bout of high-intensity work. During a sprint, shot, jump, tackle, or cut, some ATP is spent and some glucose is used to power the muscles for the hard work. Then the player recovers during a lower-intensity phase of play (walking, jogging, standing) during which ATP is replenished and lactic acid is removed. (Lactic acid is metabolized aerobically, which is one reason you breathe hard after slowing down or stopping.) This prepares the muscles for the next bout of hard work.

How long before the player is ready to work hard again depends on how quickly ATP is replenished, how much lactic acid is removed, and how a few other electrochemical processes connected with contraction are completed. What you need to understand is that the important parts of the game—the parts that define who wins, those high-intensity runs—are fueled primarily by anaerobic means, and the recovery periods are accomplished aerobically.

Recovery is an aerobic event. This is something most coaches and players either forget or ignore. The higher the player's aerobic capacity, the faster she will recover and the more frequently she can work hard, going deeper into the match before tiring. A player with poor aerobic fitness will take longer to recover from a sprint before again being able to use that blazing speed, and chances are each successive sprint will be shorter and slower. Research shows that training-induced improvements in speed are not nearly as great as training-induced improvements in endurance. That is why speed is such a highly valued trait in a soccer player, because the coach knows endurance can be improved more easily than speed. Coaches look for fast players who can improve their endurance instead of players who can run all day but need to improve speed. Yet the modern game is not about raw speed. It is about how fast a player recovers to use the speed she has over and over.

Some studies can nearly rank the final standings of a league's clubs according to each team's aerobic capacity. Aerobic capacity for rapid recovery is that important. Coaches are very adept at designing training sessions to improve endurance and the ability to recover. To raise intensity, they use short small-sided games on a small field, with restrictions to force play (for example, multiple two-minute games with limited recovery between each game; 4v4 or fewer for more ball contacts; or games in a penalty area or smaller marked area to force quick decisions, with restrictions such as overlapping every pass with a sprint). The smaller sides mean less downtime, so the body has to learn to adapt for fast recovery from the temporary fatigue induced by each sprint. For endurance, activities usually involve more players in a larger space, with restrictions that force a more constant pace of play for a longer period of time (for example, a 15- to 20-minute drill or games of 8v8 or more, in a three-quarter or full field, with restrictions such as all players in the attacking zone before a shot). A player with higher aerobic fitness can recover more quickly than an unfit player. The fit player gets to a new position faster and is ready for higher-intensity work well before the unfit player.

Jogging at a constant pace around a field or a park will improve jogging ability, but it won't train the body to do what is necessary to recover in a start–stop game. When jogging, you recover once—at the end. In soccer, recovery happens repeatedly. A well-trained soccer player will be able to keep the heads of each ratchet in the muscle well supplied with ATP to keep the ATP–PC process running and delay the influence of lactic acid on local muscle fatigue. Players who are unable to rapidly replenish the ATP for that ATP–PC cycle will be standing around waiting while other players are running past.

Muscle Fiber Recruitment

You may have heard of fast-twitch and slow-twitch muscle fibers. We are all blessed with a mosaic of muscle fibers with unique characteristics that make us supremely adaptable to a multitude of activities. Basically, the big fast-twitch fibers produce a lot of tension very quickly but can't keep producing this amount of tension for many contractions. The smaller slow-twitch fibers produce less tension at a slower rate but can keep contracting repeatedly. Think back to the description of energy, and apply that to the concept of fiber type. Fast-twitch fibers produce most of their energy anaerobically (for a rapid production of tension), while slow-twitch fibers produce most of their energy aerobically (for repeated contractions). The distribution of fast-twitch and slow-twitch fibers is, for the most part, fixed by genetics. Although some people might reason that a soccer player should have more of one type than the other, most studies show a soccer player has about a 50:50 ratio. Remember, soccer is the game of the masses, so it makes sense that no genetically predetermined factor, such as a high percentage of slow-twitch fibers in a marathoner or height in basketball, is a requirement to play the game.

Female Players

Much of the worldwide growth in soccer is due to the increased participation of women. Although the rules are the same, there are subtle tactical differences between the men's and the women's games that may not be evident to casual fans. The general pattern of work is similar but at a lower running volume and pace, although some female midfielders cover the 6 miles (9,700 m) male players do. Women have physiological differences such as a lower engine capacity. This lower capacity of females is the result of less muscle mass, smaller hearts, less total blood volume, and less hemoglobin. A female playing a match of the same duration and field size as a male and running the same distance as a male will have to play the game at a higher intensity. It isn't unusual for adult female professional players to exhibit heart rates above those of their male counterparts. They work hard.

Female athletes have other issues that can cause health problems. The female athlete triad is the interaction of disordered eating, menstrual dysfunction, and reduced bone density. Some female athletes choose not to eat appropriately, which can lead to a disruption of normal hormonal balance evident in menstrual problems. A disruption of normal hormonal balance, especially of estrogen, can reduce bone density. The repeated impact of physical training can then lead to stress fractures, mostly in the lower extremities. Because the triad begins with reduced calorie intake and possibly disordered eating, ensuring females are consuming adequate calories is imperative for maintaining normal menstrual function and healthy bones.

Females also need to ingest appropriate amounts of iron and calcium. Even athletes on a vegetarian diet can get plenty of these minerals with proper food selection. The Fédération Internationale de Football Association (FIFA) has produced an excellent booklet on the female player; see the additional resources on page 207.

Nutrition and Hydration

Our fuel for exercise comes from the food we eat. We all have plenty of fat, but carbohydrate storage capacity is limited, meaning we have to refuel carbohydrates frequently. For you to be a player in motion, you need to be well fueled, and that comes from carbohydrates. FIFA has an excellent booklet on nutrition specifically written for the nonscientific audience. See the additional resources on page 207.

Dehydration is a problem in soccer. The length of the game, the intensity of the running, the elements, and the lack of planned stoppages all contribute to players not getting necessary fluid during a match. A fluid deficit of as little as 2 percent—only 3 pounds (1.4 kg) of fluid loss in a 150-pound (68 kg) player—can negatively affect performance.

Players should take advantage of normal stoppages to drink water, sports drinks, or both. To keep fluids available, players place water bottles in or around the goal and along the touchlines and drink during injury stoppages or other dead-ball situations. Because central midfielders are the farthest from the field boundaries, they have the most difficulty taking advantage of stoppages, so they need to make a conscious effort to get to water wherever it is placed, and the coach needs to make sure that fluids get to them during such stoppages.

Players who produce very salty sweat might be inclined to choose a drink with salt and add extra salt to their meals. These players can be identified as those whose shirts show a crusty substance as the water in their sweat evaporates from their clothing. This is especially obvious when they wear dark shirts.

The other problem with soccer players is that they tend to not drink enough between training sessions or matches. There are reports that as many as 40 percent of players on a team could be clinically dehydrated even before they step onto the field.

The typical formula for fluid replacement is 1.5 pints (24 oz or 720 ml) of fluid per pound (.5 kg) of body weight lost, so know your weight and check it often. Full replenishment cannot be done in one sitting. It can take a full day. Keep a close eye on your urine color. If it looks like dilute lemonade, you are probably OK. But if it looks more like apple juice, you need to drink more fluids. See the nutrition booklet in the additional resources (page 207) for more information.

Drugs and Food Supplements

We cannot seem to separate sports from drugs, especially so-called performance-enhancing drugs, or PEDs. Although drugs seem to be endemic in sports such as cycling, soccer has little history of drug abuse. This is probably because soccer does not rely on one specific factor that could be enhanced by a PED to affect the outcome, as anabolic steroids do for weightlifters or erythropoietin (EPO) does for road cyclists. FIFA's own statistics show a trivial number of positive drug tests, and half of those positive tests were for recreational drugs, not PEDs.

A high percentage of athletes take over-the-counter, and largely unnecessary, supplements. Some reports show nearly 100 percent of Olympic athletes in some sports from certain countries take supplements. The most common supplement is a multivitamin, but that is not the point. The supplement industry does not follow the same purity rules that the FDA requires for the food and drug industries. Therefore, what is on the label may not be a full accounting of what is actually in the bottle.

Recently, the International Olympic Committee (IOC) went to some supplement stores and randomly selected supplements known to be used by athletes. The IOC tested the products and found that nearly one-quarter of them would have produced a positive drug test. In sports, the athlete is always responsible for a positive drug test. Any player who thinks college, international, or professional play is in his future will face drug testing and must be very careful about what he ingests.

If you eat a well-rounded diet, choosing from a wide variety of fresh and colorful items from all food groups, supplements will only enrich your urine and empty your wallet. The renowned sports supplement researcher Dr. Ron Maughan from Loughborough University (UK) has an axiom: "If it works, it is probably banned. If it is not banned, it probably doesn't work." Why take the chance?

Injury Prevention

Injuries are a part of all sports. The most common soccer injury is a contusion (bruise) when you get kicked, fall, or bumped. The most common location is the lower extremity, mostly between the knee and ankle. Most leg contusions do not cause a player to miss much training time or competition. The top four time-loss soccer injuries are ankle sprains, knee sprains, hamstring strains, and groin strains. In elite soccer, hamstring strains are most common. At lower levels of play, ankle sprains are number one.

There are some gender differences. Females have a higher rate of injury to the anterior cruciate ligament of the knee. Newer data suggest that females suffer more concussions than do males. The difference in concussion rates may be real, or it could be skewed because women tend to be more forthcoming than men about head injuries.

Good prevention programs, when substituted for a traditional warm-up, have been shown to reduce common injuries by about one-third. FIFA presents an excellent graduated warm-up (The 11+) that is the subject of chapter 2. For players and teams with a special concern about hamstring strains, pay close attention to the hamstrings exercise and the balance exercises. These have been shown to reduce hamstring strains. The key to any injury prevention program is compliance. Programs such as The 11+ are not an occasional diversion. Players must complete these programs at every training session and do a shorter version before competition.

Heat Illnesses

For many countries in the northern hemisphere, soccer is a fall to spring sport; summer is the off-season. In the United States, the professional game parallels the baseball season, making it a spring to fall sport. Depending on the time of year, soccer in the southern states can be played in pretty oppressive conditions. All summer leagues and tournaments need to have a plan in place to handle players suffering from heat illnesses. Players who succumb to the heat may initially show minor symptoms such as heat cramps, but problems can rapidly progress to far more serious issues such as heat exhaustion and heatstroke, which is a potentially fatal collapse of the body's ability to control its temperature. You may have read about heat-related deaths in American football players.

The body loses heat by radiation through radiant loss of heat through heat waves; convection (like standing in front of a fan or air conditioner); conduction, which is direct contact with a cooler surface (like placing an ice-cold towel on the head); or evaporation, which is the most important mechanism during exercise. Sweat production is not the loss of heat; the evaporation of the sweat results in heat loss. Any barrier to heat loss will slow the rate of evaporation. Two barriers frequently encountered in soccer include clothing, especially dark clothing that covers much of the body, and humidity. Today's sports clothing is designed to aid evaporation.

Whenever matches are scheduled during hot and humid weather, put strategies in place for making fluids available. Many youth leagues, particularly in the south, have water breaks in each half as part of the rules. If water breaks are not part of the rules, the coaches can approach the referee and ask for a break if the conditions warrant it. The referee has this authority and would probably appreciate the break as well. During the men's gold medal match at the Beijing Olympics, a water break was included in each half because of the conditions.

Fatigue

A good definition of fatigue is the failure to maintain an expected power output—you want to run fast but are unable to. Fatigue can be both general and temporary and can come from a number of mechanisms. For example, to run fast, you need muscle glycogen. When muscle glycogen levels decline below set levels, you walk. Increasing muscle glycogen stores through training and proper food selection will delay fatigue and allow you to go deeper into the match before tiring. In addition, an ample store of glucose ensures that the brain has a ready supply of the only fuel it can use. The brain can become fatigued, too. Elevated body temperature and the accompanying loss of fluids by evaporation are also factors in general fatigue. Because body temperature affects performance, it is necessary to keep fluid levels up so the body can produce sweat for evaporation and heat loss. Drink often.

Temporary fatigue is a result of rapidly altered and remedied local muscle chemistry that affects the ability of the muscle fibers to contract. Lactic acid contributes to temporary fatigue. After a few repeated fast runs, you tire, but in a few minutes you can be back and ready to go again. Any improvement in aerobic capacity will let you do more, or longer, hard runs before temporary fatigue sets in by improving your ability to recover more quickly. Training for rapid recovery minimizes the effects of temporary fatigue by speeding up the removal of lactic acid and the recovery of processes that couple the processes associated with excitation of the muscle with the muscle's ability to contract.

The Fédération Internationale de Football Association (FIFA) is the world governing body for soccer. At the 1994 FIFA World Cup, a high-level FIFA administrator casually asked the question, "Can't we make the game safer?" Everyone has to accept that participation in sport, especially a contact sport, is risky. Players will get injured. But can't steps be taken to lessen the rate of injury?

That simple question became the impetus for the development of the FIFA Medical Assessment and Research Centre (F-MARC). One of F-MARC's primary goals was to reduce the incidence and severity of injuries in soccer. Their first task was to document the true incidence of injury at the world championship level. F-MARC needed to know what injuries to try to prevent. Should they attack the most severe injuries, those that result in the greatest loss of time? Or the most common injuries, those that affect the most players? Many injury studies already existed, but the methods used were inconsistent, making comparisons and conclusions nearly impossible. F-MARC took the best methods available and started an injury surveillance program, beginning with the 1998 FIFA World Cup, that continues today at all FIFA-sponsored tournaments. This gives F-MARC a stable database on injuries at the world championship level.

When F-MARC was organized, most prevention reports were based not on research evidence but on expert opinion. Before the mid-1990s, only one experimental research project designed to prevent injury in soccer—a study out of Sweden—had been published. But that program was so extensive that it was hard to zero in on the most effective aspects to relate to the local coach.

Injury prevention research is a four-step process. First, determine which injuries should be prevented through an injury surveillance program. Second, determine the mechanism of injury (how the injuries happen). Third, devise prevention protocols. Finally, implement the protocols on a large group of players and see if the injury rate decreases. In practice, a large group of players is recruited and randomly divided into two groups. One group receives the intervention, and one group does not. All injuries are recorded over a specific period of time, and the injury rates of the two groups are compared.

That first Swedish study reported a dramatic 75 percent reduction in all injuries, but in reality, no one could comply with the number of interventions or provide the personnel required to carry out their extremely rigid program. The first F-MARC injury prevention program, conducted on mostly high-school-age European boys, showed a one-third reduction in overall injury rate, which is a level of reduction that seems to be consistent with subsequent studies. That program was the pilot for F-MARC's initial prevention program called The 11, which consisted of 10 prevention exercises and the call for fair play. (At the world championship level, nearly half the injuries to men and about one-quarter to one-third of all injuries to women are due to foul play.)

An important aspect of injury prevention is establishing the risk factors of a particular injury. Risk factors are classified as player-related factors (lack of skill, poor fitness, prior injury) or non-player-related factors (quality of refereeing, field conditions, environment). Some risk factors, such as fitness level and lack of skill, are modifiable, while others, such as gender, age, environment, and field quality, are not. Research suggests that interventions are successful at preventing injury for some modifiable factors (e.g., hamstring strength). But it is important to remember that the number one predictor of an injury is a history of that injury. A player who has had a strained hamstring has a dramatically higher risk of getting the same injury; some reports suggest the risk is increased by a factor of eight times. The obvious conclusion, then, is to prevent the first injury.

Since the original Swedish project, a number of prevention trials have been conducted and published in medical literature. Some of the trials were general and designed to lower the overall injury rate. Other trials attempted to prevent specific injuries. For example, in team sports, programs were designed specifically to prevent ankle sprains, knee sprains, hamstring strains, and groin strains. Prevention programs may be classified as primary prevention (prevent the first injury occurrence) or secondary prevention (prevent a recurrent injury). Programs that prevent hamstring strains and knee sprains are considered primary prevention but are still effective in secondary prevention, while programs that prevent ankle sprains are considered secondary prevention. To date, no prevention program has been able to prevent an athlete's first ankle sprain.

Preventing injury to the knee, particularly to the anterior cruciate ligament (ACL), has been studied intensely. ACL injuries in sports such as soccer and basketball occur at a higher rate in females than in males by a factor of three to eight times. This is a particular problem for girls in middle school and high school, but it extends into college as well. It is not uncommon for a female soccer player to have multiple ACL injuries; the younger the player when the first injury occurs, the greater the risk of another injury. A number of prevention studies have been conducted; some yielded impressive results (up to a 70 percent reduction in ACL injuries in female youth players), while others failed to show any reduction.

The key to any prevention program is compliance. These programs are quite effective when they are part of the regular warm-up for training and competition. When performed regularly, a prevention program can reduce ACL injury rates. When the prevention program is performed only sporadically, all bets are off. Most experts want to see compliance rates of 75 percent or higher.

Hamstring strains have become a huge problem in high-caliber competition. The increase in pace of the modern game has pushed hamstring strains from an insignificant injury 20 years ago to one of the top four injuries in professional soccer, sometimes the number one injury on a club. For a professional club to see six hamstring strains or more in a season is not unusual. But research shows that hamstring strains can be prevented, both the first strain as well as recurrent strains. When done regularly, the hamstrings exercise on page 30 has been shown to be extremely effective at preventing hamstring strain injury.

Groin strains are a particular problem in soccer and in ice hockey. Players typically perform static stretching to prevent groin strains. The problem is that there is no consensus on the effectiveness of preexercise static stretching in preventing injury in general, much less a specific injury such as a groin strain. The shift from static stretching to dynamic stretching has been shown to have some success at injury prevention. Static stretching is fine, but most experts suggest it be done on another day away from the performance of the sport or during the cool-down, not as part of the preactivity warm-up.

A groin strain is not the same as the sports hernia common in ice hockey and soccer. A *groin strain* is a typical pulled muscle, usually an injury to the adductor longus muscle. Most players can identify the exact moment the injury occurred. A *sports hernia*, also known as Gilmore's groin, athletic pubalgia, or athlete's hernia) is an inflammation or tear of connective tissue (not an injury to the muscles of the lower abdomen) near the location of a traditional hernia. A specific instance that caused the injury cannot be recalled. The player will complain of groin pain when sprinting or during powerful kicking. In the doctor's office, the pain can sometimes be reproduced during seated or lying resisted hip flexion or while coughing. Although a vast majority of these injuries occur in males, the sports hernia can also happen to females. The exact cause is unknown, and diagnosing this injury is a clinical challenge for the physician because so many other problems can mimic the pain.

Unfortunately, there is no definitive diagnostic test or any method of imaging that is specific for a sports hernia. Ice hockey has a prevention program for this hernia that seems to be effective, but when a modification was tried in professional soccer players, the results were inconclusive, probably due to poor compliance by the players and teams. An athlete with chronic groin pain should see a sports medicine specialist because of the difficulty in making an accurate diagnosis. Rest, massage, strengthening, medication, and more have all been suggested, but the pain frequently returns. A routine hernia repair, done more frequently in Europe than in the United States, has been shown to be a reasonably effective surgical intervention, but it may not be the solution for everyone.

As the evidence began to accumulate, F-MARC developed the second version of The 11. In the revision, the exercises were progressive, and the entire program was substituted for the typical generalized warm-up a team might do before training or a match. The result was The 11+. The 11+ was tested on female youths in Norway, with two great results. First, they showed the expected overall injury reduction of about one-third. Second, they had excellent compliance to the program because its revised design increased the interest of and participation by players and coaches. As a warm-up, The 11+ prepares players for training and competition. As a teaching tool, a number of the exercises teach players the proper techniques for landing, cutting, and pivoting. When the landing is done properly, the knee should flex over the planted foot (figure 2.1a) and not be allowed to collapse into what is called a valgus position (figure 2.1b). The coach needs to watch players do these exercises and correct players who display incorrect landing and cutting techniques.

Although a number of prevention programs are available, The 11+ has gained wide acceptance, and its use continues to grow. Because of its success and specific focus on soccer, the exercises of The 11+ have been used as the foundation for the warm-up in this chapter. (See table 2.1 on page 18.) Additional information about The 11+, including a chart that shows the entire routine, can be found at http://f-marc.com/11plus/index.html. Once a team has learned the exercise routine, the entire program can be completed in 15 to 20 minutes. Remember, The 11+ replaces a team's warm-up.

a   *b*

Figure 2.1   Landing knee position: *(a)* correct; *(b)* incorrect.

Table 2.1   The 11+ Warm-Up Routine

JOGGING EXERCISES

Exercise number	Exercise title	Page number	Sets
1	Jogging straight ahead	20	2
2	Jogging with hip out	21	2
3	Jogging with hip in	22	2
4	Jogging around partner	23	2
5	Jogging and jumping with shoulder contact	24	2
6	Jogging forward and backward	25	2

STRENGTH, PLYOMETRIC, AND BALANCE EXERCISES

Exercise number	Level 1	Level 2	Level 3	Page number	Sets
7	Static bench	Bench with alternating legs	Bench with one-leg lift and hold	26	2; 2 each leg for bench with one-leg lift and hold
8	Static sideways bench	Sideways bench with hip lift	Sideways bench with leg lift	28	2 each side
9	Beginner hamstrings	Intermediate hamstrings	Advanced hamstrings	30	1
10	Single-leg stance with ball hold	Single-leg stance with ball throw to partner	Single-leg stance with partner test	32	2 each leg
11	Squat with toe raise	Walking lunge	One-leg squat	34	2; 2 each leg for one-leg squat
12	Vertical jump	Lateral jump	Box jump	36	2

RUNNING EXERCISES

Exercise number	Exercise title	Page number	Sets
13	Running across the pitch	38	2
14	Bounding	39	2
15	Plant and cut	40	2

Adapted from The 11+, developed by F-MARC.

Three Parts of the FIFA Warm-Up

A warm-up gradually prepares the body for more intense exercise, which is important since the body operates more efficiently when warmer than when at resting temperature. For that reason, The 11+ begins with a short period of jogging.

After the jogging exercises, players move into strength, plyometric, and balance exercises. These exercises dynamically stretch the muscles and prepare them for more explosive maneuvers on the pitch.

One of the purposes of a generalized warm-up is to prepare the body for the upcoming activity. Many of the exercises in The 11+ are challenging but not very intense. Each running exercise is performed at a higher intensity, bringing the body closer to the intensity of more formal training. The pace of this running is not sprinting but a fairly hard stride. Increasing running speed means increasing stride rate and increasing stride length. Thus, the movement of the swing leg occurs faster, and the push-off by the ground leg is stronger. The actual muscles used at the various running speeds remain about the same, but the brain tells each active muscle to work harder by recruiting a greater number of muscle cells as well as by asking each cell to contract harder.

Jogging Straight Ahead

Execution

Place 6 to 10 pairs of cones in parallel lines 5 to 10 yards (5 to 9 m) apart—closer for younger players, farther for older players. (This cone configuration will be used for all of the jogging exercises.) If many players are participating, consider setting up two or more sets of parallel cones. Start with a partner from the first pair of cones. Jog with your partner to the last pair of cones. On the way back to the start, progressively increase your speed. Perform this twice.

Muscles Involved

Primary: Hip flexors (psoas major and minor, iliacus), quadriceps (vastus medialis, vastus lateralis, vastus intermedius, rectus femoris), gastrocnemius, soleus

Secondary: Hamstrings (biceps femoris, semitendinosus, semimembranosus), peroneals (peroneus longus, brevis, and tertius), tibialis anterior

Soccer Focus

One purpose of a warm-up is to raise your internal body temperature. This is important because the metabolic functions described in chapter 1 work most efficiently at temperatures above rest. Some general jogging is a simple way to start raising your internal temperature. When you break into a sweat, your internal temperature is well on the way to a range where energy metabolism is most efficient. The 11+ will effectively raise your internal temperature.

Jogging With Hip Out

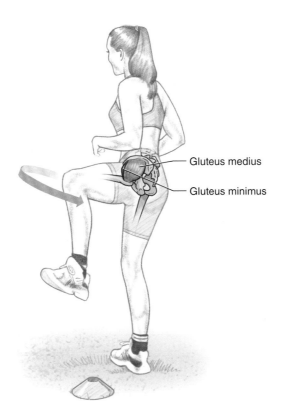

Gluteus medius

Gluteus minimus

Execution

Set up cones in the same configuration as for the jogging straight ahead exercise on the previous page. Walk or jog easily with a partner, stopping at each pair of cones to lift your knee and rotate your hip out. Alternate left and right legs at successive cones. Jog back to the start after the last cone. Perform two sets.

Muscles Involved

Primary: Hip flexors, gluteals (gluteus maximus, medius, and minimus), tensor fasciae latae

Secondary: Adductor longus, adductor magnus (posterior fibers), sartorius, piriformis

Soccer Focus

Many coaches and athletes believe static stretching will improve performance and prevent injury, but the scientific evidence shows otherwise. Dynamic stretching, which involves taking the joint through a full range of motion, does not hamper performance and has been shown to reduce strain injuries. Soccer players are prone to groin injuries and may need to perform specific dynamic stretching of the groin as a part of every warm-up.

Jogging With Hip In

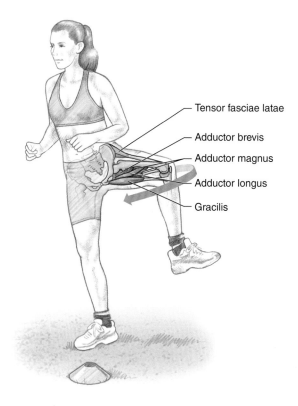

- Tensor fasciae latae
- Adductor brevis
- Adductor magnus
- Adductor longus
- Gracilis

Execution

Set up cones in the same configuration as for the jogging straight ahead exercise (page 20). Walk or jog easily with a partner, stopping at each pair of cones to lift your knee up and out to the side before rotating your hip inward. Alternate between left and right legs at successive cones. Jog back to the start after the last cone. Perform two sets.

Muscles Involved

Primary: Adductors (adductor longus, adductor magnus, adductor brevis, gracilis) gluteus minimus, gluteus medius

Secondary: Pectineus, tensor fasciae latae

Soccer Focus

Most flexibility programs emphasize opposing muscle groups. This dynamic internal rotation exercise balances out the previous dynamic external rotation exercise. With both of these dynamic flexibility exercises, be sure to move the thigh through the entire range of motion by either ending or beginning at the extremes of motion. These are effective exercises when each rotation attempts to go just a little bit farther.

Jogging Around Partner

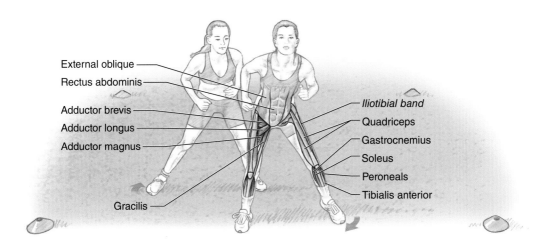

External oblique

Rectus abdominis

Adductor brevis

Adductor longus

Adductor magnus

Iliotibial band

Quadriceps

Gastrocnemius

Soleus

Peroneals

Tibialis anterior

Gracilis

Execution

Set up cones in the same configuration as for the jogging straight ahead exercise (page 20). With a partner, jog together to the first set of cones. Shuffle sideways to meet in the middle. Shuffle an entire circle around your partner as she circles around you, and then return to the cones. Repeat for each pair of cones. Stay on your toes, and keep your center of gravity low by bending your hips and knees. Jog back to the start after the last cone. Perform two sets.

Muscles Involved

Primary: Gastrocnemius, soleus, gluteus maximus, iliotibial band (push-off leg), adductors (pulling leg)

Secondary: Hamstrings, quadriceps, peroneals, tibialis anterior, abdominal core (external oblique, internal oblique, transversus abdominis, rectus abdominis) and spinal extensors (erector spinae, multifidus) for postural control

Soccer Focus

Soccer requires many lateral movements of varying distances, directions, and speeds. Lateral movement is one aspect of agility, which is a prized trait that soccer players are known for. This gentle exercise prepares players for the next exercise. Going both directions balances the load across the legs. As with all exercises that involve movement, be sure your knees don't collapse in.

Jogging and Jumping With Shoulder Contact

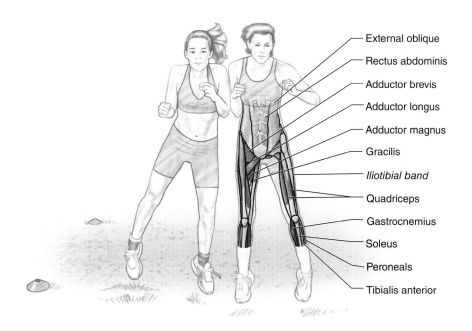

- External oblique
- Rectus abdominis
- Adductor brevis
- Adductor longus
- Adductor magnus
- Gracilis
- *Iliotibial band*
- Quadriceps
- Gastrocnemius
- Soleus
- Peroneals
- Tibialis anterior

Execution

Set up cones in the same configuration as for the jogging straight ahead exercise (page 20). With a partner, jog together to the first pair of cones. Shuffle sideways to meet your partner in the middle, and then jump sideways toward your partner to make shoulder-to-shoulder contact. Land on both feet with your hips and knees bent. Do not let your knees buckle in. Synchronize the timing of your jump and landing with your partner. Repeat at each cone. Jog back to the start after the last cone. Perform two sets.

Muscles Involved

Primary: Gastrocnemius, soleus, gluteus maximus, iliotibial band (push-off leg), adductors (pulling leg), quadriceps, hamstrings

Secondary: Abdominal core, peroneals, tibialis anterior

Soccer Focus

A key factor in knee injuries, especially injuries to the ACL, is the knee collapsing in when the player lands erect. This awkward position adds strain on the ACL that may be sufficient to tear the ligament and damage the meniscus. Many of the exercises in The 11+ teach players to control landing and cutting. This is especially important for female players from middle school age and up, the prime ages for an ACL tear. Land softly and quietly. Be sure your knees don't collapse in.

Jogging Forward and Backward

Execution

Set up cones in the same configuration as for the jogging straight ahead exercise (page 20). With a partner, jog quickly to the second set of cones, and then backpedal quickly to the first set of cones, keeping your hips and knees slightly bent. Jog to the third set of cones and backpedal to the second set of cones. Repeat through all sets of cones. Jog back to the start after the last cone. Take small, quick steps. Perform two sets.

Muscles Involved

Primary: Hip flexors, quadriceps, hamstrings, gastrocnemius, soleus, gluteals

Secondary: Abdominal core, spinal extensors

Soccer Focus

This exercise is done more quickly than the others in this group. Plant your front foot firmly, ensuring the knee stays over the foot and does not buckle in. Jog one cone forward and backward quickly, keeping good balance and posture. Plant the push-off leg firmly, and jog two cones forward quickly. Take small, quick steps, not loping strides. Maintain proper posture—flexed hips and knees—and an almost exaggerated arm action.

Bench

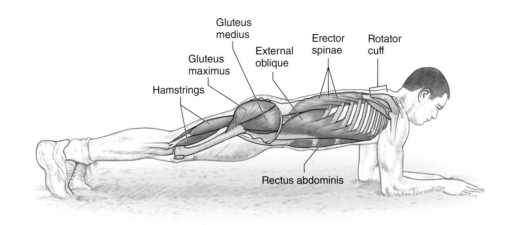

Gluteus
medius

Erector
spinae

Rotator
cuff

External
oblique

Gluteus
maximus

Hamstrings

Rectus abdominis

Level 1: static bench.

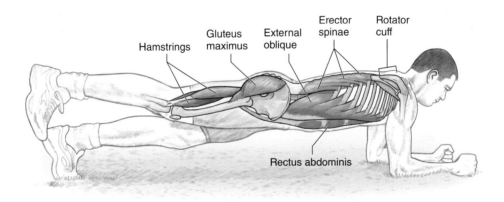

Erector
spinae

Rotator
cuff

External
oblique

Gluteus
maximus

Hamstrings

Rectus abdominis

Level 2: bench with alternating legs.

Level 1: Static Bench

Lie on your front, supporting yourself on your forearms and feet. Your elbows
should be directly under your shoulders. Lift your body, supporting your weight
on your forearms. Pull in your abdomen, and hold the position for 20 to 30
seconds. When this static position is held long enough, you will feel it throughout
the core muscles. Proper form is important, so make sure the elbows are directly
under the shoulders and your body is in a straight line from the back of the head
down to the trunk, hips, and heels. Try not to sway or arch your back. Lower
your body to the ground and repeat.

Level 2: Bench With Alternating Legs

Adding a hip extension is a simple way to make this basic core strengthening exercise more difficult. The challenge is to maintain a straight line all the way down the body. Good posture is critical. Lie on your front, supporting yourself on your forearms and feet. Your elbows should be directly under your shoulders. Lift your body, supporting your weight on your forearms. Pull in your abdomen. Lift your right leg and hold for 2 seconds. Lower your right leg, and then lift your left leg, holding for 2 seconds. Continue, alternating legs, for 40 to 60 seconds. For the best results, slowly raise and lower the leg. Keep your body in a straight line. Try not to sway or arch your back. Repeat this exercise for a second 40- to 60-second set.

Level 3: Bench With One-Leg Lift and Hold

This more difficult version of the bench combines isometrics (holding the leg in the up position) with dynamic movement (raising and lowering the leg). Holding the leg up for 20 to 30 seconds adds an additional challenge for the spine and hip extensors. Lie on your front, supporting yourself on your forearms and feet. Your elbows should be directly under your shoulders. Lift your body, supporting your weight on your forearms. Pull in your abdomen. Lift one leg about 6 inches (15 cm) off the ground, and hold the position for 20 to 30 seconds. Keep your body straight. Do not let your opposite hip dip down, and do not sway or arch your lower back. Lower the leg, take a short break, switch legs, and repeat. Do this twice for each leg.

Muscles Involved

Primary: Abdominal core, spinal extensors, gluteals, hamstrings

Secondary: Shoulder stabilizers including rotator cuff (supraspinatus, infraspinatus, subscapularis, teres minor) and scapular stabilizers (rhomboid major and minor, trapezius, latissimus dorsi)

Soccer Focus

The bench, sometimes known as the plank, is a basic core strengthening exercise. Do not skip levels 1 and 2 to get to the hardest version. When you can do a level easily, with minimal local fatigue and discomfort, progress to the next level. The advanced versions of the bench can be quite difficult if performed without some preparatory training.

Sideways Bench

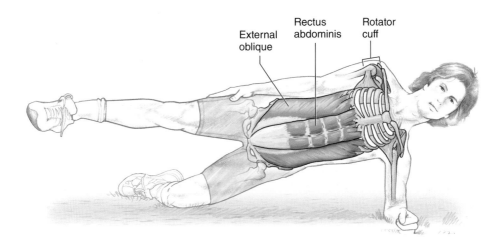

External oblique

Rectus abdominis

Rotator cuff

Level 1: static sideways bench.

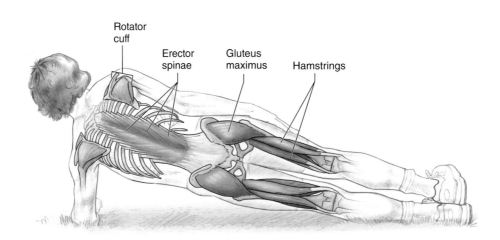

Rotator cuff

Erector spinae

Gluteus maximus

Hamstrings

Level 2: sideways bench with hip lift.

Level 1: Static Sideways Bench

Lie on your side with the knee of your lower leg bent to 90 degrees. Rest on your forearm and knee to support your upper body. The elbow of your supporting arm should be directly under your shoulder. Lift your upper leg and hip until your shoulder, hip, and knee are in a straight line. Hold the position for 20 to 30 seconds, and then lower your body to the ground. Take a short break, switch sides, and repeat. Do this twice on both sides.

Level 2: Sideways Bench With Hip Lift

The additional movement of this variation places an extra load on the core muscles. Lie on your side with both legs straight. Lean on your forearm and the side of your lower foot so that your body is in a straight line from shoulder to foot. The elbow of your supporting arm should be directly beneath your shoulder. Lower your hip to the ground and raise it again. Repeat for 20 to 30 seconds. Take a short break, switch sides, and repeat. Do this twice on each side.

Level 3: Sideways Bench With Leg Lift

Level 3 is more challenging than level 2. Raising the leg laterally is pretty tough. Lie on your side with both legs straight. Lean on your forearm and the side of your lower foot so that your body is in a straight line from shoulder to foot. The elbow of your supporting arm should be directly beneath your shoulder. Lift your upper leg and slowly lower it again. Repeat for 20 to 30 seconds. Lower your body to the ground, take a short break, switch sides, and repeat. Do this twice for each leg.

Muscles Involved

Primary: Abdominal core, spinal extensors, gluteals, hamstrings

Secondary: Shoulder stabilizers (rotator cuff, scapular stabilizers)

Soccer Focus

The sideways bench directs the effort toward the muscles responsible for lateral control of the core. To neglect this group would neglect an important functional aspect of core control. As with the three levels of the bench exercise, do not bypass levels 1 and 2 to get to level 3. When you can do a level easily, with minimal local fatigue and discomfort, progress to the next level.

Hamstrings

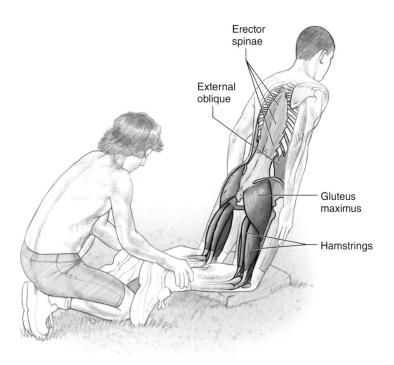

Erector spinae

External oblique

Gluteus maximus

Hamstrings

Level 1: Beginner Hamstrings

Kneel on a soft surface. Ask a partner to squat behind you and anchor your ankles to the ground. Your body should be completely straight from the shoulders to the knees throughout the exercise. You may cross your arms across your chest or simply keep your hands ready to catch your body in a push-up position. Lean forward as far as you can, controlling the movement with your hamstrings and your gluteal muscles. When you can no longer hold the position, gently absorb your weight using your hands, falling into a push-up position. Complete 3 to 5 repetitions.

Level 2: Intermediate Hamstrings

Perform the exercise as described for beginner hamstrings but complete 7 to 10 repetitions.

Level 3: Advanced Hamstrings

Perform the exercise as described for beginner hamstrings but complete 12 to 15 repetitions.

Muscles Involved

Primary: Hamstrings, gluteus maximus

Secondary: Spinal extensors, abdominal core

Soccer Focus

The pace of modern play has increased dramatically. Soccer has become a sport well suited to the high-power, ballistic sprinter. As skills and tactics evolve, so do injuries. In the 1970s, hamstring strains were rare. Today, hamstring strains are among the top four time-loss injuries in soccer. Some reports suggest a professional team can expect up to six hamstring strains or more per season. For a less severe strain, a player might be sidelined for a couple of weeks, but a more serious injury could sideline a player for four months or more. In the short, match-dense U.S. school and club-based seasons, a hamstring strain could be a season-ending injury. Thus, teams must do everything possible to prevent hamstring strains. This exercise, sometimes called the Nordic curl or Russian hamstrings, has been shown to effectively prevent hamstring strains, especially in players with a history of this injury, and should be a part of every training session. As strength improves, increase the number of repetitions you do, and try to control the descent, getting as close to the ground as possible. This exercise not only reduces the risk of hamstring strains but also strengthens the hamstrings, which helps stabilize the knee and hip when you cut or land, adding another level of protection against knee injuries.

Single-Leg Stance

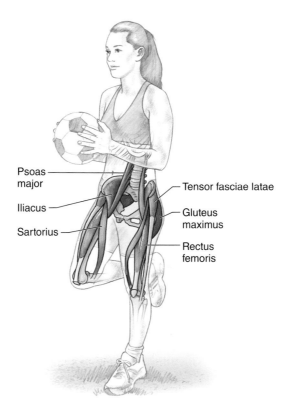

Psoas major

Iliacus

Sartorius

Tensor fasciae latae

Gluteus maximus

Rectus femoris

Level 1: single-leg stance with ball hold.

Level 1: Single-Leg Stance With Ball Hold

Holding a ball provides a small distraction, taking your mind off the act of balancing and allowing the more subconscious regions of the brain and the spinal cord to regulate balance. Balance on one leg. Hold a soccer ball with both hands. Keep your body weight on the ball of your grounded foot. Try not to let your knees buckle in. Hold for 30 seconds. Switch legs and repeat. Do this twice on each leg. You can make the exercise more difficult by moving the ball around your waist or under your raised knee.

Level 2: Single-Leg Stance With Ball Throw to Partner

Level 2 of this balance exercise adds the more demanding distraction of reacting to a ball tossed by a partner. The receiving player has to watch and track the thrown ball; predict and react to its flight; and adjust body position, balance, and posture before finally catching the ball. Stand 2 to 3 yards (2 to 3 m) away from your partner. Each of you should stand on one leg. Hold a soccer ball in both hands. While keeping your balance and holding in your abdomen, toss the ball to your partner. Keep your weight on the ball of your grounded foot. Keep your knee just slightly flexed, and try not to let it buckle in. Pay attention to controlling the supporting knee over the grounded foot to keep the knee from wobbling back and forth. Keep tossing the ball back and forth for 30 seconds. Switch legs and repeat. Do two sets for each leg.

Level 3: Single-Leg Stance With Partner Test

Level 3 of this balance exercise is even more challenging. Stand an arm's length in front of your partner as both of you balance on one foot. As you both try to keep your balance, take turns trying to push the other off balance in different directions. Try to knock your partner off balance with a gentle touch by using one or both hands to attack from different directions. You have to react quickly to the contact and respond accordingly. Try to keep your weight on the ball of your

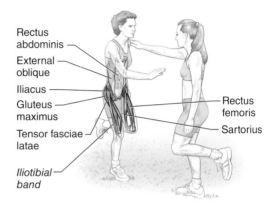

Rectus abdominis
External oblique
Iliacus
Gluteus maximus
Tensor fasciae latae
Iliotibial band
Rectus femoris
Sartorius

Level 3: single-leg stance with partner test.

foot and prevent your knee from buckling in. The goal is to maintain balance and keep the knee over the supporting foot. Keep this exercise under control; it's easy to get a bit out of hand. Continue for 30 seconds. Switch legs. Do two sets on each leg.

Muscles Involved

Primary: Hip flexors (psoas major and minor, iliacus, rectus femoris), hip extensors (gluteus maximus, hamstrings), tensor fasciae latae, sartorius, iliotibial band

Secondary: Abdominal core, spinal extensors

Soccer Focus

As upright beings, we are constantly maintaining our balance in an attempt to keep our center of mass over our base of support. When the center of gravity is outside a comfort radius around our base of support, we have to react and correct it or we fall. Balance is a complex physiological process that integrates environmental sensations with movement and reaction patterns by the brain and spinal cord. Special areas in the brain compare planned and actual movement information before reacting, all in milliseconds. Many knee injuries occur because of an inadequate response to a loss of balance, causing the knee to collapse in. The single-leg stance, the squat (page 34), and jumping (page 36) are directed at improving balance and knee control during a variety of activities.

Squat

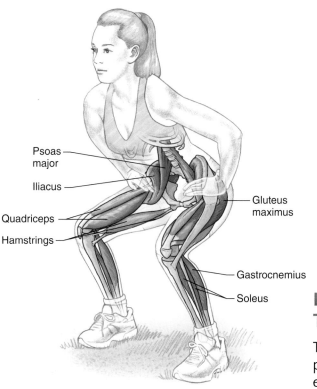

Psoas
major

Iliacus

Quadriceps

Hamstrings

Gluteus
maximus

Gastrocnemius

Soleus

Level 1: squat with toe raise.

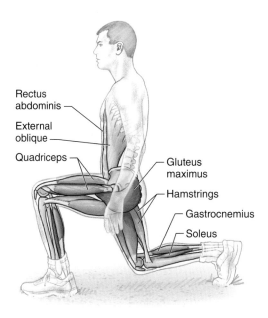

Rectus
abdominis

External
oblique

Quadriceps

Gluteus
maximus

Hamstrings

Gastrocnemius

Soleus

Level 2: walking lunge.

Level 1: Squat With Toe Raise

This is the first of three progressively more demanding exercises designed to increase leg strength. Stand with your feet hip-width apart. Place your hands on your hips if you like. Imagine you are about to sit on a chair. Squat by bending your hips and knees to 90 degrees. Do not let your knees buckle in. Descend slowly and then straighten up more quickly. When your legs are completely straight, rise on your toes and then slowly lower back to the starting position. Continue for 30 seconds. Complete two sets.

Level 2: Walking Lunge

This level 2 exercise narrows the focus to a single leg by using the walking lunge. It may help to have a coach watch your performance from the front to ensure proper technique. The walking lunge increases dynamic flexibility of the quadriceps, hip flexors, and groin. Stand with your feet hip-width apart. Place your hands on your hips if you like. Slowly lunge forward. As you lunge, bend your leading leg until your hip and knee are flexed to 90 degrees and your trailing knee nearly touches the ground. Do not let your forward knee buckle in. Try to keep your upper body erect, with the head up and hips steady. Focus on keeping the forward knee over the foot but not beyond your toes. Do not let the knee wobble back and forth. Inhale and draw in the core during the lunge, and exhale when you stand up. Many people pause briefly between each lunge. Alternate legs as you lunge your way across the pitch (approximately 10 times on each leg), and then jog back. Do two sets across the pitch.

Level 3: One-Leg Squat

The level 3 exercise is quite challenging. It is difficult to squat on one leg and keep the knee over the grounded foot. Of all the exercises, this is probably the most difficult one for many to successfully control the knee. Have a coach watch from the front and alert you if you fail to adequately control the knee. Position yourself beside your partner, each of you standing on one leg, loosely holding onto

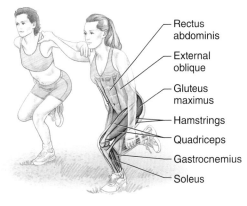

Rectus abdominis

External oblique

Gluteus maximus

Hamstrings

Quadriceps

Gastrocnemius

Soleus

Level 3: one-leg squat.

one another for balance. Keeping the trunk as erect as possible, slowly bend your knee as far as you can but no farther than a 90-degree angle. Concentrate on preventing the knee from buckling in. Bend your knee slowly, and then straighten it a little more quickly, keeping your hips and upper body in line. Repeat the exercise 10 times and switch legs. Do two sets on each leg.

Muscles Involved

Primary: Hip flexors, gluteus maximus, quadriceps, gastrocnemius, soleus

Secondary: Abdominal core, spinal extensors, hamstrings

Soccer Focus

Another part of this prevention program is controlling how players land, either during cutting or jumping. Players who are at risk for knee injuries when landing are those who land stiffly in an erect stance. To counter this, players need to learn to land softly, absorbing the force of impact with their hips, knees, and ankles. To land softly requires you to have good ankle mobility because it is hard for the knees and hips to make up for the ankles, another example of linkage as discussed in the preface. One thought is that players who land stiffly do not have the strength to absorb the force of impact.

Jumping

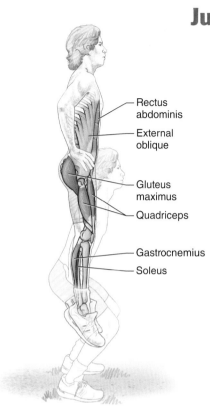

Rectus
abdominis

External
oblique

Gluteus
maximus

Quadriceps

Gastrocnemius

Soleus

Level 1: vertical jump.

Level 1: Vertical Jump

Stand with your feet hip-width apart. Place your hands on your hips if you like. Imagine you are about to sit down on a chair. Bend your legs slowly until your knees are flexed to approximately 90 degrees, and hold for 2 seconds. Do not let your knees buckle in. From this squat position, jump up as high as you can. Land softly on the balls of your feet, with your hips and knees slightly bent. Repeat the exercise for 30 seconds. Rest and then perform a second set.

Level 2: Lateral Jump

Landing on one leg is more difficult, and the level 2 exercise also adds lateral movement. Landing on one leg from a lateral jump is more like a change of direction (cutting) performed in soccer. Although the exercise is markedly slower than cutting during a match, correct form, not speed, is what is important. Stand on one leg with your upper body bent slightly forward from the waist, knee and hip slightly bent. Jump approximately 1 yard (1 m) sideways from the supporting leg to the free leg. Land gently on the ball of your foot. Bend your hip and knee slightly as you land, and do not let your knee buckle in. Also control the trunk so that it remains stable. Recent research

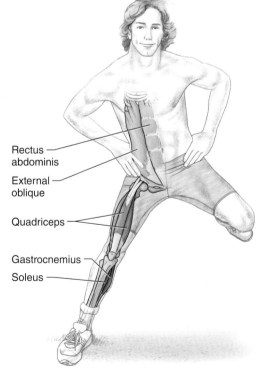

Rectus
abdominis

External
oblique

Quadriceps

Gastrocnemius

Soleus

Level 2: lateral jump.

has shown that poor trunk control precedes a wobbly knee on ground contact, yet those with good trunk control also have good control of the knee.

Maintain your balance with each jump. Watch out for errors such as slight trunk rotation, lateral flexion, or both. Also watch for counterreactions from the arms in an attempt to maintain balance. If you are having trouble controlling your trunk, reduce the distance of the lateral jump until you develop adequate control. Only then should you increase the lateral distance of the jump. Repeat the exercise for 30 seconds, rest, and then perform a second set.

Level 3: Box Jump

Level 3 combines lateral, forward, and backward movement with two-foot landings. Stand with your feet hip-width apart. Imagine that a cross is marked on the ground and you are standing in the middle of it. Alternate jumping forward and backward, left and right, and diagonally across the cross. Jump as quickly and explosively as possible. Your knees and hips should be slightly bent. Land softly on the balls of your feet. Do not let your knees buckle in. Jump from point to point on the cross you have envisioned on the ground, executing the proper landing technique. Land quietly, absorbing the shock with the ankles, knees, and hips. Repeat the exercise for 30 seconds, rest, and then perform a second set.

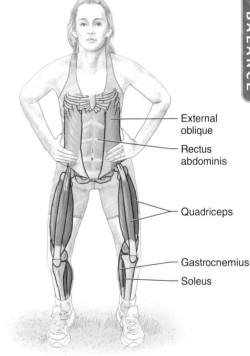

External oblique

Rectus abdominis

Quadriceps

Gastrocnemius

Soleus

Level 3: box jump.

Muscles Involved

Primary: Gluteus maximus, quadriceps, gastrocnemius, soleus

Secondary: Abdominal core, spinal extensors

Soccer Focus

Knee control when landing is a key factor in injury prevention. These three simple plyometric exercises address landing. (Plyometric exercises stretch a muscle right before it contracts.) Land softly and quietly, absorbing the force of the landing with the ankles, knees, and hips. Keep the knees over the feet, and do not let the knees collapse in.

Do not land stiff-legged when you come down from a jump. This seems to be an especially common problem in middle and high school female players. The shock of landing combined with weak hamstrings causes some players to land stiffly and erect. Landing on stiff, straight legs can cause the tibia to shift forward, putting stress on the ACL. When the knees are nearly straight, the hamstrings are at an anatomical disadvantage for resisting this forward shift of the tibia, setting up the ACL for injury. This tibial shift does not happen if you flex the knees during impact; the greater the knee flexion, the less strain on the ACL.

Running Across the Pitch

Execution

Run from one side of the pitch to the other at 75 to 80 percent of your maximum pace. Jog back and repeat a second time.

Muscles Involved

Primary: Hip flexors, quadriceps, gastrocnemius, soleus

Secondary: Hamstrings, peroneals, tibialis anterior

Soccer Focus

Chapter 1 summarizes the physical demands of soccer. About two-thirds of the game is played at a walk and a jog. Some have referred to these as *positional intensities*, when you are adjusting your position on the field in relation to ball and player movement. Faster speeds make up the other third of the game. These faster speeds—cruising and sprinting—have been termed *tactical intensities*, when you are making a concerted effort to attack or defend the goal. The warm-up is about preparing you for the upcoming training, which will include tactical training for attack or defense. Inclusion of some higher-intensity running is important to prepare your body for the harder work to come. To neglect higher-intensity running and move directly into high-intensity training would be too rapid a progression in training intensity, which increases the risk of injury.

Bounding

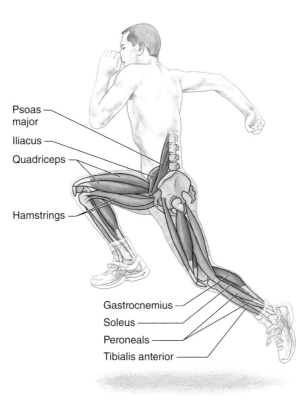

Psoas major

Iliacus

Quadriceps

Hamstrings

Gastrocnemius

Soleus

Peroneals

Tibialis anterior

Execution

Run with high bounding steps, lifting the knees high and landing gently on the balls of your feet. Exaggerate the arm swing (opposite arm and leg) for each step. Try not to let your leading leg cross the midline of your body or let your knee buckle in. Repeat the exercise until you reach the other side of the pitch, and then jog back to recover and repeat a second time.

Muscles Involved

Primary: Hip flexors, quadriceps, gastrocnemius, soleus

Secondary: Hamstrings, peroneals, tibialis anterior

Soccer Focus

Anyone who has seen a track athlete train should be familiar with this exercise. Exaggerate each step with a forceful push-off by the grounded leg and a forceful upward knee drive by the swing leg. The leg drive is aided by an exaggerated arm swing. Keep the trunk stable and erect. Do not allow the leading leg to cross the midline of the body. Keep the knee over the foot of the front leg, and do not let it go into the valgus position (see page 17) when landing.

Plant and Cut

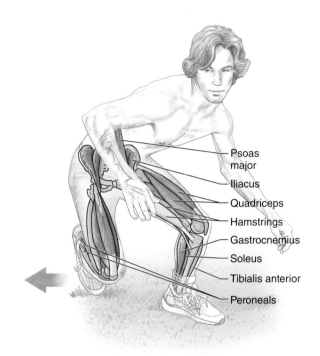

Psoas major
Iliacus
Quadriceps
Hamstrings
Gastrocnemius
Soleus
Tibialis anterior
Peroneals

Execution

Jog four or five steps, and then plant on the outside leg and cut to change direction. Accelerate and sprint five to seven steps at 80 to 90 percent of your maximum pace before you decelerate and do a new plant and cut in the opposite direction. Do not let your knee buckle in during the plant. Repeat the exercise until you reach the other side of the pitch, and then jog back and repeat a second time.

Muscles Involved

Primary: Hip flexors, quadriceps, gastrocnemius, soleus

Secondary: Hamstrings, peroneals, tibialis anterior

Soccer Focus

This exercise is about agility. Many people think agility exercises need to be done as fast as possible, but when speed is the focus, form and posture tend to falter. In this case, correct form, posture, and knee control are more important than speed. Perform this exercise quickly, but not so fast that form is sacrificed. Plant the outside foot firmly and absorb the force of impact using the ankle, knee, and hip, and then sprint off at an angle in the opposite direction.

Most fitness professionals have heard it before: Soccer is a leg game. Why should a soccer player, except perhaps the goalkeeper, pay much attention to the arms? People with these opinions should look carefully at match photos from soccer magazines or websites and note how the trunk, shoulders, and arms are used in soccer. Although the arms do not have much of a primary role in the game, the speed of play and athleticism of players today put players in such close proximity to each other that they must be able to navigate during close-quarter play. Physical contact requires adept balance, and the arms are heavily involved in maintaining balance.

Modern tactics are a combination of direct play and possession. Maintaining possession requires a player to be able to shield an opponent from the ball. Using the arms within the laws of the game helps make the player seem bigger and more difficult to displace from the ball, thereby helping him maintain possession. A system of play that is gaining popularity is the 4-5-1, in which an important trait of the single striker is the ability to maintain possession of the ball in order to play it to oncoming midfield teammates. The player who can reliably hold possession when under defensive pressure will see a lot of minutes.

If that isn't enough to convince you, look at the muscular development of some of the players on TV when they take their shirts off after a match. (If they do this in celebration after scoring, they risk getting a yellow card.) If that level of play is what you aspire to, upper-body resistance training is in your future.

Anatomy of the Upper Extremity

The upper extremity is divided into three segments. The main bone of the upper arm is the humerus, which runs from the shoulder joint to the elbow joint. The forearm runs from the elbow to the wrist. The forearm includes 2 bones, the radius and ulna. The hand and wrist make up the third segment. The wrist has 8 bones and the hand has 19 bones.

Bones, Ligaments, and Joints

The humerus is the one bone of the upper arm. The proximal end, the end toward the trunk of the body—in this case, the shoulder end of the bone—has a rounded head that articulates with the glenoid of the scapula. This is the ball portion of the ball-and-socket shoulder joint, which is discussed further in chapter 4. Around this head are areas for the attachment of muscles from the chest and upper back. As you proceed down the upper arm toward the elbow, the bone is mostly smooth, with sites for muscle attachment for the deltoid and other muscles before it widens and forms the upper portion of the elbow.

The two forearm bones are the ulna and the radius. The ulna is on the side of the little finger, and the radius is on the thumb side. A unique feature of the forearm is its ability to rotate the palm down, or pronate, and rotate the palm up, or supinate. (This is easy to remember: You would hold a bowl of soup with the palm up.) When the forearm is supinated, these two bones are parallel; when the forearm is pronated, the radius crosses over the ulna. The elbow, or proximal, end of the ulna is, for lack of a better word, a hook that wraps around the spool-shaped surface of the humerus. (When you point to your elbow, you touch the knot on the back of the joint. That knot is the ulna.) The proximal end of the radius has a flat concave disc that articulates with the rounded convex end of the humerus. Together, these two bones move around the humerus to flex (decrease the joint angle of) and extend (increase the joint angle of) the elbow. Pronation occurs when the disclike end of the radius rotates over the ulna into a palm-down position. (A similar motion occurs near the wrist.) Technically, pronation and supination occur along the forearm, not the elbow. A number of ligaments maintain the integrity of the joint and are implicated in injuries such as tennis elbow and Little League elbow. A tough ligament that lies between the radius and ulna helps keep the bones parallel and broadens the area for muscle attachment along the forearm.

The wrist and hand are very complex and are best visualized in anatomical position: palms turned forward, with the radius and ulna parallel. The wrist is made up of two parallel rows of bones (carpals), each with four small bones and small ligaments that connect both sides of adjacent bones. The proximal row of bones articulates with the distal ends of the radius and ulna, with the larger radius having the most contact. The wrist actions are flexion and extension plus the unique motions of ulnar deviation, in which the hand bends toward the ulna (decreasing the angle between the little finger and the ulna), and radial deviation, in which the hand bends toward the radius (decreasing the angle between the thumb and the radius). The distal row of carpals articulates with the five metacarpals that make up the palm of the hand. Each of these metacarpals, numbered I to V beginning on the thumb side, has a digit (finger or thumb) attached. The four fingers are made up of three phalanges (proximal, middle, and distal), while the thumb has only two (proximal and distal).

Muscles

All muscles have two attachments. The *origin* is the immobile end; the *insertion* is the movable end. In the overwhelming majority of situations, activating a muscle causes contraction that pulls the insertion toward the origin. Knowing the anatomy of the skeleton and a muscle's origin and insertion tells you the muscle's action, or how the bones move around specific joints. The muscles of the upper extremity have their primary effect on the elbow, forearm, wrist, and fingers, but in a couple of cases they also have some effect at the shoulder.

Muscles Acting on the Elbow

The elbow flexes and extends. The triceps brachii muscle (figure 3.1) of the upper arm performs extension. The word *triceps* refers to the three heads of the muscle, and *brachii* refers to the upper arm region. (Most muscle names are descriptive if you can navigate a little Latin.) The long head is the middle muscle that courses down the back of your upper arm. It originates just under the glenoid of the scapula. The medial and lateral heads originate along the long shaft of the humerus. They join together through a common tendon attaching to that knot you think of as your elbow. As the triceps pulls its insertion toward its origin, the muscle pulls on the ulna, and the result is forearm extension. The long head of the triceps also crosses the shoulder and assists in shoulder extension.

The action opposite forearm extension is forearm flexion. The biceps brachii (figure 3.2) of the upper arm performs forearm flexion. The word *biceps* refers to the two heads of the muscle. Both heads originate on the scapula. One head begins above the glenoid, opposite the long head of the triceps brachii, while the other begins on another location on the scapula underneath the deltoid. These two heads come together to form the belly of the biceps brachii, which inserts through a single tendon on the radius that is easy to see and feel.

A second forearm flexor underneath the biceps brachii is the brachialis. It begins along the anterior (front) shaft of the humerus and inserts on the anterior side of the ulna, just

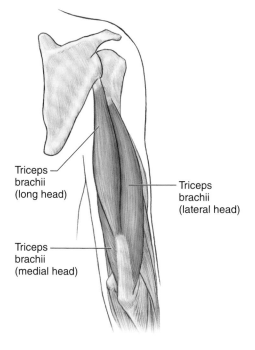

Figure 3.1 Triceps brachii muscle.

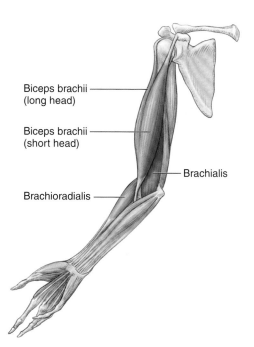

Figure 3.2 Biceps brachii, brachialis, and brachioradialis muscles.

beyond the ulna's hook. The third flexor, the brachioradialis, begins well down the shaft of the humerus and inserts on the radius down toward the base of the thumb. These three muscles work together to flex the forearm.

The biceps brachii inserts proximally on the radius. When this muscle contracts, its first order of business is to supinate the forearm. Forearm flexion is its secondary action. When the forearm is supinated, the biceps can put all its efforts into flexion. But when the forearm is pronated, the biceps tendon is sort of wrapped around the radius, so its first action is to perform supination. Pronate your right hand, and place your left hand on the biceps; feel the biceps brachii contract when you supinate your forearm.

Notice that the muscles are neatly arranged to work in opposition to each other—one group flexes and one group extends. Muscles that work in opposition to each other are said to be *antagonists*. Muscles that work together to perform the same action are called *agonists*.

Muscles Acting on the Wrist and Hand

The dexterity of the hand is a marvel of engineering. To achieve this degree of fine motor control, a large number of muscles in the forearm insert all over the wrist, hand, and fingers. The bulk of the forearm muscles (figure 3.3) originate from a common tendon coming off either the medial or lateral side of the distal humerus. These are those little bumps on either side of your elbow; you might refer to the one on the inside of your elbow as your funny bone. The tendons of the forearm pass under a tough tendinous tissue, called a retinaculum, that wraps around your wrist about where you would wear a wristband.

The muscles that perform flexion mostly originate from the medial bump and are found on the anterior side of the forearm. The extensors originate from the lateral bump and course down the posterior side of the forearm. There are a number of deeper muscles. Most forearm muscles are named for their action (flexor or extensor), location (ulnar or radial side), and insertion (carpal [wrist], digitorum [fingers], pollicis [thumb], indicis [index finger], or digiti minimi [little finger]). If you contract the muscles with *radialis* in their name, you get radial deviation. Muscles with *ulnaris* in their name perform ulnar deviation. A plethora of small intrinsic muscles in the hand assist all these muscles and also perform other actions such as spreading the fingers apart and moving the thumb.

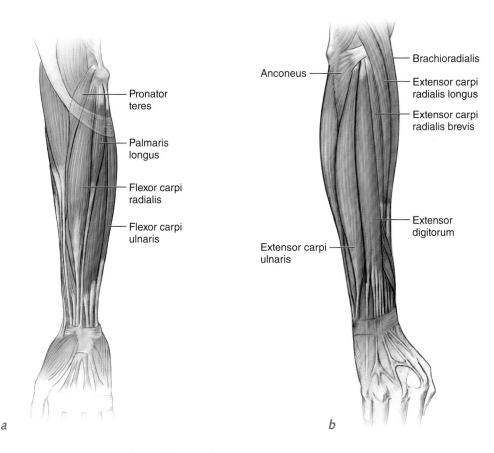

a   *b*

Figure 3.3   Forearm muscles: *(a)* flexors; *(b)* extensors.

The muscles that perform wrist flexion are the flexor carpi radialis, palmaris longus, and flexor carpi ulnaris. The muscles that perform wrist extension are the extensor carpi radialis longus, extensor carpi radialis brevis, and extensor carpi ulnaris. The muscles that perform finger flexion are the flexor digitorum superficialis, flexor digitorum profundus, and flexor pollicis longus. The muscles that perform finger extension are the extensor digitorum, extensor digiti minimi, extensor indicis, extensor pollicis longus, and extensor pollicis brevis.

Dip

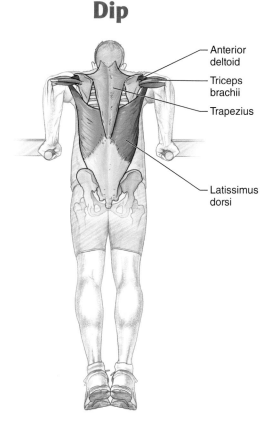

Anterior deltoid

Triceps brachii

Trapezius

Latissimus dorsi

⚠ **SAFETY TIP** Lower your body only until your upper arms are parallel to the floor. Be sure your elbows are not above your shoulders at the lowest point of this exercise. If you do the exercise properly, you should feel a little stretch across the front of your shoulders.

Execution

1. Most weight racks include supports for doing dips. Adjust the height of the supports so that your feet do not touch the ground at the bottom of the descent.

2. Grasp the grips. Jump up and extend your elbows so your arms are straight.

3. Slowly lower your body until your upper arms are parallel to the floor. Maintain correct posture, and move the spine in a straight, vertical path.

4. Pause at the lowest level and then reverse the movement, pushing yourself back up until the elbows are fully extended. Raise the body using the arms; do not push up with the feet. Your feet are for support and balance only.

Muscles Involved

Primary: Anterior deltoid, latissimus dorsi, triceps brachii

Secondary: Pectoralis major, pectoralis minor, trapezius, brachioradialis

Soccer Focus

The dip works the triceps and shoulders. Although soccer focuses on the lower extremity, nearly every challenge from an opponent must be met with resistance using the arms and shoulders. The player who neglects the arms when training will be at a disadvantage during physical contact. Players with the ball often use an arm to keep the opponent at bay. Be cautious when using the arms during such contact. A referee may call a foul if the arm moves toward or above horizontal.

VARIATIONS

On the field, you can perform a modification of the classic dip. Use two stable benches, one for your hands and the other for your feet. Lower yourself toward the ground, moving your spine in a straight line, until your upper arms are parallel with the ground. Pause and then push back up. You can also do a dip by putting your hands on two soccer balls. The depth of the dip is reduced because the balls are not as tall as the bench. Maintaining stability on the round balls adds a dimension of reactive balance as the balls move.

Elastic Band Curl

Execution

1. This exercise can be done from a standing or seated position. Choose an elastic band with the proper level of resistance for you: light (tan, yellow), moderate (red, green), heavy (blue, black), or very heavy (silver, gold). You may have to try out several bands to determine which resistance is best for you.

2. Stand in an erect posture, with your feet about shoulder-width apart.

3. Hold an end of the elastic band in each hand, and stand on the band with both feet.

4. Perform a traditional curl motion by flexing the elbows. Return to the starting position by slowly extending the forearms. You may use both arms in unison or one arm at a time. Maintain an erect posture. Do not flex the trunk, hips, or knees during the exercise.

5. As your strength increases, perform more repetitions with the same band, shorten the band to increase the resistance, or switch to a band that supplies more resistance.

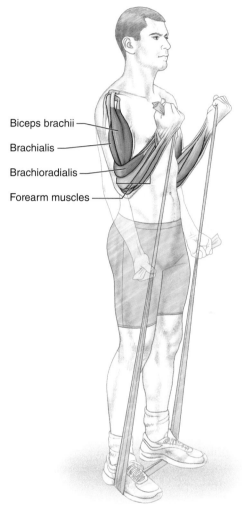

Biceps brachii

Brachialis

Brachioradialis

Forearm muscles

⚠ **SAFETY TIP** If you arch your back, develop a swinging motion in both directions, or use your back to help with the curl, you are probably using too much resistance. Reduce the amount of resistance.

Muscles Involved

Primary: Biceps brachii, brachialis, brachioradialis

Secondary: Forearm muscles (mostly wrist and finger flexors including flexor carpi radialis and ulnaris, palmaris longus, flexor digitorum superficialis and profundus, and flexor pollicis longus) to grasp band

Soccer Focus

Improving strength during training can be a challenge. Push-ups are great for strengthening the forearm extensors and shoulders. Training the forearm flexors is more difficult but still needs to be done in order to achieve muscular balance in the upper arm. In the absence of a pull-up bar, a little creativity is needed. Elastic bands are very versatile and affordable and can be used to train most major muscle groups. Elastic bands have different degrees of resistance, usually indicated by the band's color. Using a shorter band that must be stretched from hand to hand can further increase resistance. A creative coach might use this exercise as one station in a circuit of various activities.

VARIATION

Dumbbell Curl

A dumbbell curl works the same primary muscles but allows the additional actions of pronation and supination. You can raise the dumbbell in a supinated (palm up) position and lower it in a pronated (palm down) position. When the entire curl motion is performed with the forearm in pronation (palm down), the biceps is less involved, forcing more work from the brachialis and brachioradialis. Sitting on a ball adds a balance dimension not encountered when using a stable bench.

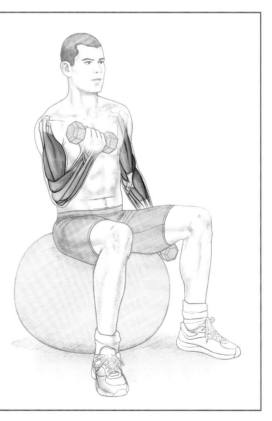

Lat Pull-Down

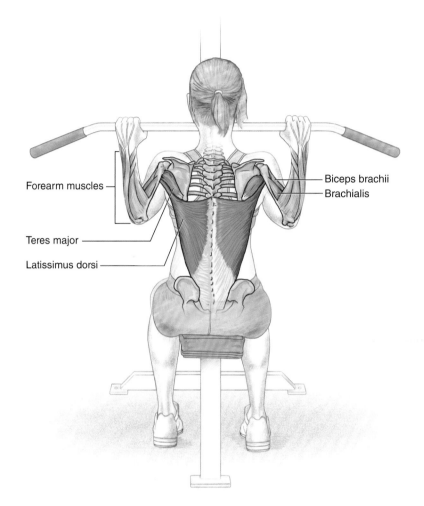

Forearm muscles

Biceps brachii
Brachialis

Teres major

Latissimus dorsi

Execution

1. Sit at a lat pull-down machine with the seat set for your body size. Adjust the seat so that the pad secures your thighs. This keeps you seated throughout the exercise.

2. Reach up and grab the ends of the bar in an overhand grip. Leading with the elbows, perform elbow flexion to start pulling the bar below the level of your chin as you squeeze your shoulder blades together. Continue to pull the bar down.

3. Slowly return the weight to the starting position.

⚠️ **SAFETY TIP** The old way to perform this exercise was to pull the bar down to touch the back of the neck, but this can increase the stress on the neck and aggravate shoulder problems. It is easy to let momentum take over when doing this exercise, so pause briefly at the end of each movement.

Muscles Involved

Primary: Latissimus dorsi, teres major

Secondary: Biceps brachii, brachialis, forearm muscles to grasp bar

Soccer Focus

Although using the outstretched arms to hold an opponent at bay is against the rules, depending on the referee, the arms and shoulders still need to be strong to resist an opponent in tight quarters. When dribbling in a crowd, you will use your arms for balance and to maintain space. The combination of the muscles of the arm and shoulder allows this. Look closely at strikers in the modern game. They have well-developed and defined arm and shoulder muscles. For

some machines that use a pulley system, you will kneel and face the device. As your strength improves and the resistance increases, you may need a partner to stand behind you and press down on your shoulders to keep you on the floor.

VARIATION

Barbell Pull-Up

Place a barbell on a weight rack high enough that you can hang from it with your feet on a weight bench. Lie under the bar and establish an overhand grip, with your hands about shoulder-width apart. Pull your body up to the bar, and then extend your arms to return to the starting position. This is sort of an upside-down push-up or bench press that also works the lats. Make sure you keep your body in a straight line when doing this. Draw in your core, too.

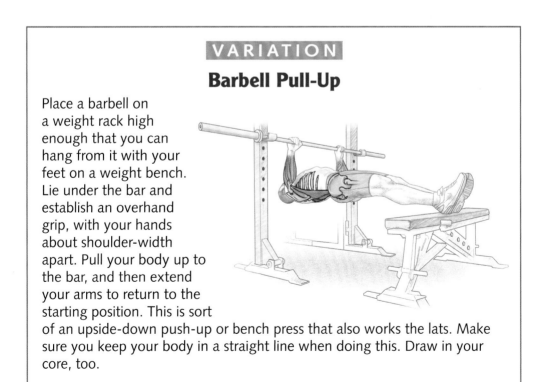

Seated Triceps Extension

Forearm muscles

Triceps brachii

Rectus abdominis

External oblique

⚠ **SAFETY TIP** Posture is important. Keep the head aligned with the spine. Keep the elbows in a fixed position, and don't drop the shoulders to help lift the weight.

Execution

1. Sit in a chair with a low back or on a bench with no back support. Spread your legs, with your knees flexed and feet flat on the floor.
2. Hold a dumbbell vertical, wrapping both hands around the inside weight of one end of the dumbbell.
3. Raise your elbows toward the ceiling. Flex your elbows so the weight is behind your head. Keep your elbows close to your ears.
4. Extend your forearms until they are in full extension.
5. Slowly lower the weight back to the starting position. Maintain good posture with an erect back during the exercise.

Muscles Involved

Primary: Triceps brachii

Secondary: Abdominal core (external oblique, internal oblique, transversus abdominis, rectus abdominis), spinal extensors (erector spinae, multifidus), forearm muscles to grasp dumbbell

Soccer Focus

Despite the size of a large soccer field (usually 110 yards by 70 yards [100 m by 64 m]), opponents may find themselves in close quarters anywhere on the field. Although raising an arm toward vertical during a confrontation may be whistled by the ref, angling the arms toward the ground and holding them in an almost isometric contraction can make it more difficult for an opponent to make a fair attempt at obtaining

control of the ball. The focus of soccer may be on the lower extremity, but the arms play a repeated role in who obtains or maintains control of the ball.

VARIATION

Triceps Kickback

A variation is the popular triceps kickback with a dumbbell. Kneel on a weight bench, and lean forward until the trunk is about parallel with the floor. Hold the dumbbell in the arm opposite the kneeling leg so the upper arm is parallel to the trunk, and then extend the forearm to full extension. Or stand in a staggered stance with the weight in the hand opposite the leg in front. Add stability by placing the inactive hand on the forward knee.

Seated triceps extensions can be made more challenging if you sit on a large stability ball. This will require you to react to the movements of the ball as you perform the exercise. Another alternative is to perform triceps extensions with a cable machine. Face away from the cable machine, and use both hands to grab the handle over your head. Extend your elbows.

Standing Push-Down

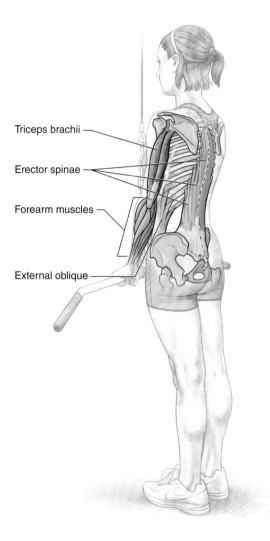

Triceps brachii

Erector spinae

Forearm muscles

External oblique

Execution

1. Stand and face a cable machine. Grasp the bar using an overhand grip, with your hands about shoulder-width apart.
2. Keep your elbows close to your body as you bring your forearms to full extension.
3. Hold the bar briefly at full extension before slowly returning the bar to the starting position.

Muscles Involved

Primary: Triceps brachii

Secondary: Abdominal core, spinal extensors, forearm muscles to grasp bar

Soccer Focus

Some sports, such as American football, favor mass, and some, such as basketball and volleyball, favor height. Soccer is a game for the masses since it does not require any particular body dimensions for those who play and enjoy the game. The typical soccer player is closer to the average height and weight for his age and gender. It is uncommon to see heavily developed players, especially in the upper body. But to neglect the upper body would mean placing oneself at a disadvantage during physical challenges.

VARIATION

Reverse Push-Down

Stand and face the cable machine. Grasp the bar in a reverse grip with the palms up. Execute the same movement. This variation works the same muscles but recruits them differently.

Barbell Curl

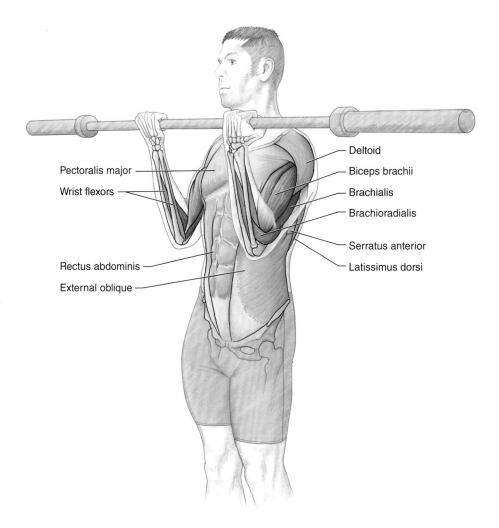

Pectoralis major

Wrist flexors

Rectus abdominis

External oblique

Deltoid

Biceps brachii

Brachialis

Brachioradialis

Serratus anterior

Latissimus dorsi

Execution

1. Stand in an erect posture, with your feet about shoulder-width apart and a barbell in front of you.
2. Grasp the bar in a supinated (palm up) grip.
3. Raise the bar by performing forearm flexion and moving the weight toward the shoulders. Lift the bar through the full range of motion. Pause briefly and then slowly lower the bar to the starting position.

⚠ **SAFETY TIP** **Keep the body aligned and the spine in neutral position. Keep the movement under control—do not let momentum play a role.**

Muscles Involved

Primary: Biceps brachii, brachialis, brachioradialis

Secondary: Wrist flexors (flexor carpi radialis and ulnaris, palmaris longus), stabilizers of the trunk (abdominal core, erector spinae) and shoulders (deltoid, supraspinatus, infraspinatus, subscapularis, teres minor, latissimus dorsi, pectoralis major), scapular stabilizers (serratus anterior, rhomboid major and minor, middle trapezius)

Soccer Focus

During free play on the field, the arms are used mostly to keep an opponent away from the ball or to gain a bit of an advantage when running with an opponent, within the laws of the game, of course. These actions generally do not require forearm flexion. It would be unwise, however, to focus strength training solely on actions specific to the game and neglect antagonist muscles. To do so would lead to muscle imbalances, which are not advisable for optimal muscle and joint function.

VARIATION

Machine Curl

A machine curl works the same primary muscles. Sit in a curl machine. Adjust the seat to allow access to the bar when you are in an erect posture and your feet are flat on the machine's platform. With the weight lowered, grasp the bar or handles in a supinated (palm up) grip. Raise the weight by performing forearm flexion and moving the weight toward the shoulder. Lift the weight through the full range of motion. Pause briefly and then slowly lower the weight to the starting position.

CHAPTER 4

SHOULDERS AND NECK

In a sport such as soccer, the attention is on the lower extremities, the legs. Soccer players move and perform the bulk of their skills with the ball using the lower extremities. Often players who decide to add resistance training to their programs focus on the legs alone, but this is shortsighted. Every section of the body above the legs is recruited during play to prevent injuries, maintain balance, increase speed, generate and transfer power, maintain space, perform throw-ins, and much more.

When choosing to supplement your ball training, realize that the entire body, not just the legs, needs to be addressed. Imbalances within and between the various regions of the body can derail performance and may even increase the risk of injury. An overall fitter player will be able to delay fatigue and go deeper into a match, increasing his chances of affecting the outcome of the match. The fitter player also is more resistant to injury, and on teams that have minimal substitutes, keeping players healthy is a prime reason for supplementing training.

Anatomy of the Shoulder Joint

A joint, or articulation, is where bones come together. The three main types of joints are immovable, slightly movable, and freely movable. Examples of immovable joints are the bones of the adult skull and the joints between the three bones that make up each side of the pelvis. Examples of slightly movable joints are where the ribs connect to the sternum. Freely movable joints are what most people think of when envisioning a joint—shoulder, elbow, knee, ankle, and others—and there are different types of freely movable joints. Two of the most common injuries sustained by soccer players damage the joint integrity of the ankle or the knee.

The typical freely movable joint is encased inside a sleeve of connective tissue called the *synovial capsule*. Thickenings of this capsule at specific locations form the ligaments. Ligaments connect bone to bone, and tendons connect muscle to bone. Most ligaments are extra-articular; that is, they are outside of the joint capsule that surrounds the two bones. The notable exceptions are the anterior and posterior cruciate ligaments, which are intra-articular and are found within the joint capsule of the knee. (Learn more about the knee in chapter 8.)

The upper arm is connected to the central portion of the skeleton, which is called the axial skeleton, through what appears to be a very simple arrangement that has a complex overall function. The humerus, the upper arm bone, articulates with the glenoid, the mostly flat surface of the scapula that is made deeper by a cartilage cup called the glenoid labrum. The scapula rides on some deep muscles of the back and can slide and rotate a bit around the curved surface of the ribs. But its only connection to the axial skeleton is by way of the clavicle, or collarbone, to the sternum, or breastbone. So what we see are three distinct joints: the sternoclavicular joint (clavicle to sternum), the acromioclavicular joint (clavicle to a specific location on the scapula, the point on the top of your shoulder), and the glenohumeral joint (the flat glenoid on the scapula to the rounded head of the humerus). You may hear of a scapulothoracic joint between the scapula and the ribs, although there is no direct bony articulation between the scapula and the ribs.

The ligaments of the sternoclavicular joint are quite strong, and this joint is not injured very frequently in soccer. The acromioclavicular joint has a number of ligaments for both stability and mobility that can be injured during soccer play, mostly from a direct blow to the top of the shoulder (e.g., falling and landing on the tip of the shoulder). The glenohumeral joint is the most mobile joint in the body and is an amazing feat of biomechanical engineering. The joint capsule thickens into a number of distinct glenohumeral ligaments. This joint dislocates most often when the arm is outstretched and forced into another direction, usually backward, leading to the humerus dislocating forward or anteriorly.

> A *shoulder dislocation* occurs at the glenohumeral joint. A *shoulder separation* occurs at the acromioclavicular joint.

The body is divided into three planes. The frontal plane divides the body into front and back sections, the sagittal plane divides the body into right and left sections, and the transverse plane divides the body into upper and lower sections. All movements of the shoulder are described according to the plane in which the movement occurs. As the most mobile joint in the body, the shoulder moves in all three planes and has a number of distinct movements (see table 4.1).

Mobility is a good thing, but it also increases the potential for injury. In soccer, collisions and falls cause most of the injuries to the upper extremity and shoulder girdle. A player with strong shoulder muscles will be able to react to and withstand impact to protect the shoulder.

Table 4.1 Shoulder Movements

Plane	Movement	Description
Frontal	Flexion	Arm raised in front of body
	Extension	Arm lowered in front of body, continuing beyond trunk
Sagittal	Abduction	Arm raised out to the side
	Adduction	Arm lowered back to the side
Transverse	Internal rotation	Humerus rotated toward the midline of the body; best visualized by flexing the elbow first
	External rotation	Humerus rotated away from the midline of the body; best visualized by flexing the elbow first
	Horizontal adduction	First the arm is abducted out to the side and then moved horizontally toward the midline
	Horizontal abduction	Arm is raised in front of body and then moved horizontally away from the midline
Multiplanar	Circumduction	Arm is held parallel to the floor and swung in a wide circle (incorporates all shoulder motions)

Shoulder Muscles

Most shoulder muscles attach to the scapula. As stated in chapter 3, a muscle has two attachments. In general the *origin* is at the immobile end, while the *insertion* is at the movable end. In the majority of situations, when a muscle is stimulated and contracts, it pulls the insertion toward the origin. Most muscles cross one joint, so its action is on that one joint, but when a muscle crosses two joints, it can have an effect on both joints. When you can picture a muscle's origin and insertion, you can reason out its action.

Deltoid

The deltoid muscle group (figure 4.1) forms the cap over the shoulder joint. There are three distinct muscles: the anterior deltoid toward the front, the lateral deltoid in the middle, and the posterior deltoid toward the back. The anterior deltoid originates on the clavicle; the lateral deltoid originates on the acromion process of the scapula (that point on the top of your shoulder); and the posterior deltoid originates on the spine of the scapula, which is on the posterior surface of the scapula. These three muscles attach to a common tendon that inserts laterally (away from the midline) on the humerus.

Together, the deltoid muscle group abducts the arm. Individually, the anterior deltoid helps with shoulder flexion, and the posterior deltoid assists with shoulder extension. Put one hand over the deltoid, and perform each action. When you raise your arm as if you were answering a question (shoulder flexion), you should feel the anterior deltoid, but not the posterior deltoid, contract.

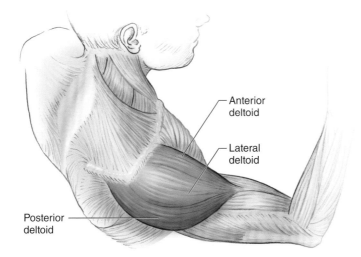

Anterior deltoid

Lateral deltoid

Posterior deltoid

Figure 4.1 Deltoid muscle group.

Rotator Cuff

The rotator cuff muscles are necessary for rotating the humerus in the glenoid, but they also are critical for shoulder stability. Unlike the hip, the shoulder does not have much in the way of structural constraints, so muscles need to provide the support. The rotator cuff (figure 4.2) is made up of four muscles. The subscapularis originates from the underside of the scapula, courses under the arm, and inserts anteriorly on the humerus. This is the main muscle for internal rotation of the humerus in the glenoid and is the muscle usually injured when a baseball pitcher tears his rotator cuff. The other three muscles of the rotator cuff are found mostly on the backside of the scapula: the supraspinatus (*supra* means it is above the spine of the scapula), infraspinatus (*infra* means it is below the spine of the scapula), and teres minor (*teres* means ropelike, and *minor* means it is the smaller of two ropelike muscles). Together, these three muscles perform external rotation of the humerus in the glenoid and assist in a number of other actions.

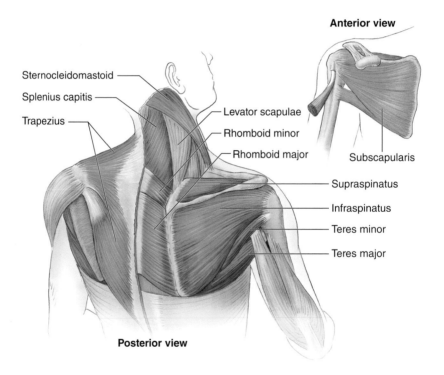

Figure 4.2 Muscles of the rotator cuff and neck.

Other Shoulder Muscles

Many other shoulder muscles help with shoulder mobility and stability:

- **Rhomboid major and minor.** These muscles originate mostly on the upper thoracic vertebrae (the vertebrae where the ribs attach) and run diagonally down, inserting on the nearby border of the scapula. The rhomboids help adduct the scapula (pull the scapula to the vertebral column), elevate the scapula (shrug the shoulders), and rotate the glenoid inferiorly (down, away from the head) because of the diagonal direction of the muscle's fibers.

- **Levator scapulae.** This muscle originates on the upper cervical vertebrae (the neck) and inserts at the upper corner of the scapula. By its name, it elevates the scapula, but it also assists in rotating the glenoid inferiorly as well as in scapular adduction.

- **Serratus anterior.** This muscle can be difficult to visualize. It originates on the lateral surface (away from the midline) of a number of ribs and follows the ribs back toward the vertical border where the rhomboids insert. When activated, the serratus anterior pulls the scapula around the surface of the ribs, away from the vertebral column. Picture the movement of the scapula when someone performs a boxing jab. This muscle is addressed again in chapter 5.

- **Trapezius.** This broad, flat muscle of the upper back is just under the skin. It originates all along the cervical and thoracic vertebral column and inserts at the lateral end of the spine of the scapula to adduct the scapula. Functionally, the trapezius is three muscles: upper, middle, and lower. The upper trapezius elevates and rotates the glenoid down, while the lower trapezius rotates the glenoid up and stabilizes the scapula to prevent rotation.

Neck Muscles

The neck is very mobile, but it is also a fragile area of the body. Because of heading, the neck muscles figure prominently in soccer. The motions of the neck include flexion (moving the chin down) and extension (moving the chin up), lateral flexion (tilting the head toward either shoulder), and rotation (turning the head). These actions can be combined for circular motions.

The primary neck flexor is the sternocleidomastoid, which originates on the clavicle and sternum, inserting on the mastoid of the skull (that knot behind your ear). The sternocleidomastoid also turns the head right or left; contracting the muscle on the right side turns the face to the left and vice versa. The main neck extensor is the splenius capitis, which originates on a number of vertebrae and inserts at the base of the skull. The levator scapulae and upper trapezius assist in neck extension. Lateral flexion is accomplished by contracting these muscles on the right or left side to move the head in the appropriate direction.

Seal Crawl

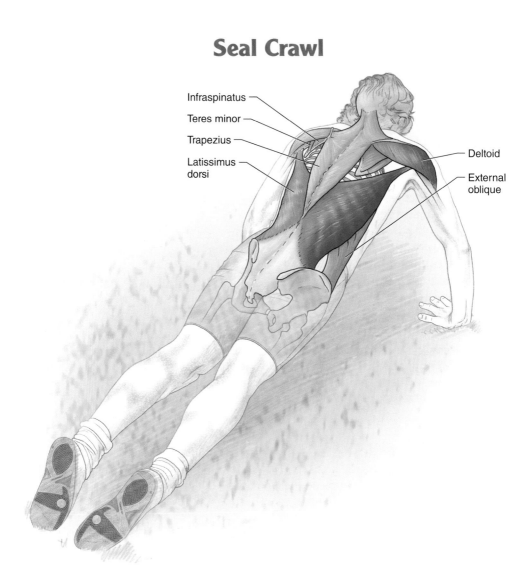

Infraspinatus

Teres minor

Trapezius

Latissimus dorsi

Deltoid

External oblique

Execution

1. Lie on the ground. Get into the up position of a traditional push-up but on your insteps, not your toes. Keep your insteps on the ground for this exercise.

2. Using only your arms for propulsion, crawl around, dragging your legs. Changing directions and speed involves more muscles, so do not crawl in a straight line. Keep your back and hips straight, and do not allow your trunk to sag toward the ground. Go farther and faster as your strength improves.

Muscles Involved

Primary: Latissimus dorsi, deltoid

Secondary: Rotator cuff (subscapularis, supraspinatus, infraspinatus, teres minor), trapezius, spinal extensors (erector spinae, multifidus) and abdominal core (external oblique, internal oblique, transversus abdominis, rectus abdominis) to maintain a straight back

Soccer Focus

The shoulder joint is very complex. Unlike the hip, the shoulder has little structural bone support. The lack of bony restraint allows for extensive motion around the shoulder. About 15 muscles attach to the scapula, clavicle, and humerus to manage this movement. Exercising each muscle and movement separately would require a lot of time and special equipment. Choose exercises that work multiple muscles in many different movements to make the most of your training time. The seal crawl requires functional motion and support from most of the shoulder, back, and abdominal muscles. This is a good general exercise for every player but especially for young players who tend to have weak shoulders.

VARIATION

Wheelbarrow

The wheelbarrow exercise requires a partner. While performing the action, you provide the pace of movement, not your partner. You pull; your partner does not push. Keep your back straight. If you have trouble keeping your back straight, have your partner hold your legs farther up toward your thighs.

⚠️ **SAFETY TIP** Even if your back sags a bit when you perform the seal crawl, try to keep it straight when performing the wheelbarrow. It is best to perform these exercises on a safe surface such as grass or the floor. Avoid surfaces littered with debris that might cut or injure the hands.

Arm Wrestling

Trapezius —
— Supraspinatus

Pectoralis major —
— Teres minor

Triceps brachii —
— Infraspinatus

— Deltoid

— Serratus anterior

— External oblique

— Rectus abdominis

Execution

1. You will need a partner for this exercise. You and your partner lie facedown on the ground with your heads nearly touching. Get in the up position for a traditional push-up.

2. On your coach's command, try to touch or gently slap your partner's hands while trying to avoid being touched or slapped by your partner. Although some movement may occur, try to stay in the same place.

3. The duration of this exercise will vary according to arm and abdominal strength. First perform the exercise for 15 seconds, and increase the time as fitness improves.

Muscles Involved

Primary: Triceps brachii, pectoralis major, deltoid, serratus anterior, trapezius

Secondary: Rotator cuff, spinal extensors, abdominal core

Soccer Focus

This is a good exercise for working a wide range of muscles—the abdominals and back muscles for posture, the muscles that attach to the humerus to maintain the desired position and balance when one hand is off the ground, and the muscles that attach to the scapula to control the shoulders as you challenge each other. This exercise improves strength, balance, and local muscle endurance of the shoulders, arms, trunk, and back. Improvements in these aspects of muscle function will help you play deeper into the match and resist fatigue. Training is not just about the legs and the heart. Training for a whole-body activity such as soccer means addressing the whole body. Focusing only on the legs is a common error when training.

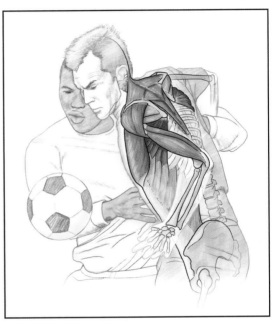

Head–Ball–Head Isometrics

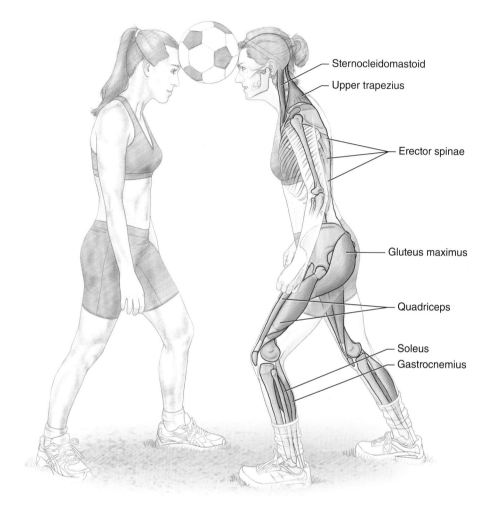

Sternocleidomastoid

Upper trapezius

Erector spinae

Gluteus maximus

Quadriceps

Soleus
Gastrocnemius

⚠️ **SAFETY TIP** Trying to best your partner could make the ball pop out and cause you to bump heads. Be careful. This isn't about winning.

Execution

1. Find a partner of similar height and weight. Stand in a staggered stance facing each other. Pin the ball between your foreheads. You may find it helpful to hold each other's upper arms.

2. Push with your legs through the trunk, neck, and ball in an attempt to push your partner back as your partner attempts to push you back. Keep the ball pinned between your heads. *This is not a competitive exercise.* You are not trying to beat your partner. The idea is to squeeze the ball.

3. At first perform a few repetitions of 10 seconds each. As you get stronger, increase the number and duration of repetitions.

Muscles Involved

Primary: Sternocleidomastoid, upper trapezius

Secondary: Gastrocnemius, soleus, quadriceps (vastus medialis, vastus lateralis, vastus intermedius, rectus femoris), gluteus maximus, spinal extensors

Soccer Focus

For very young players, heading the ball is more of a novelty that usually happens from a bounced or thrown ball. Most very young players are unable to consistently get the ball airborne or master the movements necessary to properly head the ball, making heading a pretty rare skill. As players age and grow, heading takes on an integral role in the game, making it necessary to devise ways to increase neck strength. Neck strength is important not only for heading but also to protect the head during collisions. The head is protected when the neck muscles contract to anchor the head to the much heavier torso. When the neck muscles are not strong enough, the head can jerk, causing whiplash or concussion even in the absence of a direct blow to the head.

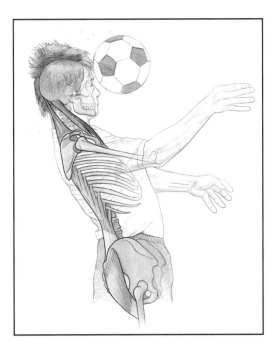

Partner-Assisted Neck Resistance

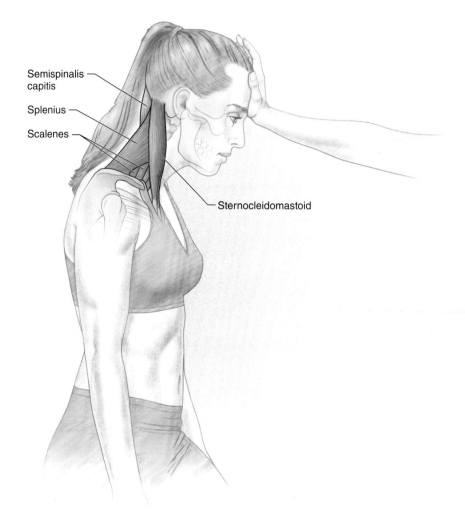

Semispinalis capitis

Splenius

Scalenes

Sternocleidomastoid

Execution

1. Find a partner of similar height and weight. Your partner will provide resistance to you as you perform the exercise. Have your partner stand in front of you with her arm extended and the palm of her hand on your forehead.

2. Flex your neck forward against the resistance provided by your partner. Your partner should provide resistance but still allow you to move through the full range of motion. The strength of this movement comes from the neck, not the trunk.

3. Repeat the exercise for all directions of movement. This can be repeated for neck extension (partner's hand on the back of your head) as well as to both sides for lateral flexion (partner's hand on one side of the head and then the other).

Muscles Involved

Primary: Sternocleidomastoid (forward flexion, lateral flexion), splenius (extension), upper trapezius (backward extension, lateral flexion)

Secondary: Neck stabilizers (such as splenius, semispinalis capitis, and scalenes)

Soccer Focus

Heading is a complex skill that does not come naturally. Why would anyone voluntarily put his head in the path of a fast-moving object? Most teams have players who will do anything to get their heads on the ball and players who will go out of their way to avoid heading the ball. Consider the difficulty of heading. When the ball is in the air, the player must decide where on the field he needs to be to head the ball and what speed and direction are necessary to get there. When he heads the ball, will he be standing or running and, if running, in what direction?

Will he have to jump? How high? Off one leg or two? Where will he redirect the ball? In the air, to the ground, to a teammate? If to a teammate, should he direct the ball to his teammate's feet, in the path he is running, or somewhere else? If the header is a shot on goal, the goalkeeper must be avoided, so where is the goalkeeper? Few of these decisions involve an opponent, and all decisions must be made well ahead of impact with the ball or the opponent. It's a wonder anyone really wants to head a ball. But when done well, heading is an electrifying skill that can thrill player and spectator alike.

VARIATIONS

There are a number of variations to this exercise. One involves a towel. Your partner stands in front of you and drapes a towel around the back of your head, holding both ends. You perform neck extension against the resistance of the towel. Your partner stands opposite the movement you perform instead of in the direction of your movement as in the main exercise. If you don't have a partner, another variation is to perform isometrics by squeezing the ball against a wall using the various neck motions.

Floor Bridge

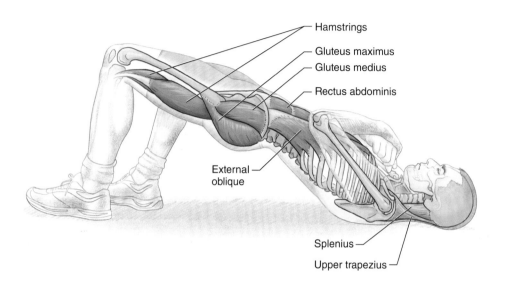

Hamstrings

Gluteus maximus

Gluteus medius

Rectus abdominis

External oblique

Splenius

Upper trapezius

SAFETY TIP At the top of the bridge, the shoulders should be in contact with the floor. This should not put any strain on the head or neck.

Execution

1. Lie on your back with your knees bent, feet flat on the floor and spread about hip-width apart. You may need to spread your arms to your sides for balance.
2. Raise your hips and trunk until your body forms a straight line from your knees to your shoulders.
3. Pause at the top position for a couple of seconds, and draw in your core. Slowly lower your trunk nearly to the ground. Hold this position and repeat. Start with five repetitions, and progress as strength improves.

Muscles Involved

Primary: Hamstrings (biceps femoris, semitendinosus, semimembranosus), gluteus maximus, gluteus medius, abdominal core

Secondary: Upper trapezius, splenius, spinal extensors

Soccer Focus

In years past, supplemental training for the neck was limited to neck bridges borrowed from wrestling. In wrestling, neck bridging is an important skill to keep from being pinned, but it is largely isometric and mostly involves neck extension and hyperextension. In soccer, a strong neck not only helps with heading but also is important for stabilizing the head during collisions with the ball, other players, the ground, the goalposts, and more. But there are other options for improving support from the neck and shoulders. Although this is most commonly thought of as a core exercise, the neck and shoulders are one of three points of ground contact and have to work against the push applied by the feet. They are also activated when the trunk is elevated. Be sure to keep the glutes contracted and the abdominals drawn in throughout the exercise.

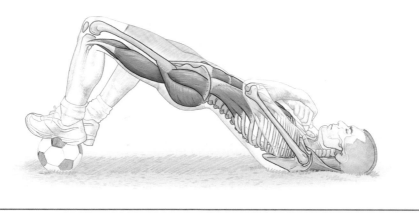

An element of balance can be added very easily. Instead of placing your feet on the ground for this bridge exercise, place your feet on a ball. Adding an unstable element and a narrower base of support greatly increases the difficulty of the exercise. In the gym, you can do this exercise with your feet on a large stability ball.

Pull-Up

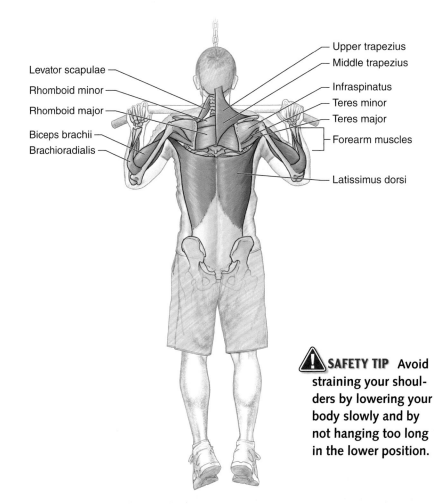

Levator scapulae

Rhomboid minor

Rhomboid major

Biceps brachii

Brachioradialis

Upper trapezius

Middle trapezius

Infraspinatus

Teres minor

Teres major

Forearm muscles

Latissimus dorsi

⚠ **SAFETY TIP** Avoid straining your shoulders by lowering your body slowly and by not hanging too long in the lower position.

Execution

1. With your hands a bit more than shoulder-width apart, grasp an overhead horizontal bar or handles on a pull-up rack, palms turned away from you.
2. Inhale and draw the navel in. Pull the body weight up until the chin is over the bar. Exhale at the point of greatest difficulty.
3. Slowly return to the starting position and repeat. Do as many as you can.

Muscles Involved

Primary: Latissimus dorsi, upper and middle trapezius, biceps brachii, brachioradialis

Secondary: Levator scapulae, rhomboid major and minor, teres major and minor, infraspinatus, forearm muscles (mostly wrist and finger flexors including flexor carpi radialis and ulnaris, palmaris longus, flexor digitorum superficialis and profundus, and flexor pollicis longus) to grasp bar

Soccer Focus

Many of the exercises in this book use body mass as the resistance. The classic pull-up is a multijoint exercise that uses body mass as resistance and is still hard to beat. For general, all-around work on the shoulders, you could do push-ups, pull-ups, and dips and expect to work almost every muscle with an attachment to the scapula and humerus. Although the pull-up increases strength, it also improves local muscle endurance because improvements are generally seen as increased repetitions. For greater strength, some athletes add resistance and intensity by hanging a free weight to a belt and wearing it around the waist.

VARIATION

Palms up or palms down? Most agree that a pull-up with the palms up is somewhat easier than a pull-up with the palms down. The reason is anatomy. The biceps brachii originates on the scapula and inserts on the radius. The brachialis originates on the humerus and inserts on the ulna. The motion of the ulna is elbow flexion and extension like the radius, but the radius also rotates over the ulna for forearm pronation and supination. The biceps is a supinator first and an elbow flexor second, while the brachialis is only a forearm flexor. When pull-ups are done with the palms up, the biceps doesn't need to supinate, so these two muscles work together to flex the elbow. When the palms are down, the biceps tries to supinate, leaving the brachialis to act without much help, making the exercise harder.

One-Arm Dumbbell Row

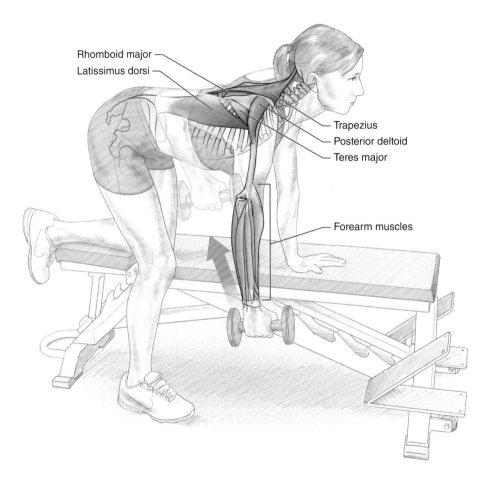

Rhomboid major
Latissimus dorsi
Trapezius
Posterior deltoid
Teres major
Forearm muscles

Execution

1. Kneel on your left knee on a padded bench. Add support by placing your left hand on the bench. Your right foot is flat on the floor, as is a dumbbell.
2. Lean forward at the hip while keeping the spine straight, and grasp the dumbbell.
3. Inhale as you raise the arm and flex the elbow as high as possible, lifting the weight to the trunk.
4. Pause at the top of the lift, and then exhale as you lower the weight until the arm is fully extended. The motion is similar to sawing wood.

Muscles Involved

Primary: Latissimus dorsi, teres major, posterior deltoid, trapezius, rhomboid major and minor

Secondary: Forearm muscles, spinal extensors for posture

Soccer Focus

Modern soccer tactics are twofold. On offense, the team tries to make the field as big as possible to give players room to maneuver and spread the defense thin. On defense, the team tries to make the field as small as possible so the team defense is very compact, and each defender is close to the ball. Players inevitably find themselves in very close quarters while competing for the ball. One of the best ways players, especially strikers, can keep a defender away from the ball is to shield the defender from the ball. This requires back and shoulder strength to make the attacking player seem bigger than he really is and avoid the wrath of the referee for unfair use of the arms. A player who is adept at screening defenders and able to maintain possession of the ball will play a lot of minutes. Possession is a big part of the game, so being able to screen defenders away from the ball is a critical and often overlooked skill.

VARIATIONS

Posture is important during rowing exercises. The standing row is a complex exercise, like many barbell lifts. You must raise the weighted bar off the floor to the thighs and then assume the specific posture before executing the row. T-bar rows, especially when performed while lying on a bench, provide support for the trunk and offer a measure of safety. Many cable machines are capable of a rowing motion that isolates the movement for safe execution of the lift.

Prone Dumbbell Fly

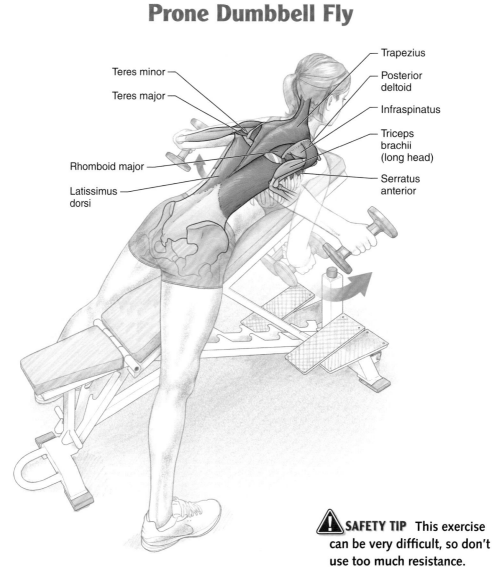

Teres minor

Teres major

Rhomboid major

Latissimus dorsi

Trapezius

Posterior deltoid

Infraspinatus

Triceps brachii (long head)

Serratus anterior

⚠️ **SAFETY TIP** This exercise can be very difficult, so don't use too much resistance.

Execution

1. Lie prone on a padded bench. Your head or neck may hang over the end of the bench. Be sure the bench is well grounded and not at all unstable. Two dumbbells are on the floor on either side of the bench.

2. Grasp the weights. With elbows slightly flexed, inhale and raise your arms to lift the weights, attempting to make the arms horizontal to the floor.

3. Slowly lower the weights as you exhale.

Muscles Involved

Primary: Trapezius, rhomboid major and minor, serratus anterior, posterior deltoid, teres major, latissimus dorsi

Secondary: Triceps brachii (long head), erector spinae, rotator cuff

Soccer Focus

Watch what goes on in the penalty area of a professional match as players prepare to receive a corner kick. The pushing, shoving, grabbing, holding off, and fighting for position in the seconds just before the actual kick might surprise you. A corner kick is a scoring opportunity that has a good enough probability for success that players will be very aggressive when establishing their positions to either deflect or defend the approaching ball. (Interestingly, the scoring probability for a corner kick is not as high as you might expect. Only about 2 percent of corner kicks result in goals. One coach told me his team went 1 for more than 100 in one season.) A striker who is being counted on to gain an advantageous position for these opportunities will not be very effective if he isn't able to use his arms within the laws of the game to maintain his position in the crowded penalty area.

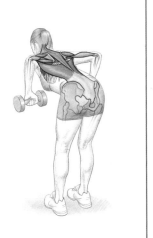

VARIATION

Bent-Over Row

A bent-over row is a good alternative to the prone dumbbell fly. Maintain good spinal posture when performing the bent-over row; don't round the back. This exercise mainly works the muscles that attach to the scapula—the muscles that help maintain good scapular motion, shoulder flexibility, and range of motion.

Neck Machine Flexion and Extension

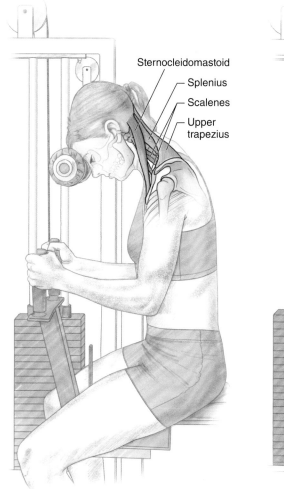

Sternocleidomastoid
Splenius
Scalenes
Upper trapezius

Flexion.

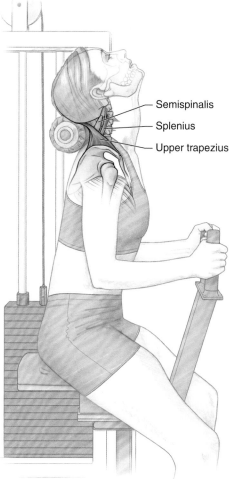

Semispinalis
Splenius
Upper trapezius

Extension.

Execution

1. Adjust the seat position for your height. Sit erect with your feet flat on the floor and grasp the handles (if your machine has handles). Begin with the neck in a bit of an extended position.

2. For flexion, place your forehead on the pad. (The pad on some machines accommodates the entire face.) Flex your neck by drawing the chin down toward the chest. Pause and then return to the starting position.

3. For extension, turn around on the seat, and place the back of your head on the pad. This time, begin with the neck in a bit of a flexed position. Perform neck extension by raising your chin toward the ceiling. Pause and then return to the starting position.

Muscles Involved

Primary: Sternocleidomastoid (flexion), upper trapezius (extension), splenius (extension)

Secondary: Scalenes (flexion), splenius (flexion), upper trapezius (flexion), semispinalis (extension)

Soccer Focus

Good neck strength is important for the skill of heading as well as for protecting the head during inevitable collisions. Despite this, surprisingly few coaches include neck strengthening in their training programs. Much of the power for heading comes from the trunk, while part of the finer touch comes from the neck's action on the head to send the ball in the desired direction. Mostly flexion is used, but rotation, which is a more complex skill, is also possible. And one cannot discount the role of a strong neck in stabilizing the head so that head acceleration during collisions is minimized.

Dumbbell Shoulder Press

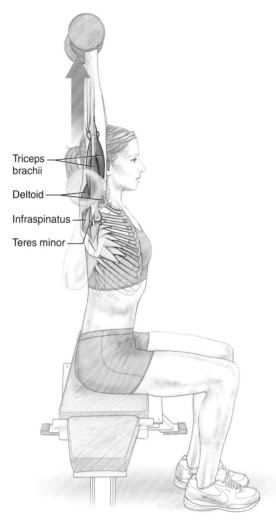

Triceps brachii

Deltoid

Infraspinatus

Teres minor

⚠ **SAFETY TIP** Begin with a low weight. You need some initial strength to be able to control the weight when it is overhead.

Execution

1. Sit on a weight bench with your back straight and your feet flat on the floor.
2. Hold a dumbbell in each hand using an overhand grip. Hold the weights at shoulder level.
3. Extend one arm vertically. Briefly hold at the top, and then slowly lower the weight to the shoulder. Exhale when raising the weight, and inhale when lowering the weight.
4. Repeat with the other arm, and do an equal number of repetitions for each arm.

Muscles Involved

Primary: Triceps brachii, deltoid

Secondary: Shoulder stabilizers (rhomboid major and minor, trapezius, levator scapulae, rotator cuff)

Soccer Focus

It is pretty hard to envision this movement as a primary action during soccer. A team picture might suggest that the goalkeeper likely has the most developed shoulders because the arms are integral to his game. That should not mean players other than goalkeepers should neglect this and similar exercises. A well-rounded supplemental strength training program will address all motions, including the shoulders, despite the minor role some motions might appear to play in any particular sport. Because of the speed of play and the amount of contact in the game, all players must be prepared for contact. As described, the dumbbell shoulder press is a unilateral exercise (one side at a time), but it can be made a bilateral exercise if you extend both arms in unison.

VARIATION

Machine Shoulder Press

As with all free weight exercises, the dumbbell shoulder press requires a certain degree of skill to perform correctly. One of the benefits of commercial machines is that you are fixed into a specific motion and the weights are supported. This provides a measure of safety for the exercise.

CHAPTER 5

CHEST

Soccer players might be hesitant to enter a strength training program for any number of reasons—lack of understanding, tradition, concern that bulking up might have a negative impact on play, and so on. One reason might be simply not having access to the equipment. Part of the purpose of this book is to show exercises that can be done either on the field or in the weight room. A player who does attempt some strength training might focus only on the legs, which could lead to imbalances throughout the body, increasing the risk of injury. Players and coaches must realize that a strength training program is for the entire body, not just the legs. All regions of the body, including the chest, must be addressed.

Many athletes think of the bench press when they think about developing the chest. Although the pectoralis major is the largest and most obvious chest muscle, others also play a role in how the shoulder girdle and upper extremities operate.

Bones, Ligaments, and Joints of the Chest

In the torso, there are 10 pairs of ribs that attach in the back to the vertebral column and in the front to the sternum, with 2 pairs of ribs that attach in the back but not to the sternum. Ribs 1, 11, and 12 have a 1:1 attachment with their corresponding vertebrae, while ribs 2 through 10 attach between two vertebrae. The bone of each rib ends at roughly nipple level and is then connected to the sternum by the costal cartilage (the Latin *costa* means *rib*) to form a cartilaginous joint that has only slight mobility. Ribs 1 through 7 are called *true ribs* because each attaches directly to the sternum through the costal cartilage. Ribs 8 through 10 are called *false ribs* because their cartilage attaches to the cartilage of the rib above before eventually attaching to the sternum. The small ribs 11 and 12 are called *floating ribs* because they have no sternal attachment. Between each pair of ribs is a pair of small muscles called the intercostals that aid in breathing. The floor of the rib cage is made up of the diaphragm. Movements of the ribs play a role in inhalation and exhalation, and their cagelike arrangement protects the heart, lungs, large blood vessels, nerves, and passages that conduct air to and from the lungs. The most common chest injury is a rib fracture from some form of ballistic impact, usually to the middle ribs.

The sternum, or breastbone, is made up of three bones that fuse during growth. If you slide a finger down your sternum you will feel a horizontal ridge one-quarter to one-third of the way down the bone. This is one of the fusion points. The third bone is a fragile extension called the xiphoid process off the bottom end of the sternum. It comes off the underside of the sternum, and the amount of covering tissue makes it difficult to feel.

The sternum is important because it is the only point of bony attachment connecting the central (axial) skeleton and the upper extremities. This sternoclavicular joint is quite strong because of the ligaments and cartilage from the clavicle to the sternum, a ligament connecting the two clavicles, and ligaments that connect the clavicle to the first rib. These all work together to maintain the integrity of this joint. Despite all these stabilizing tissues, there is some movement, so it has many of the features of the typical freely movable joint. This joint is rarely injured. Usually the clavicle fractures before this joint dislocates. But injuries can happen. Think of the rodeo rider who falls from a height, cartwheels in the air, and lands on an outstretched arm.

The scapula attaches to the clavicle. Although the scapula glides over the curvature of the ribs, there are no bony articulations between the scapula and the ribs. Muscles that originate from the sternum and ribs, however, can also have their insertion on the scapula and exercise some control over the scapula's movements.

Chest Muscles

For most everyone, chest muscles and the pectoralis major muscle are synonymous (the Latin *pectus* means *chest*). The pectoralis major muscle (figure 5.1) is the largest but not the only muscle of the chest. Because of its broad origination from the sternum and costal cartilages of ribs 2 through 6 (sternal head, or lower pectoralis) as well as the clavicle (clavicular head, or upper pectoralis), it is sometimes referred to as having two distinct origins. The muscle angles toward the shoulder, inserting on the chest side of the upper humerus. Remember that a muscle pulls the insertion toward the origin. Because it inserts on a highly mobile bone, the pectoralis major has a number of primary and secondary actions on the humerus. Primary functions include horizontal adduction (arm parallel to the ground and out to the side moves across the chest), shoulder adduction, internal rotation of the humerus, and shoulder extension. You can feel the pectoralis major contract by placing a hand on the muscle and doing any of those actions. Through the connection of the humerus with the glenoid of the scapula, the pectoralis major also assists in some movements of the scapula.

Completely covered by the pectoralis major is the smaller pectoralis minor. (In anatomy, if there is a *major* there probably is a *minor*.) The pectoralis minor originates on the outer surface of ribs 3 through 5 and, with the short head of the biceps, attaches on the scapula to abduct the scapula (move the scapula along the curve of the ribs, away from the midline), depress the scapula, and help rotate the glenoid down.

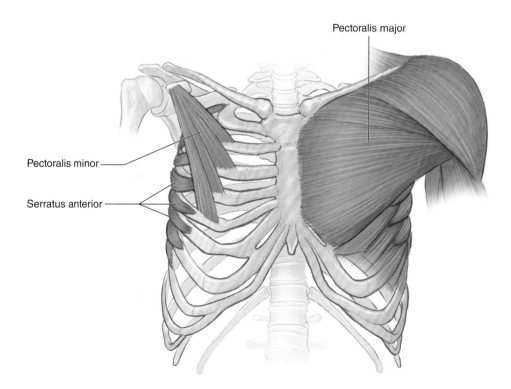

Pectoralis major

Pectoralis minor

Serratus anterior

Figure 5.1 Muscles of the chest.

The final major muscle of the chest is the serratus anterior, so called because of its serrated appearance. (Think of the serrated edge of a steak knife.) The serratus anterior originates laterally on the surface of the upper 8 or 9 ribs and courses posteriorly, following the curve of the ribs to insert on the lower half of the border of the scapula that is adjacent to the vertebral column. The muscle's primary action is to abduct the scapula (move it away from the vertebral column), but it also assists in upward rotation of the glenoid (raising your arm as if in response to a question). The serratus anterior could be considered either a chest muscle because of its origin on the ribs or a scapular muscle because of its insertion on the scapula.

Think of all the muscles of the upper back and shoulder that are fully balanced by just these three muscles. That means nearly any exercise that addresses the humerus and scapula will require these muscles, while the opposing (antagonistic) muscles can nearly be singled out by specific exercises. Although most of the motions of the arms and shoulders in soccer are meant to widen your presence and make it harder for the opponent to get to the ball, it is wise to train the opposing chest muscles to maintain neuromuscular balance.

Soccer Ball Push-Up

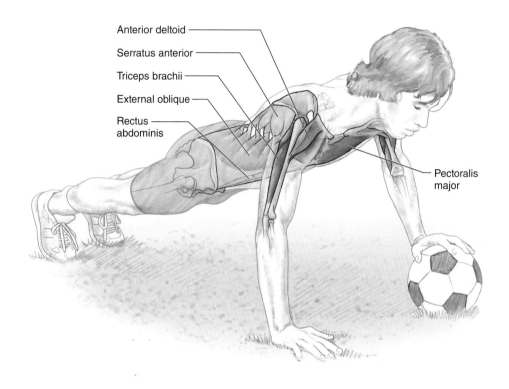

Anterior deltoid

Serratus anterior

Triceps brachii

External oblique

Rectus abdominis

Pectoralis major

Execution

1. Lie on the ground. Get into the up position of a traditional push-up, with your hands a bit wider than shoulder-width apart. Stay up on your toes with your feet together.
2. Carefully transfer one hand to the top of a soccer ball.
3. Perform a routine push-up.
4. After doing a few push-ups with one hand on the ball, stop, switch hands, and continue. Perform push-ups with the ball under the other hand.

Muscles Involved

Primary: Pectoralis major, triceps brachii, anterior deltoid

Secondary: Serratus anterior, abdominal core (external oblique, internal oblique, transversus abdominis, rectus abdominis) and spinal extensors (erector spinae, multifidus) for proper posture

Soccer Focus

The modern game is far more physical than the game played by earlier generations. The speed and athleticism of the modern player means a defender can close down a striker in the wink of an eye, and this means contact. The amount of pushing and shoving that goes on in a crowded penalty area during a corner kick would probably surprise most nonplayers. It should be intuitive that the stronger player will be better suited to handle the contact of the game. Although much of the strength necessary is initiated from the legs, the chain of actions continues up the trunk to the rest of the body. In this exercise, the height added by the ball means the body can be lowered farther than when both hands are on the ground. In addition, some reactive balance is needed because the ball can move.

Soccer Ball Push-Up With Two Balls

You can improve your skill with push-ups by doing more repetitions. Some players even devise a safe way to add weight on their backs for more resistance. Or make the exercise more difficult by going lower. Place soccer balls under both hands to be able to lower the body farther to improve strength. The balance required when using two balls is considerable.

⚠️ **SAFETY TIP** Begin with regular push-ups, and improve your strength before attempting these. Raising one or both hands during a push-up means you can go lower. The lower you go into the push-up, the greater the stress on the shoulders. Be sure to listen to your body. Because of the balance required, you may want to keep your knees on the ground until you have more strength and confidence.

Stability Ball Push-Up

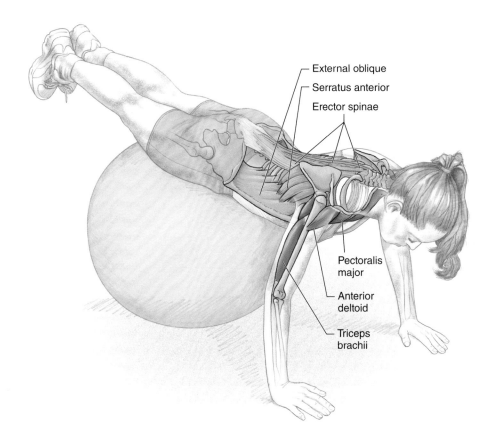

External oblique

Serratus anterior

Erector spinae

Pectoralis major

Anterior deltoid

Triceps brachii

Execution

1. Lie facedown on a stability ball. Lean forward, placing your hands on the floor.
2. Walk your hands forward until the ball is under your trunk, thighs, or feet. The exercise is more challenging the farther the ball is from your hands.
3. Get into the up push-up position with your hands on the floor, and perform routine push-ups.

Muscles Involved

Primary: Pectoralis major (especially clavicular portion), triceps brachii, anterior deltoid

Secondary: Serratus anterior, abdominal core and spinal extensors for proper posture

Soccer Focus

Strength and conditioning coaches have an arsenal of schemes to ensure that virtually every portion of any muscle can be exercised. A standard method is to change the alignment of the body in relation to the direction the resistance is being moved. In this case, the athlete tilts the body in a different way. Raising the legs effectively changes the way the pectoralis major muscle is used. In a routine push-up, the lower two-thirds to three-quarters of the muscle is addressed. Raising the legs brings the remaining upper portion of the pectoralis major muscle into the exercise.

VARIATIONS

This simple exercise has numerous variations. Using the stability ball, you can do a routine push-up with the feet on the floor and the hands squeezing the top and side of the ball. Or keep the hands on the ball, and prop your feet on a bench of the same height as the stability ball. Or leave the feet on the floor, and do push-ups with a stability ball for each hand. Also try this with the ball-height bench. Want a real challenge? Do push-ups with your feet on one ball and your hands on another. Or forget the balls altogether; keep the bench and do push-ups, placing the feet on the bench and the hands on the floor.

Bench Press

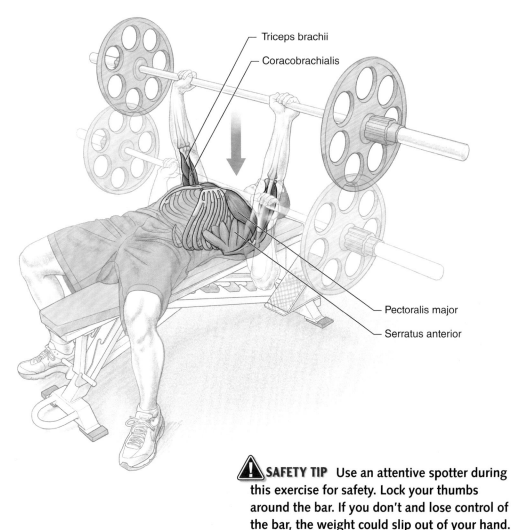

Triceps brachii

Coracobrachialis

Pectoralis major

Serratus anterior

⚠ **SAFETY TIP** Use an attentive spotter during this exercise for safety. Lock your thumbs around the bar. If you don't and lose control of the bar, the weight could slip out of your hand.

Execution

1. Lie on your back on a weight bench of sufficient length to support the body from the buttocks to the shoulders, with your feet flat on the floor. The barbell is on a rack at about nipple level.

2. Grasp the bar using an overhand grip, with the arms about shoulder-width apart.

3. With the arms extended but not locked at the elbows, lift the bar off the rack and stabilize the weight. There may be a little arching of the back at this point.

4. Lower the weight to the chest, pause briefly, and then extend the arms to lift the weight again. Keep the arms steady to support the weight, but do not lock the elbows. Inhale as you lower the bar, and exhale as you the press the bar up (blow the weight up).

Muscles Involved

Primary: Pectoralis major, triceps brachii, anterior deltoid

Secondary: Serratus anterior, coracobrachialis

Soccer Focus

In a crowded penalty area, positioning for a corner is less about pulling the opponent toward you than it is pushing the opponent away to increase the space around you. Exercises such as push-ups and bench presses are very helpful. In essence, a bench press is an upside-down push-up and recruits many of the same muscles. The major difference is that the barbell bench press is overloaded because of the added weight on the bar. This type of incremental increase in resistance for a push-up is not as simple.

VARIATION

Machine Chest Press

Most fitness clubs and weight rooms have both machines and free weights that can be used for a chest press. The machines are designed for safety. Machines that mimic a bench press can be supine, on which you lie on your back, or seated. They can also be simple (chest flys that do not use the triceps) or compound (using both the pecs and the triceps, such as a bench press).

To change the muscular emphasis of this exercise, you have many options—arch the back slightly, lift the feet off the floor, increase or decrease the width of the grip, create an incline, change the contact point on the trunk, and so on.

Dumbbell Pullover

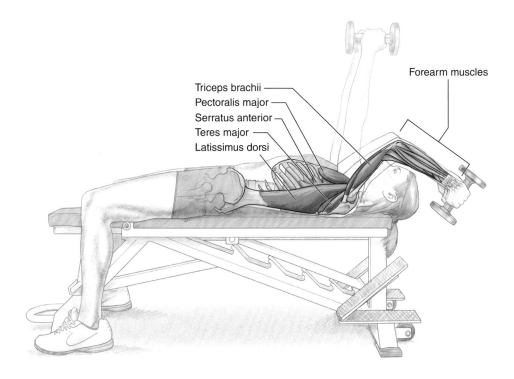

Forearm muscles

Triceps brachii

Pectoralis major

Serratus anterior

Teres major

Latissimus dorsi

⚠ **SAFETY TIP** Have a partner put the dumbbell in your hands once you are lying on the bench.

Execution

1. Lie on your back on a weight bench of sufficient length to support your body from the buttocks to the shoulders, with your feet flat on the floor.
2. Wrap both hands around the inside weight of a dumbbell. Hold your arms extended and perpendicular to the floor.
3. Lower the dumbbell over your head and down, slightly bending the elbows.
4. After a slight pause, reverse the action and return to the starting position.

Muscles Involved

Primary: Latissimus dorsi, pectoralis major, triceps brachii, teres major

Secondary: Scapular stabilizers (rhomboid major and minor, trapezius, serratus anterior), forearm muscles (mostly wrist and finger flexors including flexor carpi radialis and ulnaris, palmaris longus, flexor digitorum superficialis and profundus, and flexor pollicis longus) to grasp dumbbell

Soccer Focus

Over the years, soccer players have become bigger and more athletic. This increase in size has changed the game on a number of fronts. For example, the modern goalkeeper can routinely punt a ball to the other goalkeeper on one bounce, and a 70-yard (64 m) goal kick by a professional male player is common. Another aspect that has changed is the throw-in. In earlier generations, a defender would try very hard to send the ball over the touchline (sideline) rather than give up a corner because a throw-in to the face of the goal was very unusual, while a corner was much more dangerous. Today, most teams have one or two designated throw-in specialists just for restarts near the end line. These specialists can deliver a throw that is more like a corner kick, giving the team another offensive weapon. The movement of the dumbbell pullover is very similar to a throw-in, and you can bet a team's throw-in specialist does this exercise. The poor defender now doesn't know where to send the ball (but most everyone would still rather face a throw than a corner).

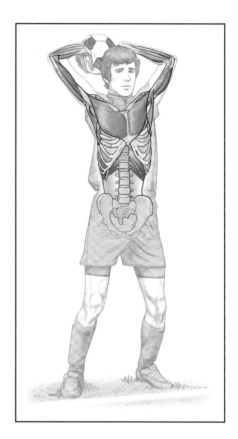

VARIATION

Machine Pullover

As with most free weight exercises, there are machine options that place the user in a fixed and safe position. Many of these machines are simple, isolating a single action such as the pullover motion, instead of compound, which allow actions across multiple joints.

Cable Crossover Fly

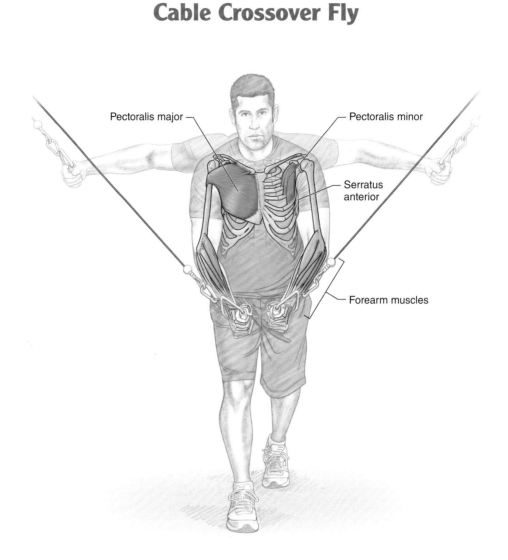

Pectoralis major

Pectoralis minor

Serratus anterior

Forearm muscles

Execution

1. This exercise usually requires a setup dedicated to this specific lift. Stand with your back to the weights. Stand with your feet staggered, with the trunk leaning a little bit forward.

2. Reach up behind you, and grasp the handles of the cable machine in an overhand grip. The arms will be extended behind you, with a little flexion at the elbows. Picture a bird opening its wings.

3. Inhale and squeeze the arms together in unison until the hands touch. Exhale when the hands touch. Try not to change the angle of elbow flexion during the movement.

4. Slowly allow the arms to return to the starting position. Be sure to keep control during the lift. It is easy to let gravity take over.

Muscles Involved

Primary: Pectoralis major, pectoralis minor

Secondary: Forearm muscles to grasp handles, scapular stabilizers (serratus anterior, rhomboid major and minor, middle trapezius)

Soccer Focus

One could argue soccer players use strength training strictly to supplement their soccer-specific training. In this case, a player could get by with a few compound exercises that train most muscles of the shoulders and arms. But just because a muscle performs a certain action doesn't mean the entirety of the muscle is being exercised. For example, the common bench press doesn't exercise a significant portion of the upper pectoralis major. Thus, a complete supplemental strength training program will include a variety of exercises to affect as many muscle fibers as possible. While the cable crossover fly is a great option that recruits most of the pectoralis major, it is also a great option to activate the pectoralis minor. The pectoralis minor lies under the pectoralis major and inserts on the scapula under the general area of origin of the deltoid. It stabilizes the scapula during movement. A stable scapula is important not only for optimal shoulder function but also to protect the shoulder when landing after a fall. This lift moves the scapula around the curvature of the ribs, which is a specific action of the pectoralis minor.

Pec Fly

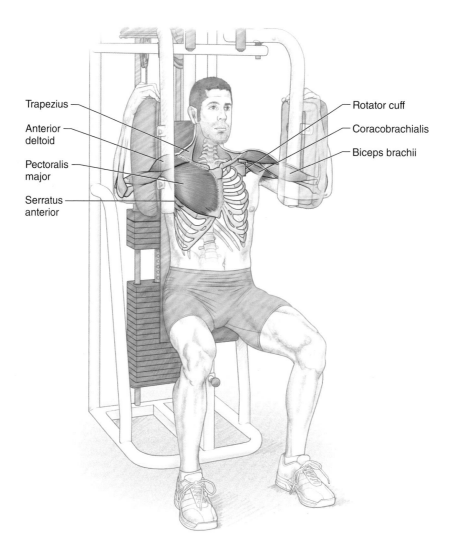

Trapezius

Anterior deltoid

Pectoralis major

Serratus anterior

Rotator cuff

Coracobrachialis

Biceps brachii

Execution

1. Make appropriate adjustments to the seat so that your upper arms are roughly parallel to the floor.
2. Open your arms and flex your elbows.
3. Place your elbows and forearms on the pads, and grasp the handles with an overhand grip. You do not need to hold the handles tightly.
4. Squeeze your arms together, pause briefly, and then return to the starting position.

Muscles Involved

Primary: Pectoralis major, coracobrachialis, anterior deltoid

Secondary: Scapular stabilizers, rotator cuff (subscapularis, supraspinatus, infraspinatus, teres minor), biceps brachii

Soccer Focus

This exercise is another option for the major chest muscles. Many athletes mistakenly believe that supplemental exercises should be specific to the sport and devise ways to mimic game actions using some form of resistance. There are many situations in soccer during which you can imagine the utility of some of these exercises, but pushing is probably not one of them. That should not be a reason to skip working the pectoral muscles. By undertaking a supplemental strength training program, you are making every attempt to improve your entire body, not just the specific movements of your sport. Exercises for the shoulders and back, which will help you maintain both your position and possession of the ball, must be balanced by exercises for the major chest muscles. An imbalance in strength between opposing muscles is a risk factor for joint injury, including injuries to the shoulder.

CHAPTER 6

BACK AND HIPS

Undervaluing the importance of the back is very shortsighted when it comes to training. Nearly every functional movement in sports is anchored to the back. Some might say that because the back is not a location of many acute injuries in soccer, we don't need to worry about it. Although the back may not be injured very often, it might surprise some people to learn that about one-third of all male soccer players have complaints about their backs. This can range from just under 20 percent of local adult-league players to more than 50 percent of top-level players. In middle and high school players, back complaints were highest among those with the poorest skill, suggesting that one way to minimize back complaints might be to improve skill.

Back complaints may not be serious enough to cause a player to miss training or matches, but they can be irritating enough to catch the player's attention. Considering the torques around the body during kicking and cutting and the fact that something in the pattern of movement in soccer changes about every four to six seconds in terms of speed or direction, it should not be surprising to learn that these actions just might be culprits in the complaints expressed by players. And there is a growing body of evidence that pain, even pain not severe enough to keep an athlete out, might be the first warning of an impending overuse injury that could sideline a player for an extended period.

Physical therapists use many effective exercises to help strengthen the backs of people with chronic back pain. But the best treatment for chronic back pain is to prevent the pain before it starts—to stop the potential pain in its tracks before it becomes a complaint. A little bit of work done each day will show great benefits in the future. You don't need to start out with terribly challenging exercises, so take your time and you'll experience results fairly quickly. The more you have to gain, the more you will gain. Since most athletes have ignored their backs, they have a lot to gain. Vary your exercise choices, and don't overload this area, or any area, too frequently or intensely.

This chapter shows a number of exercises specifically for the back. A number of these options involve a ball or are a bit competitive so they can be fun. Others involve a partner, while a few are done in a gym.

Anatomy of the Vertebral Column

The back is made up of individual vertebrae and their cartilage, which make up the spinal column; ligaments for stability between each bone; the spinal cord, which carries information to and from your brain; and an almost dizzying array of muscles most players have never considered. In total, the back can be quite complicated. Consider the spinal cord. The spinal cord is more than just a series of highways carrying information to and from the brain. It is also capable of some decision making. As one spinal cord researcher recently said, "The brain gets things started, and the spinal cord sorts out the details."

The vertebral column is a series of similar bones. There are 7 cervical (neck), 12 thoracic (chest), and 5 lumbar vertebrae (figure 6.1, page 102). These are distinct and separate bones. Below this is the sacrum, which is made of 5 fused bones, and 3 to 5 coccygeal bones that may or may not be fused. The vertebral column is not arranged in a straight line. It has three curves within the sagittal plane that curve toward or away from the front of the body, not side to side. The cervical vertebrae curve anteriorly, the thoracic vertebrae curve posteriorly, and the lumbar vertebrae curve slightly anteriorly. The ribs articulate with the thoracic vertebrae.

Although the bones of each region have their own unique look, they all have the same common features. You see a large *body*, two lateral projections opposite each other (*transverse processes*), and a third projection by itself (*spinous process*) that all surround an opening (*vertebral foramen*) (figure 6.2); the anatomical term for a projection is a *process*, and a hole is a *foramen*. The large body is anterior, and the process opposite the body that is all by itself is posterior and points down. When you run your hand up and down someone's back, those bumps are the spinous processes. There are a number of bony contacts that by themselves allow for limited movement, but summed up allow the amazing movements of the entire column demonstrated by gymnasts, divers, acrobats, and dancers.

The vertebral foramen is for the spinal cord. When you put one vertebra on top of the other, another foramen (*intervertebral foramen*) is seen on each side, and this is where spinal nerves take information to and from the spinal cord. A large cartilaginous disc sits between the bodies of adjacent vertebrae. This disc has two distinct sections. The outer ring is called the annulus fibrosa and surrounds a gelatinous center, the nucleus pulposa (picture a jelly donut). A herniated disc is one that bulges out from between its vertebrae and can cause pain if the bulge pushes on the spinal cord or spinal nerves.

Each pair of vertebrae is connected by a series of short ligaments from the process above to the process below as well as other points of bony articulations. There are also long ligaments that run the length of the vertebral column. One ligament runs along the most anterior surface of each vertebral body, while an opposite ligament runs down the smooth

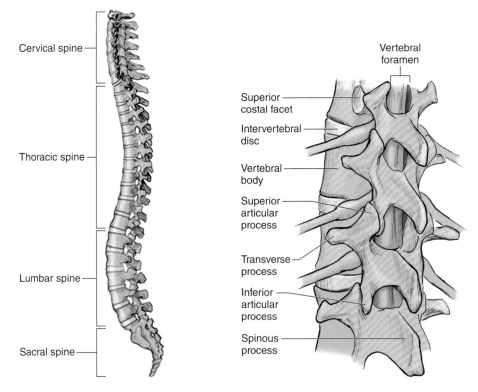

Figure 6.1 The cervical, thoracic, lumbar, and sacral regions of the spine.

Figure 6.2 The vertebrae of the spine.

posterior surface between the processes. A third ligament, the strongest of the three, the *ligamentum flavum*, runs the length of the posterior surfaces within the canal that houses the spinal cord. In total, these ligaments provide for impressive stability and mobility of the vertebral column.

The joints between each vertebra are complex and vary according to region and function. These joints can be capable of minimal movement, such as between the vertebral bodies, or can be quite movable, such as between the first and second cervical vertebrae to aid movements of the skull.

Back Muscles

The muscles of the spine are highly complex. There are long muscles that run the entire length of the vertebral column, and there are tiny muscles between each vertebra. Working individually or in groups, these muscles produce a wide range of movements. A number of back muscles with their origin on the vertebral column that attach to the scapula or arm are listed in chapter 4.

Spinal muscles differ from other muscles in that they don't really have a single origin or insertion. Most begin on the pelvis and insert along each vertebra up the column. Others begin on the vertebra below and insert on the vertebra above. Some have the opposite orientation, while still others overlap muscles up the column. Some are region specific, while others have segments both within and between sections.

The most widely recognized muscle acting on the vertebral column is the erector spinae (figure 6.3). This name is applied to a collection of muscles called the longissimus, spinalis,

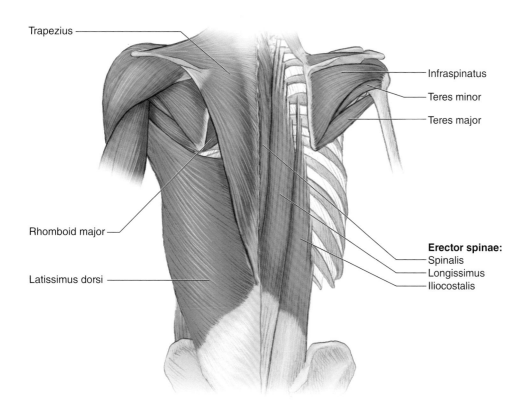

Figure 6.3 The muscles of the back.

and iliocostalis. Each of these may have region-specific portions, such as the semispinalis capitis, longissimus cervicis, and iliocostalis thoracis. As its name implies, the erector spinae extends the spine for an erect stance. Muscles pull the insertion toward the origin, so to extend the spine, the origins are low and the insertions are high on the back.

Other muscles of the back include the multifidus, quadratus lumborum, rotatores thoracis, and interspinalis. All told, there are about 30 pairs of named muscles that extend, rotate, compress, and perform lateral flexion of the various regions of the vertebral column.

Anatomy of the Hip

The pelvis, which makes up the hips, is actually three fused bones on each side (figure 6.4). The three bones are the ilium, ischium, and pubis. The configuration of the three bones can be confusing. That ridge you feel under the skin on your side is the fan-shaped crest of the ilium, or iliac bone. You sit on a specific landmark of your ischium. The two pubic bones connect with each other in the midline of the lower abdomen. These three bones are fused together, and each fused set of three bones connects with its counterpart on the other side through the pubic bones. Posteriorly, the two iliac bones articulate with each side of the sacrum to form the sacroiliac joint, a joint with surprisingly little motion.

Along with the pelvic floor muscles, the pelvis provides support from below for the abdominal organs, numerous locations for muscle attachment, passageways for nerves and blood vessels, and the site of bony articulation with the lower extremities. Injuries to this strong set of bones are not common, but there are a number of injuries to tissues that have some connection with the pelvic girdle.

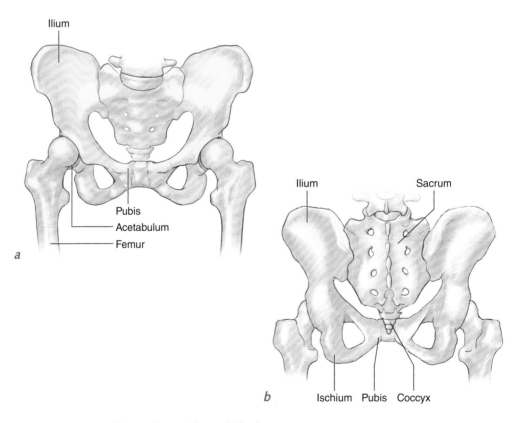

Figure 6.4   Bones of the pelvis: (a) front; (b) back.

Hip Muscles

The primary actions at the hip are flexion and extension. For hip flexion, bend your knee and raise it toward your trunk. Hip extension is the opposite motion; you move your leg behind your trunk.

Two sets of muscles create hip flexion. The primary muscles are part of a group called the iliopsoas. This group includes three muscles—the iliacus, psoas major, and psoas minor—that begin on the lower lumbar vertebrae and the deep cut of the pelvis. (Actually, half of people don't have the psoas minor muscle.) All insert through a common tendon on the femur to flex the hip and externally rotate the femur. Each psoas muscle also assists in lateral flexion of the trunk. Secondary muscles for hip flexion are the rectus femoris, one of the four quadriceps muscles of the thigh (see page 149), and the sartorius. Although these muscles are secondary for hip flexion, they are no less important. The rectus femoris begins on the rim of the socket portion of the ball-and-socket hip joint and joins with the other three quadriceps muscles to eventually insert on the tibia just below the patella (kneecap). The rectus femoris is primarily a knee extensor, but because of its origin on the pelvis, it also is a hip flexor. The sartorius is a curious muscle that begins roughly in the area where one might suffer a hip pointer (anterior superior iliac spine) and then runs sort of diagonally down the medial thigh and inserts behind the tibia below the knee, giving it numerous actions: hip flexion, knee flexion, hip abduction, and lateral rotation of the hip. If you were to check the sole of your shoe to see if you stepped on gum, you would involve all the actions of the sartorius.

Hip extension also requires two groups of muscles. The three hamstring muscles (see page 150) originate near the bony prominences on which you sit (ischial tuberosities) and insert below the knee on the back of the tibia and fibula. Their main function is knee flexion, but the pelvic attachment means they also perform hip extension. The other main muscle is the gluteus maximus, the large muscle of the buttocks. This very powerful muscle has a broad origin along the back of the pelvis and narrows to insert on the back of the proximal end of the femur. Because of the diagonal direction of its fibers, the gluteus maximus also can rotate the femur laterally as well as assist in trunk extension.

The other two gluteal muscles, the gluteus medius and the gluteus minimus, are named for their relative size and position. These originate underneath the gluteus maximus on the back of the pelvis but insert elsewhere on the femur to assist in thigh abduction (moving the thigh away from the midline of the body) and lateral thigh rotation. Depending on the position of the femur, the gluteus minimus also can help rotate the femur internally.

Prone Partner Ball Toss

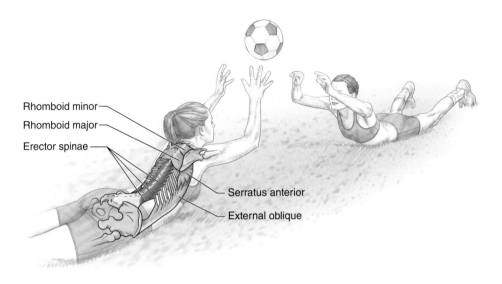

Rhomboid minor

Rhomboid major

Erector spinae

Serratus anterior

External oblique

Execution

1. You will need a partner for this exercise. Lie on your abdomen on the ground a few yards or meters away from your partner, head to head.
2. Take a soccer ball, arch your back to lift your chest off the ground, and gently toss the ball to your partner using both arms equally. Think of a throw-in.
3. Your partner arches her back to catch the ball. She tosses the ball back to you.
4. Continue tossing the ball back and forth. Toss back and forth for about 15 seconds, and add time as strength improves.

Muscles Involved

Primary: Erector spinae

Secondary: Abdominal core (external oblique, internal oblique, transversus abdominis, rectus abdominis), scapular stabilizers (such as rhomboid major and minor and serratus anterior)

Soccer Focus

We are learning more about the role of the spine in sport. Its role in the concept of the core should not be minimized, partly because we now know that some injuries to the lower extremity frequently are preceded by some minor wobble of the trunk. Add to this that a substantial percentage of soccer players have back complaints. These complaints may be enough to mention to the medical staff but not enough to keep the players off the field. The constant starting, stopping, and changing of direction in soccer twist the spine over and over again, which can lead to discomfort. Do not neglect supplemental training of the neck and spine just because you think such exercises are not soccer specific. Strengthening the muscles that attach to the spine will go a long way toward stabilizing the core, preventing injury, and minimizing back complaints. Although prone back extensions can be done individually, having the players toss a ball engages teammates with each other.

Seated Partner Ball Twist

Rectus abdominis

External oblique

Internal oblique

Erector spinae

Execution

1. You will need a partner for this exercise. Sit on the ground back to back with your partner. You may either extend or bend your legs for balance.
2. Hold a soccer ball in both hands.
3. At the same time, you and your partner twist to one side, and your partner reaches around to take the ball. Then you both twist to the opposite side, and your partner hands off the ball to you. Keep repeating the exercise for around 15 seconds, increasing the time as strength improves.

Muscles Involved

Primary: Abdominal core

Secondary: Spinal extensors (erector spinae, multifidus)

Soccer Focus

Soccer players are known for being among the most agile of all athletes. Agility is defined as being able to change speed, direction, and level quickly and accurately. The process of changing direction usually involves making a feint to get the opponent to move in one direction and then going off in another direction yourself. This feint is most effective if a twisting trunk is used to help decoy the opponent. The opponent will assume the rest of the body will follow the direction of the trunk. (An old coaching adage is to watch the numbers on the jersey in the belief they will tell you where the opponent is going.) Highly skilled and devious players know this and will use the trunk to confuse the defender. This exercise is good not only as part of a core training program but also to help a player's movements become harder to read. As players get better at this exercise, they will (usually on their own) try to do this drill faster and faster. In the gym, some swap out a soccer ball for a medicine ball, effectively adding resistance to the movement.

VARIATION

Broomstick Twist

The broomstick twist is a solo version of the partner exercise just described. The broomstick twist, a fundamental exercise in golf, requires only a stick of some kind. Try not to generate too much momentum. Perform the twist under control, with the goal of extending the limits of the trunk's range of motion, not to see how fast the movement can be performed.

Reach-Through Tug of War

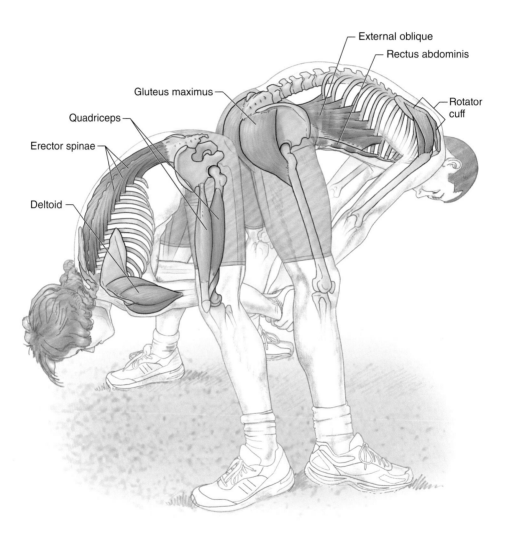

External oblique

Rectus abdominis

Gluteus maximus

Quadriceps

Rotator cuff

Erector spinae

Deltoid

Execution

1. You will need a partner for this exercise—one who is roughly your equal in size and strength. Stand back to back with your partner, both of you assuming a fairly wide stance.
2. Lean forward and reach through your legs, grasping both of your partner's hands.
3. On a "go" signal, try to pull your partner off balance as he tries to pull you off balance.
4. Break, pause for a few seconds, and repeat.

Muscles Involved

Primary: Rectus abdominis, external oblique, and internal oblique for trunk flexion; erector spinae for spinal extension

Secondary: Forearm muscles (mostly wrist and finger flexors including flexor carpi radialis and ulnaris, palmaris longus, flexor digitorum superficialis and profundus, and flexor pollicis longus) to grasp and hold hands; rotator cuff and other shoulder muscles (such as deltoid, rhomboid major and minor, levator scapulae, and serratus anterior) to maintain integrity of shoulder joint; larger hip and thigh muscles including gluteals (gluteus maximus, medius, and minimus), quadriceps (vastus medialis, vastus lateralis, vastus intermedius, rectus femoris), hamstrings (biceps femoris, semitendinosus, semimembranosus) and gastrocnemius to maintain balance, maintain standing position, and help pull on partner

Soccer Focus

This drill can be found in coaching books dating back to the 1950s and 1960s. It is very effective as a dynamic means of working trunk flexion and extension as well as balance and coordination of the trunk and spine along with the upper and lower extremities. Young players find the combination of the exercise and the competitiveness a fun way to test each other. As with other competitive exercises, players can get carried away with trying to overpower their partners and win the exercise.

On one level, this functional drill works the trunk and spine. On another level, it is a total-body exercise that requires balance, coordination, strength, and if performed long enough, some local muscle endurance, all good things for a game such as soccer.

Stability Ball Trunk Extension

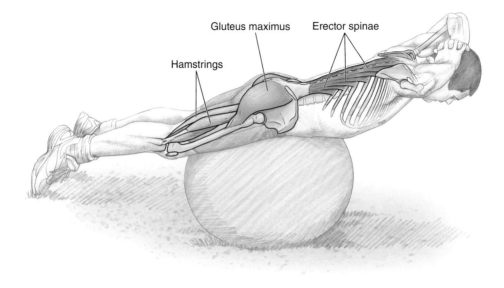

Hamstrings

Gluteus maximus

Erector spinae

Execution

1. Lean forward and place your hips on the stability ball, keeping your feet on the ground. Continue to lean forward, wrapping your trunk over the ball. Clasp your fingers behind your head.
2. Raise your chest off the ball, keeping the chin tucked in to stabilize the neck.
3. Slowly return to the starting position.

Muscles Involved

Primary: Erector spinae

Secondary: Trapezius, rhomboid major and minor, gluteus maximus, hamstrings

Soccer Focus

Acute, traumatic injury to the spine is, thankfully, rare in soccer. But that does not mean a soccer player's spine is immune to problems. When injury surveillance studies look beyond acute injury and ask players about any musculoskeletal complaints (things that bother them but do not prevent them from playing), back pain is cited by more than 50 percent of top-level adult players. And low back complaints are not just an issue for adult players—more than 40 percent of low-skilled youth players (14 to 16 years old) have low back complaints. Some researchers are investigating whether low-level pain without a specific incident may be the first warning of an overuse injury such as a stress fracture. A spinal stress fracture would lead to an extended time-loss period, so athletes should do what they can to lessen the stresses on the spine in order to keep playing.

VARIATION

Oblique Crunch

You can increase the load on the obliques by doing stability ball crunches on your side and performing lateral flexion to the side opposite the ball.

Reverse Leg Extension

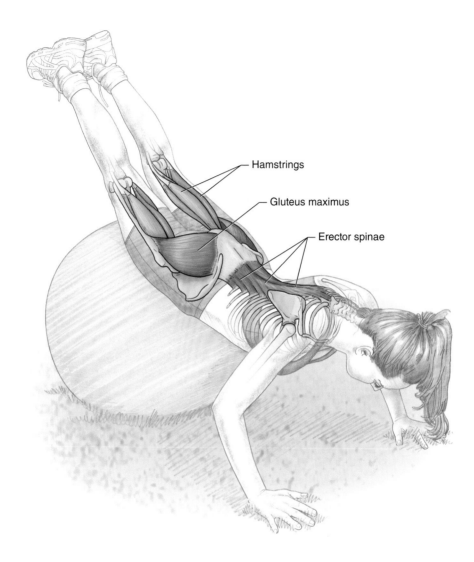

Hamstrings

Gluteus maximus

Erector spinae

Execution

1. Select a stability ball appropriate for your size: too big and you may not be able to touch the ground with the hands and feet at the same time; too small and there is little challenge.
2. Lie across the ball so that your lower abdomen is on the ball. Extend your arms, placing your palms on the ground. Your legs should be extended so that your toes touch the ground.
3. By extending your hips, raise both legs in unison as high as you can, keeping the legs straight.
4. Slowly return to the starting position.

Muscles Involved

Primary: Gluteus maximus, erector spinae

Secondary: Hamstrings

Soccer Focus

Heading is a hard skill to master. Those who are good at it are highly prized members of a team. When standing, it should be obvious that much of your heading power comes from pushing against the ground to provide the energy necessary for a successful heading opportunity. When jumping, you don't have the ground to push against, meaning you need to coordinate the hyperextension of your trunk with a rapid flexion of the trunk to apply power to the ball. In a match, this opportunity might happen only a couple of times, but heading practice (for appropriately aged players) can provide multiple opportunities for this hyperextension–flexion motion and the spinal muscles. Exercises that recruit the erector spinae muscles will help support the vertebrae during this demanding skill.

Partner Lumbar Extension

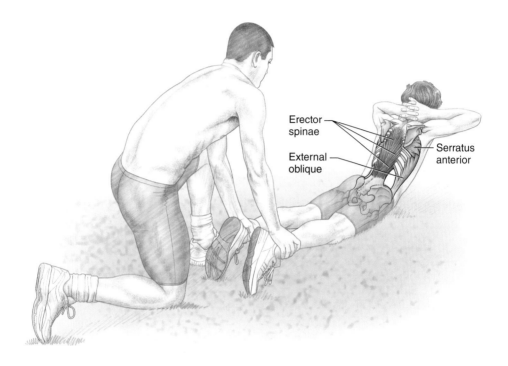

Erector spinae

External oblique

Serratus anterior

Execution

1. You will need a partner for this exercise. Lie supine on the ground, and clasp your hands behind your head. Your partner kneels at your feet and anchors your ankles to the ground.

2. Slowly extend your spine, raising your trunk and shoulders off the ground.

3. With control, lower the trunk to the ground and repeat. Do not go overboard at the beginning by attempting too many repetitions or trying to extend too far. Start with a few repetitions, and gradually add more.

4. Swap positions with your partner.

Muscles Involved

Primary: Erector spinae

Secondary: Abdominal core, rhomboid major and minor, serratus anterior, lower trapezius

Soccer Focus

Forceful kicking requires hyperextension of the back at the end of the preparatory phase. Note the degree of both hip and trunk hyperextension when preparing to kick the ball powerfully. This could happen more frequently in training or a match than what is seen during a powerful header. Add to this the very real chance that there will be some angular torque on the spine when approaching the ball from an angle, like a field goal kicker in American football. You probably have never appreciated the level to which your back is involved in soccer.

Inclined Lumbar Extension

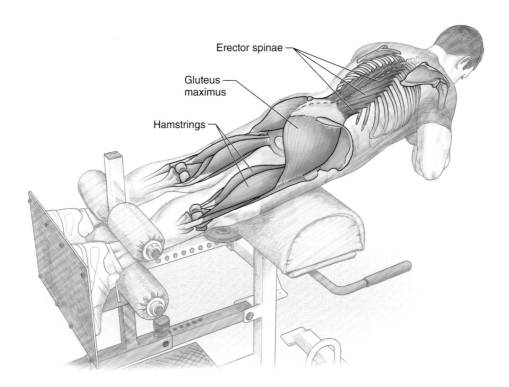

Erector spinae

Gluteus maximus

Hamstrings

Execution

1. Get into a prone position on a Roman chair by standing on the platform so that you can hook your ankles under the pads. Your thighs will be on the cushion and your arms folded across the chest. The hips need to be free to move.
2. Slowly lower the trunk to the floor.
3. Raise the trunk until it is in line with the legs.
4. Do not attempt too many repetitions. Start with a few, and gradually add more repetitions as you get stronger.

Muscles Involved

Primary: Erector spinae

Secondary: Gluteus maximus, hamstrings

Soccer Focus

A recent study looked at stress fractures to a particular area of the lumbar spine in young players. The name of the injury is a mouthful: spondylolysis (pronounced spon-de-LOL-eh-sis).The exact cause is still under study, whether it begins with a specific event or if there is a genetic component. Axial loading (pushing down on top of the bones) or repetitive twisting motions have both been suggested as potential culprits. Axial loading is not all that common in soccer, but excessive twisting is quite common. Rest is the best treatment for this condition, and most physicians expect three months or more lost to sport for complete healing. Most sports medicine specialists believe that increasing the strength of the muscles around susceptible bones and joints will go a long way toward preventing problems. This is especially true for the back, an area with a reputation for being weak and poorly conditioned.

Good Morning

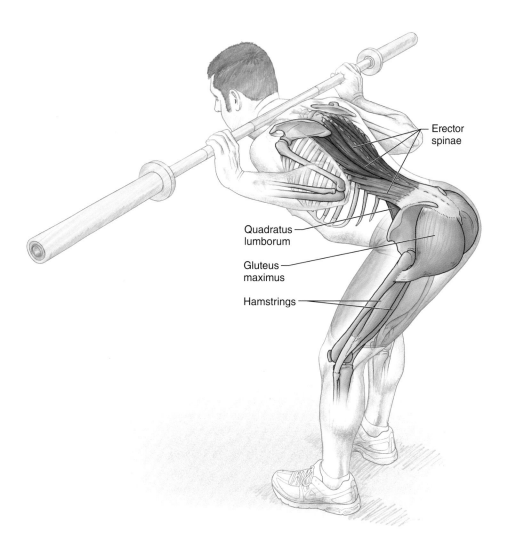

Erector spinae

Quadratus lumborum

Gluteus maximus

Hamstrings

⚠️ **SAFETY TIP** There is no need to use heavy weights for the exercise. A slight bend at the knees can make this exercise a bit easier.

Execution

1. Stand with your feet apart, with a little knee flexion. Using an overhand grip, hold a barbell across your trapezius.
2. Slowly bend the trunk forward, while keeping the trunk straight and your head up, until the angle between the trunk and thigh is about 90 degrees.
3. Pause at the bottom, and then slowly raise the trunk.

Muscles Involved

Primary: Erector spinae, quadratus lumborum

Secondary: Gluteus maximus, hamstrings

Soccer Focus

Most of the examples so far have been directed toward field players. The goalkeeper has a unique position. The goalie spends a great deal of time apart from the action, talking to his defenders about positioning and opponent movements that might not be seen by all. More important, the goalie will usually need to make three or more saves to keep his team in the game. These actions are highly ballistic and frequently quite acrobatic and can bring gasps from spectators and players alike. Stretching across the goal mouth, arching his back, and reaching out to get his fingertips on the ball to redirect the shot away from danger requires every muscle to be prepared to act in an instant. Because the goalie also is allowed to use his hands, his upper trunk and upper body have a unique role in comparison with field players. Goalies are getting bigger, with players 6 feet 2 inches (188 cm) or taller routinely manning the posts. Just the length of a goalie this size changes the torque about his joints.

VARIATION

Machine Back Extension

Machines offer a safe and stable way to isolate a muscle group. Athletes with a history of back pain or back complaints as well as athletes returning from injury should use a back extension machine as their first choice.

On many levels, the old guys were right about a great many things about soccer coaching. Drills that seem novel today often can be found in coaching books from decades ago. Just because someone coached in the 1950s or 1960s doesn't mean he didn't know the game. Although we have revised their recommendations for fluid replenishment and distance running for match fitness, their thoughts on individual ball training are being revisited as coaching methods go through inevitable cycles. Coaches of a generation or two ago would have players do sit-ups to strengthen their abdominals to withstand collisions. Today, most people, athletes included, will point to their abdominals when asked about their core, probably saying something about six-pack abs. In reality, the core is far more than just the abdominal muscles. The core refers to the body's midsection from the hips to the shoulders. Around this center, all movements occur.

A strong core is the platform around which your limbs perform. For the upper and lower extremities to move about the trunk in the most coordinated manner, the muscles of the core, of which the abdominals are just one part, need to stabilize the hips, spine, and trunk. If the trunk is not stable during movement, the limbs will have to compensate for unexpected movements by the trunk. To demonstrate this, stand on one leg, close your eyes, and note what happens to the lifted leg and your arms as your trunk shifts away from being over the support leg. Reactions like this in the frantic, uncontrolled situations of a match might lead to something unfavorable, such as an injury. In fact, high-speed videos of people who experienced noncontact knee injuries show that just before the injury the trunk wavered slightly, the player reacted a little differently than planned, and the knee failed. This is why core training is part of almost every knee injury prevention program, such as The 11+ (see chapter 2, page 18).

Over time, the core has gone from being a training afterthought ("a few sit-ups") to being a key—some might say the key—element in a training program. Because of the dozens of books, hundreds of exercise options, and thousands of websites devoted to core training, choosing training options can be intimidating.

The lower abdomen, between the rib cage and the pelvis, is like a cylinder. At its sides are the abdominal muscles, the spinal muscles, and the lumbodorsal fascia. The diaphragm above and the pelvic floor below close the ends of the cylinder.

Abdominal Muscles

The abdomen is unique in that the skeletal structure for muscle attachments is borrowed from other regions of the body. From above, some abdominal muscles originate on the ribs, and from below, others originate from the pelvis. From the back, still other muscles originate from the vertebral column and a very strong layer of tendinous tissue in the lower back called the lumbodorsal fascia (sometimes called the thoracolumbar fascia). Because of the limited locations for bony insertion for the lower abdominal muscles, portions of the muscles that wrap around the front attach to a tendon called the *linea alba* that runs from the sternum to the pelvis. This gives certain muscles an attachment to pull on. There are few traditional joints or ligaments in the abdomen. The structure of the pelvis is outlined in chapter 6.

The most obvious muscles of the abdomen are the transversus abdominis, external oblique, and internal oblique (figure 7.1). Their arrangement and functions are complex. These three muscles are flat sheets that lie one on top of another. They are named for the direction of their fibers and their location in the layers. A fourth muscle, the rectus abdominis, is embedded within the midline tendons in what is called the rectus sheath.

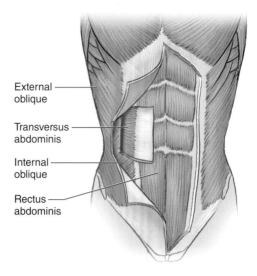

External oblique

Transversus abdominis

Internal oblique

Rectus abdominis

The paired rectus abdominis muscles run side by side and adjacent to the midline, between the sternum and pubic bones, the lowest part of the abdomen. The rectus abdominis originates where the two pubic bones join (the pubic symphysis). The fibers run up to the end of the sternum (the xiphoid process) and the nearby surfaces of the 5th through 7th ribs. This muscle

Figure 7.1   Transversus abdominis, external oblique, internal oblique, and rectus abdominis.

is unique in that there are tendons within the muscle. In most cases, a tendon is the link between a muscle and a bone, but the rectus abdominis has three tendons that break the muscle into distinct sections. When this muscle is well trained and the layer of fat under the skin is thin, the result is the highly sought after six-pack appearance associated with rock-hard abs.

The external oblique, as its name implies, is the outermost layer of the abdominal muscles that wrap around the lower abdomen. Its fibers run in a diagonal direction. It originates laterally on the outer surface of the lower 8 ribs, and the fibers run diagonally *down* toward the pelvis to insert on the iliac crest (that bony ridge on your side), the rectus sheath, and the linea alba.

The internal oblique lies just under the external oblique, and their fibers run perpendicular to each other. The internal oblique originates from the lumbodorsal fascia of the lower back and the adjacent iliac crest of the pelvis. Its fibers run diagonally *up* to the outer surfaces of the 9th through 12th ribs, the rectus sheath, and the linea alba.

The deepest abdominal muscle is the transversus abdominis. This muscle has a broad area of origin from the outer, lateral surface of the lower 6 ribs, the lumbodorsal fascia, and the iliac crest. Its fibers run horizontally to insert on the linea alba and rectus sheath. Don't make the mistake of calling this the transversus abdominal oblique. The fibers are horizontal, not diagonal, so to add *oblique* would contradict the *transversus* in its name.

These three muscles connect to the linea alba by way of fairly long, flat tendons because the actual muscle tissue ends well lateral of the midline. The only muscles per se that are on either side of the navel are the paired rectus abdominis muscles.

Many people believe the abdominals collectively perform trunk flexion and trunk rotation. But when considering the direction of the muscle fibers, it is as hard for the rectus abdominis to aid in rotation as it is for the transversus abdominis to perform trunk flexion.

Since we know the direction of the fibers, the attachments, and the rule about muscles pulling the insertion toward the origin, the actions of the abdominal muscles are predictable, if complex. Also remember that these muscles can work with their partners on the opposite side or work alone. Let's look first at the external oblique. When both external oblique muscles contract, they flex the trunk. When the muscle on the right side contracts, the trunk flexes laterally to the right. In addition, when the muscle on the right side contracts, the trunk can rotate toward the left.

The internal oblique is similar but has one main difference. Contract both sides to flex the trunk. Contract the muscle on the right side, and the trunk flexes laterally to the right. The difference is with rotation. Contract the muscle on the right side, and the trunk rotates to the right.

The transversus abdominis has different isolated actions. When activated, it increases intra-abdominal pressure and provides support for the abdominal organs.

The final abdominal muscle, the rectus abdominis, flexes the trunk and also helps perform lateral flexion and rotation.

Collectively, all four of these abdominal muscles work with each other and the long spinal muscles (see chapter 6) to provide support and stabilization for what many fitness professionals refer to as the lumbo–pelvic–hip complex.

The abdominals also play other roles. They contribute to the integrity of the vertebral column. In fact, weak abdominal muscles are often responsible for low back pain caused by poor intervertebral disc alignment. The abdominals also can aid in exhalation. When they contract, they squeeze on the underlying organs that push up against the diaphragm to increase intrathoracic pressure and help push air out of the lungs. And most people can appreciate the contribution of the abdominals in evacuating the bowels from the last time they had a lower gastrointestinal flu.

Those who choose to look further into abdominal exercises and core fitness will find dozens of exercises designed to activate very specific areas of the core such as the upper, middle, or lower abs. Such specificity will ensure that every aspect of each muscle is activated. It is easy to get both overwhelmed with the exercise options and carried away with implementing more activities at the expense of technical and tactical training for the game. Athletes are encouraged to perform their core training at a time apart from formal team training, reserving a few core exercises for the warm-up.

Reverse Crunch

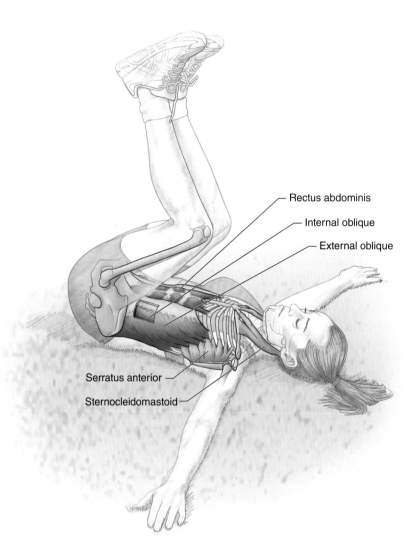

Rectus abdominis

Internal oblique

External oblique

Serratus anterior

Sternocleidomastoid

Execution

1. Lie on the ground on your back, and spread your arms to the sides for balance. Keep your head, neck, and shoulders on the ground.
2. Flex at the hips and knees, and raise the knees until they are over the hips.
3. Perform the crunch by pulling the knees in toward the head. Perform the exercise slowly. The primary movement is pulling the knees toward the head. Do not move the shoulders or head to the knees.
4. Pause and then return to the starting position.

Muscles Involved

Primary: Rectus abdominis, external oblique, internal oblique

Secondary: Sternocleidomastoid, serratus anterior, rhomboid major and minor, lower trapezius, psoas major and minor

Soccer Focus

A strong core is so important in sport for posture and general fitness, for performance and skill enhancement, and for injury prevention. A strong core anchors the movements of the limbs and minimizes extraneous motions often seen in players with poor technique. Much of the skill needed to play soccer involves rotation around an axis, and a strong core is the foundation for efficient movement. A strong core is also a factor in good posture. Muscles work best when the skeleton is properly aligned. A slouched posture increases the effort of the movement. Performance is enhanced when the body does not have to use unnecessary muscles to execute a movement. A strong core is known to have effects beyond the muscles to prevent injury. Some leg injuries, especially ligament injuries of the knee, are linked to a weak core that allows slight movements that need to be compensated for at the knee.

Soccer Ball Crunch

Adductor magnus
Gracilis
Quadriceps
Adductor longus
Pectineus
Rectus abdominis
Transversus abdominis
Internal oblique
External oblique

Execution

1. Lie on your back, arms stretched to the sides and knees bent with thighs perpendicular to the ground. Squeeze a soccer ball between your knees.

2. Pull your knees toward your chest by lifting your pelvis off the ground, trying to get your lower legs perpendicular to the ground.

3. Slowly return your hips and legs to the starting position.

Muscles Involved

Primary: Rectus abdominis

Secondary: External oblique, internal oblique, transversus abdominis, quadriceps (vastus medialis, vastus lateralis, vastus intermedius, rectus femoris), hip flexors (psoas major and minor, iliacus), adductors (adductor magnus, adductor longus, adductor brevis, pectineus, gracilis)

Soccer Focus

Core training has gone from being an afterthought to being a primary focus of training. More than just the abdominal muscles, the core includes every muscle that crosses the body's center—muscles that work together to accelerate and decelerate almost every activity in all sports. Power developed in the lower extremities can diminish as the energy passes up the movement chain, so developing the core helps transfer power to the extremities for performance. Because soccer has many abrupt changes in speed, direction, or both, a weak core could mean the trunk and upper limbs might react to changes in an uncontrolled manner, placing the lower limbs in a precarious position that could lead to injury. Awkward movements of the trunk have been reported to precede ACL injuries.

VARIATION

Captain's Crunch

Dozens of exercises are designed to strengthen the core. The soccer ball crunch can be performed on the field. A variation of this crunch focuses on the rectus abdominis and can be done in the weight room using a captain's chair. Support yourself on your forearms in the captain's chair, flex your knees, and lift your knees toward your chest.

Bicycle Crunch

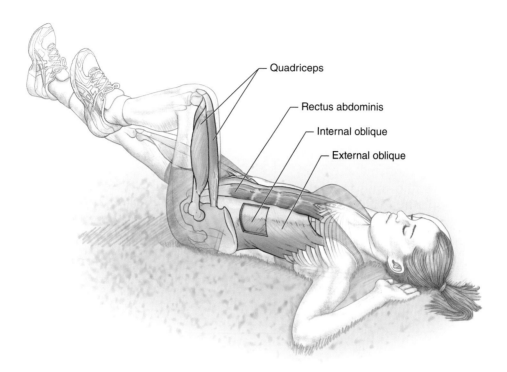

Quadriceps

Rectus abdominis

Internal oblique

External oblique

Execution

1. Lie on your back with your hands behind your head, fingers barely touching. The shoulders should be on the ground.
2. Draw one leg toward the chest so that the thigh is at about a 90-degree angle to the trunk. Draw the other leg up so that the thigh is at about a 45-degree angle to the trunk.
3. Alternate the legs back and forth as though you were riding a bicycle.

Muscles Involved

Primary: Rectus abdominis

Secondary: Hip flexors, quadriceps, adductors, external oblique, internal oblique

Soccer Focus

A number of core training exercises are performed in a slow, controlled manner. This exercise can be performed slowly or rapidly, depending on your goals. When this exercise is performed rapidly, the core is exposed to higher-velocity limb movements similar to those experienced during competition. Many experts suggest doing core training at high speed for just that reason. Increasing the speed of movement makes the exercise more functional and dynamic, which will help you prepare the core for those explosive and reactive balance situations that happen every four to six seconds. A strong core will help you transfer the power you've developed from performing the exercises in this book to the field of play.

VARIATION

Twisting Bicycle Crunch

To make the bicycle crunch more intense and increase the involvement of the external and internal obliques, bring the right elbow to the left knee and vice versa.

Vertical Leg Crunch

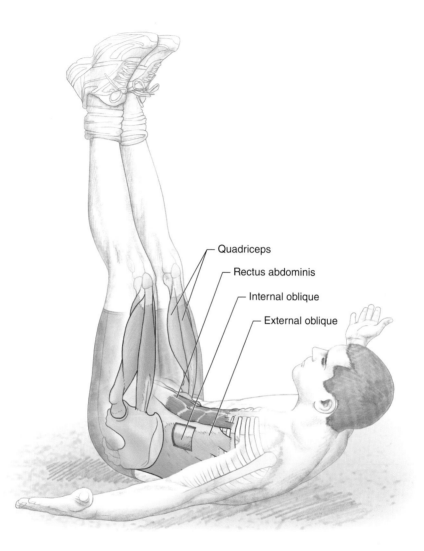

Quadriceps

Rectus abdominis

Internal oblique

External oblique

Execution

1. Lie on your back with your hands on the ground beside you.
2. Flex your hips to bring both legs vertical. You may prefer to cross your feet.
3. Slowly perform a crunch. Attempt to bring the sternum toward the thighs. Do not flex the neck.
4. Return to the starting position and repeat.

Muscles Involved

Primary: Rectus abdominis

Secondary: External oblique, internal oblique, hip flexors, quadriceps

Soccer Focus

A great deal of work has been done to determine which portions of the abdominals are used most in specific exercises. The general thought is that a routine crunch focuses mostly on the upper portion of the abdominals. When you lie back and flex the hips to raise your legs, the focus shifts toward the lower abdominals. Doing both types of crunches allows you to train a greater portion of the total abdominal mass. This is important when thinking about the transfer of power during the execution of skills. The buildup of kinetic energy for kicking begins when the planting foot strikes the ground. Power builds and is transferred up the leg through the abdomen and hips and then down the kicking leg. You can lose a lot of that power if the core fails to fully control the trunk, wasting some energy in unwanted trunk rotation or other movement. Engaging all the abs with the entire core fixes the trunk to allow the transfer of kinetic power from one link in the chain to the next. Although this is an abdominal exercise, you probably will experience some hip flexion. Try to keep your neck neutral by not letting your chin tuck toward your chest. For more resistance, hold a small medicine ball in your outstretched arms, and move the ball toward or beyond the feet as you crunch.

VARIATION

Full Vertical Crunch

This small variation changes the focus of the vertical leg crunch. Clasp the hands behind your head or to your sides for stability and perform a routine crunch, only this time push your feet toward the ceiling to give your body a U shape. This effectively shifts the focus from the rectus abdominis only and draws in more core muscles.

Single-Leg Abdominal Press

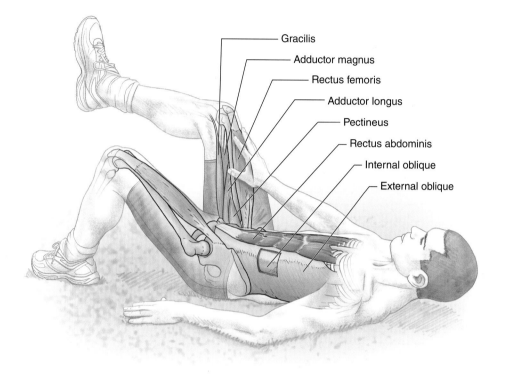

Gracilis
Adductor magnus
Rectus femoris
Adductor longus
Pectineus
Rectus abdominis
Internal oblique
External oblique

Execution

1. Lie on your back on the ground with your feet flat and your knees bent.
2. Raise your right leg so that both the knee and the hip are at a 90-degree angle.
3. Place your right hand on your thigh down near your knee.
4. Use your abdominals to further flex your trunk while resisting the movement with your hand.
5. Change to the left leg and repeat.

Muscles Involved

Primary: Rectus abdominis, psoas major and minor, iliacus

Secondary: Rectus femoris, adductors, external oblique, internal oblique

Soccer Focus

Although this is listed as an abdominal exercise, it is also an example of a field-based strength training exercise for hip flexion. Hip flexor strain injuries are becoming more common in soccer and, like hamstring strains, appear to result from the increased speed of the modern game. Strain injuries happen when a muscle contracts strongly when it has been lengthened. In sprinting, just before the trailing leg leaves the ground, the hip flexors are stretched. Once that foot leaves the ground, the hip flexes powerfully. This combination of stretch and contractile forces can tear the muscle. This can also happen when taking a hard kick, such as shooting or making a goal kick. There are about six muscles linked together as hip flexors, about half of which are classic groin muscles (adductors) that also assist with hip flexion. The other muscles, the rectus femoris (one of the four quadriceps), the iliopsoas, and the sartorius all perform hip flexion as a primary action. This exercise is designed to improve the strength of those main hip flexors. This should not, however, be the only method for preventing hip flexor strains. The walking lunge (page 34 in chapter 2) should also be performed at each training session to prevent this frustrating injury.

VARIATION

Opposite-Arm Abdominal Press

Using the opposite arm requires the trunk to twist, thereby increasing the use of the external and internal oblique muscles. In addition, this method also is thought to increase the use of a group of the lesser known, but very important, pelvic floor muscles, the levator ani and the coccygeus.

Stability Ball Trunk Lift

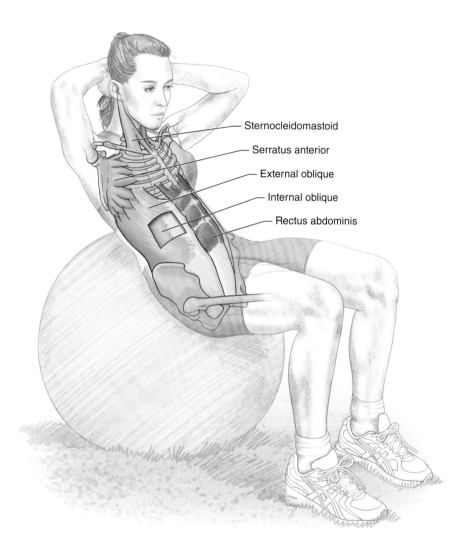

Sternocleidomastoid

Serratus anterior

External oblique

Internal oblique

Rectus abdominis

Execution

1. Lie back across a large stability ball so that the ball is under your lower back. Your feet should be flat on the ground and spread to a comfortable distance that will help maintain stability. Your thighs should be parallel to the ground, and knees should be at 90 degrees of flexion. Lightly hold your fingers behind your head.

2. Using your abdominals, slowly raise your shoulders off the ball as far as you can. Keep the neck as straight as possible to avoid tucking your chin.

3. Pause at the top of the motion before slowly returning to the starting position.

Muscles Involved

Primary: Rectus abdominis

Secondary: External oblique, internal oblique, serratus anterior, sternocleidomastoid

Soccer Focus

Years ago, the emphasis on the core was probably limited to some sit-ups and maybe some straight-leg raises. Today, the role of the core has risen from almost an afterthought to a primary focus of training. Why is the core so important? Many fitness professionals believe that nearly all movement extends from the core and most certainly passes through the core. Thus, it is difficult to coordinate the lower and upper body with each other for efficient movement through a weak core. Inefficient movements through a weak core increase the risk of injury and may lead to hip instability that must be compensated for. This reactive compensation alters normal movement patterns and can cause injuries, with the knee being the weak link in this chain of events. Practically every action in soccer—running, cutting, stopping, landing, kicking, and heading—can be performed more efficiently if you have a strong core.

VARIATION

Side-to-Side Trunk Lift

Hold a soccer ball in your hands, and add a twist to the movement to increase emphasis on the external and internal obliques. This simple variation increases the muscle mass for this exercise. Want to make this a bit harder? Use a medicine ball instead of a soccer ball. Medicine balls come in different weights. Hold a light medicine ball with your arms extended perpendicular from your trunk. Move up to progressively heavier medicine balls to increase the intensity of the exercise.

V-Sit Soccer Ball Pass

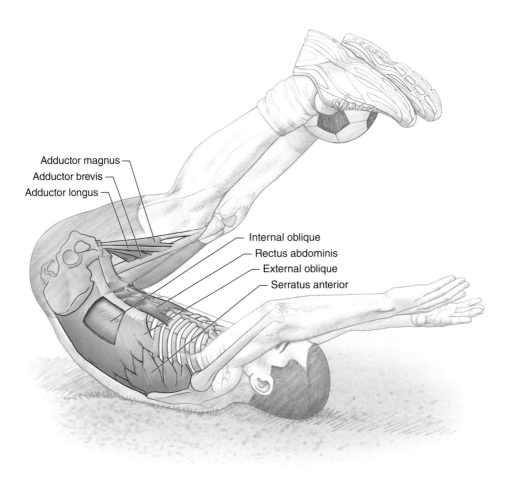

Adductor magnus
Adductor brevis
Adductor longus

Internal oblique
Rectus abdominis
External oblique
Serratus anterior

Execution

1. Lie on your back with your arms and legs extended. Clench a soccer ball between your ankles.
2. Keeping your legs straight, raise the ball over your head until the ball is over your hands, and then drop the ball into your hands. This is the first repetition.
3. Lower your feet to the starting position, leaving the ball in your hands.
4. Repeat the motion in order to retrieve the ball from the hands. This is the second repetition. At first, you may not be able to keep your legs straight throughout the exercise. As your strength improves, work on keeping the legs as straight as you can for as much of the exercise as possible.

Muscles Involved

Primary: Rectus abdominis

Secondary: External oblique, internal oblique, adductors, hip flexors, quadriceps, serratus anterior

Soccer Focus

This exercise has a long history in soccer and is described in many older coaching books. Back in the early 1970s, Pepsi partnered with the legendary Pele to produce the so-called Pepsi Pele movies that showed a number of his training methods. One of the movies featured a fitness circuit that had multiple stations for what might be considered early-generation core training. The exercises included basic sit-ups and what we eventually would call crunches. The films also showed Pele on the ground with a partner holding his ankles about waist high for a sort of inclined sit-up. The exercise that got everyone's attention was Pele lying on his back, his head between the feet of his partner and holding his partner's ankles. Pele raised his feet over his head to his partner's hands, and the partner then shoved Pele's feet toward the ground. Pele never allowed his feet to touch the ground. The audience usually groaned. Although most people would prefer exercises with less strain on the low back, one has to wonder how much of Pele's training contributed to his ability and longevity in the game. Most strength and conditioning coaches prefer to select a variety of core exercises rather than focus on just a few, as was done in the past. Doing too many repetitions of a few exercises can place unwanted stress on tissues, which can lead to overuse injury. Using the ball for some core work, such as this exercise, keeps players focused on the ball while doing the core a world of good.

Stability Ball Pike

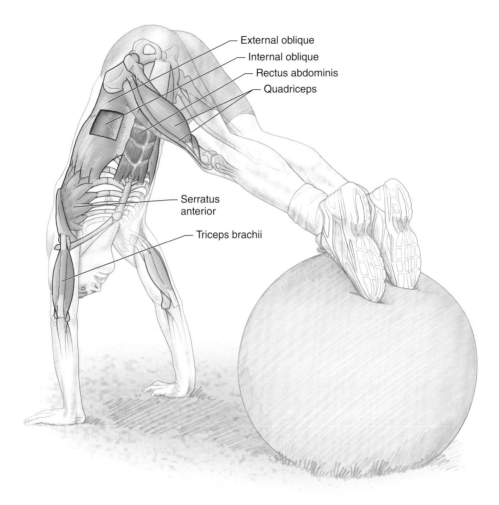

External oblique
Internal oblique
Rectus abdominis
Quadriceps

Serratus anterior

Triceps brachii

Execution

1. Get into an up push-up position with your shins on top of a large stability ball.
2. Flex to raise the hips while rolling the ball as far forward as possible from your shins to your toes. Make sure both your back and legs remain straight throughout the full movement.
3. Return to the starting position.

Muscles Involved

Primary: Rectus abdominis

Secondary: External oblique, internal oblique, serratus anterior, hip flexors, triceps brachii, quadriceps

Soccer Focus

A strong core is important for many reasons. Since your arms and legs extend from the trunk, it's only logical that a strong core will be an anchor for efficient movement of the limbs. In addition, forces for whole-body movements that are generated by the legs need to be transferred across the core to the arms for successful performance (e.g., when using the arms to make your trunk bigger when in a crowd of players maneuvering to receive a goal kick or a corner kick). When forces pass through a weak core, some of the force generated will be lost to other nonfunctional movements, meaning less force gets to its destination. The core is the link between the upper and lower body. The stronger the core, the less energy will be lost and the more force can pass between the upper and lower body for the most efficient movements.

Cable Crunch

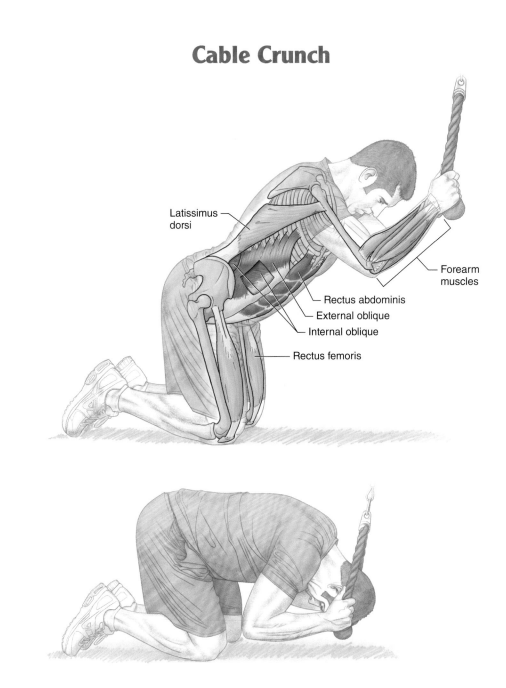

Latissimus dorsi

Forearm muscles

Rectus abdominis

External oblique

Internal oblique

Rectus femoris

Execution

1. Kneel in front of a cable machine, facing the weights.
2. Using an overhand grip, pull the rope attachment down to the shoulders and flex the hips slightly. (Your machine may have a long bar, short bar, handles, or a ropelike attachment to the cable.)
3. Inhale, and then exhale while crunching by rolling the sternum toward the pubis. Your elbows should move toward the middle of your thighs.
4. Slowly return to the starting position.

Muscles Involved

Primary: Rectus abdominis, external oblique, internal oblique

Secondary: Forearm muscles (mostly wrist and finger flexors, including flexor carpi radialis and ulnaris, palmaris longus, flexor digitorum superficialis and profundus, and flexor pollicis longus) to grasp rope, latissimus dorsi, rectus femoris, psoas major and minor

Soccer Focus

Most crunches are performed on the floor. This variation of a traditional crunch is performed from a kneeling position, and it takes a little practice to do the movement properly. The plus for this exercise is that you can increase the resistance by adding weight without having to figure out a way to hold a plate. As in all core exercises, draw in the core by pulling your navel toward your spine. You can also work the obliques by adding a slight twist during the crunch. Resist the temptation to do this exercise quickly, and you do not need to use heavy weights. Remember, this is an exercise for the abdominals, not for the hip flexors; use your abs.

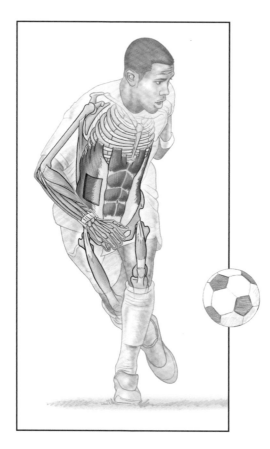

Hanging Hip Flexion

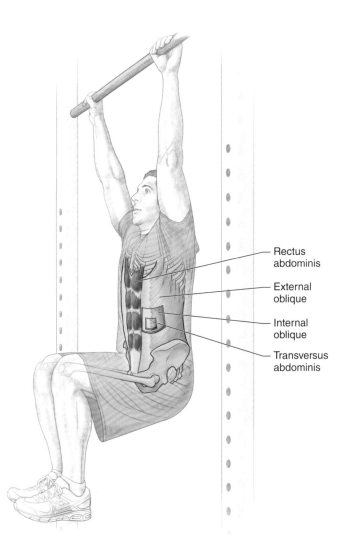

Rectus
abdominis

External
oblique

Internal
oblique

Transversus
abdominis

Execution

1. With an overhand grip, grasp a fixed overhead bar.
2. Flex the hips and knees until your thighs are parallel to the floor or higher.
3. Pause and then slowly return to the starting position.
4. Pause at the bottom before repeating to avoid generating any momentum. This exercise is about control, not about how fast you can do the exercise.

Muscles Involved

Primary: Rectus abdominis, hip flexors

Secondary: External oblique, internal oblique, transversus abdominis

Soccer Focus

This hanging exercise, like many other core exercises, involves a number of muscles. How it is done depends on what muscles are most active. For example, if the movement is just hip flexion and doesn't involve much flexion about the waist, the primary muscles are the hip flexors, and the abdominals act mostly as static stabilizers of the pelvis and waist. Raising the knees as high as possible recruits the rectus abdominis and the obliques, adding their dynamic contribution to the movement. You can add more oblique involvement by adding a slight twist to each side as you approach the end of each repetition. But don't think this exercise or any other abdominal exercise will reduce fat around the midsection. There is no proof that you can lose fat from one specific location (a process referred to as spot reduction).

LEGS: MUSCLE ISOLATION

A t last, exercises for the legs. Maybe now you'll gain the strength for that killer shot, the 60-yard goal kick, or the accurate penetrating pass out of the back that shreds the defense. Soccer is primarily about the legs. All other exercises are for support. Let's get to the good stuff.

For most sports, the power behind the activity comes from the legs. Even sports that emphasize the arms build momentum from the ground up. Problems in the legs can affect the arms and shoulders. For example, the damaged shoulder of baseball pitching legend Jay Hanna Dean, better known as Dizzy Dean, began with a toe injury. A soccer player who does not have a good foundation may soon find a lack of balance, agility, and more affecting his soccer skills. Ill-timed or poorly executed actions above the legs can be seen as poor skill execution. Players who spend too much time working their legs while neglecting the rest of the body will never be the players others thought they could be.

Players make the greatest gains in developing a stronger shot or a longer goal kick by kicking. Improvements in velocity and distance are due mostly to the coordinated timing of all the complex mechanical actions of kicking with the recruitment of the optimal muscle fibers at the instant of ball contact. Improving strength improves general motor skill performance and prevents injury.

Bones, Ligaments, and Joints of the Legs

The leg is made up of three main bones. The femur (thigh bone) is above the tibia (shin bone), which is parallel to the fibula. The patella (knee cap) has no direct bony connection to the femur or tibia because it is embedded in the back of the tendon of the large thigh muscle, the quadriceps femoris. The foot and ankle are a complex mix of seven tarsals, five metatarsals, and 14 phalanges. Although the actions and dexterity of the foot are less than in the hand, the foot is no less complex.

The hip, knee, and ankle are the three primary joints of the leg, but there are more. The hip is the classic ball-and-socket joint. It is a very strong, sturdy joint whose integrity is supported by three very strong ligaments that begin on the pelvis and wrap around the neck of the femur. The hip has good range of motion, but not as good as the shoulder. The primary actions are flexion (swinging the thigh forward) and extension (swinging the thigh back), abduction (moving the leg sideways away from the body) and adduction (swinging the leg from the side back to the midline), internal rotation (rotating the thigh in toward the midline) and external rotation (rotating the thigh away from the midline), and circumduction (swinging the leg around in a circular motion).

The knee, where the femur sits on top of the flat surface of the tibia, is the definitive hinge joint. There is also the patellofemoral joint, where the patella glides along a smooth surface of the femur. The patella doesn't *attach* to the femur per se. Although the knee is a hinge joint like the fingers, it is a very complex joint. The real magic of the knee is in its ligaments. The medial collateral ligament, or MCL, connects the femur and tibia on the medial side of the knee, between the knees. The lateral collateral ligament, or LCL, connects the femur and tibia on the lateral side of the knee, on the outside surface. These ligaments prevent the bones from getting into an extreme bow-legged or knock-kneed arrangement. The classic clip block in American football can damage the MCL.

Within the knee joint are the two cruciate ligaments. Both begin on the tibia and insert within the large notch at the end of the femur. The anterior cruciate ligament (ACL) begins in the front and runs diagonally toward the lateral wall of the notch, while the larger posterior cruciate ligament (PCL) begins in the back and crosses behind the ACL to insert on the medial wall of the notch. These two ligaments prevent the femur and tibia from twisting on each other. The ACL also prevents the tibia from shifting too far forward, and the PCL prevents the tibia from shifting too far backward.

The knee also has a pair of crescent-shaped cups of cartilage called the medial meniscus and lateral meniscus. Another cartilage, called articular cartilage, covers the surfaces of the femur and tibia and the back of the patella. The two menisci and the articular cartilage support the free movement of the knee and are frequently damaged during sports such as soccer. An injury to the meniscus can create a sharp edge that can damage the articular cartilage, and when this happens, you are on the fast track to osteoarthritis. A big problem with an ACL injury and the resulting instability is the risk of early-onset arthritis.

The main actions of a hinge joint are flexion (bending the knee) and extension (extending the knee). But the knee is more than a hinge joint because of smaller but no less important movements such as rotation of the femur and tibia with each other. Another frequently mentioned movement is a valgus (knock-kneed) or varus (bow-legged) motion that usually occurs in response to some force exerted from the opposite side. A physician can test the varus and valgus instability of a knee by prying open the medial or lateral side of the joint, which sounds worse than it is. When you hear that someone tore an ACL when her knee went into an apparent valgus, the knee looks knock-kneed, but the actual motion is a combination of knee flexion and internal rotation of the femur at the hip. The knee is far more complex in its structure and function than we yet understand. Orthopedic surgeons who specialize in the knee learn something new nearly every day.

The fibula is a thin bone that runs parallel to the tibia. The bony connection between the tibia and fibula up near the knee is quite strong, but it is not as strong down at the ankle. Those large knots on the inside and outside of your ankle (each is called a malleolus) are actually the ends of each bone. They form a sort of pincer-like grasp on the top tarsal, the talus. Ligaments connect the ends of each bone with nearby tarsals to add stability to the ankle. The primary actions of the ankle are inversion and eversion plus plantar flexion and dorsiflexion. Inversion is rolling the sole of your foot inward, and eversion is rolling the sole outward. Flexion and extension of the foot are more properly called dorsiflexion (pointing your toes up) and plantar flexion (pointing your toes down). The powerful kicking motion is done with a plantar-flexed ankle. The anatomy of the ankle makes it likely that you will sprain the outside of your ankle (an inversion sprain) far more often than the inside of your ankle (an eversion sprain). With sufficient force, the talus can force the tibia and fibula out of parallel, resulting in what is often called a high ankle sprain.

Just like the hand and wrist, the ankle and foot have a dizzying array of ligaments for proper bony alignment. The same naming conventions for the bones of the hand and wrist apply, only with metatarsals instead of metacarpals.

Muscles of the Legs

Some of the muscles that originate on the pelvis, insert on the femur, and act to move the leg are described in chapter 6. The muscles that act on the knee, foot, and ankle are the topic of this chapter.

The thigh muscles are in three primary groups. The quadriceps femoris (the four-headed muscle in the thigh, or femoral, region) has four distinct originations. The three vasti muscles—the vastus medialis, vastus lateralis, and vastus intermedius—all begin along the long shaft of the femur (figure 8.1). (*Vastus* is Latin for *huge*.) The fourth head is the rectus femoris, which begins on the pelvis around the socket where the femur articulates with the pelvis. You can easily see three of the quads, but the vastus intermedius is underneath the other three. These four muscles come together to form the common quadriceps tendon that passes over the patella and down to insert on the knot on the tibia just beyond the knee. In one of those anatomical naming quirks, once the quadriceps tendon goes past the patella, its name changes to the patellar ligament. Since a muscle pulls its insertion toward its origin, when the quadriceps contracts, the knee extends. The rectus femoris begins on the pelvis and also assists in hip flexion.

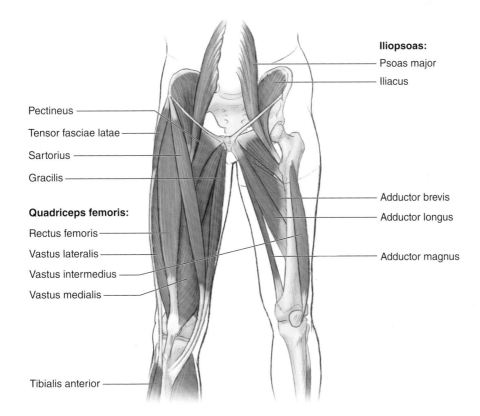

Figure 8.1 Muscles of the front of the leg.

The three muscles that make up the hamstrings (figure 8.2) are the opposite, antagonistic muscles to the quadriceps. They all begin on the pelvis. The biceps femoris is the lateral and largest of the three; it inserts down near the top of the fibula. The semitendinosus and semimembranosus run down the medial side of the thigh and insert behind the medial side of the knee. Most people can find at least two if not all three of these tendons. The main action of the hamstrings is knee flexion, but because all the muscles originate on the hip, they also perform hip extension. The hamstrings also play an important role in protecting the ACL from injury.

The muscles commonly referred to as the groin muscles all begin on the pelvis near the midline and run diagonally down and laterally to insert on the femur. Most are referred to as adductors, muscles that move the thigh toward the midline of the body. They range from quite small (pectineus) to progressively bigger (adductor brevis, adductor longus) to very large (adductor magnus) or very long (gracilis). The adductor longus is particularly susceptible to a strain injury in soccer players. All of these muscles assist in external rotation of the femur and more. You can't appreciate all these muscles do until you strain a groin and feel pain with nearly every step.

One final muscle of the thigh, sort of, is the tensor fasciae latae. The tensor fasciae latae is more tendon than muscle. This short, flat muscle originates on the crest of the hip, and the short fibers run down the outside of the thigh, ending roughly in the area of that knot felt on the side of your hip. Depending on your height, the fleshy portion might be 4 to 6 inches (10 to 15 cm) in length. From here, the tensor fasciae latae is mostly tendon all the way down the outside of the thigh, and it inserts on the mass of soft tissue that surrounds the knee. It abducts, medially (internally) rotates, and helps flex the hip.

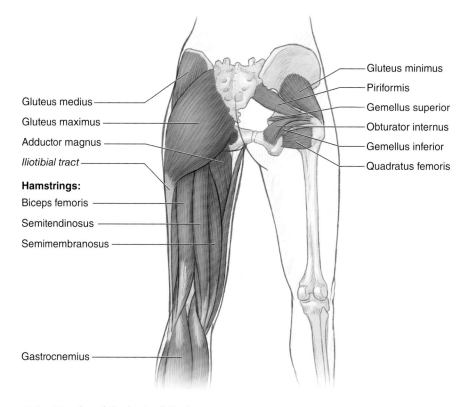

Figure 8.2   Muscles of the back of the leg.

Beyond the knee is a series of muscles that move the ankle, foot, and toes (figure 8.3). Originating along the front of the tibia are muscles that dorsiflex the ankle and others that go all the way to the toes for extension. On the lateral (outside) of the leg is a group of three peroneal muscles that originate on the fibula and mostly evert the foot but also assist in other actions. On the back of the leg are two major muscles. The gastrocnemius, which originates on the back of the femur and often is called the calf muscle, lies over the soleus, which originates on the tibia. The tendons of these two muscles join to become the Achilles tendon, which inserts on the heel (calcaneus). When these muscles contract, you rise up on your toes. They also contribute to your ability to jump and push off the ground during walking and running. These muscles are organized as distinct groups in the anterior, lateral, and posterior compartments of the leg. No muscles are considered medial.

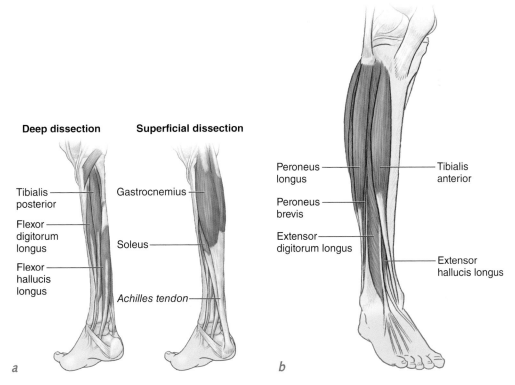

Figure 8.3 Muscles of the lower leg and foot: *(a)* back and *(b)* front.

Toe Raise Carrying Partner

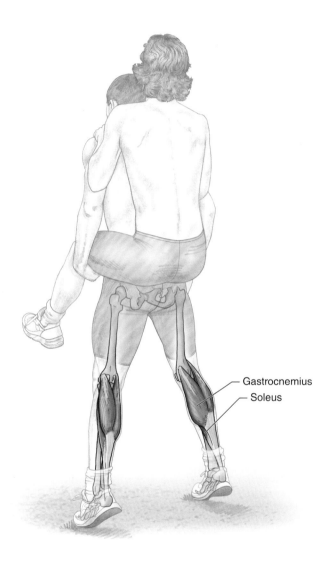

Gastrocnemius
Soleus

Execution

1. Find a partner who is about the same height and weight as you.
2. Have your partner climb onto your back in a piggyback fashion.
3. Perform slow, controlled toe raises by rising as high as possible with each attempt. Swap positions and repeat.

Muscles Involved

Primary: Gastrocnemius, soleus

Secondary: Erector spinae and other accessory back muscles (such as latissimus dorsi and external oblique)

Soccer Focus

Jumping power comes from the coordinated contribution of hip extension, knee extension, and plantar flexion (rising up on the toes). All these muscle groups need to be trained so that each can contribute appropriately during a jump. The calf muscles are also involved in running because much of the power in the push-off portion of the gait cycle comes from the gastrocnemius and soleus. This is especially true during the initial takeoff and acceleration in sprinting. The increase in stride length with faster speeds is in large part due to a stronger push-off from the gastrocnemius and the soleus. In addition, the calf muscles are strong contributors to the rigid locking of the ankle when striking the ball.

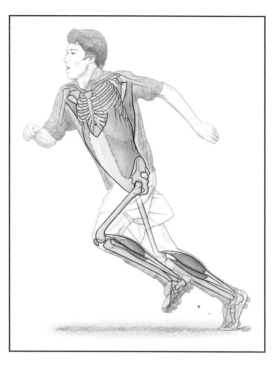

Much of the power built up in the leg during the swing phase of kicking can be lost if the foot and ankle are not rigid at ball contact.

VARIATION

Machine Toe Raise

This exercise, also known as the standing calf raise, really isolates the gastrocnemius and soleus, with the gastrocnemius producing the more force of the two. The muscles can be further challenged by standing on a board or step to add an additional stretch over a greater range of motion. The demand on the soleus muscle increases if the knees are slightly bent during toe raises.

Partner Prone Leg Curl

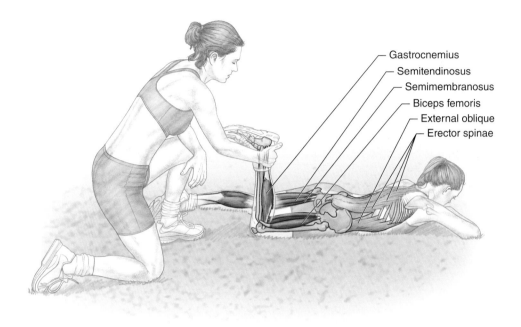

Gastrocnemius
Semitendinosus
Semimembranosus
Biceps femoris
External oblique
Erector spinae

Execution

1. Lie prone on the ground, with one knee extended and the other knee flexed.
2. Your partner kneels at your feet and holds the ankle of your flexed leg.
3. Perform knee flexion, curling the leg, while your partner resists the motion, allowing the flexion through the range of motion.
4. Switch legs and repeat with the other leg. After exercising both legs, switch places with your partner.

Muscles Involved

Primary: Hamstrings (biceps femoris, semitendinosus, semimembranosus), gastrocnemius

Secondary: Abdominal core (external oblique, internal oblique, transversus abdominis, rectus abdominis), erector spinae for core stabilization and posture

Soccer Focus

For earlier generations of soccer players, a hamstring strain was a rare injury. The pace and ballistic nature of the modern game have made this previously rare injury the number one soccer injury, according to some studies. Some studies show that professional teams see six or more hamstring strains a year. And these take awhile to heal, which means a team could be without a number of core players for an extended period of time. There are three risk factors for a hamstring strain. The strongest predictor of a strain, or almost any injury, is a history of a previous strain injury. Next, the older the player, the more likely he is to suffer a strain. Finally, poor hamstring strength increases the risk of a strain. Notice that of these three factors, the only one that can be modified is strength. Thus, it is wise to improve hamstring strength to prevent this serious strain injury.

VARIATION

Machine Knee Flexion

Hamstring strength can be improved by using a machine designed for standing, prone, or seated leg curls. Regardless of the positioning, the knee flexion isolates the motion to the hamstrings and will effectively increase strength. The greatest strength gain and reduction in strain injury come from performing the hamstrings exercise, sometimes called the Nordic curl, in the FIFA warm-up (page 30).

Lying Adduction

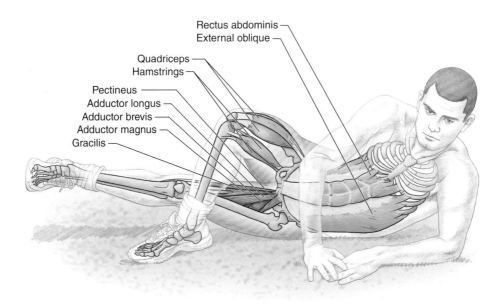

Rectus abdominis
External oblique
Quadriceps
Hamstrings
Pectineus
Adductor longus
Adductor brevis
Adductor magnus
Gracilis

Execution

1. Lie on the ground on your side.
2. Flex your upper leg, and place the foot flat on the ground in front of the thigh of the lower leg. The lower leg is fully extended.
3. Slowly raise the lower leg off the ground. Hold briefly at the highest position, and then return to the starting position.
4. Switch sides and repeat on the other leg.

Muscles Involved

Primary: Adductors (adductor longus, adductor brevis, adductor magnus, pectineus, gracilis)

Secondary: Abdominal core for posture, quadriceps (vastus medialis, vastus lateralis, vastus intermedius, rectus femoris) and hamstrings to maintain an extended knee

Soccer Focus

A sport's pattern of activity can lead to some particular deficiencies. Soccer players are famous for poor flexibility about the knee, groin, and ankle. Are these weaknesses due to the nature of the sport or the lack of attention to improving flexibility? Poor flexibility is considered a risk factor for a variety of injuries including groin strains, which can happen while defending or blocking a pass or shot; while taking a very hard shot; or during a rapid reactive change of direction. The most commonly injured groin muscle is the adductor longus. Most people don't realize how much the groin muscles are used during normal daily activities until one is injured. The leg is attached to the pelvis through a ball-and-socket joint (the hip) that allows the leg to pivot around the joint. During flexion and extension, the leg can move through a rather large cone-shaped range of motion, but the action of the adductors helps minimize the sideways motion of

the leg as it moves through hip flexion and extension. Those who have suffered groin strains usually are receptive to supplemental exercises that help strengthen the adductors to prevent or delay the next strain. Another pesky groin injury is a sports hernia, sometimes called athletic pubalgia (see chapter 2, page 16). Although the pain is situated in the groin, the actual problem can lie elsewhere, and the player may not be able to recall exactly when the injury occurred. See a sports medicine physician for an accurate diagnosis because the treatments for a groin strain and a sports hernia are quite different.

VARIATION

Cable Hip Adduction

The lying adduction exercise can be performed on the field. But the only way to continue to train the adductors on the field is to do more repetitions, increasing local muscle endurance more than pure strength of the adductors. (I have even seen some teams bring ankle weights to the field.) To really increase adductor strength, go to the weight room and use the cable machine so you can add resistance.

Fire Hydrant

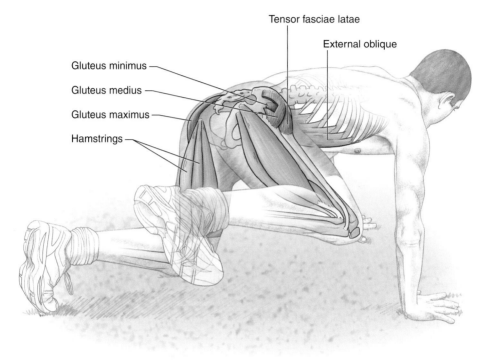

Tensor fasciae latae

External oblique

Gluteus minimus

Gluteus medius

Gluteus maximus

Hamstrings

Execution

1. Get on all fours on the ground.
2. Raise one flexed leg to the side until the leg is parallel to the ground. Pause briefly and then lower the leg back to the starting position.
3. Switch legs, raising the other leg to the side until it is parallel to the ground. Alternate legs.

Muscles Involved

Primary: Gluteals (gluteus maximus, medius, and minimus), tensor fasciae latae

Secondary: Vastus lateralis, hamstrings, abdominal core for posture and balance

Soccer Focus

The hip is a curious joint when it comes to sports injury. Not many players remember a specific inciting event, one they can pinpoint as causing the hip injury. But a substantial number of retired players have undergone total hip replacements at an age most would consider too young for new hips. It seems the lack of control of the femur within the pelvis causes minor defects in the socket portion of the joint that, over time, will wear down and eventually need to be replaced. Because strength is important in joint stability, look for exercises such as this one that can be used to improve the muscles around the hip joint. This exercise works the various muscles involved in hip abduction. At the same time, when done properly by taking the thigh through a wide range of motion, the fire hydrant is also a great dynamic stretch of the adductors. It should be easy to see where this exercise gets its name.

Machine Abduction

Most activities have both a field and a machine-based version. This machine exercise is done in a seated posture. Place your knees between the padded arms of the machine, and spread your legs as much as possible. Varying the angle of the seat is said to change the primary location of the muscle fibers being recruited.

Cable Kickback

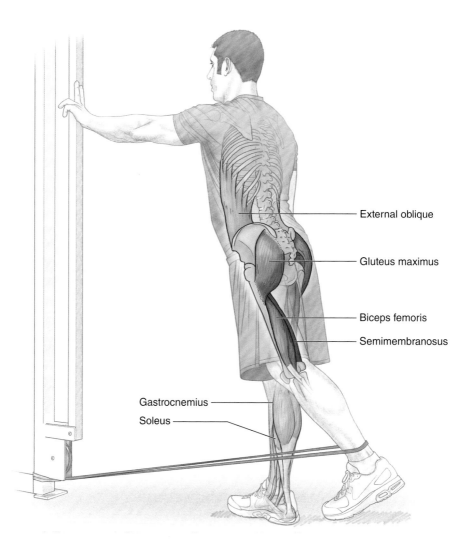

External oblique

Gluteus maximus

Biceps femoris

Semimembranosus

Gastrocnemius

Soleus

Execution

1. Stand and face a cable machine or other stable object. Loop the rope or strap or a resistance band around one ankle.
2. Keeping the leg as straight as possible, extend the leg at the hip (move it backward) as far as possible. Pause briefly and then return to the starting position. If necessary, hold onto the machine for balance.
3. Switch legs and repeat with the other leg.

Muscles Involved

Primary: Gluteus maximus, hamstrings

Secondary: Abdominal core for posture, muscles of the balancing leg (such as quadriceps, gastrocnemius, soleus, peroneus longus, peroneus brevis, and peroneus tertius)

Soccer Focus

Any movement that results in a ball being thrown or kicked requires some sort of a windup. The longer the windup, the farther or faster the ball will go. The anatomy of the hip joint as well as a specific ligament of the hip (the iliofemoral, or Y ligament) limits the backswing of a kick. Kicking is not just about the forward swing of the kicking leg. You can increase your power by increasing the strength of the hip extensors so that you use as much of the motion available for the windup as possible.

Seated Leg Extension

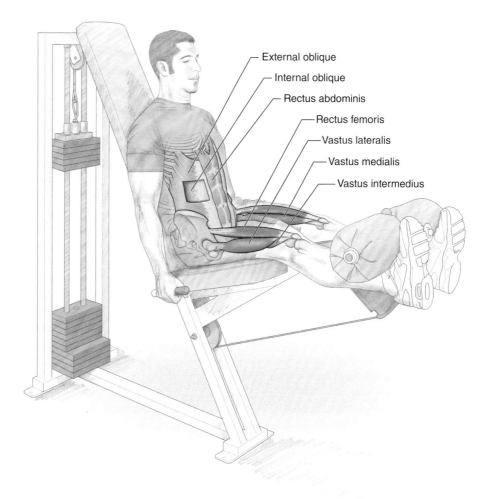

External oblique

Internal oblique

Rectus abdominis

Rectus femoris

Vastus lateralis

Vastus medialis

Vastus intermedius

Execution

1. Adjust the seat height of the leg extension machine as needed and take a seat. Hook your ankles underneath the pads.

2. Extend the knees. Pause at the top of the movement, and then slowly return to the starting position. Repeat.

Muscles Involved

Primary: Quadriceps

Secondary: Abdominal core for seated posture

Soccer Focus

Knee extension is one of the more obvious movements of kicking. Once the backswing ceases, the hip flexes while the knee remains flexed. As the knee gets close to the ball, hip extension slows and knee extension accelerates rapidly until ball contact. (Actually, the leg starts to slow just before ball contact.) The rapid acceleration of knee extension is what imparts a large fraction of the power for a shot or a long pass. Many studies have attempted to show what weight training does for kicking ability and, while it helps, it's not as much as you might think. If you want to kick the ball harder or farther, you will gain the most by kicking and a little from lifting. Be realistic about the goals of strength training. For the knee, strength training is about increasing strength to prevent injury, not necessarily to improve kicking performance.

Stability Ball Leg Curl

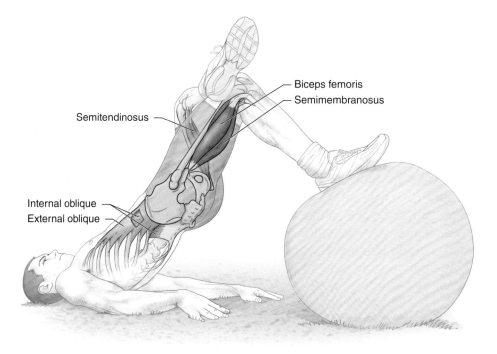

Biceps femoris

Semimembranosus

Semitendinosus

Internal oblique

External oblique

Execution

1. Lie on the ground, and place the heel of one foot high up on the stability ball. Cross the other leg over the knee. Raise your trunk off the ground, and put the weight on your shoulders.

2. Flex the knee, and roll the ball from under the heel to the sole of the foot as far as possible. Pause and then slowly return to the starting position. Switch legs and repeat.

Muscles Involved

Primary: Hamstrings

Secondary: Abdominal core for balance

Soccer Focus

The Soccer Focus section for the partner prone leg curl (page 155) covers the importance of strengthening the hamstrings to protect them from a muscle strain injury. The hamstrings also figure into anterior cruciate ligament tears. Remember, the ACL begins on the front portion of the flat surface of the tibia (leg bone) and courses back to the lateral surface within a big notch at the end of the femur (thigh bone), so it goes in sort of a diagonal direction. Think about its configuration. If you twist your right tibia in a clockwise direction, the ligament gets looser, but if you twist the right tibia in a counterclockwise direction, the ligament tightens. That's not all. If the tibia slides backward under the femur, the ligament loosens, but if the tibia slides forward, the ligament tightens. The tibia slides forward every time you land from a jump or plant a foot to make a cut. Imagine if the hamstrings contracted just as the tibia started to slide forward. What would happen? The tibia wouldn't slide forward as far, and you would have protected the ACL from being stretched through the contraction of the strong hamstrings and by calling on the hamstrings at the right time after learning how to land and cut. Strong hamstrings are very important in team sports such as soccer.

LEGS: COMPLETE POWER

Many of the exercises in this book are isolation exercises. They are designed to isolate movement to specific muscles or muscle groups. These exercises are very effective at ensuring those specific muscles and their actions get the full benefit of training.

In sports, however, actions are rarely isolated. In a game, dynamic planned and reactive movements involve multiple joints and muscles in a coordinated pattern to achieve something as simple as bending over to place the ball to take a corner kick or as highly complex as a plant, cut, and turn with one touch of the ball. It is quite impossible to mimic every action of a sport with a supplemental exercise or even with what some call functional exercises. You would spend more time on those than on the actual sport itself.

The exercises in this chapter provide a glimpse into what is possible for more complex multijoint activities. Although few of these exercises mimic any particular sport, each requires components common to most sports, including soccer. Because the power output of soccer is driven by the lower extremities, these exercises are all about improving leg power for running, cutting, stopping, jumping, maintaining static and reactive balance, and more.

It is important to include complex supplemental actions in physical training. You plan to plant your right foot and cut to the left, but your studs don't dig in as expected, or dig in too much, and you react with a slight skip or hop and adjust your posture to keep your balance during this seemingly minor adjustment. Most of the actions and reactions are handled by the cerebellum and spinal cord. If all your supplemental training activities were simple single-joint, single-muscle-group actions, your body would miss a valuable opportunity to train adaptations to support skilled performance. This is why you hear a lot about functional training.

A common adage, if a little simplistic, is the so-called 10-year and 10,000-hour rule, which says that the truly elite achieved that elite status after putting in about 10 years and 10,000 hours of deliberate practice in their chosen fields. Although a great deal of the learning involved over the years is tactical, much of neuromuscular learning is the ability to use only those muscle cells necessary to perform a skill. Think of children learning to bounce a ball. They use their entire bodies—trunk, hips, legs, shoulders, and arms. Everything parallels the up and down movement of the ball. As they improve, they learn to rule out unnecessary muscle cells, eventually using the bare minimum. Watch professionals play, and you will see a midfielder on the run place a pass right in the stride of a running teammate. The passer had to gauge her own speed and the speed of her teammate, decide how to pass the ball (with or without spin, on the ground, in the air, with what part of the foot), and determine how hard to hit the ball (not so hard that it outpaces the receiver and not so soft that the receiver runs past the ball). I guarantee that not one of those decisions was done consciously. All had been pushed to the subconscious and used only the muscle cells necessary to make a difficult pass look simple. One part of that 10-year, 10,000-hour rule is that motor skills become mostly rote and unconscious so the conscious brain can focus on planning, predicting, reacting, adjusting, and anything else that might fall under the executive function heading of *tactics*. All our midfielder did consciously was choose whom to pass to, a tactical decision. The rest was automatic.

Back-to-Back Squat

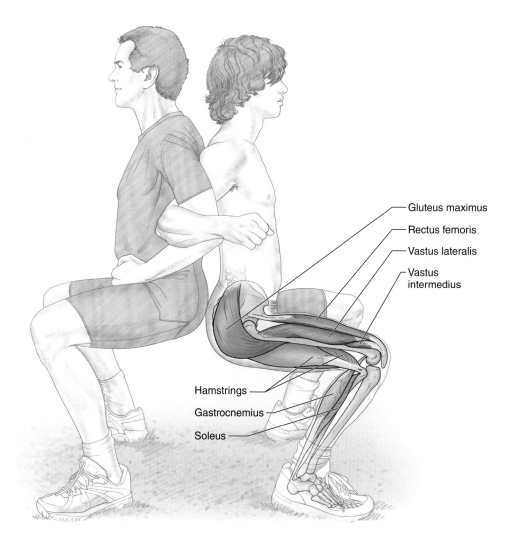

Gluteus maximus
Rectus femoris
Vastus lateralis
Vastus intermedius

Hamstrings
Gastrocnemius
Soleus

Execution

1. You will need a partner of similar height and weight for this exercise. Stand back to back with your partner, feet about shoulder-width apart.

2. Hook elbows with your partner, and lean back into each other as if leaning against a wall. There should be about 2 feet (.6 m) between your heels and your partner's heels.

3. In unison, squat down until your knees form 90-degree angles. Return to a standing position.

Muscles Involved

Primary: Quadriceps (vastus medialis, vastus lateralis, vastus intermedius, rectus femoris), gluteus maximus

Secondary: Hamstrings (biceps femoris, semitendinosus, semimembranosus), adductors (adductor longus, adductor brevis, adductor magnus, pectineus, gracilis), erector spinae, gastrocnemius, soleus

Soccer Focus

Soccer requires explosive movements at a moment's notice: the goalkeeper pushing hard against the ground to dive across the face of the goal and make a save, the defender jumping high to clear a cross, or the striker leaping to head a shot. All of these require high power output from the hip extensors, knee extensors, and ankle plantar flexors. A coordinated pattern of movement from strong muscles is needed for maximum jump height and distance. All players would be wise to perform squats like these because the increased strength and power will be used frequently in a match. Although each muscle group can be trained separately, a compound movement such as a squat better simulates conditions faced in competition.

VARIATION

Racked Squat

Use a barbell and perform traditional squats within a safety rack. The rack supports the bar. Step under the bar, position it appropriately in the correct posture, and then stand up. The safety supports are removed, and the exercise begins. Safety stops are positioned a little below the level of the shoulders when the knees are bent to about 90 degrees.

Partner Carry Squat

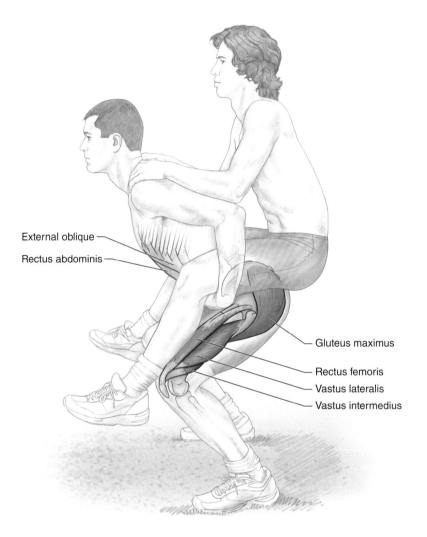

External oblique

Rectus abdominis

Gluteus maximus

Rectus femoris

Vastus lateralis

Vastus intermedius

Execution

1. As in toe raise carrying partner (chapter 8, page 152), choose a partner of equal height and weight. Be careful when choosing a partner because this exercise can be demanding on the knees. This exercise isn't just about up-and-down strength; it is also about balance. Have your partner climb on your back in a traditional piggyback position.

2. With your legs comfortably apart and your partner centered on your back (you'll probably be leaning forward a little), perform a partial squat to about a 45-degree angle at the knees. Do not squat beyond 90 degrees of knee flexion.

3. Squat slowly. Pause briefly at the bottom of the squat before returning to the starting position and repeating. After finishing your repetitions, switch places with your partner.

Muscles Involved

Primary: Quadriceps, gluteus maximus

Secondary: Adductors, erector spinae and abdominal core (external oblique, internal oblique, transversus abdominis, rectus abdominis) for posture

Soccer Focus

The traditional squat exercise has numerous variations. One reason squat exercises are often included in any supplemental training program for sport is that they activate multiple muscles and several joints to perform the movement and maintain balance. The primary muscle groups for the movement are the quadriceps femoris for knee extension and the gluteus maximus for hip extension. One of the most important aspects of performing any squat is posture. Correct posture activates the abdominal core and erector spinae muscles during the squat. Widening the stance increases the involvement of the adductors. Never discount the importance of the force produced by these muscles during close physical contact during play. The player with the stronger hips, back, core, and quads will be at a distinct advantage during tackling and other player-to-player challenges.

Split-Leg Squat

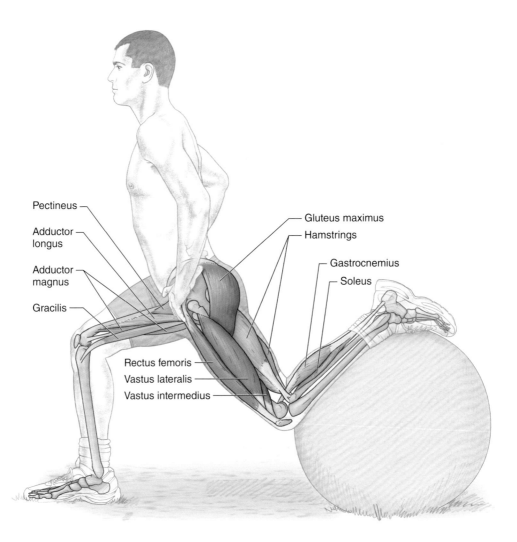

Pectineus
Adductor longus
Adductor magnus
Gracilis
Gluteus maximus
Hamstrings
Gastrocnemius
Soleus
Rectus femoris
Vastus lateralis
Vastus intermedius

Execution

1. Stand on one leg. Reach back with the other leg, placing the ankle or shin on top of a stability ball.
2. Flex the forward knee to about a 90-degree angle while rolling the ball backward with the trailing leg.
3. Return to the starting position.

Muscles Involved

Primary: Quadriceps, gluteus maximus

Secondary: Hamstrings, adductors, erector spinae, gastrocnemius, soleus

Soccer Focus

Flex the forward knee, and roll the ball back a bit to prevent your forward knee from going beyond your foot. Motor control of the knee is emphasized repeatedly in soccer, and this exercise is a good test of your ability to control your knee during a functional movement. The knee should not waver to the right or left, nor should it completely cover the foot. The strength and balance required by an exercise such as this should help control the lower body during the ballistic and reactive actions of cutting and landing from jumps, adding even more protection to the knee. Use a spotter or support if needed when assuming the starting position. Good balance and quad strength are needed for this exercise, so if either is lacking, this might not be the best initial option until you have improved both. Carrying dumbbells in each hand or an unloaded barbell on the shoulders, adding weight as strength improves, can make this exercise even harder.

Low Hurdle

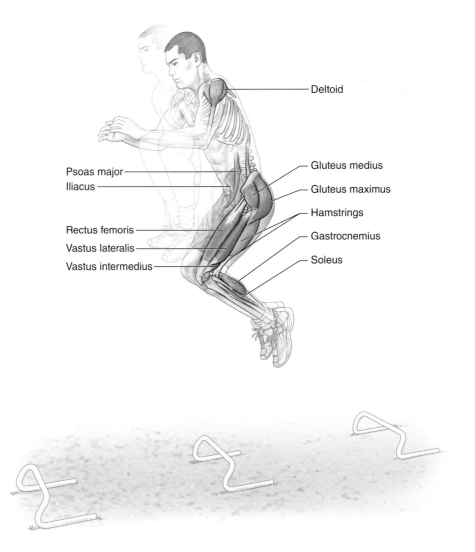

Deltoid

Psoas major
Iliacus

Rectus femoris
Vastus lateralis
Vastus intermedius

Gluteus medius
Gluteus maximus
Hamstrings
Gastrocnemius
Soleus

Execution

1. Set up a series of hurdles in a straight line, 3 to 5 feet (about 1 to 1.5 m) apart.

2. Approach the first hurdle with a step or two, and jump over the hurdle. Use a two-foot takeoff and landing. You will need to tuck your legs up to your chest to clear each hurdle.

3. Jump the subsequent hurdles with as little time on the ground as possible between hurdles. Think of this more as a series of rebounds than separate jumps.

Muscles Involved

Primary: Gluteus maximus, gluteus medius, quadriceps, gastrocnemius, soleus

Secondary: Hip flexors (rectus femoris, psoas major and minor, iliacus, sartorius), erector spinae, deltoid, hamstrings

Soccer Focus

Repeated jumping is a common training task across generations of soccer players, and it benefits players in many ways. For example, each takeoff helps improve leg strength for jumping. Each landing teaches the player how to land safely if the coach is watching and offering advice on landing form. Functional and reactive balance is required throughout the task. An understanding of the length of the legs and the force needed to just clear each hurdle keeps the player from falling or working too hard. The plyometric aspect makes this task one of the best functional exercises for improving jumping ability. (Plyometric exercises apply a stretch right before the muscle contracts. This makes the subsequent jump higher. If you squat and hold the position and then jump, you will not jump as high as if you squatted and immediately jumped with no pause. The pause negates the effect of the stretch during the squat.) This exercise features reciprocal jumps over hurdles, but the same concept can be used with a speed ladder or back and forth or side to side movements across a line. Some coaches still ask players to jump over a ball, but this is not advised because landing on the ball can cause any number of injuries.

Step-Up

Erector spinae

Gluteus medius

Gluteus maximus

Rectus femoris

Vastus lateralis

Hamstrings

Vastus intermedius

Gastrocnemius

Soleus

Execution

1. Stand in front of a bench or box that is between shin and knee height. Using an overhand grip, hold an unweighted bar on your shoulders.
2. With the lead leg, step up onto the bench or box. Continue the step-up until the lead leg is straight, but keep raising the trail leg, knee flexed, until the thigh is parallel to the ground. The trail leg does not touch the bench or box.
3. Step back down, leading with the trail leg.
4. Switch legs and repeat, leading with the opposite leg.

Muscles Involved

Primary: Quadriceps, gluteus maximus, gluteus medius

Secondary: Erector spinae, hamstrings, gastrocnemius, soleus, adductors

Soccer Focus

We all know that the dominant hand is the one we write with. But which is your dominant leg? Is it the leg you use for your hardest goal kick or the leg you use to take off for a long jump? Most of us have a dominant leg that works more than the nondominant leg when both legs are active at the same time. Single-leg exercises have some advantages over exercises that work both legs simultaneously. When the legs work one at a time to provide all the force, each leg gets worked equally without one picking up the slack for the other, although the entire exercise does take a little longer. And the benefits are not just for strength. Each leg is required to apply motor control of the knee and whole-body balance, two important factors for preventing injury, especially to the knee. Pay close attention to posture for safety as well as core stability.

Forward Lunge

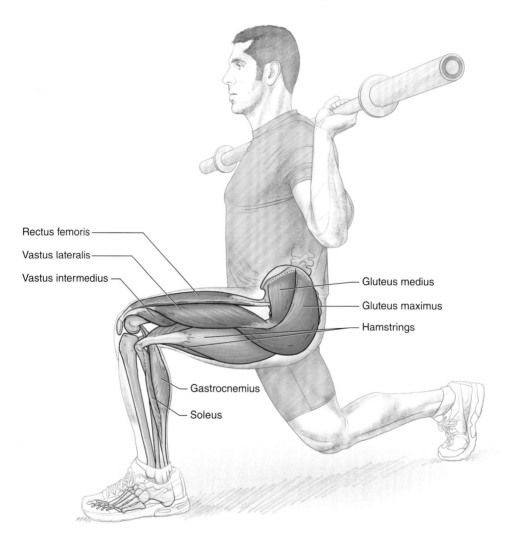

Rectus femoris

Vastus lateralis

Vastus intermedius

Gluteus medius

Gluteus maximus

Hamstrings

Gastrocnemius

Soleus

Execution

1. Hold a barbell in an overhand grip. Stand and place the barbell on your shoulders.
2. Step forward far enough so that when the lunge is complete, your leading knee is at a 90-degree angle and that thigh is parallel to the floor. The trailing knee will likely be just above the floor.
3. Step back to return to the starting position. Repeat with the opposite leg. Alternate legs on each lunge.

Muscles Involved

Primary: Gluteus maximus, gluteus medius, quadriceps

Secondary: Erector spinae, hamstrings, gastrocnemius, soleus, adductors

Soccer Focus

This exercise differs slightly from the lunge in chapter 2, which is used for dynamic flexibility of the hip and groin. In this version, you stay in one place and use a bar. This variation is more of a strength exercise and is highly valued by conditioning experts who create programs for the eccentric, concentric, and balance requirements of a number of different sports. Keep the back straight, and keep the head up and looking forward. At the end of the lunge, do not allow the leading knee to go beyond the toes or wobble across the long axis of the foot. Poor strength or fatigue can affect proper execution. If you struggle to perform the lunge correctly, reduce the load being carried, shorten the length of the lunge, or allow more recovery time between lunges to prevent fatigue.

VARIATION

Side Lunge

Being able to control the knee during a change of direction is an important feature of knee injury prevention. When doing a side lunge, the knee of the leading leg must be over the supporting foot and not wobbling back and forth.

Goalies

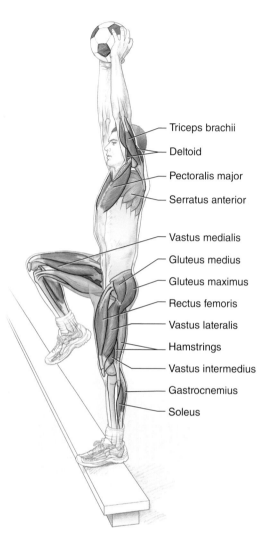

Triceps brachii

Deltoid

Pectoralis major

Serratus anterior

Vastus medialis

Gluteus medius

Gluteus maximus

Rectus femoris

Vastus lateralis

Hamstrings

Vastus intermedius

Gastrocnemius

Soleus

Execution

1. Stand in front of a low bench. Hold a soccer ball in both hands.
2. In a smooth motion, step up onto the bench with your lead leg, continuing the step-up until the knee of the lead leg is fully extended. Swing the trailing flexed knee as high as possible as you fully extend both arms overhead.
3. Reverse this smooth movement to return to the starting position.
4. Switch legs and repeat, leading with the opposite leg. Alternate legs with each repetition.

Muscles Involved

Primary: Quadriceps, gluteals (gluteus maximus, medius, and minimus), gastrocnemius, soleus, deltoid, triceps brachii, pectoralis major

Secondary: Hamstrings, erector spinae, trapezius, serratus anterior

Soccer Focus

As the name suggests, this exercise is great for goalkeepers, but it also is useful for all players. Think about all the key movements needed to run and jump for a ball in the air. The main difference between a field player and a goalkeeper is that the goalie gets to reach up with the arms and hands. Both the field player and the goalkeeper must approach the area, plan the timing, decide which is the best takeoff leg, gather for the jump, extend and push off to leave the ground to contact the ball at the top of the jump, and then safely land. The emphasis of this exercise includes everything up to the takeoff and is an efficient way to apply the various individual lower-extremity exercises into one functional task.

VARIATION

Stadium Stair Goalies

A reasonable alternative uses stadium or bleacher steps, and you carry dumbbells instead of a ball. Take every other step, pressing the dumbbell in the hand opposite the stepping leg. You may choose to raise both arms on each step.

Rebound Jump

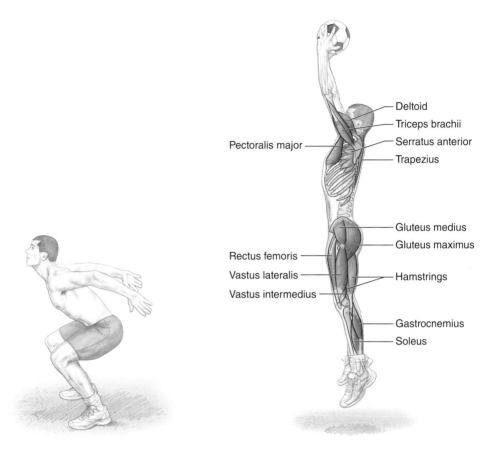

Deltoid

Triceps brachii

Serratus anterior

Pectoralis major

Trapezius

Gluteus medius

Gluteus maximus

Rectus femoris

Vastus lateralis

Hamstrings

Vastus intermedius

Gastrocnemius

Soleus

Execution

1. You will need a partner for this exercise. Face your partner. Your partner is holding a soccer ball.
2. Your partner forcefully bounces the ball on the ground. Using a two-leg takeoff, jump and catch the ball at the top of your jump.
3. Make sure you stick the landing. Do not let your knees wobble back and forth over your feet when you contact the ground.
4. To avoid fatigue from frequent maximal jumps, it is best for you and your partner to alternate jumps.

Muscles Involved

Primary: Quadriceps, gluteals, gastrocnemius, soleus, deltoid, triceps brachii, pectoralis major

Secondary: Hamstrings, erector spinae, trapezius, serratus anterior

Soccer Focus

The rebound jump exercise might be considered a functional extension of the goalies exercise (page 180), which did not require you to actually leave the ground. The rebound jump exercise requires significant timing because so much has to happen in order for you to get to the takeoff point, jump, and catch the ball at the peak of your jump, as a goalie might do during a match. This usually requires some movement on the jumper's part (the bounce rarely goes straight up) and correct timing to coordinate the ball's descent and your takeoff so you can catch the ball as high as possible. But it doesn't end there because you have to land safely. Many of the exercises in this book require that the knees flex and be over the feet when landing so that the knees do not wobble back and forth. Although all your attention is on the jump and catch, you can't forget about the landing. Try to land quietly, absorbing the shock of impact. Most players like the challenges—the bounce, the jump, and the landing—of this exercise.

VARIATION

Single-Leg Rebound Jump

A simple variation is to use a single-leg takeoff. In most instances, the two-leg rebound jump is done when the ball is bounced nearly straight up. For this variation, the ball should be thrown to the ground in such a way that you have to run a little and jump for the ball from a single-leg takeoff, landing on both feet.

Lying Machine Squat

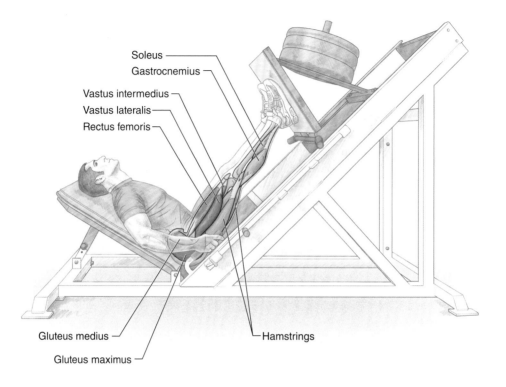

Soleus
Gastrocnemius
Vastus intermedius
Vastus lateralis
Rectus femoris
Gluteus medius
Gluteus maximus
Hamstrings

Execution

1. Adjust the machine so that when you get in, your knees are bent a little less than 90 degrees and your feet are about shoulder-width apart. You may prefer to point the feet out slightly.
2. Position your feet on the platform so that your knees do not obscure your feet. Rest your back and head on the sled, with your shoulders pressed into the shoulder pads. Grasp the handles.
3. As you exhale, press against the platform through the balls of your feet, and move the sled until your hips and knees are extended.
4. After a brief pause, inhale and slowly return to a knee angle of 90 degrees. This is not as far a movement as the initial starting movement.
5. After the last repetition, slowly return the sled back to the starting position.

Muscles Involved

Primary: Quadriceps, gluteus maximus, gluteus medius

Secondary: Gastrocnemius, soleus, adductors, hamstrings

Soccer Focus

The value of the squat cannot be overstated. It works multiple muscles and joints over a wide range of motion while requiring posture and balance—a big strength bang for the training buck. The modern game is more congested than ever as bigger and faster players compete on the same size field using defensive tactics designed to make the field even more compact. Contact is inevitable, and the stronger player will be better prepared to withstand the contact and either gain or maintain control of the ball. No one wants to see the individual brilliance of a player stifled and smothered by big, strong players. Neither does anyone want to see that brilliant player put out of play because of an injury. While nothing says that a smaller player will always be more skillful and entertaining or that a bigger, stronger player can't be as skillful, both players need to be well prepared for the unavoidable contact that is common at higher levels of play.

Woodchopper

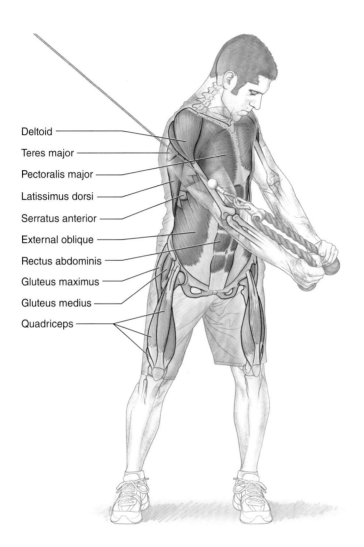

Deltoid
Teres major
Pectoralis major
Latissimus dorsi
Serratus anterior
External oblique
Rectus abdominis
Gluteus maximus
Gluteus medius
Quadriceps

Execution

1. Stand sideways to and a slight distance from a high pulley. Lift your arms to grasp the rope, strap, or handle with both hands.

2. Start by pulling the rope down and across your body. As your hands pass your shoulders, twist the trunk and crunch your abs. Flex your knees slightly as you continue this diagonal pull toward the opposite knee.

3. Slowly and under control, reverse the movement to return to the starting position. After completing the desired number of repetitions, turn around and repeat the exercise in the opposite direction.

Muscles Involved

Primary: Rectus abdominis, external oblique, internal oblique, deltoid, latissimus dorsi, pectoralis major

Secondary: Quadriceps, gluteals, teres major, serratus anterior

Soccer Focus

This whole-body exercise has many benefits. The action recruits the arms, trunk, gluteals, and quads in a stepwise, coordinated movement. There are no shortcuts, as one action must precede the next. On the surface, the arms and abs seem to be the focus, but the legs also play an important role as the base around which the actions occur. Pay attention to the position of the knees over the feet, and don't let the knees wobble back and forth. This is a very good functional exercise that involves multiple muscles and actions. Multijoint activities such as this are very useful supplemental exercises for the whole-body demands of team sports such as soccer. Some instructions do not include trunk flexion and the squat, making it an arm extension and trunk rotation exercise.

VARIATIONS

On most machines, the pulley system can be reversed so the action is low to high. This exercise can also be performed while seated, using a medicine ball instead of a pulley system.

WHOLE-BODY TRAINING FOR SOCCER

Throughout this book, the strength training focus has been on isolating a movement and the muscles involved in that movement. The strength training shelf of any commercial bookstore or library will display dozens of books that show how to train muscles in isolation. This concept ensures that every muscle is fully activated and will adapt to the new imposed demand.

The next step is to incorporate the muscles to function as part of a whole system, sort of the athlete's version of the whole being greater than the sum of its parts. Athletic performance is not done in isolation. Rather, the whole of performance is greater than the result of the sum of the neuromuscular parts. Performance in sport is a combination of the technique required for that sport, the specific fitness (physical and psychological) for that sport, and the unique tactics for success. Some of these are planned and some are reactions to the opposition, but all evolve over time as advances force the sport to change. Any opportunity to involve multiple parts of the whole system will move the player closer to being able to execute the coach's vision of the sport. This is especially crucial in team sports since the outcome is influenced by so many things—each individual player, the interactions of small and large group play, the style of play, the style of the opposition, the referee, the environment, the crowd, and more.

The options presented in this chapter have one common thread: They all require multiple joints, muscles, and muscle actions. No exercise is done in isolation. Coaches who have experience with or exposure to earlier training methods might recognize that similar field-based exercises formed the core of fitness circuits found in coaching books dating back to the 1960s and earlier.

Although players from the old country might remember similar exercises in their training programs, those programs were deficient in the basic training fundamentals: frequency, intensity, duration, and progression. They might have done comparable exercises but can't recall doing things as frequently or as intensely or for as long as what is currently in vogue. And their training certainly was not periodized over a long competitive calendar. What is seen today is a reincorporation of earlier modes of training into modern training principles.

The goal of these and other whole-body activities is to prepare players for the strategic actions that will lead to success either in scoring or preventing goals. Those actions frequently require high power output for jumping or sprinting. Repetitive jumping is a plyometric activity, and various versions are used to take advantage of the stretch–shortening cycle that is known to improve power output not just in jumping but also in sprinting. If improvement in sprinting is a goal (and it should be), look at what track sprinters are doing and you will see plenty of exercises directed toward repetitive jumping.

Incorporating whole-body training tools helps in coordinating the body during the random actions that occur every few seconds in a soccer game. Players will jump, hop, skip, leap, and cut at a moment's notice, often without any conscious thought at the time to the action or reaction. Although it is difficult to plan training to mimic what actually happens when facing a real opponent (as opposed to a teammate in training), it is not difficult to prepare each player's neuromuscular system to be ready to make sudden reactions to unforeseen circumstances during a match. And it's the responsibility of the coach to make sure each player is as prepared as possible. This is why it's more the norm today to see players doing guided activities that on the surface appear unrelated to the game. These might involve benches, hoops, hurdles, speed ladders, and other tools of the trade that will teach players to use their bodies efficiently with as few unnecessary movements as possible. Although the running form of a soccer player will rarely be mistaken for the smooth and efficient form of a sprinter, a comparison of soccer video clips from a few decades ago to today's game should be proof enough that the training, coordination, and athleticism have advanced considerably.

Despite all the training advances of the past 25 years, none of them will produce the desired benefit if coaches and players fail to heed the lessons of experts in other supplementary aspects of performance. Consider the following:

- Research has shown that as little as 2 percent dehydration can lead to impaired performance. Don't use the running clock in soccer as an excuse not to drink during a match. There are plenty of dead-ball opportunities to take a drink. On really hot days, the ref has the authority to stop play for a fluid break. A water break is part of the rules in numerous youth leagues during hot and humid conditions. Did you notice the water break in each half of the men's gold medal game at the Beijing Olympics?

- It has been reported that between 25 and 40 percent of soccer players are dehydrated before they even step on the field for training or competition because they have failed to adequately rehydrate after the previous day's training or competition.

- Muscle requires fuel, and the primary fuel for a sport such as soccer is carbohydrate. Restricting carbohydrate will only hinder performance. Players who enter the game with a less than optimal tank of fuel will walk more and run less, especially late in the match when most goals are scored. For some reason, team sport athletes are not as conscientious about their food selections as individual sport athletes are.

- Injuries increase with time in each half, suggesting a fitness component to injury prevention. One aspect of injury prevention is to improve each player's fitness. Players should arrive at camp with a reasonable fitness level so that the coach can safely raise the fitness of the players even further through directed preseason training. Many teams have a very dense competition schedule, making it hard to raise fitness further during the season. Those who try to improve fitness each week with too much high-intensity work during a match-dense season risk acute and overuse injury, poor performance, slow recovery, and the possibility of overtraining.

- Some reports suggest that less skilled players suffer more injuries than do more highly skilled players. Thus, another way to prevent injuries is to improve skill.

- Take the time to do a sound warm-up such as The 11+ outlined in chapter 2 (page 18). Tangible rewards should be realized when a warm-up is included as a regular component of training. There are no guarantees when it is done infrequently. Most coaches are good at planning a training session, but neglect guiding the team through a good warm-up.

- The most dangerous part of soccer is tackling. Research has shown that the most dangerous tackles involve jumping, leading with one or both feet with the studs exposed, and coming from the front or the side. (Head-to-head contact is also dangerous. See the next item.) A simple axiom to remember is bad things happen when you leave your feet. Players should stay on their feet and not imitate what they see in professional games.

- Don't take head injury lightly. Head-to-head, elbow-to-head, ground-to-head, goalpost-to-head, or accidental ball-to-head impacts are dangerous. You cannot see a concussion like you can see a sprained ankle. A player who experiences one of these head contacts should be removed from the game immediately and not be allowed to resume play until everyone is sure about his safety. The best advice is: When in doubt, keep them out.

In the United States, many states are following the lead of Washington state, passing laws requiring written medical clearance before a player is allowed to return from a concussion. Don't mess around with head injuries. No game is that important.

• Exercise some common sense when it comes to training. For example, use age-appropriate balls. Older players shouldn't train with younger players. The younger ones will get run over or hit with high-velocity passes and shots. Next, the best predictor of an injury is a history of an injury, so an injured player should be fully recovered before returning. An incompletely healed minor injury often precedes a far more serious injury. Be smart and stand on a chair or ladder to put up or take down nets. The combination of jumping, gravity, rings, and net hooks is an invitation to a pretty severe laceration. Finally, never allow anyone to climb on goals. There have been serious injuries and even deaths because kids were playing on unanchored goalposts.

Knee Tuck Jump

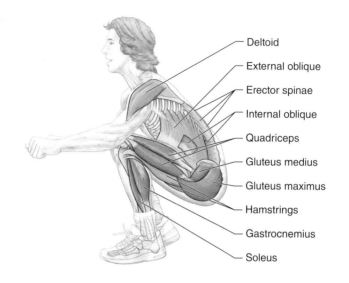

Deltoid

External oblique

Erector spinae

Internal oblique

Quadriceps

Gluteus medius

Gluteus maximus

Hamstrings

Gastrocnemius

Soleus

Execution

1. Choose shoes with good cushioning, and jump on a forgiving surface.
2. Using a two-foot takeoff, jump as high you can. Bring your knees as close to your trunk as possible. Use the arms for balance during flight.
3. Land softly to absorb the impact, and then quickly take off again. Spend as little time on the ground as possible. This exercise is simply reciprocal vertical jumps.

Muscles Involved

Primary: Quadriceps (vastus medialis, vastus lateralis, vastus intermedius, rectus femoris), gastrocnemius, soleus, gluteus maximus, gluteus medius, hip flexors (psoas major and minor, iliacus, rectus femoris, sartorius)

Secondary: Abdominal core (external oblique, internal oblique, transversus abdominis, rectus abdominis), erector spinae, hamstrings (biceps femoris, semitendinosus, semimembranosus), deltoid

Soccer Focus

Most books state that soccer is an endurance activity. With a 90-minute running clock (even though the ball is in play for only 70 minutes at most) and no stoppages, the game does have a significant endurance component. But games are won and lost by high-power bursts of activity—executing a short 10- to 20-yard (10 to 20 m) dash to the ball or outjumping an opponent for a corner, for example. Although these opportunities do not occur very frequently, players need to be ready when the time comes to execute high power output multiple times during a match. Many exercises train for high power output. Some involve an apparatus, and others are deceptively simple but very effective. Other exercises in this book involve jumping. Performing this exercise effectively requires you to jump as high as you can, pull your thighs up to your trunk, and then land softly and quietly. One jump is tough enough, but multiple jumps are very challenging. As you develop more power, you will find yourself jumping higher with each jump. As your legs develop local endurance, you will find yourself able to do more repetitions. Perform this exercise sparingly, when you have two or more days to recover before the coming match.

Repetitive Jump

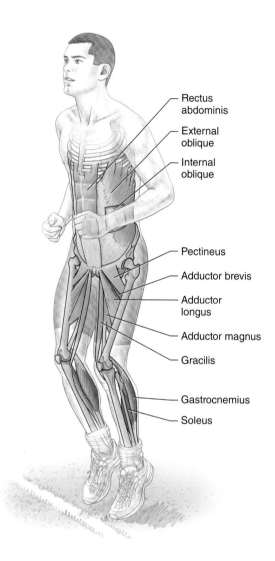

Rectus abdominis

External oblique

Internal oblique

Pectineus

Adductor brevis

Adductor longus

Adductor magnus

Gracilis

Gastrocnemius

Soleus

Execution

1. Stand facing or right beside the touchline or end line on the pitch.
2. Using a two-foot takeoff, jump back and forth or laterally just barely across the line.
3. Upon ground contact, jump back across the line as quickly as possible. This movement is very rapid, with little flight time and minimal ground-contact time.
4. Rather than count the number of ground contacts, do these jumps as rapidly as possible for a defined number of seconds, adding time as fitness improves.

Muscles Involved

Primary: Gastrocnemius, soleus

Secondary: Abdominal core, erector spinae, adductors (adductor longus, adductor magnus, adductor brevis, pectineus, gracilis)

Soccer Focus

Endurance, power, speed, agility—soccer requires virtually every aspect along the spectrum of fitness. Fast footwork is quickly becoming a part of skill training programs. You are asked to do a wide range of activities with as many ball contacts as possible in a short period of time. The player who has done these exercises knows that the physical demands of fast footwork training can be very tiring. Short, rapid touches in a very short time tax the ability of the body to produce energy rapidly. Exercises performed as fast as possible in a confined space prepare you for this kind of work.

VARIATIONS

This exercise simply takes you back and forth across a line on the ground. You can think up any number of variations such as traveling up and down the line; performing two touches on each side of the line; or imagining a shape on the ground and touching each corner, forward and back, adding a half spin. Use your imagination; just remember the keys—minimal flight and ground time. Increase the duration as fitness improves. You will be surprised at how fast you see improvements.

Depth Jump

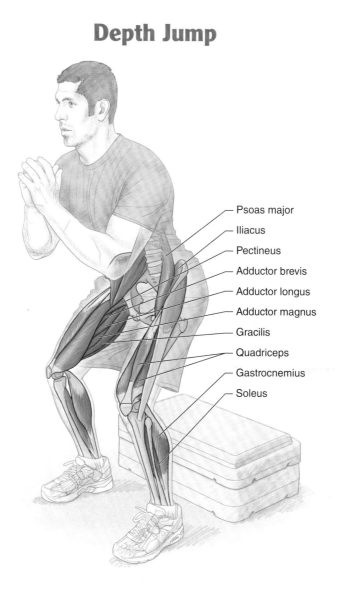

Psoas major
Iliacus
Pectineus
Adductor brevis
Adductor longus
Adductor magnus
Gracilis
Quadriceps
Gastrocnemius
Soleus

Execution

1. Choose a low box, about 12 inches (30 cm) tall.
2. Stand on the box with your legs about shoulder-width apart, hands and arms at your sides.
3. Step straight off the box. Land on both feet at the same time, bringing your hands up in front of you.
4. Absorb the impact of the landing by bending at the ankles, knees, and hips, sticking the landing so there are no adjustments to the impact.
5. Return to the box and repeat.

Muscles Involved

Primary: Hip flexors, quadriceps, gastrocnemius, soleus, adductors

Secondary: Erector spinae, abdominal core

Soccer Focus

Injury prevention is a theme of this book. Prevent injuries to keep playing and improve your game. At the core of injury prevention is neuromuscular control of the knees and the surrounding joints such as the ankles, hips, and trunk during demanding activities such as landing from a jump or cutting to change direction. Your goal for this exercise is to control the impact and not allow the knees to wobble right or left when landing. In addition, it is important to begin absorbing impact at the ankle and to not let the trunk waver during landing. If either of these surrounding joints shifts inappropriately, the knee must adjust, and this adjustment could put the knee in a poor position that could cause damage. Your coach should watch you when you perform this exercise to make sure your form is correct. Remember, these are single landings. Do not try to jump after stepping off the box.

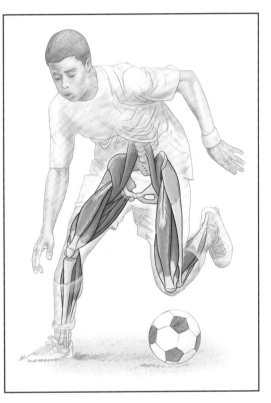

VARIATION

Rebound Depth Jump

This is more of an extension of the depth jump than it is a variation. After landing, immediately jump up to another bench of similar height. This changes the depth jump from a shock-absorbing eccentric exercise to a plyometric task.

Speed Skater Lunge

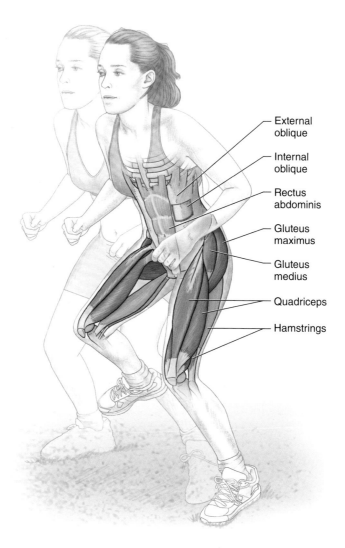

External
oblique

Internal
oblique

Rectus
abdominis

Gluteus
maximus

Gluteus
medius

Quadriceps

Hamstrings

Execution

1. Stand with your legs about shoulder-width apart, with your hands on your hips or out to the sides for balance.
2. Keeping your trunk erect and straight, jump slightly and lunge to your right, landing on your right foot. Your left foot is off the ground, and you are balanced entirely on your right foot.
3. Pause briefly and repeat, jumping and lunging to your left.

Muscles Involved

Primary: Gluteus maximus, gluteus medius, quadriceps

Secondary: Erector spinae, hamstrings, abdominal core

Soccer Focus

This really is a whole-body exercise because it requires the legs to propel the sideways lunge; the core to stabilize the trunk during takeoff, flight, and landing; and the arms and shoulders for balance. With time you will begin to notice improvements in lateral quickness and agility. During a match, you don't do much conscious thinking about your movements. You may find yourself dribbling at speed when a defender you didn't notice pops up to challenge you. In an instant, you plant a foot and lunge far in the opposite direction while redirecting the ball into your path. But you never actually think about the movement; it just happens. The pace of your play and the ability to veer quickly and decisively away from your opponent can be drastically improved with simple exercises such as this. You will soon see an increase in the distance of the lateral lunge and the stability of landing as strength and neuromuscular control improve.

Floor Wiper

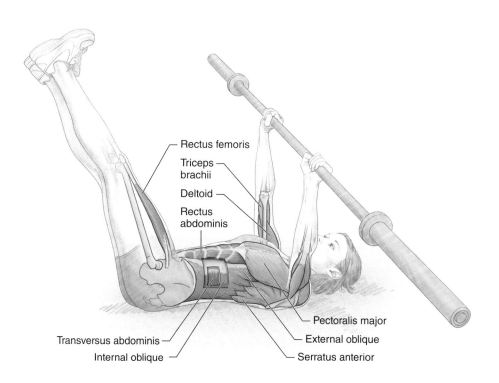

Rectus femoris

Triceps brachii

Deltoid

Rectus abdominis

Transversus abdominis

Internal oblique

Pectoralis major

External oblique

Serratus anterior

Execution

1. Lie on your back, holding an unweighted barbell above your chest. Arms are straight.
2. Without moving the barbell, raise your straight legs up toward one end of the barbell.
3. Keeping your legs straight, lower them back to the floor.
4. Repeat, raising your legs to the opposite end of the barbell. Moving the legs right and left counts as one repetition.

Muscles Involved

Primary: Abdominal core, rectus femoris, psoas major and minor, iliacus

Secondary: Sartorius, pectoralis major, triceps brachii, deltoid, serratus anterior

Soccer Focus

In the Soccer Focus section for the V-sit soccer ball pass (page 139), I mention a series of movies from the 1970s referred to as the Pepsi Pele movies. Within this excellent series of training films was a group of abdominal exercises that were part of a Brazilian circuit training protocol. This exercise is very similar, only instead of holding the ankles of a standing partner as the Brazilians did, you hold a barbell overhead and perform hip and trunk flexion combined with a little trunk rotation. Most of the abdominal exercises in the Pepsi Pele movies isolated the abs, but this exercise recruits multiple muscles of the core, making it a good bang for your exercise buck. Don't take this exercise lightly. It is quite challenging, especially when you realize the hard part of the action restricts your breathing. Don't forget that the bar stays overhead the entire time.

VARIATION

Floor Wiper With Dumbbells

This is the same exercise but with dumbbells. Holding a weight in each hand requires the arms and shoulders to balance each arm individually. Keep the arms overhead and the elbows extended as you perform the exercise as you would with a barbell.

Box Jump

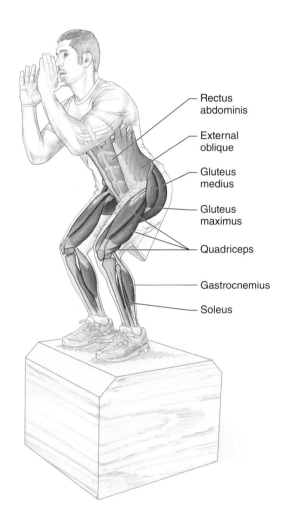

Rectus abdominis

External oblique

Gluteus medius

Gluteus maximus

Quadriceps

Gastrocnemius

Soleus

Execution

1. Stand in front of a sturdy box—one that will not tip over—that is midshin to knee height.

2. Using a two-foot takeoff, jump high onto the box, landing on both feet. Don't jump just high enough to land on the box. Jump higher so you are coming down on the box.

3. Jump back to your starting point, landing softly and quietly to absorb the force of the landing.

4. Repeat in a continuous, nonstop motion. Start with 5 to 10 seconds, and add time as fitness improves.

Muscles Involved

Primary: Quadriceps, gluteus maximus, gluteus medius, gastrocnemius, soleus

Secondary: Abdominal core, erector spinae, hip flexors

Soccer Focus

Modern soccer is a mix of high-power-output activities surrounded by more endurance-oriented running. A sought-after trait is the desire and ability of each player to press everywhere on the field. Upon losing possession, the player, often with one or two teammates, will press the opponent on any number of levels (e.g., to immediately regain possession, to close down in order to occupy the opponent and keep the ball in front, to rapidly close down to force an errant pass, or to close down a player and delay forward movement, allowing teammates to recover). In each case, pressing the opponent requires a fast, controlled approach featuring a short-term period of very high power output. This kind of work is very intense, but it can have important and nearly immediate outcomes when the opponent makes a mistake and a teammate collects the ball. The challenge is to develop sufficient fitness in order to press, and press appropriately, when the need arises. Nearly every coach will say how hard it is to get a player to press when that player has lost possession of the ball. Part of this is frustration or disappointment at having lost possession, but it also may stem from a lack of fitness. Jumping exercises such as this require a very high power output that when used in combination with similar work on and off the ball should help put a team into the position of being very effective at pressing.

Romanian Deadlift

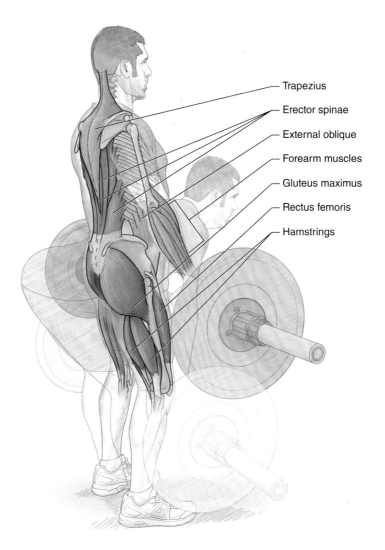

Trapezius

Erector spinae

External oblique

Forearm muscles

Gluteus maximus

Rectus femoris

Hamstrings

Execution

1. With the barbell on the floor, stand with your feet flat on the floor, shoulder-width apart or slightly less, and toes under the bar and pointed slightly out.

2. Move into a deep squat. With the arms straight, grasp the bar in an overhand grip, palms down. Your back should be flat or slightly arched. Pull your shoulders back and your chest forward.

3. Look forward and take a breath. Pushing through your heels and contracting your quadriceps and gluteals, pull the weight off the floor. Keep your back flat and the bar close. Stand erect, but don't lock your knees. Exhale.

4. Inhale and slowly lower the bar by returning to the starting position.

Muscles Involved

Primary: Erector spinae, rectus femoris, gluteus maximus, hamstrings

Secondary: Scapular stabilizers (such as trapezius), rectus abdominis, external oblique, internal oblique, forearm muscles (mostly wrist and finger flexors including flexor carpi radialis and ulnaris, palmaris longus, flexor digitorum superficialis and profundus, and flexor pollicis longus), vastus lateralis, vastus medialis, vastus intermedius

Soccer Focus

The deadlift is a whole-body exercise found in nearly every training manual across the sporting spectrum. It demands power output from the legs, hips, trunk, and back. If you have never done this lift before, you may think it looks easy, but the use of a barbell increases its complexity by making a smooth motion more difficult. It is a good idea to get some personal instruction to ensure you are doing this lift correctly and safely. Rounding the back during the lift exposes the intervertebral discs to possible herniation, so keep your head up. Looking at the bar leads to a rounded back. Also, do not try to flex the forearms during this lift because it can place unnecessary strain on the biceps. Posture is the key. Don't take any shortcuts with the deadlift.

ADDITIONAL RESOURCES

From FIFA

Health and Fitness for the Female Football Player: www.fifa.com/mm/
document/afdeveloping/medical/ffb_gesamt_e_20035.pdf
F-MARC Nutrition for Football: www.fifa.com/mm/document/
afdeveloping/medical/nutrition_booklet_e_1830.pdf
The 11+: http://f-marc.com/11plus/index.html

From the National Strength and Conditioning Association (NSCA)

Position statement on youth resistance training: www.nsca-lift.org/
Publications/YouthResistanceTrainingUpdatedPosition2.pdf
Position statements on other aspects of resistance training:
www.nsca-lift.org/Publications/posstatements.shtml

From Human Kinetics

Resistance training catalogs: www.humankinetics.com/
personalstrengthtraining
www.humankinetics.com/youngathletes

EXERCISE FINDER

Legs: Complete Power

Whole-Body Training for Soccer

ABOUT THE AUTHOR

Donald T. Kirkendall is uniquely positioned to author *Soccer Anatomy*. He earned a PhD in exercise physiology from The Ohio State University and went on to teach human anatomy, physiology, and exercise physiology as a faculty member at the University of Wisconsin at Lacrosse and Illinois State University. In 1995 he was recruited to join the sports medicine program at Duke University Medical Center and then at the University of North Carolina at Chapel Hill. His research interests focus on sports medicine and physical performance with an emphasis on team sports—especially soccer. Since 1997 he has written a sport science column for the monthly magazine *Southern Soccer Scene*.

Dr. Kirkendall began competing in soccer during middle school and continued to play during high school and junior college and at Ohio University, where he competed in the NCAA tournament. He continues to play today in adult recreational leagues. He has coached soccer at various levels from U10 youth leagues to assistant coach at Ball State University in Indiana and earned the USSF B coaching license.

Dr. Kirkendall is a member of FIFA's Medical Assessment and Research Centre (F-MARC) based in Zurich, Switzerland. The Fédération Internationale de Football Association (FIFA) is the international governing body for soccer. F-MARC conducts and collaborates on medical studies to reduce soccer injuries and promote soccer as a healthful activity. Dr. Kirkendall is also a member of U.S. Soccer's Medical Advisory Committee. Because of these affiliations and his expertise in applying sport science concepts to soccer, he is in demand around the world as a speaker on soccer-related sport science topics. He frequently lectures at coaching clinics and to local and national coaching organizations, and he has lectured to audiences in all six of FIFA's confederations.

ANATOMY SERIES

Each book in the *Anatomy Series* provides detailed, full-color anatomical illustrations of the muscles in action and step-by-step instructions that detail perfect technique and form for each pose, exercise, movement, stretch, and stroke.

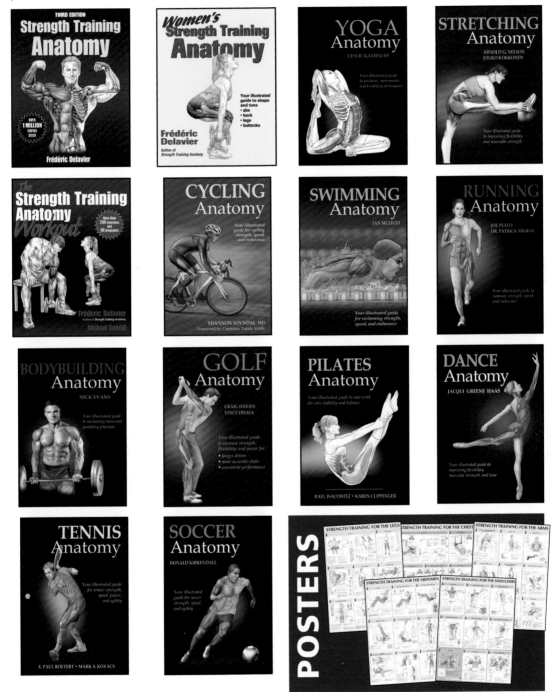

To place your order, U.S. customers call TOLL FREE **1-800-747-4457**
In Canada call 1-800-465-7301 • In Europe call +44 (0) 113 255 5665 • In Australia call 08 8372 0999
In New Zealand call 0800 222 062 • or visit **www.HumanKinetics.com/Anatomy**

HUMAN KINETICS
The Premier Publisher for Sports & Fitness
P.O. Box 5076, Champaign, IL 61825-5076

You'll find other outstanding soccer resources at

www.HumanKinetics.com/soccer

In the U.S. call 1-800-747-4457

Australia 08 8372 0999 • Canada 1-800-465-7301
Europe +44 (0) 113 255 5665 • New Zealand 0800 222 062

HUMAN KINETICS
The Premier Publisher for Sports & Fitness
P.O. Box 5076 • Champaign, IL 61825-5076 USA

eBook
available at
HumanKinetics.com